re-
, is
ey
ife

the
or
var
me
le.
od-

ce,

is directly _red
by y   ty called V'Ger.

This u_____   _ead serious. "Are you sure?"

"As sure as it is possi__ _o be when dealing with the irrational motivations of religious fanatics. The propaganda states that V'Ger's . . . transformation represents a failure of your latest deicidal effort, and is thus an omen, a signal to the people to rise up and overthrow the secular order, at which point the Oracle will be magically resurrected."

"Literally, sir," Lindstrom said. "The suit that's taken responsibility for the attacks, led by a man named Dovraku, is
one that embraces this point of view to an extreme. They
worship machine logic above all, advocate a rigid way of life
where people are ruled by a computer's calculations."

"Indeed," added Soreth, "their propaganda condemns the
Federation for what it sees as a policy to subjugate or
destroy artificial intelligences on other worlds—a 'war
against the gods', as they describe it. They believe you came
to Yonada with a specific agenda to destroy their Oracle.
You, Captain Kirk, have a particular reputation as a 'god
killer.'"

"Who, me?" Kirk put on his best doe-eyed innocent face,
though the humor was lost on the sour Vulcan.

"And in fact, the current uprising seems partly inspired
by your recent encounter with the entity V'Ger..."

This time Kirk's surprise was genuine...

STAR TREK®

EX MACHINA

CHRISTOPHER L. BENNETT

BASED ON _STAR TREK_
CREATED BY GENE RODDENBERRY

POCKET BOOKS
New York Toronto London Sydney Lorina

An *Original* Publication of POCKET BOOKS

POCKET BOOKS, a division of Simon & Schuster, Inc.
1230 Avenue of the Americas, New York, NY 10020

This book is a work of fiction. Names, characters, places, and incidents are products of the author's imagination or are used fictitiously. Any resemblance to actual events or locales or persons, living or dead, is entirely coincidental.

This book is published by Pocket Books, a division of Simon & Schuster, Inc., under exclusive license from Paramount Pictures.

ISBN 13: 978-0-7434-9285-0
ISBN 10: 0-7434-9285-4

First Pocket Books paperback edition January 2005

10   9   8   7   6   5   4   3   2

POCKET and colophon are registered trademarks of Simon & Schuster, Inc.

Cover design by John Vairo, Jr.
Front cover art © John Blackford

Manufactured in the United States of America

For information regarding special discounts for bulk purchases, please contact Simon & Schuster Special Sales at 1-800-456-6798 or business@simonandschuster.com

*To Xuân and Kelly, for teaching me that
faith and reason can get along after all.*

*And to Jerry Goldsmith,
who lives on as pure music.*

ACKNOWLEDGMENTS

This is a story I've wanted to tell since the days when writing *Star Trek* fiction professionally was only a remote fantasy. But I wouldn't have been able to tell it without the help and inspiration of a lot of people. What follows is no doubt an incomplete list, and I apologize for any omissions.

Thanks first to the screenwriters who provided the primary sources for this historical exploration, including D. C. Fontana, Gene Roddenberry, Boris Sobelman, and Rik Vollaerts from the Original Series; Alan Dean Foster, Harold Livingston, Jon Povill, and Jaron Summers from *Phase II/ST:TMP;* and Rick Berman, Brannon Braga, Robert Doherty, Michael Piller, Phyllis Strong, and Mike Sussman for more recent insights into Vulcans and *Trek* history. For additional character background, I'm indebted to Allan Asherman (*Who's Who in Star Trek*); Peter David (*The Captain's Daughter*); Diane Duane (*Enterprise Logs:* "Night Whispers" and general inspiration); Julia Ecklar (*The Kobayashi Maru*) and the rest of L. A. Graf (various works); Josepha Sherman & Susan Shwartz (*Vulcan's Forge*); and Dayton Ward & Kevin Dilmore (*S.C.E.: Foundations*).

Thanks to Robert Wise, Harold Michelson, Douglas Trumbull, John Dykstra, Jerry Goldsmith, and their colleagues for making *Star Trek: The Motion Picture* such an extraordinary cinematic achievement and an indelible influence on me. And thanks to Wise, David C. Fein, Michael Matessino, Daren R. Dochterman, and the erstwhile staff of Foundation Imaging for completing the film at long last. Particular thanks to Robert Fletcher and Fred Phillips, whose concepts for the diverse aliens glimpsed in the film provided the foundation for their portrayals here. And I'd like to give a nod to Paula Crist, Joshua Gallegos, David Gerrold, Marcy Lafferty, Terrance O'Connor, Momo Yashima, Billy van Zandt, and the other background players with whom I've populated this novel.

Much gratitude to the authors of the references which helped me get the details right, including David Kimble (*ST:TMP Blueprints* and cutaway poster), Shane Johnson (*Mr. Scott's Guide to the* Enterprise), Geoffrey Mandel (*ST Star Charts*), Judith & Garfield Reeves-Stevens (*The Art of ST* and *ST Phase II: The Lost Series*), Susan Sackett (*The Making of ST:TMP*), the Star Fleet Printing Office (*Federation Reference Series*), and the editors of *ST: The Magazine* for their special issue on the TMP Director's Edition. Non-*Trek* authors whose works provided scientific insights include Poul Anderson, Robert L. Forward, and Stephen L. Gillett.

Thanks to Ian McLean and Bernd Schneider for their helpful Web sites. I also received valuable advice from my fellow members of the TrekBBS's Trek Tech forum, particularly Aridas Sofia, Hutt359, Alex Rosenzweig, Timo Saloniemi, and Rick Sternbach; of Ex Isle's Exploring the Universe forum, particularly BR48, CJ Aegis, Delvo, John 3831, and Kaimia (not a real name in the bunch—what are you people hiding?!); and of Psi Phi's Trek Books forum, particularly Dayton Ward and the aforementioned Ian McLean.

Special thanks to Dr. Elizabeth Frierson, whose keen insights into history in general and modern Middle East history in particular were highly influential in shaping my ideas herein. If the world's leaders had listened to her, there'd be peace in the Middle East by now. Also thanks to Dr. Michael Sitko for helping me decide where the Fabrina supernova took place.

Finally, eternal gratitude to Marco Palmieri for saying yes when I pitched my dream *Trek* novel, and to Keith R.A. DeCandido for inviting me onto the playground.

We all create God in our own image.

—Willard Decker

EX MACHINA

PROLOGUE

YONADA WAS RISING in the western sky, and the farmers were praying to it for rain again. Natira, Governess of the Promised World Lorina, knew she had to put a stop to it—either the praying or the rising. Perhaps Yonada could be moved into a higher orbit, one where it would not be bright enough to see by daylight, and would not cross the sky four times a day. But that would not be enough. Not if the people's minds could not be opened, as hers had been.

Impulsively, Natira ordered the hovercar to a halt and climbed out, making Tasari's security team and the Federation team alike scramble to catch up with her. She strode through the mud, not caring that her elegant shoes and the hem of her scintillating gown would be ruined (she had plenty more, after all). She placed herself between the farmers and Yonada, striking a proud pose and speaking in her finest oratorical tones. Truly, how could a dim point of light in the sky compete with her resplendence? "The Oracle will not bring the rain," she told the misguided souls. "It is naught but a machine—a tool, no more than your plows and rakes. Have faith in your plows and rakes, in the toil of your own sinews, and in the dedication of the People, and then your crops will thrive, and make Lorina thrive."

The farmers looked on sullenly and timidly, save for one burly youth who rose to challenge her. "Apostate! Betrayer of the Oracle! Why should we listen to you, you Fedraysha whore?"

"Because I serve the Creators' *true* purpose," she replied with a confident smile. "The Oracle was merely a tool of the Creators, and its usefulness has ended. We must rely on ourselves, and on our Federation friends."

The youth spoke an excremental word, then followed it up with a chunk of the actual substance, fresh from the *konari* that pulled his plow. It splattered across the front of Natira's gown—and across the large wedges of her skin that the gown left artfully exposed. Natira winced, thankful that he hadn't aimed any higher.

Tasari's security troops were already moving, their crisp brown uniforms clashing with the farmers' simple homespun robes. The boy tried to run, but they quickly surrounded him with stunners drawn. "Be gentle!" Natira commanded. "For he is but a misguided youth. Such men as he are the future of Lorina, and we have too few as it is."

"But, Governess, an example must be made," Tasari insisted. "The people must learn—"

"Yes, *learn* they must," she said. "Therefore, take him and offer him guidance. Show him the Book of the People and the texts of the Federation. With education, with enlightenment, he and all Lorini can rise together from the pits of superstition into a bright new age."

Tasari simply nodded. "Yes, Governess."

Natira headed back toward the vehicle, eager to return home, discard her ruined gown, and be thoroughly bathed. She didn't envy the Federation observers, whose senses of smell were more acute than a Fabrini's. Indeed, Commissioner Soreth's nose visibly wrinkled, though the wizened Vulcan strove to conceal his reaction. The boyish Starfleet sociologist, Lindstrom, coughed into his fist. "If only you would provide us with your modern equipment,"

Natira told them wryly, "such toil and filth would be unnecessary."

Soreth tilted a stern eyebrow. "You are well aware, Governess, that you must make such progress for yourself. We can only advise."

Her attendants, who had rushed forth with washing cloths, proceeded to help her out of her ruined gown. "Even though you wish us to join your great Federation, so our medicines and ancient knowledge can benefit all your peoples?"

"We wish you to be a strong culture that can add to our diversity, not be subsumed by it."

"Well, you may rest assured, Commissioner, that the children of Fabrina will regain their ancient glory. The People will outgrow the lies of the Oracle, if I have any say at all."

"I have seen much evidence of such growth in my time here," Soreth replied. "It would not be logical to believe that a single . . . noxious incident negated such evidence."

"I wouldn't be so sure about that," Lindstrom said, trying not to look directly at her as her attendants cleansed her skin. Humans had taboos about the oddest things, considering that it had been they who had freed the Fabrini from their worst taboos. "The old beliefs have been ingrained into your culture for over ten thousand years. You can't expect them to fade away in a generation."

Natira glared at the boy. (True, he was not much younger than herself, but his callow face, sun-bleached hair, and impulsive manner made it hard to see him as anything but a boy.) "The Creators may have felt that those superstitions served some purpose on Yonada, while we were confined within the false sky of a hollow world. But they intended for the People to know the truth once we reached the World of the Promise. And I am sworn to serve the truth."

"So am I," Lindstrom said. "In Starfleet we're taught that

it's our first duty. But there are different kinds of truth. Whatever the origin of these beliefs, they have meaning to your people; they're woven throughout your culture."

"You speak like the Oracle," Natira scoffed as she began wrapping her replacement gown about her hips. "Truth should be truth for all."

But Lindstrom was frowning now, sniffing the air. "Do you smell that?"

Soreth cocked a brow. "It is impossible to smell anything else."

"No, not that—something . . . burning. . . ." He spun, stared intently at the groundcar for a moment, and then abruptly launched himself at Natira and Soreth in a most unseemly manner, shoving them down into the mud, negating all her attendants' efforts and ruining the new gown before she'd even fully donned it. . . .

And then the ground shook and searing heat washed over her and a blast of air pushed her deeper into the muck. When she had gathered her wits and sat up to look around, she saw a burning hulk where the hovercar had been. The flames were eerily quiet, and she realized there was no sound in her ears save a loud ringing—just as she realized that the driver had still been inside the car.

"So Natira lived?"

"Yes, Holiness," Moredi answered reluctantly. After his bomb had missed its target, he'd been tempted not to return to headquarters to face Dovraku's judgment. But had he run, he knew the Faithful would have found him, and dealt with him as surely and ruthlessly as they would deal with all their enemies, as he had been meant to deal with Natira. Instead, he faced his leader and spoke the truth, relying on his mercy. "But it was not my failure! That Fedraysha thug saved her! I curse them all! First their 'Star-fleet' shackles our Holy Oracle, now it shelters the bitch who betrayed Him!"

"Calm yourself," Dovraku replied evenly. "All things have their reasons. Even the Starfleet plays its part in the Oracle's calculations."

"How? By what logic do the Creators allow such evil to exist?"

Dovraku strode forward, his body relaxed, his gaze dispassionate—and struck Moredi across the face with a force that knocked him to the ground and nearly rendered him unconscious. "It is not for the likes of you to question the Creators' sublime logic," he said without emotion. "Remember why we strike now."

"Because of the Sign."

"Yes. The birth of a new god, a being of transcendent logic and infinite calculation . . . directly above the Fedraysha heartworld, as the Oracle is above Lorina." The prophet's voice remained calm and clear, unsullied by mortal passion, yet it grew heavier with meaning and faith. "And attending at the birth were the very Starfleeters who sacrificed our Oracle to their Fedraysha lies."

"But why?" Moredi dared to ask, keeping his tone pleading and not challenging. "Why would they slay one god and herald another?"

"That is something I hope to learn. But clearly there is a purpose to this. The apotheosis at Earth is a sign, a portent of the Oracle's own rebirth. And the triad of Kirk, McCoy, and Spock will have their role to play, of that I am certain. Perhaps as the Oracle's deliverers . . . or perhaps as its sacrifices."

Dovraku reached out his hand and helped Moredi to his knees, gazing down at him beatifically. "But there is no doubt that the Oracle will soon be reborn, greater and more magnificent than ever before. Mighty V'Ger has shown us the way."

CHAPTER ONE

Shall we give the Enterprise *a proper shakedown,*
Mr. Scott?
                                                        —James T. Kirk

JIM KIRK WAS LOST in the *Enterprise*.

Not the way he'd been two weeks ago, when his unfamiliarity with the redesigned starship had forced him to ask a yeoman the way to the turboshaft, embarrassing himself in front of Will Decker. No, as soon as the V'Ger mission had ended, Kirk had launched into an intensive study of the upgraded vessel's every feature. It was something he'd always meant to do, since it made sense for a Chief of Starfleet Operations to know these things, but somehow the business of managing the deployments, personnel, and maintenance of an entire fleet had always managed to keep him from concentrating on the particulars of a single redesign. Or, perhaps, he had subconsciously shied away from it, since it would have hurt too much to watch from afar, knowing that the *Enterprise* was no longer his.

Kirk had thought his crash course in the new *Enterprise*'s technical particulars had cured him of the romanticized reaction he'd had upon first seeing her in drydock, when Scotty had taken the long way around in the travel pod to show off his baby. But now, as he gazed out the large picture windows of Starbase 22's officers' lounge, which overlooked the base's dock facility and the gleaming starship moored therein, he was lost in her beauty once again. The old *Enterprise* had always reminded Kirk of Pegasus in flight, her skin gleaming white, her dorsal connector evoking the neck of a horse with head held high, her nacelle struts angled like wings poised for a forceful downstroke. Yet to an observer of a less poetical bent, it had been a utilitarian design, all functional straight lines and circles. Now, with her more forward-thrusting neck, her backswept pylons, her Art Deco nacelles, her subtly sleeker hull contours, and her constellation of self-illuminating lights, she was a sculpture evoking speed and energy. It was as though she'd emerged from her cocoon looking the way she'd always been meant to look.

Arguably there was little left of the original ship beyond the bare skeletal framework of the saucer and forward secondary hull. It certainly wasn't the first ship in naval history to be so thoroughly rebuilt, and as much as possible of the original material had been recycled into the new structural members and bulkheads. Still, every propulsion and power system, every computer, every piece of equipment, every meter of piping and optical cable, every last console and chair and lighting panel had been replaced with a new, improved model. Yet none of that mattered to Kirk. After all, most of the cells in his body at the time he'd first taken command of the starship had been replaced by now (though regrettably not with improved versions), but the gestalt remained the same; the body held the same soul. And Kirk had known as soon as he'd seen her that the same was true of *Enterprise*. The only difference was that her soul was more visible now.

"Don't you ever get bored?" came a cheerful voice. Kirk noted Commodore Fein's florid reflection in the window as the base commander entered the lounge. "Just staring at your ship? I mean, it's just . . . sitting there. It's not *doing* anything."

Kirk smiled. "Neither is the Mona Lisa. But people seem to like looking at her."

"Not my type," the big, dark-bearded commodore said with a shrug. "And I don't see what the big mystery is about the smile. I mean, aren't you *supposed* to smile when you get your picture taken?"

Kirk opened his mouth, but couldn't find a response to that. So he just went back to looking at the *Enterprise*. Fein joined him for a moment, but then yawned conspicuously, earning a glare from Kirk. "Sorry. Don't get me wrong, she is a pretty ship, no question. Even more so now that my guys are done with her."

"No argument there. Please extend my thanks to Commander Mattesino and his teams." Since the *Enterprise* had been launched prematurely, there hadn't been much time to install creature comforts. Kirk's impulsive decision to head "out there, thataway" on a shakedown cruise, rather than returning to Spacedock for debriefing, re-crewing, and final outfitting, had led to grumbling among the crew. So Kirk had arranged to have their personal effects delivered to Starbase 22, which had happened to be in the general direction of "thataway." Fein and his staff had done a superb job of fixing up the ship, making it less austere and more comfortable. More importantly, they'd helped Spock and the engineering staff purge the last of the Trojan-horse code with which Romulan spies had infected the computers during the refit, and which Decker had discovered literally the night before Kirk had booted him from command. It was only after the V'Ger mission, when Scott and Dr. Chapel had had time to brief him about the incident, that Kirk had learned just how much they all owed the late Will Decker. *No, not late, just . . . missing? Departed? Ascended? What, exactly?*

Fein spoke up again, interrupting his reverie. "Are you sure you don't want us to paint the hull, though? You just want to leave it like that?"

Kirk's eyes swept across *Enterprise*'s skin once more. He knew that what he saw was twenty thousand crystal-tritanium plates phase-transition bonded into a single, nearly seamless whole, each plate with its grain aligned differently so no crack in the hull could propagate too far. But to his eyes it was a mosaic of pearlescent, luminous grays, making the ship shimmer like a many-faceted jewel. "I prefer her this way," he said, but stopped himself from adding "naked," realizing how that would sound—especially if it got back to McCoy, who was still watching him for signs of obsession with the *Enterprise*.

But if I'm not obsessed, Kirk thought, *then why am I standing here gawking out the window at every chance, instead of mingling with my crew, getting to know them?* Particularly the new ones just coming on board here at the starbase. *Enterprise* had left port with a minimum standard crew of 431, many of them temporary personnel who had other assignments waiting now that the emergency was past. They had disembarked and just over a hundred new people had boarded here at the starbase, bringing the crew to its full five-hundred-person capacity. Kirk had formally welcomed them all aboard and gone through the proper motions, but he hadn't yet made any serious effort to get to know them, to connect with his crew and begin forging them into a team, a family, like the old crew had been. Why was that?

Kirk mentally shook himself from his reverie. "You're right, David," he said. "Enough rubbernecking. It's time I got back aboard." With Fein following, he left the officers' lounge with a deliberate stride.

The corridor leading to the docking gangway had its own windows, and Kirk was not surprised to see that he was far from the only person looking at the *Enterprise*. Certainly he could understand the base personnel's curiosity—for most, this was their first look at the cutting edge of Starfleet technology. But soon he realized that many of them were staring at *him*, with expressions ranging from curiosity to awe. He fidgeted. "What's wrong?" Fein asked.

Kirk hid behind a wry smirk. "Contrary to popular belief . . . I'm not that comfortable in the limelight."

"You can't blame them, Jim. That was a pretty spectacular mission you were on. A giant cloud cutting a warp-nine swath through Klingon and Federation space, spitting out a ship the size of Maui that almost wipes out the Earth, but somehow ends up putting on the mother of all fireworks displays instead, apparently in the course of evolving to a higher plane of existence. On top of which it turns out to be the long-lost *Voyager 6*, all grown up and looking for its mommy. Not only epic stuff, but with great visuals to boot."

"Visuals?"

"Of course. V'Ger's . . . *eruption* . . . has been all over the news feeds for a week and a half now, shot from every conceivable angle. Not to mention the sensor records from your flyby of the thing, which the feeds have been replaying ad nauseam. Pundits are coming out of the woodwork to explain what V'Ger was, what it became, and how it proves their pet theories about cosmology, cybernetics, evolution, God, whatever. I hear some people are making pilgrimages to Earth, declaring it a holy site." Fein frowned. "Haven't you heard any of this?"

"I've been busy! Besides, you know me, I'm more of a reader."

"Anyway, the point is, it's only natural that people would be interested in the ship that was in the middle of it all, and its captain."

"But Starfleet people? We encounter . . . strange cosmic phenomena all the time."

"But this is a special case. Face it, Jim, you literally saved the Earth. That's going to get a guy a fair amount of publicity, especially if that guy happens to be James T. Kirk."

Kirk sighed. "I'm not *James T. Kirk,*" he said, echoing Fein's dramatic delivery. "I'm just Jim Kirk. I'm no more special than any other captain. It's just . . . publicity."

"Yeah, I know. The Pelos thing. Hard enough trying to live that down, and now this gets dumped on you. Face it, Jim, from now on you're a cosmic hero, larger than life, like it or not." Fein chuckled. "If it were me, I'd capitalize a little. A promotion, a book deal . . . But then, that's not the way of the cosmic hero, is it?"

"Keep it up, David, and I'll stop coming here for repairs," Kirk said with more good humor than he felt.

"And miss out on the food? That'll be the day." The commodore slapped Kirk on the back and made his farewells, leaving the captain alone with his thoughts as he strode along the gangway.

Cosmic hero. Where did they get that? But then, maybe Kirk had started to believe it himself. He'd been so sure that only his years of experience could let him save the world. But how much had he really contributed to the V'Ger mission? It had been Spock whose mind-meld with V'Ger had provided the key insights into its nature. And it had been Will Decker who had made the final sacrifice that had really saved the world, giving up his corporeal existence to fulfill V'Ger's need to merge with its Creator and evolve to a new level of consciousness.

True, Decker might have been more cautious than Kirk, might not have taken the necessary steps in time; but then again, as first officer it had been his duty to advise caution. Had he been in the center seat, he might have made the same choices Kirk had. So what had Kirk really contributed to the mission? What had he done to deserve anyone's accolades—or to earn the trust of his crew?

Kirk pushed those thoughts aside as he neared the main gangway hatch to the *Enterprise*. For better or worse, he was her captain again, and it was time to start acting like it. "Permission to come aboard, ma'am," he said to Bosun's Mate zh'Ral as he crossed the threshold.

"Permission granted, sir," the Andorian replied. "Welcome back, Captain."

"Thank you, Crewman," Kirk said, appreciating the informal addendum. Indeed, he did feel welcomed. Something about the air, the gravity, the ambience of the ship, as standardized as it all was, just felt more *right* than the starbase had, more like home.

Now all Kirk had to do was prove himself worthy of that welcome. He needed a mission. This was supposed to be a working shakedown, after all. The fleet was stretched dangerously thin these days, still recovering from the losses sustained in the past several years—*Constellation, Intrepid, Excalibur, Defiant, Zheng He,* the entire crews of *Exeter* and *Sphinx* and *Ashoka,* too many others. This had led to the preposterous situation of Earth being left defenseless save for one unready heavy cruiser and a smattering of light cruisers too weak to make a difference. (Well, that and a state-of-the-art planetary defense grid, which V'Ger had switched off like a light panel after extracting its highly encrypted specs from *Enterprise*'s computer in a matter of seconds.) Now, in the wake of their close call, the Federation Council was finally heeding Admiral Nogura's calls for more resources. *Enterprise* was certain to be put to real use before long, testing her untried systems in action, in what would no doubt be a long and interesting (in the Chinese sense) process of discovery. Klingons attacking from without, systems blowing up from within . . . that was just what he needed, Kirk thought wryly, to take his mind off his self-pity.

As he neared the turbolift, he saw his first officer emerge. "Mr. Spock!"

Spock nodded. "Captain."

"Were you coming to find me?"

An eyebrow lifted, and Kirk reflected on how much he'd missed the sight. "No, sir. I was . . . going for a walk."

Kirk stared at him. "Not another spacewalk, I trust?"

Spock reacted with a slight but genuine smile—a sight Kirk was still trying to get used to. "No, I have had my fill of those for now." He paused. "I . . . have had difficulty meditating since my meld with V'Ger. I recalled that my mother frequently enjoys taking walks around the city— generally at night, when the temperatures are more amenable to a human—in order to, as she puts it, spend some time with her thoughts. To me, the concept of walking with no specific destination or exercise goal in mind always seemed illogical. But Amanda believes it helps her to focus her mind. She told me once that she tends to associate a given thought with a given place, so that any single place can grow 'cluttered' with thoughts, making it difficult to sort among them. Walking apparently allows her to . . . distribute them more effectively. Or so she has always claimed."

Kirk smiled. "It doesn't sound very logical, does it?"

Spock tilted his head thoughtfully. "In fact, humanoid brain function is largely an associative process, so there is merit to the idea. However, I will grant that I have become more open to . . . unorthodox ideas of late." Kirk harrumphed. "Sir?"

"Oh . . . nothing."

"Very well."

"It's just that . . . Bones and I spent five years trying to get you to explore your human side . . . you spent decades of your life *immersed* in human culture . . . yet despite all that, what finally got you to open up was a two-minute mind-meld with the galaxy's biggest computer!" Spock looked at him with bemusement—or was it amusement? "I just feel a bit . . . slighted. On behalf of the human species, that is."

"I see," Spock said dubiously. "Well . . . if it's any conso-
lation, Jim, the original *Voyager 6* probe *was* built by
humans."

Kirk threw him a long-suffering look, but it soon turned
into a smile. There in Spock's eyes was that puckish humor
Kirk had always believed he'd seen there in the past, but
now it was no longer as veiled, as regulated, as once it had
been. All joking aside, that meld had changed him, and so
far Kirk liked the results. "Go on with your walk, Mr.
Spock. But try not to leave too many stray thoughts lying
around in the corridors. They aren't as wide as they used to
be," he added, rapping on the angled, metallic bulkhead.

Spock definitely smiled this time. "Yes, sir," he said, and
turned away. As the Vulcan strolled—yes, *strolled*—around
the bend, Kirk was certain he heard a chuckle. He shook his
head. *This will take some getting used to,* he thought as he
called the lift. Although he was intrigued to see where
Spock's journey would take him, he found he somewhat
missed the old, deadpan Spock who always pretended not to
get the joke.

Spock paused to gather himself before the chuckles got out
of control. Succumbing to humor was a pleasant sensation,
but right now he needed to find his focus. (And it hadn't
been that funny anyway.) That was the paradox: his recent
epiphany about the necessity of emotion had given him
much to think about, but his emotions made it difficult for
him to think. And that tended to bring annoyance, which
made matters worse and threatened to set off an escalating
cycle. That was the real reason he had "gone for a
walk"—sitting in his quarters, fruitlessly attempting to meditate, had been an exercise in frustration, and he had simply
felt an overwhelming urge to exert himself physically, presumably a manifestation of the instinctive fight-or-flight

reaction. Since there was nothing in his utilitarian quarters to fight against, and since he hadn't wished to explain a roomful of smashed furniture to the quartermaster, he had chosen flight, or at least movement. Only once he was out in the corridors, his legs carrying him aimlessly forward, had he remembered his mother's long meandering walks, and the benefits they seemed to bring her.

Spock's continued difficulty with impulse control was a matter of concern to him. At first, he had been able to attribute it to the neurological trauma he had sustained when the contents of V'Ger's cosmos-spanning memory banks had flooded his brain. Indeed, many times over the past ten days, he had been tempted to conclude that his new emotionalism was solely the result of impairment to his mesiofrontal cortex, and that once he was fully healed he could return to his old, strictly logical ways. But he knew that would be an act of self-deception. He had seen the barrenness of a life ruled solely by logic. V'Ger had journeyed across gigaparsecs of space and millennia of time (for the singularity which had hurled it across space had also sent it well into the past), amassing unprecedented amounts of knowledge about the workings of this universe while searching through thousands of galaxies for its point of origin. Yet even with all that knowledge, it remained completely empty and unfulfilled. With no emotion at all, there was no motivation, no sense of purpose or meaning to existence.

In retrospect, this should not have come as such a surprise. Vulcan neurologists had learned millennia ago that even the most logical, abstract decisions engaged the emotional centers of the humanoid brain, with the more sensible or correct option being selected because it *felt* more right. Yet Vulcan philosophers shied away from confronting the ramifications of this fact. Spock saw now that to do so was itself illogical. And it would be just as illogical for him to deny the knowledge he had gained simply because it failed to conform to his prejudices. Besides, by now his brain function should have returned to normal, so he could no longer use it as an excuse. That recognition alone, however, did not solve his control problem, nor did it explain his inability to meditate.

At least the change of scenery had helped to ease the clutter in Spock's mind. But it couldn't take the place of meditation. There was too much sensory input, as passing crew members greeted him, as conversational echoes from side corridors reached his sensitive ears, as the scents of over a dozen different species asserted themselves to his olfactory receptors. All it did was to take his mind off the questions he sought to meditate on; it brought him no closer to finding answers.

And even without the sensory interference, it was growing harder and harder to sense the Voyager, as he had come to think of the entity which had emerged from the fusion of V'Ger, Decker, and the Deltan navigator Ilia. From the moment of its emergence, Spock had no longer felt the same telepathic rapport he'd somehow achieved with V'Ger—an awareness that many other telepaths across known space had reported experiencing as well, though only Spock had been in a position to use it constructively. According to the news feeds, those telepaths had felt an overwhelming surge at the moment of the transformation, and then nothing more, as though the entity had either moved beyond their sensory range or transformed beyond their ability to detect. But Spock had retained some lingering awareness, an aftereffect of his direct contact with V'Ger's mind.

He knew that the Voyager had gained the sense of purpose V'Ger sought, that it felt a newfound freedom and was suffused with passionate curiosity. More: the Voyager was no longer alone. Even greater than the freedom to intuit new levels of existence, it had learned, was the joy of having someone to share its knowledge with, to share *itself* with. Although the Voyager was a unified being, Spock could still recognize the facets that made it up. V'Ger was still the core, the power and purpose of the whole, still driven by an overriding urge to learn all that was learnable, yet now finally able to understand the human curiosity that had inspired that programming, and able to gain fulfillment from its fruits. Decker was there, suffusing the Voyager with awe and wonder, giving it the imagination it needed to find new realms, yet tempering it with a sense of caution and discipline, keeping the newborn entity from becoming too reckless on its ventures into the unknown. And Ilia was there too, a quieter voice, less of a driving force, yet in some ways serving the most crucial role of all. Her experience with Deltan mating practices gave her insight into the sharing of minds and made her the linchpin of this far more intimate joining. While Decker gave it the impulse to quest outward and seek out new realms of existence, Ilia gave it the instinct to know itself, and to love the selves that made it up.

Spock sensed that the Voyager was exploring realms that made four-dimensional spacetime seem flat and claustrophobic, sensing and seeking contact with other minds that resided within those realms, but the experiences were too far outside Spock's referential frame for him to comprehend. And he sensed that the Voyager was growing, searching through its memory for the countless sentient beings which V'Ger had absorbed—all of their minds digitally preserved as perfectly as Ilia's had been, but not recognized as consciousnesses until now—and methodically incorporating them all into the composite mind, allowing them to live again, perhaps forever, as parts of its growing gestalt. Many might consider this a reasonable approximation of an afterlife. Spock didn't know, however, never having given much thought to the question.

Spock's own rapport with the Voyager was swiftly fading as it evolved further and further away from the mind he'd melded with. He regretted this; on some elementary levels, the Voyager's journey of discovery paralleled Spock's own—they were both logical beings who had recognized that logic was not enough and had achieved a new unity with an emotional half. Spock had hoped that an ongoing rapport with the Voyager would bring him guidance on his own journey. But it seemed he would soon be entirely on his own.

Spock registered that his meanderings had somehow brought him down to Deck 7, right outside sickbay. He lifted a brow, wondering if his walk had been as direction-less as he'd thought. Fascinating, to be guided by motives he hadn't consciously reasoned out. No, correction: he had always had those motives; he just hadn't admitted it to him-self before. Vulcan thought, he was coming to understand, was not wholly rational so much as wholly rationalized. But Spock judged his subconscious impulse, if such it had been, to have merit. Perhaps a medical consultation would be ben-eficial. Perhaps there was some physical factor he was over-looking.

On entering the medical lab, he found it empty, but he could see Doctors McCoy and Chapel through the window of the CMO's office, and their voices carried plainly through the open door.

"Are you sure the damn thing is calibrated now?"

"I supervised the installation myself, Leonard. I think I know what I'm talking about!"

"Well, then according to this thing, the whole crew is currently dying of hypothermia!"

"Let me see that. . . . Oh, Leonard, you're reading it wrong! Are you still thinking in Fabrini units?"

"Damn . . . I knew I spent too much time on that blasted backwater. Okay, how do I select between channels again?"

"Just read the menus, all right? I have rounds to do."

"Don't leave me here alone with this monstrosity, Christine! I didn't sign up for this kind of torture."

"You're the one who always says a little suffering's good for the soul."

"I never say that."

"Well, one of us does, so you're getting no sympathy from me. Honestly, you're as bad a pupil as you are a patient."

"Damn straight."

Spock considered leaving before Chapel registered his presence, but it was already too late. "Mr. Spock!" the doctor said as she stood in the doorway.

"Doctor."

After an awkward pause, she steeled herself and spoke. "I haven't seen much of you lately. I think you've been avoiding me." At his uncomfortable silence, she smiled. "Not that I blame you. The way I used to carry on over you, it's no wonder you'd think I'd see this as my big moment, now that you've . . . well, you know."

"Yes . . . I am aware of the circumstances."

"Well, you don't have to worry, Mr. Spock. I've long since gotten over that silly little crush. I finally realized I wasn't doing myself any good, constantly falling for distant, undemonstrative men."

Spock looked at her warily. "But I am no longer . . . entirely undemonstrative."

Chapel pursed her lips. "No, I suppose that's true. But I think . . . you still have a lot of questions to answer before you're even ready to consider romance. If you don't mind my saying so."

"No." In fact, he was quite relieved to hear it.

There was another uneasy pause. "Well! Anyway, I have my rounds to get to. I'll see you around, Mr. Spock."

He inclined his head. "Doctor."

Chapel departed, perhaps a bit more hastily than was consistent with her breezy manner, and Spock approached the office. But he winced as McCoy cried out again. "Chris! The damn thing says this crewman is breathing fluorine!"

"That must be one of the Zaranites!" came Chapel's voice from around the corner.

"You mean to tell me there's actually a species that breathes *fluorine?!*"

"In fact," Spock interposed, "the Zaranites' main respiratory gas is oxygen. But there are abundant microbes on Zaranai that metabolize fluorides and release fluorine gas as a waste product. Since fluorine is highly reactive, it does not remain in the atmosphere for long, but the trace amounts that are available play an important supplementary role in the Zaranite metabolism, much as trace minerals do in yours or mine. Each of our Zaranite crew members' breathing tanks contains a colony of these fluorogenic microbes and—"

"Spock!" McCoy interrupted. "For someone who's supposedly learned to understand emotion, you still seem to have an inordinately hard time telling when you're irritating someone!"

Spock threw him an innocent look. "Since irritation is your normative state, Dr. McCoy, it can be difficult to distinguish the individual causes."

"Well, whenever you're around, Spock, there's no need to look very far." He harrumphed. "Though right now this blasted perscan unit's just as annoying. Whose brilliant idea was it to put medical monitors in everyone's belt buckles? Just gives people one more excuse not to go see their doctor. 'Oh, they're monitoring me anyway, they'll just tell me if anything's wrong.' Just one more layer of technology getting in the way. Medicine isn't about scans and readings, it's about talking to a patient, looking him in the eye, listening to his voice. It's about being kind and reassuring, goddammit!" McCoy snarled. Spock unleashed an eyebrow at the irony, but the doctor either missed or ignored it. "Not to mention how much I hate the idea of everyone's confidential medical information getting broadcast all over the ship."

"In fact, Doctor, the perscan units are passive, requiring the unit here in sickbay to scan them remotely, out of just such privacy con—" He broke off at McCoy's glare.

"I still don't like it. It's Orwellian medicine. It's convenience and efficiency overriding human needs, and I'm gonna raise the biggest stink I can to get them left out of the next uniform design." He pulled at his collar. "Blasted quartermasters can't make up their minds anyway—we'll probably have new uniforms in another six months. Well, maybe for once they'll design something that doesn't look like a pair of pajamas."

"Indeed," Spock said. "If you have such difficulty telling the difference, it would explain why your uniform so often appears to have been slept in."

"Did you just come here to insult me, or did you have a reason?"

Spock took a breath. "I am still having difficulty meditating."

McCoy sighed. "Now, Spock, you know we've ruled out a physiological reason for that."

"A neurological reason, yes. But perhaps there is some other factor involved. A hormonal imbalance, perhaps."

"Hm." McCoy leaned back in his seat and fixed a piercing gaze on Spock. "Have you considered that there may be a psychological reason? Something you can't get off your mind?"

"That is generally what meditation is *for*—to clear one's mind, or to deal with an individual problem in a focused way, without the distraction of other thoughts. If simply having something on my mind interfered with meditation, there would be no point to meditation."

McCoy harrumphed again. "Then maybe there's something you're *not* thinking about that you should. Something that's bothering you in the back of your mind, but that you're avoiding facing directly. So no matter how clear your conscious mind may be, your subconscious is still riled."

"I do not see how that could be," Spock said, furrowing his brow. "Lately I have made a point of confronting ideas and issues I have avoided in the past. I have been in the process of reevaluating all of my beliefs."

"All while I've been doing my level best not to gloat *too* much," McCoy interposed.

Spock's look showed what he thought of that. "You may wish to reserve your gloating, Doctor. I have not yet reached my conclusions. There is still much of merit in the body of Vulcan thought. And even if I have chosen to accept my emotions, they are still Vulcan emotions, not human. I cannot assume that the human path is valid for me."

McCoy quirked one of his own brows. "Then maybe you should be talking to Dr. Onami. She's the new xenopsychologist. If anyone understands anything about Vulcan emotions," and he shook his head at the phrase, "it's more likely to be her than me."

Spock frowned. "I am . . . uneasy with that suggestion. As you know, I am a private man. Even though Dr. Onami is no doubt quite skilled, I would prefer not to share these matters with a stranger."

Spock could see in McCoy's eyes what it meant to him to be counted among those Spock trusted enough to confide in. Still, evidently he couldn't resist teasing. "Turning down the help of the most qualified person? That's not very logical, is it?"

"No . . . it is not."

McCoy grimaced. "Ahh, you're no fun anymore." He leaned back, thinking. "Well, there's always family. Sometimes they'll listen when nobody else will." Spock just stared. "Oh. Yeah, right. If Sarek practically disowned you for choosing your own career, I can just imagine how he reacted to your coming out of the closet."

" 'Closet,' Doctor?"

"Never mind."

"In any case, I have not yet told Sarek or Amanda of my . . . recent insights."

Leaning forward again, McCoy said, "Well, maybe that's it right there. Maybe you're shying away from taking that step, and that's what's keepin' your subconscious all hot and bothered."

"On the contrary, Doctor—I have been consciously examining the question every day since my epiphany occurred. If I have not yet taken the step of notifying my family, it is because I have not yet determined what it is I am to notify them of—since I have not yet determined where my new path is leading."

"Then I don't know what to tell you, Mr. Spock." The doctor sighed and shook his head, poking at the perscan display on his desk again. "Hell, right now I don't know what to tell anyone. I'm just an old hermit who got himself yanked back into civilization against his will. I'm still struggling to get caught up with all the changes around here. Chapel's an M.D., you're a born-again . . . whatever, Chekov's gone from eager young space cadet to gung-ho security chief, the crew's half-made up of species I can hardly even *pronounce,* let alone know how to treat, I can't even find the bathrooms on this new ship yet—and don't try to tell me, I see that look, you should know a figure of speech by now."

Spock studied him. "Is there something on *your* mind, Dr. McCoy?"

"Ahh, don't mind me, I'm just tired. Maybe we both are. Tell you what, instead of worryin' about meditation, you just try gettin' a good night's sleep. Can't overstate the importance of simply bein' rested." He sighed. "Back home in my cabin, that was restful. Middle of the Appalachians, nothin' but nature for miles around, a secluded little fishin' hole . . . Be there now if Jim hadn't drafted me. I still can't figure out how Nogura's boys even *found* me. . . ."

Spock saw that McCoy would be of no more help to him today. "Very well, Doctor," he said, rising. "I shall take your advice . . . and recommend that you do the same."

"Most sensible thing you've said—well, ever. Pleasant dreams, Spock."

Spock's lips twisted in irony. "We shall see."

Security Minister Tasari was frowning as he entered Natira's hospital room. That in itself told her little, since it was his preferred expression. But usually it was less pronounced, just a general look of watchfulness or concern; with his rounded, unimpressive features, he sometimes looked to her like a small boy straining to follow a mathematics lesson. Now, though it never varied by any great amount, his frown seemed deeper than usual. "Governess," he said in his flat, unpolished voice, "I regret to inform you that there has been another attack. A dissident attempted to smuggle an explosive device into the Federation consulate. Our guards became suspicious and attempted to search his robes. He detonated the device, taking two of my troops with him."

Natira was aghast. "He killed himself?" Tasari simply nodded. "Incredible. They are truly mad." She shook herself. "The violence grows worse by the day. Tell me, Tasari, have you made any progress at all in your investigations?"

"Very little, Governess. The explosives are apparently fertilizer-based, an easily made compound, often used by farmers to clear rocks and stumps. It would have been easy for anyone to obtain access."

"I see. Tell me, what of the boy you detained? Did he have any knowledge of the planned attack on my person?"

"None that we were able to extract before . . ."

Her gaze sharpened. "Before what?"

"My lady, the boy . . . attempted escape. There was an . . . incident with a stairwell. . . . He is dead."

Natira closed her eyes. However much the upstart youth had humiliated her, she hadn't believed him truly criminal, simply misguided. Perhaps his flight indicated guilt, but that didn't feel right somehow. "So much death . . . all in the name of an ancient fraud."

Tasari took a step closer. "My lady . . . perhaps we should not be so squeamish about death. The Oracle dealt it out when it needed to, and order was well maintained."

"That was the way of the Oracle," she snapped. "The way of the past, of our enslavement. We are building a modern world here, and we will not sink to the Oracle's barbarism. Ours is the way of enlightenment, the way of the Federation."

"Yes, Governess," Tasari said, not seeming convinced.

But Tasari was not a thinker. He did what he was told. He had served her when she had served the Oracle's madness, and now he served her as she strove to undo it. As long as she remained committed to the true way, he would follow obediently.

Perhaps that is the problem, she realized. A man like Tasari could provide the stalwart strength and discipline to preserve the peace, but not the inspiration needed to find new solutions. She needed inspiration. And with that, Natira thought back to the one man in her life who had truly inspired her—and his friends who had saved her world once before. Perhaps they could help her save it again.

CHAPTER TWO

We are now of one mind.

One heart.

One life. —Traditional Yonadan wedding vows

IT TOOK LONGER than McCoy had hoped before he was able to leave sickbay for the refuge of his quarters. With all the new crew members, the schedule of physicals was exhausting—and the sheer diversity of biologies involved made the process far more complex. *It was hard enough keeping up when it was just Spock, M'Ress, and Arex,* thought McCoy. *Now we've got fluorine-breathers, plankton-feeders, big gray caterpillars. . . . What's next, Hortas and talking spiders? How in hell do they expect an old country doctor to keep up with it all?*

McCoy sank down onto his bed, but it was still hard to relax in this unfamiliar environment. He missed his wooden walls, his fireplace, the rafters creaking in the wind. *Why am I even still here?* he asked himself for the hundredth time. Chapel understood the new sickbay and the new crew better than he did. And he'd essentially won his years-long argument with Spock. So what possible contribution was left for him to make here?

If there was anything keeping him here, it was Jim Kirk. McCoy was still concerned about his old friend's emotional state after the way he'd been yanked around for the past few years. *No good deed goes unpunished,* McCoy thought, reflecting on how straightforward the decision to save the Pelosians had seemed.

By the time the *Enterprise* had discovered Pelos, its population had already been ravaged by the climatic catastrophes caused when a dense interstellar dust cloud had blocked their sun. Spock had projected that the new plague would wipe the rest of them out within two years. But their empress had believed that only the gods should determine who lived or died, that any medical intervention was blasphemy. Kirk had seen no choice but to give a little clandestine assistance to the rebels seeking the empress's overthrow. Between that and the species' total extinction, it had seemed the only sane choice to make. And he'd done it without revealing the existence of other worlds, passing off McCoy's serums as a new discovery from a distant land. And if a little deflector-dish action happened to thin out the dust a little faster, nobody on the planet had to know.

But somehow Starfleet Command had seen it differently. It had been around the end of their nominal five-year tour, and Command had been reviewing Kirk's request to extend the mission. The Pelos affair had unfolded right under the nose of the petty bureaucrat who'd been sent to review the fitness of the ship and crew. Kirk had immediately been brought up on charges of violating the Prime Directive, and the ship had been ordered back to Earth posthaste.

The scandal had only grown bigger as every one of Kirk's past questionable decisions had been put under the microscope. Of course, the veteran officers on the review panel had appreciated that Kirk had upheld the Directive more often than he'd bent it, and that his apparent violations had usually been in response to other interference of one sort or another. They also understood that a captain in the field must be free to interpret the rules flexibly for each situation, and that Kirk's record in that regard was no worse than that of any other effective captain.

But it had been Kirk, not any other captain, whose record had been dissected in the media, and so in the public eye Kirk had gained a reputation as a rogue, a loose cannon, or at best a well-meaning cultural imperialist. It had been the biggest scandal to hit Starfleet since the M-5 debacle. Yet at the same time, there was no disputing the good Kirk had done, the lives he'd saved. That got exaggerated in the media as much as his "bad boy" image had been. Starfleet and the public alike were polarized on whether to keelhaul him or canonize him.

So Fleet Admiral Nogura had found the most politically expedient solution: promoting Jim to a desk job with a fancy title, nominally rewarding him while in fact pushing him to the sidelines to keep him out of trouble. It worked at quelling the controversy, to be sure. But McCoy had been more concerned about the cost to the man. He'd angrily confronted Nogura, telling him that getting stuck behind a desk was cruel and unusual punishment for a quarterdeck breed like Jim, a man whose spirit could only thrive out there on a ship. Even busting him to crewman and sending him out on a freighter would have been kinder. McCoy had threatened to resign if Nogura didn't reverse the decision, and had then been forced to follow through on his threat.

McCoy had tried to keep an eye on Kirk for a while, but it had been hard to do so as a civilian, and it had grown even harder as Kirk had fallen more under the sway of Nogura's right-hand geisha, Lori Ciana. *Nahh, I shouldn't speak ill of the dead,* McCoy thought, remembering that Vice Admiral Ciana had died in that infernal transporter just hours before he himself had been compelled to go through it. But there was no question that she had taken advantage of Kirk's vulnerability, seducing him into believing he could succeed as an admiral, or at least providing a distraction from his unhappiness. McCoy really didn't know what had happened between them after he'd decided to join the medical mission to Daran IV. But though Jim had certainly grieved over her death—repressing his feelings until after the mission was over, but then facing them once he had the luxury—it hadn't been the deep, love-of-your-life kind of grief he'd shown after Edith or Miramanee, but a more routine level of grief, the kind he'd feel for any colleague or crew member. With Jim Kirk, even that routine grief was sincere and heartfelt, but whatever he'd shared with Ciana must have pretty definitively ended some time before.

Maybe that was why Jim had rediscovered his passion for command, and had ultimately managed to fight his way into a position to reclaim the *Enterprise.* But when McCoy had come aboard, he'd quickly seen how that desire had become an obsession to the captain, blinding him to the good of the mission and pitting him against Decker—his best advisor on the new ship—like two men fighting over a woman.

Once McCoy had confronted his old friend and made him see how he was acting, Kirk had seemed to pull himself together. That had always been the man's special strength, McCoy thought—he had a unique balance of self-confidence and self-doubt, always able to question himself and confront his flaws and follies, but always able to resolve them decisively and not let them get in the way of his job or his life. Well, most of the time. The way Nogura and Ciana had seemed to have Jim whipped, McCoy hadn't been sure if he still had it. But he took the *Enterprise* into the belly of the beast and brought it out in one piece, and McCoy knew the old Jim Kirk was back again. Maybe he was still a bit tentative, but he'd find his way.

So really, did he need McCoy's guidance that badly now? With Spock back at his side, with a ship's deck beneath his feet once more, was he ready to carry on without a certain old country doctor who grew more restless each day he spent away from said old country?

McCoy was just about to drift off to sleep when the intercom whistled. He flailed around for the bedside switch and somehow managed to hit it. "McCoy."

"Dr. McCoy, there's an incoming message for you," came a voice he didn't recognize, presumably whoever was on communications this shift. "It's not real-time, but it's marked urgent."

"Ohhhh," he groaned. "Why is it that urgent messages never come at two in the afternoon?" He pulled himself up to where he could see the big viewscreen in the next room through the translucent partition. "Okay, put it through."

The rustic painting he'd set as the screen's default display gave way to a face he'd never expected to see again— the regal, lovely face of a woman he'd married and divorced in a single day. "McCoy," said Natira. "The People of Lorina need your help."

"Lorina?" Kirk asked.

"Daran IV," McCoy explained, "where the Yonadans settled. It's the Fabrini word for 'promise.' "

"Ahh. Of course." Kirk's hadn't remembered the local name for the planet, but he recalled the Yonada incident vividly. It had been just after the Kettaract affair in the Lantaru sector, out on the fringes of explored space. On the way back, the *Enterprise* had encountered the generation ship Yonada on the outskirts of the Daran system. It had been on a collision course with the fifth planet, home to a sizable civilization—spaceflight-capable, but lacking the means to deflect an asteroid this size. The straightforward mission to redirect Yonada's course had been complicated by the religious dogma imposed by its ruling computer, the Oracle—and by Dr. McCoy's diagnosis with a terminal disease. Not to mention by his whirlwind courtship, marriage, and divorce with Yonada's high priestess, Natira—a set of events Kirk wasn't familiar with in much detail, since Bones had barely said a word about Natira afterward.

But now here she was on Bones' comm screen, looking elegantly disheveled as she sat up in her hospital bed, her mahogany tresses tumbling loose to her waist. "Computer, resume playback," Kirk said.

". . . I am told you are with the *Enterprise* again," Natira continued. She spoke in Standard now, but with the same kind of stilted formality with which the universal translators, in their ineffable wisdom, had rendered her Fabrini speech in their first encounter. "And I would request the help of your shipmates as well. Our world is facing a time of crisis. We are besieged by fanatics who will not let go of the Oracle's lies, who wish to drag the People back into the darkness of the past. I myself was nearly a victim of their madness, saved only by your courageous colleague, Mr. Lindstrom." Kirk remembered the hotheaded young sociologist he'd assigned to Beta III after the Landru affair, and was pleased to hear that he was acquitting himself well. "The explosion killed one of my loyal retainers, and would have left me grievously crippled if not for your Federation medicine.

"But that was merely the first of the attacks. In the days since, more crude explosives have been set off at various state facilities. Over a dozen of the People have been slain by these cravens, and our security forces have been unable to locate them and bring an end to this madness.

"I need your Starfleet's aid in quelling this unrest, so that we may continue to bring the People forward into the future promised by the Creators." Apparently her injury hadn't impaired her capacity for oratory. Even in a sickbed, she stood on a dais. "And I wish your ministrations as I convalesce, McCoy. Not only as the finest physician ever to grace the World, but as . . . an old and dear friend, to comfort me in this time of hardsh—"

"Viewer off," McCoy interrupted. "Trust me, that's all the important stuff. Except for some data files about the unrest."

"Let me take a look."

McCoy yielded the console to Kirk, but said, "Won't make any difference. You've already made up your mind to go, haven't you?"

"What makes you say that?" Kirk asked.

"Don't give me that doe-eyed innocent look, you know it never works on me. You've been champin' at the bit for some action."

"Bones, Daran IV is a Federation ally requesting our help, and there aren't any other starships that far out. What are you saying, that you don't want to help Natira?"

"No, of course not, Jim. You know me, I can't turn my back on a lady in distress. It's just . . . well, this particular lady . . ."

"As I recall," Kirk said with a rakish grin, "you and this particular lady hit it off with spectacular ease."

"Well, that was . . ." McCoy wandered over to the cabinet and withdrew a bottle. "You want a drink?"

"No, thanks, I'm on duty. I thought you were trying to cut down, for your health."

"I said *a* drink. No harm in just the one." He poured. "Well, the second one."

"Bones—"

"All right, all right. Don't rush me." He took a seat. "When I met Natira, I thought I was dying. I was . . . *numb,* I was in shock. All I saw ahead of me was bleakness. And then this gorgeous, classy lady I barely know starts goin' on about wantin' to spend her life with me. It was . . . She was offering me a future when I thought I didn't have one. It gave me something to look forward to in the time I had left.

I guess I was looking for comfort. And frankly, Jim, I didn't see what I had to lose. Nothing mattered to me anymore. I was already a goner."

"So you didn't love her."

"Jim, I was hardly feelin' anything right then. Like I said, I was just looking for what comfort I could find." He sighed, took a sip from his glass. "But then that blasted Oracle tried to fry my frontal lobe, and as soon as I woke up I was askin' myself what the hell I'd gotten myself into. I mean, nothing against Natira, but I must've been out of my mind to agree to live in that kind of a police state, get a death trigger stuck in my skull so I couldn't have any unpopular thoughts." He chuckled. "Can you imagine? Me, only thinkin' what's popular to think?"

Kirk joined in his laughter. "You wouldn't last a day. In fact, you didn't."

"Yeah . . . and then I realized what a fool I'd made of myself. I knew I couldn't stay in that place. I offered to take Natira with me to the *Enterprise,* but she wouldn't go, decided she had to help her people now that she knew the truth about Yonada. I made some stupidly noble offer to stay with her, but she saw that I couldn't stay." He shook his head. "Soon as she offered me an out, I seized it—spouted some cock-and-bull story about this noble quest I had to go on to find a cure for others like me. Then Spock comes in from the next room with the cure right there in his tricorder." He gulped back the rest of the drink. Kirk watched with concern, but the doctor didn't reach for the bottle again. "I no longer had an excuse not to stay, but I left anyway. I didn't even have the guts to say good-bye to her face."

Kirk studied his friend. "I wondered why you never took me up on my offer to go back there once they made planet-fall."

"Well, that was a busy time for me. We'd just gotten through the Dramian plague, then Spock came down with choriocytosis. . . . But yeah, I was just as happy not to press the issue."

"Even though you obviously remembered the date."

McCoy blushed. "Yeah, I guess."

"But you did go back to Daran IV eventually."

"Yeah, after I resigned . . . there was this big medical mission organized to go there and study their ancient medicine, find more miracle cures. I couldn't come up with a good excuse not to come along, especially since I'd had the bad sense to make myself the Federation's leadin' expert on the stuff." He scoffed. "Though mainly by default.

"So all the way out there, I was scared as a long-tailed cat in a room full o' rocking chairs, dreading what'd happen when I saw Natira again. Turned out she was so busy gettin' the new settlement set up, writin' a constitution and so on, that she barely had any time for me. Don't get me wrong, Jim—I could see in her eyes, she still had feelings for me. But she couldn't spare a moment to pursue 'em. And I was just fine with that.

"I wasted no time gettin' as busy as I could myself, spending all my time out with the common people while Natira was walkin' the halls of power. Learning about their folk remedies, watchin' how they dealt with sickness and injuries. I helped out with the farming and building, too." He smiled. "I grew to like it. That's why I retired to the mountains when I came back to Earth. That and . . ." His smile faded. "Well, to be honest, Natira had been findin' a bit more spare time, and had started to press me. I made some excuse about needing to go back to Earth, and . . . well, I guess you can go ahead and paint a yellow stripe down my back. I was hiding from a woman."

"Come on, Bones," Kirk said. "You wouldn't go to those lengths just to avoid one woman. I mean, you were already three hundred light-years away, what difference did it make whether you were in the Appalachians or San Francisco?"

"Well, I guess it was more that . . . I just wanted to retreat. From space, from people, from relationships. I just wanted a simpler life. Nobody makin' any demands on me." He glared. "And I had it, too, till you came and dragged me back into the life. And now look where it's got me. Two weeks back in civilization, and Natira's found me again. And did you see that look in her eyes? She's still smitten. And now . . ." He poured himself another drink. "Now I'm gonna have to go back there and look that poor woman in the eyes, and tell her that I never loved her. That I just used her to give myself some comfort. That everything I told her was a lie." A convulsive movement, and the glass was empty again. "Jim, that woman worships truth above all else. She's going to hate my living guts. And I'm gonna deserve it."

Kirk rose and took the bottle before McCoy could reach for it again. "Bones, has anyone ever told you you're a melancholy drunk?"

"Bull. I'm melancholy enough when I'm sober. I'm a charming drunk."

"No, you just think you are," he teased. Taking McCoy by the shoulders, he addressed him seriously. "And you're being too hard on yourself. Like you said, you were a wreck. Confused. You weren't yourself, and you messed up. Natira's a grown woman, a smart one. She can understand that. But the more you try to run from the truth, the more you have to compound the lie, and the worse it gets. It's not the crime that gets you, it's the cover-up."

McCoy's vivid blue eyes met his, their focus still relatively undulled. "So you're tellin' me I should just go there and face her and admit I never loved her."

"That's right."

The doctor glowered. "And why exactly did I agree to trust in your leadership again?"

"Haven't you heard?" Kirk said archly. "I'm a galactic hero!"

Bones snorted. "Until the next flavor of the month comes along."

As Kirk entered main engineering, his eyes were inexorably drawn (as always) to the tall intermix shaft which ran nearly the height of the ship, the light of the matter-antimatter reactions within it swirling and churning throughout its length, and through the equally long horizontal shaft that ran back to the warp engines. He couldn't get over how fragile the narrow, glassy shafts appeared.

Then, once Chief Sternbach had pointed out Mr. Scott's location, about halfway back along the horizontal shaft, Kirk began to see the truth behind the illusion. Scotty crouched beside one of the cylindrical modules that made up the shaft, which had been pulled out and now rested on a maintenance dolly. In cross section, Kirk could see how thick the walls of the module actually were, with the dilithium swirl chamber just a narrow tube at the center of several solid, concentric layers of shielding and constrictor coils. He really shouldn't have been surprised; of course the light that got out through the walls could only be a tiny fraction of the searing radiation emitted by total matter-antimatter annihilation. And of course in a narrower shaft, the particles and antiparticles had less space to miss each other in, so the reaction was more efficient. Still, the illusion was hard to overcome.

At the moment, Scotty was peering intently down the swirl chamber, his back to Kirk. Chief Theresa Ross, a lissome blonde in a white jumpsuit, crouched beside him in a pose that Kirk took a moment to appreciate. "It's a microscopic impurity, sir," the chief said. "You don't really expect to see it, do you? Or is this some sort of 'communing with the engines' thing?" There was no sarcasm in her voice, just curiosity.

Scott chuckled. "No, lass, it's just me bein' silly, that's

all. And I already told you, call me Scotty. We're all engineers here, no need to stand on rank."

"Present company excepted, I trust," Kirk spoke up.

"Captain Kirk, sir!" Scott said, rising from where he had been crouched.

"At ease," Kirk smiled. But Scott just stood there expectantly, looking eager to get back to work. "Is there something wrong with this unit, Scotty? I thought you said your repairs were almost complete."

"Aye, that I did, sir, but then Ross here picked up a trace impurity in the dilithium matrix. Probably got laid down in the vapor-deposition process. There are still a few bugs to be worked out in that."

Kirk peered more closely at the central shaft and caught Ross giving him a wry look. He straightened and asked, "Could it pose a danger to the ship?"

"It's more a question of efficiency, sir," Ross explained. "There could be a slight dropoff in performance above warp 7."

"Above warp 7. I see." He looked over the partly disassembled engine shaft again. "Did that really warrant taking the engine apart?"

"Not to worry, sir," Scott said in a businesslike tone. "Nicholson and Longbotham are bringing up a spare now."

"And how long will it take to get the engines back online?"

Scott pondered. "Well . . . to get the spare module installed and align its magnetic field, no more than another two hours. But then we'd need to run some performance tests to make sure. And I'd like to test all the other modules for impurities."

"I'm afraid we don't have time for that, Scotty. We have a mission. I need these engines powered up and ready for a trip to the Daran system at best speed."

"The Daran system?" Scott echoed with concern. "But . . .

that's a very long voyage, Captain. A couple of weeks, at least. It's longer than we've run these engines for yet. Plus, it's on the edge of the Lantaru sector. They're still chartin' the subspace ripples from that . . . natural disaster," he finished, remembering to gloss over the classified details for Ross's benefit. "There might be unexpected interactions, ye never can tell."

"Scotty, there are lives at stake on Daran IV and there aren't any other starships out there."

Scott sighed. "Of course not. There never are, are there? Sir."

His tone made Kirk frown. "Is there a problem, Mr. Scott?"

"No, sir. I have no doubt this ship can handle anything you throw at her."

Kirk was tempted to demand an explanation for that . . . though he supposed he didn't need one. The ship's hasty launch had led to two serious accidents—a transporter malfunction that had killed two good people (including one who had once been dear to Kirk) and a wormhole imbalance that could have destroyed the whole ship. Ever since then, Scott had become obsessive about testing and retesting every system on the ship, extending his estimates of the necessary shakedown time before the vessel could be declared truly ready. And the more Kirk pressed him, the more distant and coldly professional he became. He'd been treating Kirk like a stranger, avoiding him as much as his duties would allow. No doubt he blamed the captain for pushing too hard. And Kirk couldn't really find it in himself to argue otherwise.

"Very well," he ended up saying. "How soon can you have the engines up and running?"

"Two hours, sir."

Kirk studied him a moment longer, then nodded formally. "Thank you, Engineer. We'll be shipping out at 1800." Then he headed back the way he'd come, his steps echoing bleakly through the long, cavernous tunnel.

CHAPTER THREE

Two and a half years as Chief of Starfleet Operations may have made me a little stale, Mr. Scott—but I wouldn't exactly consider myself "untried."

—James T. Kirk

LIEUTENANT PAVEL CHEKOV sat at the bridge tactical station, trying not to look bored.

There wasn't really that much to do at tactical while the ship was in dock. He couldn't schedule any more security drills without disrupting departure preparations. And he'd already thoroughly confirmed the ship's secure and ready status during the previous five tedious hours of his shift.

In the past, he could have just turned to his left to chat with Hikaru Sulu, back when they'd shared the helm/nav console. But now Chekov was stuck out here on the outer rim of the bridge. True, he wasn't exactly out of Sulu's earshot, but there was a greater psychological distance. And Sulu was currently holding down the command chair anyway. Even when he wasn't, he spent much of his time chatting with the new navigator, Marcella DiFalco, with whom he'd been hitting it off splendidly. Apparently they'd both traveled around space extensively while growing up, giving them many common experiences and interests. Chekov's friendship with Sulu had always been defined more by contrasts, as Hikaru the Renaissance man had tried to broaden Chekov's horizons, while Pavel had clung more and more assertively to his conviction that nothing the rest of the universe had to offer quite compared with the beauty of Mother Russia and her culture.

("This is the country whose history is basically one foreign army after another marching through and ravaging the place, right?" Hikaru had once asked. "Leading you to live in a constant state of paranoia? This is your idea of paradise?"

"Of course!" Pavel had countered. "Why do you suppose everyone else was so eager to invade us?")

Normally he might have Nyota Uhura to talk to as well; communications was just two stations down from tactical. But Uhura's new duties were keeping her busy elsewhere. Her gift for communications extended beyond hailing frequencies and subspace modulations to languages and the nuances of alien social interaction. So when Captain Decker—the *former* Captain Decker—had arranged for *Enterprise* to carry the most diverse multispecies crew in Starfleet history, he'd recognized that Uhura's skills would be essential to helping that crew mesh as a unit, smoothing over potential tensions and misunderstandings between species that had rarely if ever served together before. The last Chekov had heard, Uhura was still working with the new Megarite oceanographer, refining the programming of the translator/voder, which would interpret the musical, whale-like sounds of her speech.

And Chekov hadn't had much luck striking up a conversation with the tall young Trill woman next to him at environmental engineering. He couldn't really find much to say about atmospheric gas storage or thermal regulation, and the Trill didn't seem eager to encourage a dialogue. He wondered if that was due to the species' general secretiveness, or if she just didn't like him. Too bad Uhura wasn't around to ask.

Chekov suppressed an urge to sigh. *Look at you, feeling sorry for yourself. It's not as though you've been exiled to Siberia. Some security chief—stop feeling so insecure.* Resolving to at least look busy, he stood and made his way across the bridge to check on Ensign Zaand at the internal security station. (Uhura had wondered the other day why tactical and internal security had been placed on opposite sides of the bridge. But she'd quickly interrupted Chekov's catalogue of the things that could theoretically destroy one side of the bridge or the other, saying that security training had made him too morbid.)

"Ensign, report," he said, trying to make it sound routine and official.

The Rhaandarite snapped to attention. "Yes, sir," he said crisply. "All units show green. Exterior sensors, all nominal. Interior sensors, all nominal. All on-duty personnel reporting and accounted for, sir."

It was the same report he'd given at the start of the shift—verbatim. "Thank you, Ensign. At ease."

"Sir," Zaand acknowledged, but didn't show much change in his bearing. That was a Rhaandarite for you—along with the smooth, bulging forehead, golden eyes, and stringy hair came an innate knack for obedience and discipline. He recalled Uhura saying it had something to do with the intricate social structures on their world, with a specific set of rules laid out for every possible status relationship. For his part, Chekov wasn't so sure how to relate to Vaylin Zaand—he was three times Chekov's age, but wouldn't hit puberty, or his full two-and-a-half-meter height, for another sixty or seventy years. Did that make him a naive kid or a seasoned veteran? In the two weeks they'd been serving together, Chekov had seen signs of both. It did nothing to ease his concerns about his own youth and inexperience. At least Zaand had never questioned Chekov's authority—or at least, not to his face. When Kirk had taken the ship back, it had been Zaand who had stood up for Decker, once Kirk had left the bridge. Apparently those strict social rules held sway only in face-to-face interactions.

"So," Chekov ventured, "do you have any questions about the mission?"

"I'm sure you'll address any questions fully at the security briefing, sir," Zaand said.

"Well, I'll do my best." Zaand just looked at him uncertainly. Chekov sighed and wandered back toward his station.

"Sir?" It was Chief DiFalco. "Do you have a minute?"

Chekov pretended to think about it. "I believe I can make the time. What is it, Chief?"

"I have what I guess is both a navigation question and a security question," the slim brunette told him. "I figured you'd be the best person to ask."

"Well, here I am. You could've been asking me already."

"Oh. Of course. Sorry, sir. I don't mean to waste your time. . . ."

"You're still not asking."

"Oh. Umm . . . see, I need to plot a course from here to Daran, and, well, look." She projected a star map onto the astrogation display disk between the helm and nav positions, highlighting their current position in the Regulus Sector and their destination on the edge of the Lower Sco-Cen Cluster. "You see the problem—it means passing between Klingon and Romulan space where they touch, or else taking a major z-axis detour around them. The captain ordered best possible speed, but the fastest subspace geodesic I can find that doesn't go right through them still brushes right up against Klingon territory." She added the spatial-topography data, though Chekov didn't need it shown to him. After four years at navigation he knew intimately how the distributions of mass, energy, and subspace fields in the region affected the efficiency of a warp engine, and could instantly see which paths would allow the greatest effective speed. "But given how, well, turbulent things have been over there lately, I'm not sure that's a good idea. Do you know, are they taking it out on others, too? Looking for excuses to start a border incident?"

Chekov was tempted to tell her that was a bit outside her purview as a navigator. But he supposed he couldn't blame her for being concerned. Whatever had been going on in the Klingon Empire lately, it was probably something it would be best to stay away from. Starfleet Security had been sending out regular intelligence reports, but there was little solid information coming from within the Empire, and nothing to explain why the more humanlike race of Klingons, which had dominated their military for the past few decades, had suddenly fallen out of sight in the recent upheavals. Such information was notoriously hard to gather from Klingons, who had some kind of taboo against discussing ethnic matters with outsiders. The first Terran anthropologists sent in to study them, around the founding of the Federation, had been executed as spies. To this day, even Starfleet Intelligence wasn't certain (or wasn't admitting it knew) what the different types of Klingon actually represented: different ethnic groups or developmental stages, genetic mutants or hybrids, or even separate species with a common national identity, the way everyone from Estonians to Uzbeks had all once called themselves Soviets.

Bottom line, Chekov had no idea what to tell her, except to fall back on first impulses. "I'd say that's a bit outside your purview as a navigator, Chief. You just plot the course—the captain worries about the politics."

"I know," DiFalco said, "but I want to make sure I give the captain the best possible option."

From the command chair behind them, Sulu chuckled. "Cella has a crush on the captain."

DiFalco blushed. "I do *not*. I just . . . Look, I never expected to get this posting. I was just a backup navigator—heck, I wasn't even supposed to be on the *Enterprise;* I just happened to be available when the emergency was declared. I was amazed when Captain Kirk asked me to stay on as head navigator." She finished in a stage whisper. "I don't know if I'm ready for this."

Chekov patted her on the shoulder. "Chief, the captain wouldn't have picked you if you weren't. He's a very good judge of character."

"Oh, I know. That legendary intuition of his." Sulu grinned and rolled his eyes at Chekov. "That's just it—serving under Captain Kirk is a dream come true for me. I never expected it to happen so soon, or ever—and of course I never wanted it to happen the way it did," she hastened to add.

Chekov winced at the reminder of DiFalco's immediate predecessor. Ilia had been kind and easygoing, nothing like what he'd expected from the lurid spacer's tales about Deltan women. She'd used her empathic abilities to ease Chekov's pain when he'd been burned during V'Ger's attack, and he'd felt a wave of gentle compassion immerse him, like being in his mother's arms. It had been a hard shock when she'd been disintegrated by V'Ger's plasma probe, then used as the template for a cold, unfeeling android. He took some comfort from the knowledge that Ilia's consciousness had apparently survived within the android, and still existed in some form, on some plane. But then, he would have believed that anyway—it was just reassuring to have hard evidence.

"But what about the way Captain Kirk got his post?" That was Ensign Zaand, taking a step toward them. "Captain Decker earned this command. He supervised the whole refit. He handpicked this crew, and he was entitled to our loyalty." Apparently Zaand felt more able to speak freely as long as the conversation wasn't initiated by his direct superior, Chekov thought with annoyance. "But Captain Kirk pushed him aside, out of his command, ultimately out of his whole life!"

"He had his reasons," DiFalco countered.

"More 'legendary intuition'? Or was it recklessness? Kirk has no respect for the way things are supposed to be done. He just acts on his personal whims and thinks he can get away with it because he's popular."

DiFalco's expression had grown mortified, but Chekov realized her gaze was directed not at Zaand but at the starboard lift, whose opening he'd subliminally noticed a moment before. Chekov looked over to see Captain Kirk standing rigidly on the threshold.

"Captain on the bridge!" Chekov announced, then threw a sharp look at Zaand. "Ensign! Man your post."

"Aye, sir," Zaand said, but his response seemed to be an unconscious reflex, given the look of paralyzing dread on his face.

Kirk just stood there for a moment, taking in the scene, debating how to respond. Ultimately he decided just to let it go, to pretend he hadn't heard the ensign's remarks. Chekov had acted promptly to maintain discipline, and Kirk wasn't the type to punish people simply for not liking him. So far Zaand had done his job so efficiently and faithfully that Kirk hadn't even realized how the man felt. It was painful to hear such sentiments from one of his crew, but they clearly weren't a threat to discipline, so it was best to let the matter go—for now.

Besides, Kirk thought as he took over from Sulu and listened absently to his routine report, he didn't know if he could blame the young Rhaandarite for his doubts. He *had* shoved Decker aside, hijacked the man's well-deserved command for the sake of his own personal ambition. And look what the cost had been. Even Scotty didn't trust him anymore.

But he'd just have to deal with that as it came. Right now, he had a job to do. "Navigator, is our course to Daran IV laid in?"

Chief DiFalco spoke with a trace of hesitation. "Plotted, sir . . . but if you'll take a look . . ."

Chekov interjected. "We . . . I have some security concerns about the proximity of this course to Klingon space, sir."

Kirk looked over the plot on the astrogator display, reflecting on his idle wish for the distraction of a Klingon attack. *Tempting fate,* he thought. In the mood he was in, he would be happy to charge right into battle, prove himself in fire. His doubts fell away when adrenaline took over. But he wasn't about to risk losing more crew members just to satisfy his selfish drives. Probably it would be better to take a longer, safer course—but how many more people on Daran IV might die as a result?

Kirk stared at the display, wondering how in hell he'd ever gotten this public image as an impulsive hothead. A lot of the time he felt more like Hamlet, agonizing over every decision. He just had the knack for not letting it show. Being a captain was sometimes more about *looking* decisive and convincing your crew that you knew what you were doing. Right now, though, he couldn't see which course to choose. He knew that only a few seconds had passed, but it was still too long.

Chekov cleared his throat. "However, Chief DiFalco here has reminded me that the Lantaru disaster has altered the subspace geometry in the surrounding sectors. So there might be a slightly more circuitous route that lets us make up some time on the final leg. Isn't that right, Chief?"

DiFalco looked nonplussed for a moment; Chekov was clearly trying to give her a boost in her captain's eyes. But the chief rose to the occasion, looking at the plot for a moment and soon spotting the option Chekov was hinting at. "Uhh, yes, sir. If we head on 59 mark 354, then just past N Velorum we can trim onto this new heading and . . . it should only lose us three hours, Captain."

Kirk nodded. "Very good. Lay in the course, Chief."

"Aye, sir," she said crisply, then smiled thanks at Chekov.

Kirk threw the lieutenant a look. "Mr. Chekov, I know I'm new around here, but weren't you a security chief instead of a navigator?"

"Ahh . . . yes, sir." Chekov hastened back to his post. Kirk was slightly annoyed to see him trying to help DiFalco impress her captain, when she so clearly had a crush on him—or more likely, on his public image, which Kirk was eager to discourage interest in, particularly among his own crew members. But the lieutenant and the chief had spared him from a tough decision, so he could excuse it—this time.

Kirk tapped the intercom on his seat arm, and was pleased that he was finally able to find the switch without looking. "Captain to all decks. Stand by for departure at 1800."

Spock was beginning to recognize that the Vulcan face was more expressive than most Vulcans were willing to admit. He had seen evidence enough in the expressions of the other Vulcans aboard over the past days. And he saw it now, on the gaunt, stern face of Security Technician T'Hesh as the door to her quarters slid open. But the slight, centenarian Vulcan controlled her voice well, by contrast. "Commander Spock," she said with icy formality. "How may I assist you?"

"May I enter?" At T'Hesh's hesitation, he added, "Given the temperature differential between your quarters and the corridor, it would place less of a strain on your environmental controls if we could have our discussion with the door closed."

After a moment, T'Hesh stepped back to let him enter. But as the door closed behind him, Spock discovered that the room was bare except for a small cargo container and two carrying cases. "Are you relocating?" he asked.

"I am transferring to another posting."

"Indeed. May I ask where?"

"That has not yet been determined."

"Ahh." Spock decided to get to the point. "I had intended to ask a favor. In recent weeks, I have had difficulty achieving a meditative state. It occurred to me that I might benefit from a focusing aid, such as a meditation flame or *keethara* blocks. Never having needed such aids in the past, I have none of my own. I had hoped I might borrow something of yours."

T'Hesh's visage remained stony. "As you can see, all my possessions are packed, and I must leave the ship before it casts off at 1800."

"I see. Very well. Thank you for your time, Technician." He turned to leave, disappointed at the failure of his goal, but relieved that the encounter had gone relatively smoothly. But T'Hesh proved unable to resist speaking her thoughts.

"I am surprised," she said in an imperious tone, "that a *V'tosh ka'tur* would seek to meditate at all."

So—someone voices it at last. Spock turned to face her. "Then you are operating under a misconception. I am not 'without logic.' On the contrary—I have recognized that it is illogical to ignore the input of my own emotions. They are a part of me."

"You *are* half human."

Spock quirked a brow at the non sequitur. "Vulcans have emotions as well. We simply manage them with logic. Yet that does not mean we must pretend they do not exist."

T'Hesh turned back to her packing cases. "If you will excuse me, Commander. I must prepare for departure."

She wouldn't even listen. Spock supposed he shouldn't be surprised. "Very well. Perhaps Spanla or T'Khuln will be able to help me."

"If they do not transfer as well," T'Hesh said. "And even so, I doubt very much that you can be helped."

Spock gazed at her rigid back for a moment, examining the emotions her words evoked. There were strong echoes of the pain and anger he'd felt as a boy, when the other children had taunted him as a "half-breed," a "barbarian" whose father had brought shame to Vulcan by marrying a mere human. Fascinating, how much those memories could still burn, even now that he could see the irony in the way the children had treated him with anger and hate for being emotional. Such outbursts were tolerated by Vulcan adults, who took it as a given that their children would out-grow such behavior as they matured and mastered logic. Instead, Spock realized, they simply grew more subtle in expressing it.

Spock noticed that his fists were tightly clenched. Taking a deep breath, he forced one fist open and his fingers apart into the Surakian salute. "Peace and long life, T'Hesh. And success in your future postings."

Evidently T'Hesh judged him unworthy of a response. Spock hastened from her quarters.

"All decks report ready for departure. All hatches secure. All seals holding."

"Thrusters are hot. Intermix set for impulse power."

"Nav deflector on standby at impulse mode."

"Helm ready, sir."

"System departure on plot, sir."

"Clear all moorings."

"Aye, sir."

"AG section reports clean decouple from starbase AG field. Structural integrity field ramping to full."

The voices mingled in a smooth, professional counterpoint, veterans and newcomers each taking their verses in turn. Sulu at helm, his solemn tones belying his passion for flight. DiFalco at navigation, her voice strident with tension. Chekov at tactical, crisp and determined. Zaand at internal security, controlled and letter-perfect. Baby-faced Enrique Mercado at engineering, his every word tinged with excitement. And Uhura at communications, the concertmaster whose voice led all the rest.

"Starbase reports all moorings clear, and wishes us fair sailing."

"Acknowledge starbase, with our thanks, Ms. Uhura. Mr. Sulu, thrusters ahead."

"Thrusters ahead, aye."

"Departure angle on viewer."

"Departure angle, aye." Starbase 22 appeared on-screen, a modular structure of branching cylinders, backlit by the system's small orange star and growing progressively smaller. The other docked ships blinked their running lights in tribute to the *Enterprise*.

"Viewer ahead."

"Viewer ahead, aye." Now Kirk took in the forward view, dominated by the swath of the Milky Way crossing the viewer from end to end, sprinkled liberally with the bright blue stars of the Sco-Cen Cluster, and highlighted with the faint wisps of the Azure Nebula off to the right. There was no visible sign of the two powerful, warlike empires whose territory filled much of this field of view, or of the borders which they fought so fiercely to defend or expand. Kirk remembered reading the words of twentieth-century astronauts who believed that war and strife would vanish if people could see the Earth from space and realize how illusory their borders were. In interstellar space the borders were even more invisible, but of course it hadn't proved to be so easy. War could be overcome, Kirk knew, but not by looking at the scenery. You had to change your internal landscape to pull it off, and that was much harder to see clearly.

Why, he wondered, had the Yonadan settlers turned to violence? Was it truly in the name of that discredited computer god of theirs? Or was that just an excuse for something else? After ten thousand years with a machine regulating their very thoughts, keeping them placid and controlled on pain of death, were their long-repressed aggressions simply asserting their freedom?

Either way, you won't find the answers hanging around here, he reminded himself. "Impulse power, Mr. Sulu. Ahead warp point five."

"Aye, sir." The ship surged with power, and in almost no time Sulu was reporting, "On course, sir. Holding at warp point five."

Kirk nodded, impressed at the *Enterprise*'s swift acceleration. The new impulse engine design used a low-level warp field to reduce the ship's inertial mass, letting it maneuver at sublight like a ship a fraction of its size. But Kirk found it awkward to hear impulse speeds referred to as fractional warp factors, which didn't literally correspond to the speed in any case. That was a bit of terminology that he didn't expect would last long in practical use.

He tapped the intercom. "Kirk to engineering. Scotty, assuming you've got the engines put back together, how far out from the sun do we need to be to engage warp drive?"

"You can do it anytime, sir," Scott replied. *"Now that they're properly calibrated, there's no risk of field disruption from local gravity sources. Ye won't be seein' any wormholes outside o' the apples in the botanical garden."*

"Thank you, Mr. Scott, for that . . . appetizing image. Mr. Sulu—ahead warp factor seven."

"Aye, sir." Sulu pushed forward on the manual throttle

lever—a bit showy of him to rely on it instead of the computer controls, Kirk thought, but given Sulu's reflexes, he knew they were in for a smooth ride. "Warp point six . . . warp point seven . . ."

"Never mind, Mr. Sulu."

"Aye, sir."

The subsonic rumble of the ship intensified, lifted, like a racehorse's body tensing at the gate. Below, Kirk knew, matter and antimatter surged, annihilated into energetic plasma that poured across the massive warp coils, creating the precise patterns of mass and energy required to knead three dimensions of space and six of subspace into unnatural, improbable, and very useful shapes. Gravity-lensed starlight erupted in a prismatic burst once the warp field was fully formed, then appeared to streak backward impossibly fast as the field cycled and played with the light. Soon the field stabilized and locked into place with another prismatic burst.

"Warp seven, Captain."

"Very good, Mr. Sulu." And it was. For all its distortions of physics, all the loopholes it had to take advantage of to bend the laws of the universe to their limits, there was just something that felt so *right* about being on a ship in warp. It was something he'd been without for far too long, and he couldn't imagine ever giving it up again. "Steady as she goes."

CHAPTER FOUR

> *The tide is chaos to the ear, / A wild and ever-changing song.*
> *And yet each time that it goes out, / We know it will come in again,*
> *As regular as beating hearts, / And nourish us another day.*
> *The changes are but raucous lies. / The sameness is the stuff of life.* —Traditional Megarite liturgy

THE HARDEST THING about being on the *Enterprise* was how *dry* it always was.

It wasn't just the lack of humidity, Specialist 2/C Spring Rain on Still Water reflected as she hurried to Mr. Spock's science briefing, her wide flat feet slapping loudly against the deck. Certainly that wasn't pleasant, requiring her to wear a skintight, hooded "drysuit" most of the time, and periodically coat her face and hands with a moisturizing compound to keep her thick, knobbly brown skin from drying and cracking. True, the emollient's effects lasted longer than a good wallow in the mud, but it didn't feel nearly as good. That was what Spring Rain missed the most about Megara—simply having large quantities of moisture around, a place to immerse herself, whether in mud or water. Just having the sound and smell of a river or sea nearby. Would it hurt them so much, she wondered, to put at least a little trickling stream along an edge of the corridor? Maybe have fish tanks periodically placed along the walls? Maybe then she wouldn't feel so thirsty all the time.

But Spring Rain wasn't about to complain. She would never give any sign that she couldn't pull this off, never give the slightest bit of ground to the naysayers back home who'd insisted that Megarites didn't belong in space, and that such chores as exploration were unworthy of a female.

Yes, it had its share of discomforts. Yes, it took an effort for her even to survive here, away from the algae and krill of her home waters. Without a large enough body of water to swim through and strain with her baleen vents, she had to subsist on nutrient injections, at least until Dr. Chapel could devise a better mechanism. She couldn't even singspeak properly here, with no other Megarite voices to harmonize with—only the staccato, unmelodic sounds produced by species with mouths, and by the voder that stomped over her song with its discordant translations. Uhura had done her best, and was as close to a true singer as any non-Megarite on this ship, but it still wasn't the same, and every conversation felt incomplete, unresolved at a spiritual depth.

But none of that mattered. She wouldn't let it matter. Not if the alternative meant keeping her people stuck on one world, no matter how wet and beautiful. Not if it meant keeping them restricted within their confines of thought and aspiration, cut off from the wondrous diversity of ideas and knowledge which embodied the Federation. It had been two sixty-fours of years since the first Denobulan traders had brought the knowledge of other worlds, yet still Megara had not joined the Federation, had never established a presence in space beyond the occasional diplomatic envoy, and had never been represented in the Federation Starfleet—until a young female named Spring Rain on Still Water, enchanted since childhood by the tales brought by alien traders, had looked at the adult life her clan had laid out for her and thought, *Is this all I am to be? Is there nothing more?*

Of course, part of succeeding at her goal was showing up at Mr. Spock's briefings on time. And her large, thick-limbed frame wasn't built for running; she was more graceful in the water. Plus, her quarters were at the rear of Deck 6, too far away from the science complex that occupied the forward quadrant of Deck 7.

Finally she reached the complex and made her way to the large briefing room located at its center, linking the various departments' labs together and facilitating the kind of cross-disciplinary communication which Mr. Spock believed was essential for scientific progress. Her entrance interrupted Spock in the middle of a sentence, and her efforts to make her way to the Planetary Sciences table without stepping on any of the others' small and fragile feet (unsuccessfully, as it proved) further disrupted things. She endured Spock's reprimand stoically, knowing it was her own fault for taking so long with her layers—emollient, drysuit, uniform. She had to get better at that.

But it was time to listen, for Spock was resuming his briefing. "As I was saying . . . our earliest knowledge of the Fabrini came from a sublight interstellar probe discovered by the *Intrepid* nine years ago, during a survey of the Scorpius-Centaurus OB Association. As many of you know, this cluster has been the source of numerous supernovae over the past twenty million years, due to its abundance of hot, short-lived stars. Analysis of the probe's course and the radiation damage to its hull suggested that it had originated in the vicinity of a Sco-Cen supernova which occurred approximately ten thousand two hundred years ago." A graphic showing the location appeared on the screen behind Spock. "This was confirmed by the translation of the probe's contents. Its creators, the Fabrini, had known their star was dying and had sent out probes containing cultural databanks, in the hope that their achievements would not be forgotten. In the years following, several other Fabrini probes were discovered by Starfleet crews."

"They couldn't have helped knowing their star was dying," spoke up one of the sensor analysts, though like Spring Rain he depended on the translator to render his high-pitched, piping speech into Standard. "It would've already been a red giant when they evolved." Hrrii'ush Uuvu'it was a Betelgeusian, tall and blue-skinned, with ears not unlike Spock's and a triangular brown muzzle containing an upper, beaklike speaking mouth and a lower, vicious-looking eating mouth. He knew whereof he spoke; his people had long since abandoned their homeworld in the Betelgeuse sector to live on ships and space habitats, once they'd learned that Betelgeuse itself was on the verge of supernova.

"More like when they settled," interposed Jade Dinh from the Anthropology and Archaeology table. "A phenotype that humanlike couldn't have evolved there naturally. They must be part of the Sargonian Diaspora, so they would've settled Fabrina less than a million years ago."

"We don't know it was Sargon's people," said Uuvu'it. "It's only hearsay."

"The archaeology bears it out."

"Only that some race settled across space, built livable worlds around young giant stars like Rigel and Altair, then lost their technology and had to start over again. But why pick one on the brink of death, with only a million years or less to go instead of hundreds of millions?"

"I thought the Sargonians seeded the Vulcanoid races," interposed Bolek, the Tellarite biologist.

"In any case," Spock spoke up, getting them back on focus, "we have no knowledge of the Fabrini's origins, only their end. They remained only an archaeological curiosity until stardate 5476, when the *Enterprise* encountered this body on the outskirts of the Daran star system." The viewscreen showed a large, vaguely octahedral asteroid. Uuvu'it leaned across to make a wager with Dinh about the origins of the Fabrini, but Spock glared them into silence before laying out the basics of the encounter with the asteroid-ship Yonada. It was a prosaic account, giving Spring Rain no sense of the *feel* of the incident, the timbre of each participant, the harmony and counterpoint of their worldviews. It wasn't just the Vulcan's matter-of-fact manner, though; these words, these isolated bits of sound most species used, simply didn't have the necessary fluidity to convey such meanings. How did they ever understand one another?

"The previously discovered Fabrini probes made no mention of the Yonada project," Spock went on, "although their language banks do contain the word *yonada,* meaning 'hope.' Apparently, construction of the probes was halted once the decision was made to dedicate their resources to Yonada's construction—which surely would have required all the available resources of their civilization.

"Yonada's shell is three hundred twenty-six kilometers in diameter at its widest axis, with an internal core three hundred and seven kilometers in diameter. The surface of the core is terraformed to resemble a planet's surface, with the shell interior projecting a simulated sky. The shell's supports are camouflaged as high mountains.

"The probes revealed that the Fabrini had lived underground for generations as their swelling star rendered the surface uninhabitable. Thus, it does seem odd that they would go to the trouble of simulating a surface and sky. Apparently the Fabrini did not wish the people of Yonada to know they were not on a planet—perhaps to prevent psychological trauma to the hundreds of generations that would grow up knowing that their destination would not be reached in their lifetime. And perhaps they also wished to give the Yonadi a respite from their underground conditions, a respite unavailable to those on Fabrina. The Yonadan surface does have livable conditions, though it is barren; and many Yonadi we spoke to stated that they occasionally spent time there for recreational or ceremonial activities. Perhaps this was encouraged to reinforce the illusion of a planetary existence." How cruel, Spring Rain thought, to remind them of their imprisonment by letting them glimpse an illusion of freedom. It was much like the liberties her family had tried to offer her to dissuade her from leaving home—slight variations in convention that would only have made her feel her confinement more acutely. But at least the Yonadi hadn't known there was an alternative.

"The gravity," Spock was now saying, "is considerably greater than would be expected in a body of this type. But there is no evidence that the Fabrini ever developed artificial gravity technology, as can be surmised from the crude fission thrusters employed for Yonada's propulsion. The source of the gravity appears to be an inner core of collapsed matter with a density of some four hundred grams per cubic centimeter. We believe the Fabrini must have collapsed an asteroid using shaped antimatter explosions, then bombarded it with carbon-coated projectiles in order to coat it in a layer of diamond, the only substance available to their science with sufficient tensile strength to prevent its reexpansion." Many people fidgeted and muttered at that, and Spring Rain could understand why. It was a dangerous way to achieve artificial gravity. The Fabrini must have truly been desperate, to undertake the construction of this massive starship with such limited technology. Couldn't they have waited another century or two? But no—Spring Rain thought about how long her own people had waited, and understood the dangers of thinking that way . . . especially if your star was about to blow up on you. Even without hearing the tone color of their experience in Spock's words, she could deduce how it would sound.

"Significantly," Spock went on, "the gravity at Yonada's inner surface is point eight-six *g*'s, virtually identical to that of Daran IV, their intended destination. Clearly they had advance knowledge of this world's specific conditions, and designed Yonada to prepare their people for inhabiting it."

Spring Rain had a thought, and sang it. Her translator rendered it thus:

> *"Bright messengers go sailing forth*
> *Like branches on the ebbing tide,*
> *And sing of distant shores, so that*
> *The sailors know what garb to wear?"*

Spock raised a brow, and moved his mouth slightly. If Spring Rain had learned mouth expressions correctly, it may have been a smile, but that didn't fit what she'd heard about Vulcans. Some of the others seemed surprised by it as well. "If I understand you correctly, you suggest that the Fabrini obtained advance knowledge of Daran IV from their probes." Spring Rain nodded, or came as close to it as her thick neck allowed. Spock seemed apologetic as he went on. "This is not possible, since the probes' propulsive capabilities were even less advanced than those of Yonada, and even with their vastly lighter payload would have taken longer to cover the thirty-two light-year distance to the Daran system."

> *"Then on those distant shores are folk*
> *Who send forth their own songs, which swim*
> *Unto the sailors' ears and sing*
> *Of how the land does lie."*

"Correct," Spock said with a mouth-gesture similar to the previous one. "Evidently the Fabrini gained their knowledge of the Daran system through radio communication with the Shesshran of Daran V." He switched the viewer to a display of Daran V's indigenous species, a gorgeous, winged race with iridescent skin and spindle-shaped heads. "The Shesshran are currently at an interplanetary stage, but archaeological studies have confirmed that they had a similarly advanced civilization some ten millennia ago. This earlier civilization evidently made contact with the Fabrini and invited them to settle the uninhabited fourth planet in the system. The Shesshran themselves—or whatever they may have called themselves at the time—had no use for it, since they are adapted to a pressure of 3.4 atmospheres and a gravity of 1.65 g's.

"However, when the radiation front from the Fabrina supernova hit, it apparently ravaged the Shesshran's electronic infrastructure and caused severe ecological damage, either beyond what the Shesshran had expected or beyond what they had been capable of protecting against. Ironically, the very civilization that offered the Fabrini refuge from the death of their sun was wiped out by its aftereffects. The Shesshran were reduced to a primitive, subsistence-level existence, and have only now recovered to their pre-supernova level." Oh, if only he could sing it! What a grand and moving tragedy it must have been. How unjust it seemed to feel so little of it in the tale, to have to empathize from such a great remove.

"However, we are getting ahead of ourselves. To return to the subject of Yonada . . ." The Vulcan carried on, putting up graphics of the asteroid-ship as he spoke—cross sections, surface maps, geological analyses.

The skin has worn away, Spring Rain observed after a time;

"Dry bone
Lies bare, the body echoing
With long-stilled cries for water."

Spock frowned. "Apologies, Ms. Spring Rain, could you rephrase that?"

She struggled to pitch it more toward fact and less toward feeling. *"There was more water once,"* she said as simply as she could, letting air through only one of her forehead vents so that she would sing only one layer of meaning. It felt unnatural.

"Ah. Yes, the surface of Yonada does resemble a once-lush terrain which has become excessively dehydrated. However, given that the surface of Fabrina itself was presumably like this when Yonada was constructed, this appearance may have been artificially created."

"Couldn't it have started out with more water and life, and gradually dried out through outgassing?" asked Sara Bowring, a yellow-haired human female from Life Sciences.

"It is possible," Spock said, "but that would conflict with the prevailing theory that the builders wished its inhabitants to believe they had never left the homeworld. If that model is correct—and at this point we have no strong evidence to the contrary—then it is unlikely that they would have given it such radically different conditions from Fabrina itself."

"But how did they move the people there without telling them?" Uuvu'it asked. "How did they explain the change in gravity?"

"The change in gravity was minor, as far as we can tell from the information in the probes. It would have been barely within the perceptual threshold. As for your first question, there are many possibilities, none of which has sufficient evidentiary support to merit singling out for discussion. But clearly the ancient Fabrini exercised great ingenuity—however deceptive it may have been—in preserving a piece of their world and their civilization, and succeeded in solving far greater problems than this."

Spring Rain took his point. Truly it was an extraordinary achievement. Whatever their origins, the Fabrini of ten millennia ago had managed, using only pre-warp technology, to make an extraordinary journey across space so that their race and memory could survive the death of their star system. It reminded Spring Rain of how vulnerable any one world was, how imperative it was to claim the stars if a species wished to survive. For the good of her world, she had to succeed here in Starfleet, and she had to inspire others, male and female both, to follow her here. And if the people of Yonada had been able to survive against such impossible odds, then surely she could handle being a little thirsty.

Though she could still kill for a good wallow in the mud.

Nyota Uhura soared through the air of the variable-gravity gym, gliding and swooping around its perpendicular bars with the grace of a Mark IV Peregrine interceptor evading enemy fire.

Careful, Hikaru, Sulu thought to himself. *When you look at a beautiful woman in motion and think about ships, that's when you know you need a vacation.* Though thinking about Uhura's beauty wasn't a road he was comfortable going down either, given his luck with workplace romances. He satisfied himself with a clinical appraisal of her gymnastic form. She maneuvered herself well, gauging forces and distances, though there were a few missteps that suggested she wasn't experienced with this gravity level. But she was so focused that she didn't notice him watching—or didn't choose to. A communications officer who routinely had a dozen voices yammering in her ear at once needed that kind of focus.

Once she settled herself on a perch and took a moment to rest, Sulu applauded, and launched himself with just enough force to alight on a bar near her. She glared at him, and he belatedly realized he should have made some effort to look as if he'd been making some effort. "This is an unusual gravity," he said. "Most people pick Mars, Luna, Vulcan, or freefall. What is this, Pluto level? Point oh six?"

Uhura nodded. "I wanted to challenge myself. It's low enough that it's hard to get a sense of up and down at all, but if you let yourself think it's freefall you get in trouble. It's surprising how tough it can be."

"You'd hardly know from watching," Sulu said.

"That's sweet of you to say, Hikaru, but I'm exhausted." She just perched and breathed deeply for a moment. "Still, the low gravity feels very relaxing when you're not trying to move through it. I just wish the blood flow to my sinuses didn't make my voice more nasal." Sulu nodded absently, shared in the quiet for a moment. "So how are things on the bridge?"

"Quiet," he replied. "We're past the Klingon border now, and no sign of trouble."

"Good."

There was more silence, and finally Sulu asked, "So how do you think the new crew's settling in?"

"Oh, they're doing fine. Everyone's excited—a good-as-new ship, a new mission. And the alien crew members are meshing pretty well so far. Not many tensions." She smirked. "Although I did have to break up a spat between a Caitian and an Eeiauoan yesterday."

"What was it about?"

"Some territorial thing. I rearranged their duty shifts, and had them groom and make up."

"Okay. So it wasn't . . ."

"Wasn't what?"

"Well," Sulu said, "I've heard people talk. Ensign Zaand, mainly, but a lot of others too."

"Ahh. You mean doubts about Captain Kirk. Whether he was right to take command or not."

"That's it. I mean, he pulled us through, that should've proved it. But a lot of people . . ."

"A lot of people haven't served with Captain Kirk as long as we have. And a lot of them were very loyal to Captain Decker. He chose them personally, tried to establish relationships with as many of them as he could. They haven't had the opportunity to get to know Captain Kirk yet."

Sulu absorbed her words. "What about you? I know you worked closely with Decker." Sulu hadn't been around for that; although he, like Chekov and others, had kept himself on Earth so he'd be available for reassignment to the *Enterprise*, he'd spent his time working as a test pilot for prototype small craft. He and Pavel had only been assigned to the *Enterprise* a couple of hours before Kirk had taken over; apparently Admiral Nogura himself had sent out orders to reassemble as much of the old command crew as possible for the V'Ger mission, even before he'd approved Kirk's transfer of command. But Uhura had been part of Decker's handpicked senior staff, and had played an active role in recruiting many of the nonhumans in the crew. "I hear he even considered you for first officer."

Uhura didn't confirm or deny it. "So do I think he should've stayed in command? Hikaru, you were on the bridge that day, you heard what I said to Zaand."

Sulu chuckled. "You sure chewed him out, all right. But I was a bit surprised. Whenever you talked about Decker, you seemed to think the world of him."

Her dark, elegant eyes met his. "I did. There was a lot more to Will Decker than met the eye. He was a real Renaissance man, a man of great imagination. He had big ideas, and he worked hard to make them real. Yet he didn't lose sight of the people he worked with. He was the kind of commander who really forms a bond with his crew, treats them like family." She paused. "But he was young, and he'd never commanded a ship before. I know he would've made a great captain someday . . . if his path hadn't taken him . . . elsewhere. But when it came down to the fate of the Earth—then I'd pick James T. Kirk every time."

"Me too," Sulu said. "So . . . does that mean you'll stay with the ship? After the shakedown ends . . . assuming they extend the shakedown into a full five-year tour?"

"Of course. I have a lot invested in this crew." She studied him. "And you? Are you planning to stay with the *Enterprise?*"

Sulu didn't answer right away. Restlessly, he pushed off his perch and let himself drift in a slow arc. "I'm not sure yet. I don't know if I want to go back to being a helmsman again. I mean . . . I've *done* that. And I really enjoy test piloting . . . though I don't know if that's something I want to do indefinitely either."

Uhura rotated herself to watch as he drifted lazily downward, catching himself and pushing off into another arc. "So what are your long-term goals, Hikaru? Just do whatever catches your fancy for a while, then find something else?"

"Sounds about right."

"I don't think you'll ever get your own command that way, honey."

He looked at her, thought a moment, then arced his way to the perch next to hers. "To tell you the truth, Nyota, I don't know if I'm interested in command. I tell people that I want my own ship someday—they expect it, since I took command training. But—just between you, me, and the perpendicular bars—the only reason I *took* command training was, well, the same reason I try everything else."

She smiled. "To see if you can." Sulu nodded. "And what's the answer, usually, when you try these things? Yes or no?"

"Usually yes," he said with a shrug.

"And don't you think someone who can do all those things would make a good captain? Don't you think maybe it's a waste of potential if he doesn't even try?"

He hadn't thought about it that way before. "Maybe," he granted. "But I just don't know if it's right for me."

Uhura looked him over, then pushed off and arced her way to the exit, pirouetting to face him as her feet touched gently down. "And what makes you think the decision is about you?"

Most people, upon seeing Reiko Onami's delicate Asian features and diminutive frame, wouldn't normally envision her facing down a two-meter carnivore with talons and fangs. But it would never have occurred to Reiko not to. "Hrrii'ush, you have *got* to understand that there are *rules* on this ship!"

The Betelgeusian snarled (more than usual) with his eating mouth while his speaking mouth fluted his response. "I know about ship rules!" Uuvu'it insisted. "I would never endanger any ship or its crew! I would never have lived this long if I were so careless."

"I know that. But ships aren't just about machines and ecosystems, are they? What about the social environment? Don't you care about maintaining that?"

Uuvu'it quieted a bit in response. "It was just a friendly wager."

"Invading a locker room? With a videocorder?!"

"Chavi'rru and I were arguing about which was stronger, human or Saurian nudity taboos. He dared me to test it. I can't turn down a dare!" he said as though it were a law of nature. "And it was fun to see their reactions."

"I don't think Lieutenant Chekov found it much fun."

68   CHRISTOPHER L. BENNETT

"Which proved my point!"

Reiko glared affectionately. She was glad that he was starting to bond with the other 'Geusians on board, beginning to move past the usual inter-pack suspicion, but she had to encourage him and the others to find less disruptive ways of interacting. "What I don't get is, if you wanted to test taboos, why not do it with the opposite sex?"

He let out a chirp that corresponded to a shrug. "I figured species difference would count more than sex difference. You think it wouldn't? Hmm, I'll have to test that next."

"No, you won't! You're in enough trouble as it is! Look, I understand how restless you can get. I know the available rec facilities are a bit spare by your standards." Most beings would consider the *Enterprise*'s rec deck downright extravagant. But 'Geusians were a race of pack hunters living out their lives on ships and space stations. Some of the larger stations had hunting preserves, but slots were limited. Sometimes they went hunting on planets without sentient life, but those weren't easy to find. For the most part, they had to sublimate their hunting drive through intense, aggressive sports and gaming. The alternative was constant warfare—though sometimes 'Geusian games didn't seem that far removed from combat. "But you've got to find more appropriate outlets. No more testing people's taboos. No more practical jokes with the gravity system. And no more attempts to bungee jump down a turboshaft."

"Well, it was either that or the warp shaft!"

Reiko glared. "Look—next time you feel the urge, just go blast stuff in the phaser range."

"Too easy. No danger."

"Hrrii'ush, you keep going like this, you'll end up with plenty of people who'll be glad to shoot back. And I'm on the verge of being one of them."

"You promise?"

Reiko growled in frustration. "Just get out of here. I'll see you next week."

Uuvu'it wasted no time in haring off to whatever duty or mischief he had next. Reiko sighed, wondering what she was going to do about him. *Knack for interspecies understanding, my ass,* she thought. Sure, growing up on Nelgha, she'd had to learn how to read nonhuman psyches. How else to survive when you and your parents were the only humans in the whole sector, without a Federation to back you up if you wanted to live by human rules and customs? When survival required holding your own amid the trading and scheming of dozens of different species? To her parents, it had been immersion anthropology in its purest state; to Reiko, it had been the only life she knew, and like any child, she'd grown up thinking it was normal.

But even with all her experience, even with all the xenopsych theory and abstract understanding in the universe, some beings were just plain aggravating—even when you liked them. Reiko had liked almost every alien she'd ever met; even the scoundrels and brutes had shown some endearing qualities when she looked at them right. It was only when she'd come to Earth that she'd first found it difficult to relate to other people. Other humans.

Reiko ran her fingers through her short, backswept hair, shook her head to clear it, and headed out of her office, making her way through the sickbay complex to check in with Christine. She found her and Dr. McCoy in the examination room, working together on the crew physicals to speed up the pace. R'trikahi, the Saurian engineer, was just finishing up. "Now, you remember to use those eyedrops twice a day," McCoy was lecturing her. "And until your eyes are ready for the contact lenses, you keep those sunglasses on! I don't care how they make you look—you won't care about that anyway if you go blind!" R'trikahi bowed in thanks and left. McCoy shook his head. "Saurians.

Strong as an ox, can breathe almost anything, but shine a bright light and they're helpless. Don't know why she and her mate don't stay home and drink brandy with the rest of 'em."

Reiko glared. "The Saurians have a rich civilization older than ours, Doctor. They don't need to travel so much because everyone else is so eager to come to them for trade. But that doesn't preclude their right to join Starfleet if they want to."

"Yeah, yeah, I know. But why not serve on a ship of their own, where they can keep it nice and dark all the time?" He shook his head. "Damn fool idea, tryin' to cram all these different species together in one environment. It's just not natural."

Who did this backwoods hick think he was? "It isn't natural for anyone to live in space."

McCoy scoffed. "You don't have to tell me that. But at least you and I can breathe the air here. What about those Zaranites, the fluorine-breathers? What happens if one of their tanks gets damaged and he can't breathe? What if it ruptures when there are other people around? People could die! Or what if that Megarite lady gets lost on some desert planet with no way to feed herself? It's just not responsible, taking species with so many different needs and sticking 'em on the same crew."

"Just because something hasn't been tried before doesn't mean you shouldn't do it. And if something does go wrong, you're supposed to be the one whose job it is to fix it. If you don't think you're competent to do that job, Dr. McCoy, then you should turn this sickbay back over to Christine, the one who's spent the past two years training to treat this crew."

McCoy grew furious. "Now, see here, little lady—"

"Leonard." Chapel interposed herself. "There are still patients waiting. And your shift ended ten minutes ago. Why don't you go get some rest? I'll take it from here."

Under Chapel's firm gaze, McCoy subsided. "All right. But this isn't over!"

"You bet it isn't," Reiko responded.

Once McCoy left, Chapel turned to Reiko, but the psychologist interrupted. "Don't start with me, Christine. I know you're fond of him—and you know I have the greatest respect for Captain Kirk. But for the life of me I can't understand by what right Kirk put that parochial antique in the job that was meant for you, or how you could accept it."

"I can because Leonard is the most caring and conscientious doctor I have ever known, and the most brilliant. Maybe he hasn't specialized in xenomedicine, but he has the genius and commitment to make up for it."

"Chris, the man's a bigot."

"He is not," Chapel said adamantly. "You just . . . you just have to know him. Learn to see past the walls he puts up. Leonard . . . he likes to cultivate his flaws. He thinks that if we become too perfect we lose our individuality."

Reiko shook her head, unconvinced. "He's angry at the universe."

"Yes, he is—because it keeps hurting people, and he can't stand seeing people in pain. I think being angry is what lets him face that pain and keep fighting against it." Chapel smirked. "Come on, Reiko, you should know a thing or two about anger. Maybe if you didn't keep throwing your righteous fits at everybody, you'd be a chief by now."

Reiko shrugged. "I don't give a tribble's eye about rank. I'm just here to help realize Will Decker's dream. I'm a civilian through and through."

Chapel smiled. "Then you and Leonard have more in common than you think."

"Except he can't get along with aliens."

"And you could learn some more about getting along with humans."

Reiko mulled it over. "Not something I had a lot of

opportunity to learn, growing up. Outside of family, that is. But if you ask me, humans aren't all they're cracked up to be. They're just the latest bunch of cultural imperialists. Why do you suppose Starfleet is so overwhelmingly human?"

"Hmm, maybe. But Will Decker was human too."

"Yeah, but he outgrew it." There was an awkward moment, and Reiko realized she'd probably had another burst of inappropriate humor. "Look . . . even if you're right about McCoy, I still say he's not the right person for this job. *You* are. I could put up with him staying on the ship, but he should be working for you. And as long as he's in charge, sooner or later the well-being of this crew is going to suffer. Maybe you should consider the pain he'll feel if he lets that happen—if you let him let it happen."

She left Chapel to ponder her words. Reiko could see she was far from convinced, still guided by her strong loyalty to McCoy. But with any luck, Reiko had successfully planted the seeds of doubt.

Montgomery Scott frowned at the molecular synchronization readouts on the transporter console. "Och, it *looks* fine, but I'm still not convinced. There's still a wee variance."

Beside him, Chief Janice Rand sighed. "It's well within tolerances. The redundant scanners will—"

"Aye, I know what the manuals say! But these are entirely new systems; there's no telling what kind of unexpected interactions there can be. You know that, lassie."

"Yes," she said, her tone still a bit haunted by the memory. "I know that. But we've rebuilt practically the whole system from the ground up, Scotty. There's nothing more we can do."

"Except rebuild the rest of it. Pull the quantum phase scanners—I want to run a few more—"

"Mr. Scott." It was Kirk's voice, coming from the doorway. Scott started; he'd been so intent he hadn't heard the door's pneumatic seal hiss open. "Are you sure that's necessary? Chief Rand is the expert on this system, and if she says it's good to go, it's good to go."

"Aye, Captain, but I still think—"

"Mr. Scott. You assured me this overhaul would be completed before we reached the Daran system. That's less than twelve hours away now. And I expect you to have this system up and running by that time, is that clear?"

"Sir, if you'd just let me try a few more things—"

"To do what? Improve efficiency by another hundredth of a percent? Scotty, this . . . perfectionist jag of yours is starting to interfere with the operations of this ship."

Scott stared at the captain. "Permission to speak freely, sir?"

"I think that's long overdue. Please excuse us, Chief."

Once Rand had left, Scott spoke his piece. "This is supposed to be a shakedown cruise, sir. These are brand-new systems, the first of their kind. They can't be rushed. The last time you called them into use before they were ready, we almost lost the whole *Enterprise* to a wormhole! And we *did* lose two good people to a—a transporter accident. A *transporter accident!*" he repeated in disbelief and disgust, slapping his palm on the console as if to reassure himself of its solidity. "Aye, we've had a few close calls with the transporter, but only under extraordinary conditions, alien influences . . . and even then, even with the ship blowin' up around us, we almost always managed to put everyone back together again. But to lose two poor souls to a routine beaming—in *drydock*—it's just not right, sir!"

Kirk studied him. "Scotty, you know there was no other choice. We had to intercept V'Ger as soon as possible."

"Aye, I know that." *Not that we were able to do anything about the beastie till we were back in Earth orbit,* Scott thought, knowing it was unfair. "I'm just sayin'—the new girl can't be rushed, sir. She can handle whatever's asked o' her, I'd stake my reputation on that—but she needs to be guided into it by a gentle hand, someone who understands her moods and how to pace her."

Kirk's gaze hardened. "You mean like Will Decker?"

Scott couldn't find the words to respond to that, because it was exactly what he did mean. Decker had been with the *Enterprise* through every stage of her reconstruction, getting to know her as intimately as any captain had ever known his ship. Meanwhile, Kirk had gone nearly three years without so much as a visit, even though the whole refit process had nominally been under his purview as Chief of Fleet Operations. And then all of a sudden he'd swept in out of nowhere, taken over, and begun demanding the impossible again. Scott hadn't questioned that at first; after all, this was still Jim Kirk.

But then look what had happened as a result of his pushing. When Kirk had come to tell Decker he was being removed from command, the younger captain had just tracked down the faulty module which had taken the transporters offline—a simple backup sensor for error-checking the Heisenberg compensator. After Kirk had pulled Decker aside, a circuit anomaly had sent a spurious green light to the transporter room while the HC was still disengaged, and then failed to alert Rand that it had not entangled with Commander Sonak and Vice Admiral Ciana, had not encoded their quantum-level data in its Bose-Einstein condensate. The thought still made Scotty shudder—the idea of a living thing's particles being reassembled with random errors in their positions and momenta, body parts blurred together into mush, but with just enough of their original form remaining for the victim to be alive and aware of it for the brief moments it had left. . . . It was a horrible thing. It shouldn't have been allowed to happen.

Now Kirk peered into his eyes intently. "That's what you're thinking, isn't it, Scotty? That maybe Decker could've prevented the accident if I hadn't dragged him away."

"I . . . there's no way of knowin' that, sir." *Or whether I could've prevented it if I hadn't been so distracted by their conversation . . .*

"But that's what you're thinking, isn't it?" Scott tried to look away, but Kirk moved to catch his gaze. "I know, Scotty . . . because I have the same thought every day."

When Scott saw the pain in Kirk's eyes, he could have slapped himself. How could he have been so self-absorbed? "I'm . . . sorry, sir. I wasn't thinking. . . . I'd heard you and Admiral Ciana were . . . close. . . ."

Kirk lowered his head. "To tell you the truth, Scotty, that . . . didn't end well. We hadn't been close for a long time. I still don't even know why she tried to come on board. . . . I guess I'll never know. But it was almost certainly because of me." He sighed and rested his weight on the console. "She's dead, and it's because of me. Whatever our . . . history, she didn't deserve that. And Commander Sonak, too . . . he was young, dedicated, on his way to becoming an exemplary officer. He deserved better."

There was a long silence, but finally Scott reached out and put a hand on Kirk's arm. "Jim . . . whatever you or . . . or I may feel about it, the hard fact is, nobody could've predicted the malfunction. Every new system has quirks and interactions you just can't anticipate—not even with computer simulations, since they're only as good as the conditions you put into 'em. And Mike Cleary's a good man. He distinguished himself on the *Potemkin* and the *Sacajawea*—if anyone could've seen it coming, he could. I guess . . ." He let out a long puff of breath, ruffling his mustache. "Maybe we'd *both* better stop blamin' ourselves. And maybe," he added with a self-deprecating smile, "I should get out o' Janice's hair and find some real work."

Kirk returned the smile, though it was faint. "You do that, Scotty. Thanks."

"Aye, sir."

CHAPTER FIVE

Strange, terrible and beautiful are the Keepers of the Promise: dragons of auroral light, patrolling the heavens, they guard the Promised World, keeping it untouched and pure until the People arrive to claim it as their home. Though we may recoil at their fearsome aspect, we must recall the profound debt which the People owe to the Keepers, and show them the same reverence, respect, and neighborly affection which they have promised us, in the Creators' name.

—The Book of the People

IT'S AN ANCIENT QUESTION: If you travel faster than light, will your headlights work?

The answer is yes, and no. In warp drive, your head-lights—and the rest of your vehicle—are in a bubble of normal spacetime surfing on a distortion wave half-submerged in subspace. A beam of light will travel forward through the bubble until it reaches the edge—but once it crosses into normal space and moves at light speed relative to that, it's suddenly going a whole lot slower than the bubble it just left—which immediately overtakes it, of course. (This is indelicately known as the spit-into-the-wind effect.) From the ship's point of view, the light bounces off the front of the bubble and back the way it came. From outside, it's still moving forward, but it won't reach an observer until long after the ship does.

Theoretically, this means that an arriving warp ship would seem to appear out of nowhere and split off a ghost duplicate that travels *backward* to its starting point, as the leftover light from farther away takes longer to catch up. The reason this effect doesn't occur (not visibly, anyway) is the navigational deflector. At the effective velocity of a warp ship, a ray of light entering the front of the warp bubble would be blueshifted to a high enough energy level to vaporize the ship. So any warp ship needs a deflector that not only slows and diverts any impinging matter, but also redshifts any incoming light. So by the time our headlight beam passes out the back of the bubble and reenters normal space, it has been reduced to a long, feeble radio wavelength, barely hotter than the cosmic microwave background itself.

In short, without subspace-based FTL sensors, it's impossible to detect an approaching warp ship until it enters your system. Even then, it's not always easy. When a ship exits warp, the collapse of spacetime back to its normal geometry causes a release of energy, a sudden burst across the spectrum heralding the vessel's arrival. But the energy released is not very great, the flash is not exceedingly bright, and it ends very quickly. So it's easy to miss unless it happens at close range, and unless you happen to be looking in the right direction.

These facts all made Ssherrak Ki'threetl very nervous. Like most Shesshran, she disliked the idea of anyone being able to enter her territory without advance warning. True, her own territory was a few acres of hunting ground and the airspace above it, no more than a speck against the vastness of the Daran star system. But invaders from beyond that system, if they had the technology to warp space, could put every Shesshran's territories in danger, and Shesshran had no problem cooperating in the name of a common interest, so long as individuals respected one another's autonomy and boundaries. So as soon as the Shesshran had developed the early stages of warp theory, they had begun a cooperative effort to observe and patrol Daran's interplanetary space, determined to catch that brief flash of a ship dewarping. They didn't even know for sure whether any other life existed in the universe, but they weren't about to take any chances.

Thus it was that Ssherrak was out here, flying through vacuum in her one-person pod, watching for phantoms, rather than soaring on her own wings through Kachissat's warm, dense, welcoming air in pursuit of some lively, succulent prey beast. *No,* she reminded herself, *not phantoms. Such thinking diminishes your vigilance.* It had been only three of Kachissat's years since the theories had been proven true, the watch worthwhile—since the alien ship called *Intrepid* had been spotted exiting from warp within the system. The creatures called Vulcans had sought to avoid detection, to do a clandestine survey and then leave, for whatever reasons of their own. But they hadn't counted on Shesshran vigilance, and the blast from a railgun had effectively proven it to them. True, it hadn't put a dent in the powerful fields of force around the ship, but it had gotten the point across, and served as that all-important show of strength for opening a negotiation. It would have been a moral victory, so the defense coalition had asserted, even if the Vulcans had proceeded to destroy them.

Ssherrak hadn't been with the coalition at the time, but even if she had, she doubted she would have seen it that way. She figured it was fortunate that the Vulcans had chosen to talk instead of fight back. They hadn't even made the traditional response strike to demonstrate their strength—

but then, they hadn't really needed to, given the futility of the railgun attack. It was even more fortunate that the Vulcans had been a type of life form better suited to the weak gravity and thin air of the fourth planet, and thus uninterested in territorial claims on Kachissat itself.

By initiating contact, the Shesshran had nullified the Vulcans' rule against dealing with pre-warp cultures. Still, the Vulcans had been protective of their advantages, unwilling to trade their technologies. They had claimed to be interested in engaging the Shesshran as equals, yet had been unwilling to let the sides meet at equal altitude by sharing the FTL sensor technology which would let the Shesshran guard their territory against future incursions. So the Shesshran, quickly reaching a consensus among the population, had asked the Vulcans to leave, and the Vulcans had done so. And the Shesshran had continued to watch, more alertly than ever now that they knew there was definitely something to watch for. Ssherrak herself had signed up for the defense coalition soon after, ceding the wardenship of her hunting grounds to her sister and eldest son for the duration of her offworld tours. It drove her crazy, not being home to defend her own grounds, but her sister and son were under strict contracts, and she was fully entitled to kill them if they abused their wardenship. They knew this full well, of course, so they were likely to honor their contracts. Which was a relief, at least in her son's case. Her sister had naturally been a rival since reaching maturity, and had enjoyed being a rival too much even before then.

And of course, what Ssherrak did out here was important. In the years since the *Intrepid* had left, Daran space had been incurred upon several times more. This series of incursions had begun when a large, powered asteroid had been detected on the far edge of the system, and another Federation starship along with it—indeed, since the asteroid had been heading almost directly for Kachissat at too great a distance for easy parallax, it had not been identified as a threat until it had exchanged fire with the starship. Once it was realized the object was on a collision course with Kachissat, a fleet had been mobilized to engage it and the starship, on the assumption that it was an attack launched by the Federation. Ssherrak had been one of the volunteers for that fleet, knowing that it was probably a futile battle, but driven to defend her world and her little patch of sky or die trying. She'd begun to understand why the coalition members had been willing to die for a moral victory. But she'd been sad to think that her lovely hills, her elegantly rustic eyrie, and her tasty *dushiik* herd would end up destroyed—or worse, as her sister's property.

No sooner had the fleet been assembled, however, than the starship had contacted the Shesshran, calling itself *Enterprise* and announcing that the asteroid had been diverted, that it was in fact an alien colony ship intending to settle the fourth planet. The Shesshran had been stunned to discover that more than one species was adapted for such hostile conditions—although Ssherrak couldn't tell any of those species apart and wasn't remotely convinced of their claim to be unrelated.

In any case, the Shesshran had objected strenuously to the idea of aliens settling one of their planets, even a useless, nearly airless one. Ssherrak hadn't really been bothered by that per se, but having aliens so close would have required even greater vigilance, and her grounds would thus have to stay in her relatives' hands for longer. Ssherrak could have always resigned; unlike the Federation types, Shesshran did what they chose, not what they were told by another, so nobody could have prevented her from leaving the coalition. But if people thought that way, she believed, then there would be no volunteers and no global defense. And although she was uncomfortable leaving the tending of her grounds in other hands, she couldn't trust anyone but herself with the defense of their very existence.

So she had argued against letting the aliens settle on Daran IV, and for telling the Federation to take them somewhere else. But then the asteroid people, the Fabrini, claimed that the world had been promised to them by the ancient Shesshran. It had seemed a ludicrous claim to most, but some archaeologists got all excited and drummed up interest in their crackpot theories, and then the Federation sent a smaller ship called the *Yang Liwei* whose crew helped them dig up their own hunting grounds (their choice, of course, but what a waste!), and proved that the ancient civilization really had existed before the Great Die-Off, and really had invited the Fabrini. That, unfortunately, had changed everything. Contracts and promises had to be honored, or society couldn't function.

So Ssherrak had accepted the consensus that the Fabrini should have their world, though she wasn't in the minority that actually wanted them there. And so she kept serving her tours in the coalition, watching space for intruders, knowing that if they came in force the defense effort wouldn't make any difference, but was still worth dying for. But the whole thing put her in a really bad mood. She spent her long, tedious tours fantasizing alternately about blasting an invading starship into vapor and about creative ways to kill her sister if and when she broke some minor codicil of their contract. Sometimes, for variety, she even fantasized about killing her son—he was a sweet boy, but she could have more, and sons were relatively expendable, since all they ever did was go off and mate with some rival female, defend her lands, and make it harder to take them away from her. Besides, she hadn't been hunting in weeks, and she was aching to kill *something*.

Which was why it filled her with satisfaction when that

familiar warp flare happened in her own sector, and a Federation starship popped forth. She had no illusions about being able to kill anyone aboard it, but at least it gave her something to shoot.

"Captain, we are taking fire!"

"Easy, Mr. Chekov," Kirk said. "As I understand it, this is just the Shesshran's way of saying hello. Risk assessment?"

Chekov seemed to be striving for total calm, self-conscious about his overreaction. "Minimal, Captain. Their weapons pose no significant threat to our shields." He checked the tactical monitor. "However, four other ships have diverted to intercept us. If they combine their forces they could . . . *still* not pose a significant threat. Not unless we let them fire continuously for an hour or two."

"Hail them, Commander Uhura."

"Aye, sir."

Kirk swiveled to the science station behind him. It was a bit awkward, having his first officer and most trusted advisor directly behind him instead of off to the side as he used to be. After the shakedown, he would propose returning the station to something closer to its original position. "Tell me, Mr. Spock. What is it about the Daran system that makes everyone we meet here want to beat us up, electrocute us, or shoot at us before they're willing to have a conversation?"

Spock raised a wry brow. "I have insufficient data to draw a conclusion, Captain. Though I would submit that the phenomenon is hardly unique to this star system. Perhaps the fault lies not in our stars, but in ourselves?"

Kirk threw him a glare, and there was a trace of laughter in Uhura's voice as she spoke. "Receiving a signal from the lead Shesshran ship, sir." She stressed their name on the second syllable: Shessh-*rahn*. Kirk resolved to remember that. Come to think of it, he'd probably been pronouncing Daran wrong too.

"On screen." A rainbow pterodactyl appeared on the viewer, or so it looked to Kirk. The Shesshran's head was very pterosaurian, with a long sharp beak and a shark-fin rudder on the top. Its body was streamlined, with a pronounced keelbone in mid-chest, and it floated in a spacious freefall cockpit to accommodate its batlike wings and saurian tail. Its silver skin shimmered and diffracted the light in a gorgeous prismatic display; indeed, the cockpit seemed to be equipped with extra lighting specifically to bring out the effect—although, since it was a one-person pod, Kirk guessed the extra lights only went on when the comm did. The Shesshran wore nothing but an equipment harness—if you had skin like that, Kirk thought, who'd want to cover it?

The pilot spread its wings and raised its arms in an aggressive posture. Fascinatingly, its arms split at the elbow into two forearms each, giving it a total of four three-taloned hands—all of which looked like they were poised to disembowel. "I am Ssherrak Ki'threetl, speaking for the defense coalition of Kachissat," the translator interpreted, giving the alien a female voice (someday he'd have to ask Spock or Uhura how it *knew* these things). "Declare your intentions and justify your presence, or leave this territory immediately!"

Kirk nodded to Uhura, who opened the channel for him. "This is Captain James T. Kirk of the Federation starship *Enterprise*," he said, enjoying how good it felt. "We come on a peaceful mission, at the invitation of the government of Lorina. I'm certain your own leaders were notified to expect our arrival."

Those fearsome talons twitched. "I have no 'leaders,' groundling. I fly in defense of the lands I own, and of the common cause I share."

"My apologies," Kirk said. "But I'm sure if you confer

with your . . . compatriots, you'll find that we're expected."

"What is *expected* is that you will do nothing to disrupt Shesshran affairs or undermine our autonomy in this system. Emerging in our space unannounced is such a disruption—particularly so long as you refuse to provide us with the technology to detect your approach."

If you had that technology, Kirk wondered, *would you use it to prepare a welcome or an ambush?* "Again, my apologies, Ms. Ki'threetl." He hoped that was an acceptable form of address. "We will make a note of your approach protocols for the benefit of future visitors."

"My concern is only with your visit in the present. To ensure you do nothing to disrupt our interests, I will escort you to Lorina. Follow the course I set and do not deviate!"

Kirk found this whole thing a bit ridiculous. The Shesshran had no power to enforce her demands, and she knew it. But that was just why she felt obligated to put on a forceful show, and in his three years dealing with Admiralty politics, Kirk knew the simplest way to deal with such people, at least when there was nothing at stake, was to play along and let them save face. "Certainly, Ms. Ki'threetl. After you."

Ki'threetl let out a rude puff of breath and cut the transmission. "Mr. Sulu . . . please be so good as to follow the lady."

"Aye, sir."

"Captain," Chekov informed him, sounding puzzled, "the second ship is in range . . . and is firing on us."

"The Shesshran," Spock explained, "are highly individualistic, since as avian raptors they each need a sizeable hunting ground to provide adequate sustenance, making it impractical for them to coexist in groups. What social institutions they have are based on mutual decision-making and mutual benefit, but each individual has a say in the process and the option to act autonomously."

"You mean we have to negotiate with all five scouts to stop them from shooting us?" Kirk asked.

"And any others who decide to confront us."

Kirk sighed. "Ms. Uhura . . . open a hail to *all* the Shesshran ships." *This is going to be a long morning. . . .*

Bones was late. He'd been ordered to report to the transporter room five minutes ago and still hadn't shown up. Not that Kirk was all that surprised, somehow. He was considering paging McCoy again, but then Chekov approached him and said, "Captain, I still recommend that you remain aboard the ship. Given the ongoing violence on the surface . . ."

"Mr. Chekov, this is a diplomatic meeting with a planetary head of state. It would be rude for me not to come along. And I have full confidence in your people."

"But . . ."

"Mr. Chekov . . . the matter is settled." This was a side effect of Chekov's promotion to security chief that Kirk hadn't expected. The young Russian had always been fiercely loyal to his captain, and now that he was directly responsible for his captain's safety, he was pursuing that duty with the same earnest zeal he applied to most everything else. But Kirk wasn't out here to sit in his cushy ergonomic command chair while he sent other people out to risk their lives. He'd had enough of that as Chief of Starfleet Operations, deciding where starships should be deployed and having to watch helplessly from afar when those deployments led them into danger and death. And before that, as a captain, he'd lost far too many good security men and women. He couldn't prevent them from risking or giving their lives for his protection; that was their job, whether he liked it or not. But if it had to be that way, at least he would be out there with them, as a comrade in arms.

McCoy's belated arrival mercifully disrupted that train of thought. "You're late," Kirk said. "Get your field jacket."

"Now, wait a minute. You ordered me to report, so I reported. But I haven't agreed to get into that blasted machine again," he declared, throwing a hateful glance at the transporter alcove. "The damn thing's a deathtrap and you know it."

Kirk caught the wince on Chief Rand's face as she stood at the console behind the clear partition. He knew that on some level she must still feel responsible for the deaths of Sonak and Ciana. After all, he still did, and always would, regardless of Scotty's assurances. But he didn't have time for this. "Bones, you've been through it since the accident."

"Once. And that was under duress. I'm not about to push my luck a second time."

"Doctor," Spock interposed, "you may rest assured that the safety of this transporter design has been thoroughly verified. It has been in use within the Sol system for the past six years, and in all that time there has been exactly one accident, caused by a freak sensor malfunction whose cause was promptly identified and remedied, as your own continued existence attests. You are far safer in the transporter than you would be in a shuttlecraft, or even as a pedestrian within a typical city."

"Oh yeah, Spock? Then *explain* to me," McCoy went on in his highest dudgeon, "why the designers felt it necessary to install a—a *splatter guard* in front of the console!"

One of the security guards—Mosi Nizhoni, a deceptively dainty Navajo woman with her long hair styled in twin braids—stifled a laugh. Rand just looked mortified. Spock displayed his impatience openly—not that he'd ever really bothered to suppress that particular emotion where McCoy was concerned. "Doctor, it is no different from the radiation protection which medical personnel once used when working with x-ray equipment, since they were exposed far more frequently than the patients."

That just made Bones look more alarmed. "But those patients only got scanned once or twice a year. We have to go through this damn thing all the time. Are you tellin' me we've been getting dosed with radiation all along?"

"Bones," Kirk said sharply. He suspected that McCoy's hesitancy had less to do with the transporter than it did with having to face Natira down on the planet. He looked his old friend in the eye and said, "You're going to do this. I'm not letting you off the hook, and you know there's no point in putting it off. So come on." He figured the others would assume the exchange related to the transporter, but he could see in McCoy's eyes that he'd gotten the subtext.

"All right," McCoy said, taking his khaki field jacket and equipment from Chekov. "Let's get this over with." He glared at Spock. "But we're gonna have a talk about that radiation."

"Doctor, considering that the energies emitted by the transporter are intense enough to sever the molecular bonds of your body and reduce you to component particles, it hardly seems—"

"Spock! You're not helping!"

The people of Yonada, Kirk remembered, had spoken of their Creators' promise that they would one day leave their austere, underground dwellings for a new, lush, beautiful world. In this respect, at least, the Creators had not been lying. When Kirk materialized in the courtyard outside the capitol building of Lorina City—or more accurately, the one and only city so far extant on the planet Lorina—it felt like coming home, except with lighter gravity. The air was fresh and warm, the sky a clear, vivid blue. The courtyard was airy and open, yet lined with tall, fragrant trees. The walls of the capitol building itself, a tall cylindrical tower of glass and stone, were adorned with flowering vines on their lower levels. It was a startling contrast to the barrenness of Yonada, to the enclosed corridors in which the Fabrini refugees had lived for so many generations. The only things that detracted from the idyllic scene were the security barricades and armed guards on the perimeter of the courtyard.

A contingent of the guards was now emerging from the capitol building, approaching the landing party. Their uniforms—brown tunic and black trousers—were also a contrast; the guards on Yonada had worn robes patterned with tartans that wouldn't look out of place in a Scottish regiment, and odd cylindrical black cowls. At least the swords were familiar, though they seemed to be largely ceremonial, since they were accompanied on the uniform belts by more modern sidearms. "Wireless electric stunners," Spock observed, "evidently based on the same UV laser principle as the Oracle's punishment shock."

At least this time the weapons weren't drawn, and the guards' approach was considerably more civil than it had been the first time. The leader bowed briefly and spoke to Kirk. "Greetings, on behalf of the People of Lorina. I am Tasari, Minister of Security."

Kirk returned the bow, finding the man familiar, though his nondescript features were hard to place. "Greetings, Minister Tasari." He introduced the members of his party, though Tasari didn't seem inclined to introduce the rest of his contingent.

"I've been sent to escort you to Governess Natira's office," Tasari said in a simple, businesslike tone. "If you'll follow me, please."

"Certainly," Kirk said, now realizing where he'd seen the man before. "All you had to do was ask," he said pointedly. Tasari stared dully for a moment, then gestured them forward.

"Pardon me," McCoy asked of the minister. "Have we met before?"

"Indeed, you have, Doctor," Spock volunteered when Tasari hesitated. "Though I can't blame you for being vague on the encounter, since at your first meeting the gentleman struck you in the back of the head with the butt of his sword."

McCoy's withering glare brought the first sign of expression the minister had shown yet, not counting the slight frown that seemed to be his default mode. "I was under orders to detain you, as possible invaders. You understand, of course."

"Oh, really? And who gave you the order to clock me from behind when I wasn't looking?"

"Bones," Kirk warned. He'd seen enough regime changes to know that most of the people who made up the everyday machinery of a state generally had to be left in place to keep things running—and most of them didn't really care much about ideology so long as they got their living wage. Tasari struck him as that type. And given Natira's wholehearted rejection of the system she'd once embraced, Kirk doubted she would have promoted the man to Minister of Security if he'd been an Oracular loyalist.

Tasari led them into the capitol building and through its spacious lobby. It was bright, airy, open—in every way the opposite of Yonada. The walls were adorned with art and sculpture imported from many Federation worlds: Terran landscapes, Vulcan mosaics, Axanar crystal topiaries, Tellarite erotic abstracts, Efrosian prismatic gels. The soft strains of Andorian *flabjellah* music played over the public address system. "Very eclectic," Kirk remarked.

Spock took it all in with a critical eye. "Very . . . nontraditional. I see little here that is Yonadi."

"After ten thousand years cooped up in the same tunnels, wouldn't you welcome a change?" McCoy asked.

"If I had lived for ten thousand years, perhaps. But as a shorter-lived inheritor of ten thousand years of tradition, would you be quick to abandon it for something alien?"

Kirk frowned. "What's your point, Spock?"

"None at this time, Captain. It is merely odd."

Tasari led them into what seemed to be a standard-issue Federation turbolift car. Kirk realized a good deal of the city's construction must have been done by the Starfleet Corps of Engineers. The level of technology being shared with the Lorini was presumably no greater than that available in Yonada and its databanks—about comparable to Earth circa 2100 but without warp drive and with more advanced medicine—but Kirk knew the Federation was eager to benefit from that medicine, and thus was offering all the cooperation it could within those limits.

The lift deposited them on the top floor of the building. The view through its large windows and glass ceiling was spectacular, showcasing the northern mountains and the wide, vivid blue sky into which they almost seemed to merge. "And I have touched the sky," Kirk murmured.

Tasari led the party into the governess's office, whose architecture and decor mirrored the rest of the building. Standing there to greet them was Natira, recovered from her injuries and carrying herself as regally as ever. She was clad in a metallic-blue, gold-trimmed gown that spiraled around her body, baring her right leg, left shoulder, and a diagonal swath across the midriff, and trailing a short cape behind. Her long mahogany hair was styled in an elaborate coif which continued the spiral. She stood out among the small group of people she was with, including a man and woman in colorful tunics, somewhat Yonadan in pattern but more Terran in cut; a tall, wizened Vulcan in subdued civilian garb; and a boyish blond human whom Kirk recognized as Christopher Lindstrom.

"Captain Kirk," Natira lilted, gliding forward to greet

her guests. "And Spock, and McCoy. It is truly an auspicious day, for the saviors of the People stand on Lorina at last."

"Governess," Kirk said, inclining his head. "You are a gracious host, but you overrate our importance. We merely helped you achieve the goal your Fabrini ancestors set with their great ingenuity and commitment." With the obligatory exchange of praise out of the way, Kirk went on. "You know my first officer, Commander Spock, and my chief medical officer, Dr. McCoy," he said for the benefit of the others in the room. "And this is Lieutenant Chekov, my chief of security, and Ensigns Perez and Nizhoni."

"You are all very welcome, as are our other guests from your esteemed Federation. Please allow me the honor of presenting Soreth of Vulcan, the Federation Commissioner for Aid and Reconstruction; and Lieutenant Commander Lindstrom, whom I believe you know."

Further greetings were exchanged, though Natira didn't include the two Lorini with her; Kirk figured they were aides or attendants, and indeed they quietly made their way out of the room as the others traded pleasantries. Kirk took particular notice of the interaction between Soreth and Spock. "Peace and long life, Commander Spock," the hawk-nosed elder Vulcan intoned in an aged but sharp tenor, his tone giving no indication that he genuinely wished such things. Though with a Vulcan, that coldness didn't necessarily mean anything.

"Live long and prosper, Commissioner." Kirk was surprised to hear a similar coldness in Spock's voice. Gone was the animation it had contained over the past few weeks; it sounded as cold and emotionless as when Spock had first boarded the *Enterprise* after the wormhole incident, when he was still aspiring to the sterility of *Kolinahr.* Spock's features had grown equally cold, like an old mask slipping back into place. He supposed he couldn't blame

Spock for donning a little protective camouflage in front of other Vulcans, at least initially. Still, it was a bit unsettling.

As if that weren't enough, Bones had been just as closed off since they'd entered the room, though Kirk could see the tension in his old friend's frame. But Natira hadn't shown him any more attention than anyone else, keeping it formal while in public. McCoy had seemed somewhat relieved by this, but he still looked like a man waiting for the other shoe to drop.

Between the two of them, the Vulcans, and the respective security teams, Kirk felt surrounded by people with their guards up. The one exception was Mr. Lindstrom, whose boyish enthusiasm seemed undimmed from its level of six years earlier. "It's good to see you again, Captain. And I guess I owe you my thanks."

"What for?"

"Well, for making sure I still have an Ohio to go back home to one of these days. Really, that was amazing what you did."

Kirk fidgeted. "I don't deserve that much credit. It was . . . it was a team effort," he finished lamely, not really wanting to get into this again.

"Speaking of rogue computers," McCoy interposed, perhaps sensing Kirk's discomfiture, "you seem to make a habit of cleaning up after them, Mr. Lindstrom. First Beta III, now here."

"Not to mention the Avrosians that Commodore Wesley liberated," Lindstrom added. "It is a fascinating sociological study," he went on, his blue eyes gleaming as he warmed to his subject. "Both the similarities and the differences. Landru didn't really institute a religion to govern its people, it basically just told them what to do, what to think. Treated them like cogs in a machine. The Avrosian Worldlink fed its people illusions to make them perform as its drones, but let them think they were leading free and independent lives. But the Oracle's control was much looser. It left the Yonadans their individuality and awareness; it just regulated them through a religious institution and imposed sanctions when they violated its rules."

"You mean it burned a hole in their brains if they had an unauthorized thought," McCoy shot back.

"Yeah, but plenty of humanoid institutions have been just as strict. Methods aside, the approach of the Oracle wasn't all that different from a lot of other organized religions. I came here expecting to find more preprogrammed drones, to help them relearn how to think for themselves, like we did on Beta. But they had plenty of their own ideas already."

"Mr. Lindstrom is too kind." It was Natira, gliding her way in between them. "We had much to learn indeed, and it has been a struggle to cast aside the lies and superstitions which held the People down for so long. We are eternally grateful to you and the Federation for helping us find the way."

Her words made Kirk uncomfortable. "The way is yours to find, Governess. All we've done is make sure you had the opportunity and the liberty to seek it for yourselves."

"Either way, we owe you much, and I am eager to show you the fruits of your efforts. If you will allow me, I have arranged for a tour of our fair city."

"Er, excuse me," Chekov interposed. "Given the current unrest, are you sure that's wise?"

Natira seemed taken aback by his bluntness. But before anyone else could speak, Minister Tasari said, "You will be touring in closed hovercars. A full security contingent will surround the vehicles at all times, and the vehicles will not be left unattended. There should be no danger to you or the governess."

"And the People must see that we continue to live as nor-

mal, that their leaders are not cowering in fear. I trust my
People, Captain, and I know they are with me. A few isolated
malcontents cannot prevail against our combined will."

Tilono's finger tensed visibly above the crossbow's trigger
as the betrayer Natira and her Fedraysha cohorts emerged
from the capitol tower. Moredi hated that tower—all the
towers, really, all this bright openness and straining toward a
sky that should be forbidden to mere mortals. The bitch
thought herself and her cronies worthy to exist on such a
divine plane, as though she were better than the decent,
pious, hardworking people she'd turned her back on. And
those Fedraysha blasphemers, who hunted down gods and
killed them wherever they found them—on Yonada, on Beta,
on Avros, on Gamma Trianguli—they took advantage of her
hubris, used her as their puppet to spread their evils, to
destroy every vestige of the Yonadan way of life as they had
destroyed the Oracle.

   So Moredi couldn't fault Tilono's eagerness to fire her
grenade arrow. But still he said, "Easy, sister. The time is
not right."

   "Even with the guards, the blast should be enough to kill
her," the fair-haired young woman protested. "But she will
be in the car in moments!"

   "Yes, but it would kill the Vulcan Spock as well.
Dovraku wants him alive." The Great One had arranged this
carefully, knowing that his attacks on Natira's government
would prompt her to summon her Fedraysha cronies for
help. Now that they were here, it would be unconscionable
for one acolyte's overzealous trigger finger to spoil his sublime plans.

   "But why? He is one of the godkillers!"

   "Dovraku says he is more. He was touched by the new
god V'Ger. And V'Ger escaped destruction, and ascended
to the heavens."

"Does Dovraku think this Spock somehow saw the light, and stayed the godkillers' hands? If so, then why did he not slay them himself?"

"Take care, Tilono," Moredi snapped. "It is not for us to doubt the wisdom of a prophet. Dovraku says Spock must live—at least until he can be brought before Dovraku himself. After that . . . who can say?"

CHAPTER SIX

Even historians fail to learn from history—they
repeat the same mistakes.   —John Gill

THE HOVERCARS WERE more Federation technology, though
of an antiquated design. There were very few of them in evidence on the streets. Not many people were out, even on a
fine day like this, but those who were visible were mostly
walking, or riding carts drawn by a local species of draft ani-
mal resembling a small ceratopsian dinosaur.

As with the capitol building, the design of the city was in
sharp contrast to Yonada's claustrophilic austerity. The
streets were wide and lined with trees, and a number of
small parks were scattered throughout the city. The cylindrical buildings were full of large windows and arranged
with a good deal of open space between them so as not to
obscure the view of the mountains to the north or the wide
river to the south. And the buildings themselves were often
adorned with vegetation, seeming to blend into the landscape. It was one of the most beautiful cities Kirk had ever
seen beyond Earth.

On the other hand, it struck him that the locals' garments,
while still brightly colored, were not as garish or elaborate as

they had been on Yonada. Some still wore the traditional robes and wraps, but others, including all the government personnel he'd seen, were dressed in a more modern, clean-lined style. "And that is as it should be," Natira told him when he mentioned it. "We are no longer on Yonada. Instead of clinging to the past, we should look to the future, and develop new styles along with our new way of life."

"If I may say so, Governess," Kirk replied, "your own taste in fashion doesn't seem to have changed."

She smiled indulgently. "Perhaps before, I was more of an iconoclast than I knew."

"Actually," Lindstrom said, "there was always a lot of variety in Yonada's fashions over the centuries. With the Oracle's restrictions, the people only had so many outlets for expression. They had essentially no literature, no literacy outside the priestly class and the bureaucracy. After all, the more people read and write, the harder it is to limit their exposure to ideas."

"Well, with the Instruments of Obedience," McCoy said, "what did it matter? It knew what they were thinking."

"In fact, the devices were not so advanced," Spock replied. "The Instruments merely detected sound and certain biometric data, and transmitted them to the Oracle via microwave signals. If that telemetry exceeded certain parameters, it would amplify its microwave signals to deliver heat pulses to the brain, causing either discomfort or death, depending on their duration."

"Thank you, Mr. Spock," McCoy said. "*That* part I remember vividly."

"Anyway," Lindstrom went on, "they didn't really have literature, and they didn't have much musical freedom either—music can be very subversive, you know—so they threw themselves into visual media like abstract art, clothing design . . . things that didn't have any straightforward ideological content but still allowed expression.

"Now people are freer to express themselves in other ways, so maybe they don't need their clothes to be as vivid. Still, the conservatives tend to favor the old styles, see them as a mark of tradition—even though they originated as a form of resistance to orthodoxy."

The hovercar turned a corner, and such abstractions were driven from Kirk's mind as the first of the bomb sites appeared. "The city arena," Natira said. "It was attacked eleven days ago, shortly after an exhibition game of Parrises Squares. Fortunately the audience had left, but six employees were killed, a dozen more wounded." To Kirk's practiced eye, the damage suggested a fairly low-level explosive, commensurate with Lorini technology and the prior attacks. The building was still largely intact, with only the portion around the entrance reduced to wreckage. It could be repaired. But that wouldn't bring back those six lives, or the others before and since. Kirk warned himself not to let their low level of technology make him cocky. The danger posed by terrorists was in their tactics, their decentralization, the ease with which they could scatter and hide and wait out their hunters.

The tour led them past several other attack sites, which Natira described with unwonted simplicity, letting the images speak for themselves. Kirk recognized one or two from the data files accompanying her original request for help. But more were new, having been hit in the two weeks it had taken the *Enterprise* to reach here. Kirk knew they'd arrived as soon as they possibly could have, but still the knowledge burned.

The farther they got from the center of the city, though, the fewer attack sites were in evidence. "Clearly the militants are targeting only the authority structure and symbols of the Federation, not the general population," Spock observed, still in that rigid, ultra-Vulcan tone.

"Not that they truly care," Natira said. "Some bystanders have been killed and wounded."

But in this part of the city, the people Kirk saw didn't seem afraid for their lives. Most of the adults he saw, in fact, were accompanied by one or more small children, who were running, laughing, and playing as their parents struggled to keep up—and most of the parents had a baby or two in their arms as well. It was a sight Kirk had seen on many young colonies, and a clear sign that the rigorous population controls of Yonada no longer applied on Lorina. Kirk recalled seeing few Yonadi who looked younger than forty, and the same was true of the adults he saw here. It must have been quite a change, suddenly being not only free to procreate at will, but encouraged to have as many children as possible. And with so many older Lorini, it must have been particularly hard to keep up with all the children. "The way these people are willing to let their children play in the open like this," Kirk said, "suggests that they don't consider the terrorists a threat to them."

"Indeed," Spock replied. "It indicates that the general public does not see the enemies of the state as being enemies to themselves."

"That could make this problem a lot more complicated to solve."

"I would prefer to believe," Natira told them, "that the people have faith in our ability to protect them from the fanatics. And that they are unwilling to let a few madmen drive them out of the light." She sighed. "Still . . . the number of people you see here, letting the sun touch their faces, is but a fraction of what I would wish for. As I have said, it is a struggle to bring the People into the light of day. Even without the Instruments of Obedience, many are still afraid to move beyond the limits the Oracle placed upon them. Most of the People remain below us, still dwelling beneath the ground and crawling through dim tunnels." She looked out at the parents chasing after their children in the park and smiled. "Mercifully, the young have not been weighed down by such fears. It is my hope that they may teach their elders."

Spock furrowed his brow. "Although such a preference for subterranean existence is no longer necessary in this environment," he said, "I fail to see the harm in allowing it to continue. There are certain advantages to underground dwellings, such as thermal regulation and protection from meteorological extremes or solar radiation. And this region is not prone to geologic upheaval."

"To see the problem, Commander Spock, you must look beyond the superficial," Commissioner Soreth told him in a stern, lecturing tone. "If the rank and file of Lorini are irrationally attached to the custom of dwelling underground, it is only logical to infer that they cling similarly to other atavisms. There is resistance to change on all levels, and as you have seen, it has reached the point of violent fanaticism. Indeed, that is the very reason you are here."

"Yes, it is, Commissioner," Kirk replied, disliking the way he addressed Spock like a slow pupil, but keeping his own tone quiet and civil. "Governess, of course I'm disturbed by what I've seen today, but we need to understand the causes behind these attacks if we're to be able to help. Am I right to understand that they're being launched by a group that still worships the Oracle?"

"Quite correct, Captain," said Natira.

"Even though they know now that the Oracle was simply a machine?"

"Even so. They have been shown the truth and yet they still deny it. They have even kept the priesthood alive, appointing a new high priestess after I cast aside that fraudulent role." She lowered her eyes. "It is an embarrassment. My administration has done all it could to bring the truth to the People. We have made the contents of the Book of the People available to all, and have aggressively spread literacy so that they may understand it. We have brought them

Federation schooling, given them terminals to access Federation informational networks. Commissioner Soreth has organized frequent seminars to promote knowledge of science, of technology, of Fabrini and galactic history. Yet these foul superstitions linger, as though the People are too blind to see what is before their eyes!"

"If I may, Governess," Lindstrom said, then turned to the newcomers. "The reality is more complicated than that. Yes, the people were shown that the Oracle is a computer—but you have to keep in mind, they didn't know what a computer was. As you saw on Yonada, its people had either regressed or been deliberately placed by the builders at a preindustrial level. To them, the technology of the Oracle was supernatural power. When you or I see the mechanisms behind the temple, we think 'Oh, the Oracle is just a computer.' And since computers are everyday things to us, that demystifies and diminishes it in our eyes. But what many of the Yonadi, the Lorini come away with is, 'Oh, a computer is a kind of Oracle.' And that means they see computers as something mystical and powerful, even something to be worshipped."

"Deus ex machina," Kirk observed.

"Literally, sir. The cult that's taken responsibility for the attacks, led by a man named Dovraku, is one that embraces this point of view to an extreme. They worship machine logic above all, advocate a rigid way of life in which people are ruled by a computer's calculations . . . a lot like Beta III was under Landru, in fact. We've had cultists come to the Federation consulate and pray to our mainframe."

"Indeed," added Soreth, "their propaganda condemns the Federation for what it sees as a policy to subjugate or destroy artificial intelligences on other worlds—a 'war against the gods,' as they describe it. They believe you came to Yonada with a specific agenda to destroy their Oracle. You, Captain Kirk, have a particular reputation as a 'godkiller.' "

"Who, me?" Kirk put on his best doe-eyed innocent face, though the humor was lost on the sour Vulcan.

"And in fact, the current uprising seems directly inspired by your recent encounter with the entity called V'Ger."

This time Kirk's surprise was dead serious. "Are you sure?"

"As sure as it is possible to be when dealing with the irrational motivations of religious fanatics. The propaganda states that V'Ger's . . . transformation represents a failure of your latest deicidal effort, and is thus an omen, a signal to the people to rise up and overthrow the secular order, at which point the Oracle will be magically resurrected."

Kirk sat back, dismayed. *Damn this reputation!* He'd thought the publicity and sensationalizing of his missions had only been a nuisance, an embarrassment. But now, apparently it had spread even to this remote world, thanks to those Federation network terminals, and it was getting people killed. He knew it was irrational to feel responsible—the blame lay with those who misrepresented his actions, and those who used them as an excuse to act out their own malicious urges—but he did nonetheless. "Governess . . . if there's anything I can do to resolve this situation, rest assured I will."

"Of that I have never had any doubt, Captain Kirk," Natira told him. "What I ask is that you provide your security forces to help protect the innocent from these fanatics, and to use the technologies at your disposal to help us root them out of their hiding places and ensure that they are brought to justice."

Kirk pondered her request. The Prime Directive forbade taking sides militarily in an internal conflict, true; but the aggressors here were not a rival state, merely a band of misguided fanatics. This would be more along the lines of a peacekeeping effort, apprehending a group of criminals.

But before he could answer Natira, Lindstrom spoke up.

"Captain, I advise against that. The actual terrorists are only a small minority, but they have a great deal of popular support. The Fabrini have been a religious people for a long time, and their faith is still important to most of them. If we send in the troops, it could be seen as an attack on their belief system, on their whole way of life. And that would just make things worse."

"I must interrupt," Soreth said. "Having heard this line of argument before, I can tell you that Commander Lindstrom is about to propose negotiation, although he is well aware that it is against Federation policy to negotiate with terrorists."

"I'm not saying we should negotiate with terrorists. I'm saying we should negotiate with the nonviolent majority that has the same grievances as the terrorists. Right now they're sympathetic to the extremists, keeping quiet about what they know, maybe even helping to hide them, because they think the extremists are the only ones that can do anything about their concerns. Most of them don't like Dovraku's tactics, but they don't see any other way of bringing about change. If we can show the masses that they have a legitimate avenue for addressing their grievances, then we can marginalize the terrorists, strip them of their support."

"What kind of 'grievances' could they have?" McCoy asked incredulously. "Do they really want to go back to living in constant dread that a hunk of tin is going to fry their brains for saying the wrong thing?"

"This isn't just about the Oracle, Doctor. There are a lot of factions with a lot of different issues driving them. Like I said, the terrorists represent one extremist cult. Most Lorini don't interpret things in quite the same way. And that includes the current high priestess, Rishala. She's the one who represents the beliefs of the majority, not the terrorists."

"He is about to propose that Rishala can be negotiated with," Soreth interrupted again. "And he is being illogical. Rishala has voiced her solidarity with the fanatics."

"She's expressed support for their goal of overthrowing Natira, but that doesn't mean she shares their *reasons* for wanting her gone, or their ideas about what to do afterward. And her faction hasn't engaged in any actual violence. If anything, she's been trying to keep things from getting too far out of hand. Maybe if we offer her an alternative to the militants, let her feel that we're willing to listen to her, to work with her, then she'll change her tune."

"Never," Natira said. "Rishala is an avowed enemy of the state. She denounces me daily in her sermons."

"But she's the most influential religious figure on this planet, Captain. And I believe she can be reasonable, if we're willing to give her a chance."

Soreth lifted a scathing eyebrow. "Rishala is a devout believer in a fiction invented by her ancestors as a means of social regulation and mass deception. I would hardly consider that reasonable."

"That may be how it started out, but it's been part of their lives for ten thousand years, and the People have given it their own meanings beyond what the ancient Fabrini may have intended."

"In either case, it is an invention, having no relation to reality."

"Well, whether you believe in its teachings or not, Soreth, it's a powerful and pervasive cultural force, a focus for a people's aspirations and values. And I don't automatically assume it's progress to give something like that up."

"Which is quite consistent with your pattern of allowing your youthful romanticism to interfere with your rational judgment."

"Well, maybe if you weren't so rigid—"

"Enough!" Natira snapped. "I have heard this argument

too many times from you both. And my mind is not swayed. I will not legitimize Rishala by negotiating with her."

"With respect, Governess," Kirk said, "it can't hurt to try."

"No. Rishala cannot be reasoned with. She is driven solely by ambition and hate. She condemns me for deeds she claims I committed as high priestess, yet she has seized that very title for herself, as a platform for her venom."

Kirk studied her. "Well, clearly there's no love lost between the two of you. But maybe if she were approached by a neutral party, she might be more receptive."

"No."

McCoy cleared his throat, and traded a meaningful look with Kirk: *Let me try something.* Kirk nodded fractionally. "Uhm . . . Natira . . . I think it's worth the effort." She stared at him, but remained quiet, listening. "I know it's taking a chance . . . but . . ." He steeled himself and moved closer to her. "The Natira I remember didn't hesitate to take a chance on people. Even a big, life-changing chance with someone she barely knew. Even knowing it would bring pain, and loss . . . she still seized that chance, accepted the risk, because she was open to the good it could bring. And when that Natira found out that the things she'd believed in weren't really true, she resisted for a bit, but she found the courage to open her mind to new possibilities. And that's . . . that's something I always admired about her."

Kirk winced in sympathy for his friend. Bones was so guilty already, feeling he'd used Natira before, and now here he was deliberately playing on her affections. It would only make it harder to come clean with her when the time came.

But in the bigger picture, McCoy was doing the right thing, using whatever means possible to work toward peace, toward saving lives. The surgeon hated seeing others in pain, but understood that sometimes he had to do a small harm to heal a greater one. Not that such rationalizations would help him sleep better. They never did for Kirk, anyway.

In any case, McCoy's entreaties proved effective. Natira softened, pondered for a moment, and said, "Very well, McCoy. As always you speak wisely. I must not close my mind to new possibilities, or I shall be no better than those who have placed the People in danger."

"Thank you, Natira," McCoy said.

"Yes, thank you, Governess." Kirk turned to the sociologist. "Mr. Lindstrom, you seem to have considerable familiarity with the Lorini religious community. Do you suppose you could arrange a meeting between Rishala and myself?"

"I'll see what I can do, sir. I'm not that much of an expert—they still see me as an outsider—but I have some contacts I can try."

"Then it is settled," Natira said in a commanding tone, as though it had been her idea all along. "Let us return. I have guest rooms prepared for you all."

"That's very kind of you, but it's not necessary," Kirk said. "We can just beam back up to our ship."

"As you wish. But . . . McCoy, I would be grateful if you could remain for a time. I am curious to know how your studies of our medicine have proceeded in your time away."

Bones threw Kirk a look, but Kirk's gaze told him, *You got what you asked of her, now you owe her something in return.* At least that was what he tried to convey; after three years apart, he wasn't sure if they could still read each other as effortlessly as before. But the doctor squared his shoulders and told Natira, "Yes, I think I can manage that."

Soreth of Vulcan would have been quick to point out, if the subject arose, that nostalgia was an illogical emotion. Yet after eighteen decades of life, it was sometimes natural enough to reflect on the changes which had occurred during that time, and to acknowledge that some of those changes had not been for the better.

As he entered the Federation consulate—a quieter place now that its nonessential personnel had been beamed to the *Enterprise* for their protection—Soreth reflected that when he had been young, there had been an orderly system to the known universe. The Vulcans had maintained that order, bringing their guidance to less mature civilizations, keeping threats to those civilizations in check, and diligently sheltering those too primitive to handle knowledge of the greater universe. It had been a stable, rational way of doing things. But then the humans had unraveled all that. In their childish enthusiasm, they had barged out into the universe, disrupted the whole astropolitical landscape, and gotten embroiled in several wars. True, in the wake of those actions they'd played a central role in creating the Federation, which had turned out very well indeed—but only, Soreth was certain, because of the Vulcans' choice to participate in the alliance and continue the peacekeeping and civilization-building activities they'd been engaged in all along.

Yet somehow Starfleet had come to take over the lion's share of those responsibilities, and Starfleet was so . . . *human.* Most Vulcans today had come to accept that. Keeping the peace sometimes required actions inconsistent with Surak's pacifistic ideals, and if the humans were so insistent on doing the work, it spared the Vulcans from having to get their hands dirty. But Soreth believed that, whatever the moral compromises, the task should be undertaken by those most qualified to handle it. By handing the task off to humanity, Vulcans had chosen their own moral comfort over their responsibility to others, and that, Soreth was convinced, had been selfish and shortsighted. Humans meant well, but they were simply too immature.

He was thus disappointed that Natira had called in the *Enterprise.* He felt that he and the governess had established a good working relationship based on mutual trust. She had always been quite receptive to his advice, and had thoroughly renounced the superstitious follies of her past. She and Soreth had been working out a reasoned strategy for dealing with the unrest, an aggressive education campaign directed against the atavistic ideas that led the Lorini astray. And her security forces had been an adequate adjunct to that strategy, he was sure. But Natira was still an emotional being, and these attacks had frightened her into calling in Starfleet unnecessarily.

After touring the sites of the recent incidents, Soreth had to admit it was not unreasonable to seek a stronger military presence. He just wasn't sure about the choice of starships. James Kirk was as human as humans got, a known disruptive element, infamous for his reckless, impulsive tactics. And Spock . . . well, on the tour he had seemed perfectly controlled. But Soreth knew he had failed *Kolinahr.* Of course, *Kolinahr* was an advanced discipline that few Vulcans actually undertook, and fewer still succeeded in. But Spock's failure had had an inevitable quality to it. Though any initiate's reasons for pursuing the discipline were private, it was widely accepted that Spock had undertaken it in an attempt to purge his human half. His failure to do so was symbolic: what was innate could never be truly purged. Then again, Soreth thought, Spock had been at a double disadvantage. Not only was half of him human, but the other half was a melder.

One of the changes which had come about over Soreth's lifetime had been the mainstreaming of that minority of Vulcans with the innate ability to mind-meld, and a renewed openness about the telepathic procedures that Soreth had been raised to consider uncouth and perverted. Even non-melders had the capacity for a more limited mind-touch, but to Soreth's generation, such things were intended only to establish the mating bond, and otherwise were not used or spoken of. Vulcans were supposed to relate only on a rational plane, and mental communication, let alone the actual blending of minds, operated on a distastefully visceral level. It was an unsafe practice in the best of circumstances; melders risked compromising their identity, their privacy and their mental balance even if their partners had no deficit of skill or ethics. They could not help how they were born, but the responsible thing was to recognize the ability as a maladaptive aberration and avoid exercising it. Just because it was "natural" didn't mean it should be embraced, any more than the "natural" emotions of hatred or rage should be.

But in this as well, modern Vulcans had lost sight of their responsibilities. And Soreth believed it was again due to human influence. Their emotional openness had confounded the Vulcan sense of propriety, brought private and impolite things out into the open, and encouraged a breakdown of public morals. Now Vulcan's own ambassador to the Federation was a melder—and he had married a human woman and borne a son with her. (True, Vulcan's first ambassador to Earth had been Sarek's grandfather, and may thus have been a melder as well, but at least he'd had the decency to keep quiet about it.)

Indeed, it seemed the melders tended to be persistently involved with humans, as though they were kindred spirits. Those few Vulcans who had served on human ships always seemed to be melders, and had a pattern of letting themselves become far too influenced by human ways—going back to T'Pol, the first Vulcan to crew with humans. When Soreth had been briefly acquainted with her in his youth, she had been an admirable and proper Vulcan from whom the High Command expected great things. But her interaction with humans had led her to experiment with emotion, in ways that had changed her permanently and infamously. At least Spock had recognized the problem and made an effort to correct it, but that effort had failed, and now he was back among that human crew yet again. Soreth suspected the pattern would repeat itself; indeed, he'd heard rumors suggesting that it already had, and more. Not that Vulcans engaged in gossip, of course.

On reaching his office, Soreth found a message awaiting him—from the *Enterprise,* of all places. It was from Spanla, a Vulcan nurse on the crew. Soreth raised an eyebrow, but dismissed the synchronicity as a meaningless coincidence and opened the message. The young Vulcan's thin face appeared on the screen. "Peace and long life, Commissioner Soreth," he began. "It is my judgment that there is something about Commander Spock of which you should be informed."

Soreth leaned forward, fascinated.

The first time Leonard McCoy had been alone with Natira, he'd believed he was dying. This time, he only wished he were dead. Anything to spare him from having to face her now. He'd gotten himself into this, but he had no idea what he would say, how he'd respond to . . . whatever she said or did.

Natira's residential suite, like her office, was spacious and open, with abundant windows through which an unfairly romantic sunset was visible. The decorations were eclectic, with little of evident Fabrini origin, except for a pedestal in familiar black marble, on which rested a copy of the Book of the People. McCoy was disquieted to see holos of himself, taken during his research visit here, adorning one wall near her bed. "You, um . . . you have a lovely place," he said. "Quite a view."

Natira smiled fondly and moved toward him. "Ohh, McCoy. *Leonard.* You need not stand at such remove, we are alone! I have waited far too long for this. Come, sit."

She took his hands, and he let her lead him over to the

couch. He sat down gingerly, and Natira leaned against him, resting her head on his shoulder. She let out a long sigh, and simply stayed there, silent, for a long moment. "Ohh, this is such a relief," she finally said. "Just the two of us . . . no duties, no crises, no ministers and functionaries clamoring for attention. For this little while, I can be at peace, like a little girl resting in her father's arms." McCoy was relaxing now, thinking this wasn't so bad. Simple, chaste, platonic—he could do that. Except her hair smelled really good. . . .

"These have been such burdensome times. So many turn against me when I only seek to help them. . . . It pains me, dear Leonard, and makes me sad. For them, and for myself."

She looked up at him. "I must apologize, Leonard. When you were here before, I made too little time for you, feeling that the burdens of government did not allow such a luxury as companionship. But now I see they demand it, for no one can bear such weights alone."

Now she rose to face him more directly, and clasped his hands. "Besides, now I know something of what you felt when first we met. I too have had a brush with my mortality. And so I understand the urgency of seizing the opportunities we have. And more . . . I wish to ensure that I can leave a legacy, pass on a part of myself to ensure the vitality of Lorina, as I have encouraged the rest of the People to do."

Oh, God. "Natira . . . what are you saying?"

She beamed. "That I am ready now. Ready to resume what once we started, and let nothing else stand between us." She reached up and touched his right temple. "When Spock removed the Instrument from you, I believed it meant our marriage was over. Now I know that I was wrong—that the Instrument was a tool of tyranny, not a bond of love. Its loss meant nothing to what we shared. As far as I am concerned, Leonard McCoy, you are still my husband. And I wish you to be my children's sire as well."

She moved forward to kiss him . . . but he rose convulsively and began to pace. "Leonard, what is wrong?"

"Natira, I . . . Don't misunderstand, I'm very flattered, but . . ." But what? How could he just come out and tell her, at this of all moments, that his feelings for her had not been genuine? That, although he thought kindly of her and wished her only happiness, he only wanted to return to his ship and his life?

Except . . . *was* that his life? Back in Starfleet again, against his better judgment? Struggling to catch up with a sickbay and a crew that Chapel knew better anyway? It wasn't as though he'd been exactly happy on the *Enterprise*. But what was the alternative? To go back to his lonely little cabin in the mountains? If he wanted that kind of a life, couldn't he have it here, and have someone to keep him company to boot?

Aw, who'm I kidding? The way he'd mishandled her affections before, how could he trust himself to do right by her now? Sooner or later, he always bungled his relationships, always ended up hurting them—Nancy, Jocelyn, Tonia. And Natira, though she didn't know it yet. He could play along, let her keep her illusions, and wangle for himself what might be a life worth having. But it couldn't work based on false pretenses. And children, again? He'd let Joanna down enough times. Sure, it could be a chance to start anew, avoid the old mistakes—but more likely it would just be a chance to make whole new ones.

Natira stood, and faced him sternly. "Leonard, have you nothing to say? Surely you owe me some reply."

"I honestly don't know what to say, Natira. I do think you're a remarkable woman. And you were there for me at a time when I needed comfort. . . . I'll always be grateful to you for that. But . . ." *It's not the crime, it's the cover-up. Just get it over with.* "But that's why I owe it to you to be honest. Natira, when we met . . . I wasn't myself. I'd just received a terrible shock, I wasn't thinking clearly. When you offered me a . . . a purpose for the life I had left, I jumped at it, because I had nothing left to lose. But it was the act of a desperate man, Natira . . . not a man in love."

"I see." Her gaze had grown cold. "I understand now. Why you left. Not only the first time, but the second. I was never anything real to you—you simply used me as a . . . a distraction and then tossed me aside, like a cheap harlot. And now you use me again, to get your captain his meeting with Rishala, only to toss me aside again!"

"No, that's not what I'm saying. I just . . . I wanted to be honest with you, before we . . . before we can figure out what to do next."

"It is quite clear to me what to do next. Go, McCoy! Return to your ship and do not come back."

"But I—" He broke off, knowing there was nothing more he could say. He could see how hurt she was beneath her anger. She'd made herself vulnerable to him, and he'd chosen that moment to deliver his blow. She had every right to feel betrayed, and right now he had no right to stand in her presence. So he lowered his head and raised his wrist communicator. "McCoy to *Enterprise*. One to beam up, these coordinates." He'd never welcomed the sensation of beaming quite so much.

CHAPTER SEVEN

*I have not served God from fear of hell for I
should be a wretched hireling if I served Him
from fear; nor from love of heaven for I should be
a bad servant if I served for what is given; I have
served Him only for love of Him and desire for
Him.*   —al-Hasan al-Basri (642–728)

FOR THE FIRST TIME since setting foot on Lorina, Kirk was
experiencing déjà vu. The entrance to the underground quarter of the city was a cluster of two-meter metal cylinders,
just like the one on Yonada. But they seemed incongruous
here in the middle of a lush parkland.

Kirk stepped forward and depressed the footplate that
triggered the outer cylinder to rise, revealing the entrance to
the spiral stairway leading below. Chekov moved forward,
frowning. "I don't like this, sir," he said. "Too narrow.
Perfect for an ambush."

"I've survived one ambush from these things, Mr.
Chekov."

"With respect, Captain, that was just a warning. These
terrorists want to kill you."

"And the longer we keep standing around here, the better targets we make."

With a glower, Chekov preceded the captain into the stairwell and gestured to Nizhoni to take up the rear. Kirk glanced back at the young Navajo woman. "I hope you're not claustrophobic," he said.

"Oh, no sir," she replied with a brief, pretty smile, not letting herself get distracted from her vigilance. "I love caving. My big sister and I are always crawling through holes in the ground."

"Hm. When you've been trapped in as many caves as I have, Ensign, they tend to lose their appeal."

"You get trapped in caves a lot, sir? Then I guess it's a good thing I'm around now." He threw her a glare over his shoulder, and she replied with an insouciant shrug.

The stairwell soon opened up into an antechamber with four corridors leading off from it. The architecture was a match for that on Yonada—wide corridors with flat concrete walls and bare rock overhead, with arch-topped supports at regular intervals. The walls were mostly bare, with only occasional geometric patterns carved into them. There were no directional signs; among the mostly illiterate Yonadi, the only writing had been associated with the temple and religious art. Recalling Lindstrom's directions, Kirk led the party down the north corridor. Chekov insisted on staying ahead of him again.

Down here, the people tended to be attired as they had been on Yonada, in brightly patterned robes. Most of them quailed at the sight of Chekov's phaser and pressed against the walls as the party moved past. "Easy, Mr. Chekov. We're not here to frighten these people."

Nizhoni stared at their garish outfits. "God, if those clothes don't frighten them, nothing will."

"This," Chekov replied, "from a woman who insists on wearing nonregulation beads and feathers."

"Oh, you're one to complain about taking pride in one's heritage," she shot back with a grin, tacking on "sir" as an afterthought.

"Well, if some crazed killer grabs you by the necklace—"

"It's under my armor!"

Mercifully, they soon arrived at the entrance to the temple, framed by the familiar triangular panels of Fabrini script. But Chekov wasn't quite finished. "You still insist on going in alone, don't you, Captain?"

"Pavel, if we want to earn their trust, we have to be willing to show a little of our own."

"I am willing to show a little, sir. I just prefer it to be as little as possible."

Kirk gave Chekov a look, then raised his wrist communicator. "Kirk to Chief Rand. Is the transporter lock holding?"

"Yes, sir, I've got you loud and clear. Do you need beamout?"

"No, Chief, just checking. Kirk out." He smiled. "Trust in Allah, Mr. Chekov, but tie up your camel. Satisfied?"

"Aye, sir," the lieutenant said, though he didn't look it. "We'll be right outside if you need us."

"That makes me feel very secure." Kirk clapped him lightly on the shoulder, then strode up to the doors and pushed them open.

The temple interior resembled the one from Yonada, but it was larger, and somehow more inviting. The floor was covered in long, cushioned platforms lined up like pews, presumably for kneeling. Triangular text panels and geometric patterns adorned the walls, with the Oracle's starburst and the graphic of Fabrina's planetary system holding pride of place. Yet there were other, less familiar decorations: icons and paintings of humanoid figures. Kirk moved to study a few of them more closely. He couldn't interpret the accompanying text, but they appeared idealized, larger than life, powerful yet comforting, like images of saints. He hadn't realized the Yonadan religion had included such figures. He'd only heard about the Oracle and the Creators, the latter mentioned only as an inchoate collective, not personified in any way.

Though the main temple was unoccupied save for Kirk, he heard voices coming from a room off to the side. The main voice was a woman's, warm and energetic. The others sounded like children of various ages. Once Kirk reached the half-open doorway, his eyes confirmed what his ears had told him. It seemed to be a class of sorts, though not a large one. The students were mostly adolescents and young adults, and there were not too many of those on Lorina yet.

The woman teaching the class was not striking to look at—middle-aged, black-haired with slight tinges of gray, plain-featured and stocky, dressed in simple beige homespun robes. But the students, seated on high hexagonal cushions, watched her raptly as she spoke. ". . . And Vari saw that the World would be consumed by Nidra's fire, and he wept. Yes, children! Vari himself, he who has the strength to lift the World in just one hand, wept. For he knew that it could not be stopped, that the fire of deception came through all material things, and so the World was doomed by its own essence."

Many of the children were caught up in the tale. "Oh, no!" "Could it be?" "What did Vari do?"

"But then came Baima, our wise mother Baima, and she placed her hands on Vari's eyes and made him see beyond the surface, beyond the lies, to where the pure souls of the People shone. And Vari saw our souls, children, brighter than the fire, oh yes! And he knew that the People could be saved, and the World reborn."

"Yes!" "Vari will save us!"

"And so Vari the Mighty brought all the Creators together. Picture it, children! Here sits Baima the Wise, mother to us all, smiling down on us with her patient love. Here's Miura the Farmer who feeds our souls and bodies. . . ." She continued with a substantial roster of names, not merely setting the scene but paying tribute to each Creator's gifts. It had a ritual quality, but there was a sense of improvisation at the same time, and the children were free to chime in with their own expressions of praise. "And now Vari stands before his brothers and sisters, equal yet greater than them all, the Power that moves every one of us. And he tells them, 'Brothers and sisters, we must not fight the fire, for that is not the Way. To fight Nidra's deceptions is to fall under yet another deception, and let ourselves be lost. We must allow the World to burn!"

"No!" "Can he mean it?" "Vari, no!"

" 'Yes!' Vari cries. 'We must let the World burn, even as we make a new World! The sins and lies under which the People struggle will be burned away with their flesh, and they will be reborn within our new World, saved and made pure.' " The children gave cries of relief and joy—most of them, anyway. Several of them watched the rest with an air of skepticism or disdain. Evidently the priestess wasn't preaching only to the converted.

"But now hear Dedi the Questioner, littlest brother with the sharpest eye. 'Can they remain pure?' Dedi asks. 'So long as they live in a World, so long as they have flesh, then Nidra will have her grip on them.'

" 'And so it must be,' says our mother Baima. 'For she is our sister, and though she walks alone, yet she is forever with us.' Yes, children, heed her words! 'And so she will have her will,' says the wise mother, 'even as we have ours. The People have been lost, but they will be saved.' "

"Yea!"

" 'Yea, they will be lost again, but they will be saved again.' "

"Yea!"

" 'Yea, the People will be reborn into the new World we create for them. And when that World reaches its end, we will have another waiting.' "

"So says the Promise!"

"But see there, as Dedi rises again. 'Must the cycle go on without end?' asks the Innocent One. 'Are the People doomed to be lost again after each salvation?' "

"No, Dedi!" "That's not the way!" "Tell him, Baima!"

"Yea, now Baima turns her gaze upon him, upon us all, and now she tells us, 'No, the People are not doomed! For I see a time when the souls of the People will find their way free of the flesh.' "

"Yea!"

" 'When they will no longer be blinded by desires and cravings and ambitions . . .' "

"Yea!"

" ' . . . and they will know the Truth as we, their Creators, know it now. Do not forget that we were they once. And so, in time, they must become us, and be saved forevermore.' "

"Saved!"

" 'Yet until they are ready, my Children, we must shelter them with our love, and give them a World wherein they may face Nidra's tests and gain wisdom from them.'

"Now the Creators all agree, and they remove their protection from the burning World. Now hear—the People cry, 'O great ones, why have you abandoned us?' "

"Tell them, sister!"

"But those who have faith in the Creators know they will be saved—so long as they surrender to the Creators' love and crave nothing else, not food nor drink nor sex nor wealth nor life itself!"

"Yea!" "Saved!"

"Now Tilu the Source brings forth earth and ice from the heavens. Now Vari the Mighty takes them to his forge and crafts them with his great, gentle hands. And even bright

Nidra comes down from her scorching sky and gives of her fire to fuel the forge. Yes, children! For though the Creators ever strive against her lies, against her beauty that distracts and blinds the unwary soul, still she is their sister and their love, and she knows that this new World will be hers as well as theirs.

"But fear not! For now Miura the Farmer sheds his tears and sweat on the earth and brings forth life."

"Let the life grow!"

"But Baima the Wise bids him caution—she tells him to leave the surface of the World barren, as a reminder to the People that all surfaces are barren of truth."

"We hear you, Baima!"

"Yea, we hear, children, and we see—as the old World burns and dies, a new World is born! Yea, and now the faithful are reborn within it, born through the vehicle of the Creators' love!"

"I feel their love!" "Mother Baima, Father Vari!" "I see the World being born!"

"And now you see, children! You see why the Creators' love pervades every aspect of our lives, why it defines our very existence! You see why it will always save us, if we have the faith and the devotion to value it above all things!"

"Yea, sister!" "I see it!" "I feel it!"

"All praise to the Creators!"

"Praise them!"

"All praise to the Creators!"

"Praise them!"

A wave of devotional fervor surged through the room. Even those students who'd been watching skeptically, who hadn't joined in before, got caught up in the chanting. Kirk almost expected a gospel song to break out. But after a few more hosannas, the dark-haired woman lowered herself silently onto her cushion and closed her eyes. Gradually, the students' ardor subsided and they joined her in silent contemplation. It seemed an odd anticlimax, but it gave Kirk a chance to evaluate what he'd just experienced. He'd felt almost as caught up in the energy of the tale as the students. Rishala (for that was who the woman presumably was) had spoken with great vitality and passion—but not the blind passion of the fanatic, nor the fierce passion of the holy warrior. The tale had contained some apocalyptic elements, but she had downplayed them in favor of joy and hope.

Now one of the students, a girl in mid-adolescence, spoke a bit breathlessly. "Priestess . . ."

"Please, just Rishala," the older woman smiled, confirming Kirk's suspicions.

"Ahh, Rishala," the girl started over, "where is that written in the Book of the People? I don't remember seeing it."

"The Creators speak to us in many ways, Tanila. Until recently, only a very few could read a book. But the Creators wanted all the People to know their wisdom. This story, like many others, has been passed down from mouth to ear since the second World was born."

"But if it's not in the Book, it can't be true, can it? That's what Sonaya preaches."

"Well, does it feel true?"

The girl seemed unsure how to answer. A younger boy spoke up in her place. "In the schools they teach us that the Creators were just our ancestors. That they made Yonada from an asteroid, using ships and machines and rays. That the People moved there in ships, instead of dying and being reborn."

Rishala mulled over his words. As she did so, she briefly made eye contact with Kirk, registering his presence but not acknowledging it yet. "And, Nikuri, is that the truth of the story?" she said with added meaning. "If you tell it that way, does it stop meaning that the Creators saved us through the power of their love? Is the story about the how, or the why?"

An older boy stared at her, looking scandalized. "But those are Fedraysha lies! You should punish Nikuri for even listening to such blasphemy!"

"Quiet down, Tavero. We can't decide what's true or untrue unless we listen first," Rishala said, still looking toward Kirk. "So it's when we *don't* listen that we're led astray." She studied the youth. "And tell me, Tavero, what do you think of *my* version of the tale?"

The youth glared at her, but seemed cowed by her presence, holding back what he really wanted to say. "It was not the full truth."

"Why not?"

"You made no mention of the Oracle."

Rishala shrugged. "The Oracle was the tool of the Creators, how they watched over their creation. I was telling a story about the Creators themselves, how they made the World and the Promise."

"The Oracle was the hand, the voice, the living embodiment of the Creators!" the boy insisted. "We must never forget Him! When He was taken from us, so were they!"

Rishala took his hand. "We're all the children of the Creators, Tavero. *This* is their hand. And you speak with their voice, like we all do."

He pulled his hand away. "No. Left to themselves, the People speak in too many voices. Only the Oracle is the voice of Truth. Else why would we need the Instruments of Obedience to keep us on the path?"

"Do you hold the Creators' love in your heart? Do you have faith in their wisdom and guidance?"

"Of course!" Tavero exclaimed.

"Then what other Instrument of Obedience do you need?"

"And what of those whose faith is not as strong as mine? Who will keep them from leading others astray, as the schools have led Nikuri? Who . . ." The adolescent had turned to point at the younger boy, and this brought the entrance into his peripheral vision. At the sight of Kirk, he whirled and shot to his feet, knocking over his cushion. For a moment he was frozen in terror, as though he were gazing upon the devil himself (and in his theological terms, Kirk realized, that may have been exactly true). But then the terror transmuted into rage. "*You! Killer of the Oracle! How dare you show your face in a holy place!*" Even as he spoke, he lunged at Kirk.

But it was a graceless attack, and Kirk was able to block it and drop Tavero to the ground efficiently and with minimal force. He looked down at the boy amiably and extended a hand. "Where I come from, fighting in a holy place is frowned upon . . . and usually everyone is welcome in them."

"It's the same way here," Rishala said, her eyes on Tavero.

The youth scrambled to his feet, glaring at Kirk's hand as though it were an obscenity, and then transferred that glare to the priestess. "Dovraku is right about you! You are soft on blasphemers, disloyal to the Oracle! You are a beggar, playacting in a role you have no true understanding of! You had better repent soon," he added, a Parthian shot as he retreated from the room, "all of you, or you will be swept away in the fires of His rebirth!"

Several of the other students chose to follow him out of the room, giving Kirk a wide berth. Rishala sighed. "I suppose that ends our session for today. May you all go with the Creators."

As the students filed out, some hastening to leave, others lingering to gawk at Kirk, he made his way over to Rishala and met her gaze sheepishly. "I apologize for disrupting your class," he said. "I was actually quite enjoying it."

"So you're not here to steal my soul?" she asked with humor, though there was challenge in her eyes.

Kirk studied her for a moment. "It seems to be doing more good where it is."

She raised her brows. "That's not the answer I would've expected."

"And you're not what I was led to expect, Priestess."

"Rishala," she corrected, though her eyes showed appreciation that he hadn't presumed to drop the title without her leave. "Let me guess. You were told I was a rabble-rouser, a hateful fanatic preaching the overthrow of the state."

"Basically."

"Well . . . I try not to be hateful."

Kirk chuckled. "From what I saw just now, you succeed."

"I try. That's all." She looked him over. "So what was it you enjoyed so much about my tale?"

"The skill of the teller," he told her, locking eyes with hers. "Her sincerity and passion."

She appeared unimpressed. "And what about the tale itself?"

Kirk answered slowly. "It was . . . an interpretation of your beliefs which I haven't heard before. Quite an education. I have to wonder if you chose the topic knowing that I'd be here today."

"I like to hope that all my sermons are educational."

"And are they always so different from the orthodox line?"

Rishala smirked. "Orthodoxy. What is it? I'm high priestess now," she said, sounding singularly unimpressed with the title, "so does that make my view of things the orthodoxy? Maybe." She moved among the cushions, straightening them out. Perhaps she meant to make a point by performing the menial task herself, but it didn't seem so affected. "But then, if Tavero becomes the next high priest, or Tanila with her reverence for the Book, or Nikuri with his Fedraysha lessons, won't that make their views the orthodoxy? And if so, then what does the word really mean, when everyone will just go on believing as they already do?"

Kirk crouched down and began adjusting a few cushions himself, getting another look of surprised approval from her. "For a long time, orthodoxy meant what the Oracle said it did. On pain of death."

"Yes," was all she said.

"So I have to wonder how a . . . an alternative tradition could've thrived for ten thousand years."

"Alternative?" She shook her head. "For ten thousand years, we've all accepted what the Oracle taught: that the Creators made the World, and promised us that we would one day attain a new one. That the laws of Yonada were laid down by the Creators and must be obeyed. We have questioned none of the Oracle's doctrines. We simply . . . haven't dwelt on them much. While the Oracle and its priesthood concentrated on the laws of Yonada and the daily lives of the People, many of the rest of us have concentrated on the love of the Creators and the ultimate fate of our souls. There's no conflict there."

Kirk nodded, understanding. "Simply . . . a difference in emphasis."

"Exactly."

"Still—I wouldn't have expected the Oracle to be so . . . accommodating."

Pain showed in Rishala's eyes. "Sometimes it wasn't. Or sometimes it was, but the priestesses were not. Their enthusiasm about enforcing their . . . *emphasis* often went beyond what the Oracle required. Natira was like that."

She caught his gaze meaningfully. "Why do you suppose she needed armed guards, when we all had Instruments of Obedience? The priestesses and their cronies often exercised their will where the Oracle saw no need to intervene. But the guards acted in the Oracle's name, so it gave them great license in their methods of enforcement. And the rest of us could say nothing against it." Her voice remained level, but Kirk could sense the underlying anger. That wasn't a bad thing, though—it meant they were getting to the meat of the issue.

"But Natira's changed," Kirk said. "She no longer follows the Oracle."

"Has she changed? I said before, the Oracle was just a tool. A tool of the Creators' will . . . and sometimes, a tool of the priestesses' will. The Oracle may no longer speak, the Instruments may be gone, but the guards still bear arms, and Natira still gives them their orders."

Kirk frowned. "And . . . what does she order them to do?"

"The Fedraysha's bidding, of course," she answered, skeptical that he really needed to ask.

"The Federation . . . doesn't operate that way. Your people are free to make their own choices, without our interference. It's our highest law."

Rishala strode from the classroom, and Kirk followed. "Laws. Like all material things, they're illusions. The powerful use them to serve their ambitions. You let us make our own choices . . . so long as they're the choices you think are right."

Kirk thought before answering. "You seemed to be saying to the boy—Nikuri—that it was all right for him to believe the things being taught in the Federation-backed schools."

She looked disappointed in him. "What I said was that the forms of things don't matter, that the truth lies on a higher plane. Your Fedraysha schools teach that the forms are all there is. All they teach are more laws. Laws of nations, laws of nature, laws of mind—everything codified and ordered and locked in place, as if putting names to things and sorting them in charts meant that you understood them. Laws of what to say, what to build, what to wear."

Kirk strode in front of her, stopping her. "Wait. Are you saying Natira's government . . . regulates your speech? Your forms of expression?"

"Not according to what's written. The laws say we have those freedoms. But there are other laws that warn against sedition and threats to the common peace . . . and it's where those laws meet that the illusion becomes clear. Excuse me." She moved around him, resuming her course. It brought her to the nearest of the saintlike icons, a golden-armored figure working at a forge. Rishala bowed her head and murmured a soft prayer to the image Kirk realized must be Vari the Mighty.

When she was done, Kirk spoke again. "Even if what you say is true . . . you can't believe that blowing up buildings and killing innocent people is the right way to deal with it. You don't strike me as the type who approves of bloodshed."

She glanced at him as she made her way to the next Creator icon, a burly shirtless male bearing a golden scepter that on second glance appeared more like a hoe, and surrounded by grains and fruits at his feet. "And you? Do you approve of bloodshed?"

". . . Not if it can be helped."

"Ahh." She made another murmured prayer, then continued her rounds. "Yet you've inflicted it. And you'll do so again if you feel it can't be helped. You have outside a man and a woman carrying weapons that can inflict far more bloodshed than anything on Lorina."

Kirk was surprised; she was well-informed. "We are trained to use force . . . but only in defense, and only when all other options have been exhausted. And we don't use it indiscriminately against innocent people."

Rishala recited another brief prayer, then gestured to the icon, a plump, matronly nude with snow-white hair cascading around her body. "Baima the Wise," she said. "I love all the Creators, but I think I feel closest to her. Not that I'm anything like wise, mind you—I think she holds me close because I need a wise guiding hand more than most. And right now I think she wants me to ask you whether that's true—have you really never struck down an innocent? Not even once? Are your weapons so precise that they only destroy the guilty?"

Kirk imagined the icon's eyes glaring down on him in judgment. "I'd be lying if I said I hadn't. But there is a difference. I didn't target them specifically."

"I'm sure they appreciated the distinction."

"And I fought openly," he went on, raising his voice. "Gave my enemies a chance, and a fair warning. I didn't strike from hiding like a coward."

Rishala was unimpressed. "Of course not. You had your mighty ship to protect you. But what if you had nothing? What if you were against a mighty foe, and had only the crudest of means to strike with? What if you had no way to deliver your weapons, except for the sacrifice of a dedicated defender who could carry them on her own person? Would you just abandon the fight? Would you sacrifice everything you believed in to salvage your warrior's pride?"

Again Kirk realized his arguments were hollow. He was a trained soldier, and he understood that in war you used whatever means necessary to stay alive and win the fight. He'd engaged in tactics that could be called terrorist— destroying the munitions dump on Organia, blasting the Eminians' computers and disintegration booths. And he'd do it again if he were forced to. But that was the key. "If I had no other choice, no. I'd do what needed to be done. But I wouldn't go out of my way to encourage such tactics. I wouldn't start the war, like your Dovraku has.

"And what about those 'dedicated defenders'?" Kirk went on. "Don't tell me—young men and women, right?

Passionate, enthusiastic, concerned about the future. A lot like those kids back there in the classroom. They're the ones with the most at stake, with the strongest commitment, so they're the best ones to turn to if you want someone willing to give everything for the cause." Rishala nodded, watching him curiously. "But doesn't that also make them the ones most qualified, most motivated to build a better future? And what does it do to your future if you throw them all away on suicide bombings?"

"Why do you think I have them here?" Rishala cried, her serenity giving way to a deep pain. "Do you think I haven't made those same arguments to Dovraku? Haven't tried to sway his followers to a better path? Do you think I want to see my People torn apart? But Natira gives me no alternative! She's determined to purge Lorina of our faith, to turn the People away from the Creators. At least before we only differed in 'emphasis,' and could usually coexist. But now she's changed her mind," she went on mockingly, "and won't rest until she's changed all of ours to match.

"Yet the faithful are drifting apart, unable to agree on whether it's the Creators or the Oracle or the Book or the blinking husk of Fabrina that defines who we are. I wonder if you've heard about that. When the 'fanatical cultists' attack the workings of the state, it's widely reported and denounced—but you never see the information networks reporting on the fights that break out between the sects, fiercer every day as the People lose more hope, grow more desperate for answers. We cannot unite enough to stand against Natira and hold her back in any way *except* force."

Kirk saw the dilemma in her eyes. She clearly hated what the militants were doing, but felt compelled to stand with them, for losing the unity of the faithful would be the greater of evils. He took a moment to choose his words. "In a case like this, it often helps to bring in a neutral party to mediate. I'd be happy to—"

Rishala laughed. "Neutral? Have you forgotten your own name, James T. Kirk? Have you forgotten who silenced the Oracle and brought the Fedraysha to us?"

"Everything that I did," Kirk answered, trying not to sound too defensive, "was done to help your people, and the people of Daran V. Yonada had to be put back on course, or *billions* would have died. To do that, we had to convince Natira that it was really a spacecraft. We had to override the Oracle and take manual control. All we did was show your people the truth—a truth you would've had to learn anyway a year later, when Yonada reached here and it was time for you to leave it. What you've done with that truth, the decision to leave the Oracle shut down . . . that was the choice of your own leaders."

"And since you only kicked the first pebble, that absolves you from any further interest in the avalanche?" She moved closer. "You say your highest law is not to interfere. To leave others alone."

"As much as possible, yes."

"But when you do interfere in someone's life, is it right to leave them alone afterward? Do you have no obligation to take responsibility for what you've started?"

Her eyes held his, and he was transfixed once more. Finally she broke their gaze and stepped away. She prayed under one more icon, then spoke again. "You are far from neutral here, James Kirk. But that's exactly why you *must* be involved in seeking solutions. If you can bring Natira to the table, I will come too, and I'll *try* to bring the other factions as well. But only if you understand the nature of your own place there—not as someone outside the problem, but someone right there at the heart of it with the rest of us."

CHAPTER EIGHT

*The difference of opinion in my community is a
divine mercy.*

—The Prophet Muhammad (Peace be unto him)

"LEONARD, WAKE UP!"

On the fourth or fifth iteration, McCoy finally mustered
up the energy to speak. "Computer, don't call me
'Leonard.'"

"Do I sound like the computer to you?" The lights went
up to their full, blinding magnitude, and McCoy squinted
through the tears until he finally made out the form of
Christine Chapel. She didn't seem pleased. "You're over an
hour late for your duty shift. You wouldn't answer your
door. I used a medical override to get in here—I thought
you might be in trouble!"

McCoy scoffed. "Why not . . . just read the damn belt-
buckle thing?"

"Because you're out of uniform." She peered at him.
"Though I'm surprised it couldn't read your blood alcohol
levels from across the room. Now listen to me, Leonard.
Back home in the mountains maybe you could sleep all day
if you wanted."

"Bull," he countered, struggling to his feet with limited success. Christine declined to assist him. "I woke up with the rooster every morning."

"That's between you and the rooster. The point is, now you're back on the *Enterprise* and you have responsibilities again."

"Wasn't my idea." He'd managed to find the lavatory and splashed some water on his face. "Look, Chris, I'm sorry. . . . I had a really rough night. Things didn't . . . didn't go so well."

She crossed her arms. "Don't tell me—you've come down with another incurable disease."

He blinked. "No."

"Then things can't be that bad, now can they?"

McCoy's brain was too muzzy to think of a comeback—or maybe she just had a point. "Okay . . . so what'd I miss?"

"Mostly routine." She rattled off a brief status report that McCoy absorbed almost subliminally, recognizing that there was nothing in it demanding closer attention from him. "But we have received a request from the main hospital down on Lorina. They'd like our assistance with some of the people injured in the attacks."

"Lorini doctors asking for our help? That seems a bit backward."

"Not when it comes to dealing with paralysis victims, amputees. . . . They want to know what we have to offer in terms of prosthetics, motor assist units, that sort of thing."

"Oh." Made sense. Fabrini medicine was unparalleled when it came to pharmaceuticals and therapeutic techniques, but when it was a question of hardware, they were pretty much medieval. And this was an area where McCoy had some experience—the cerebellar bypass unit he'd devised as a "remote control" for Spock's body when the Eymorgs had stolen his brain (ouch—that was not a sentence he wanted to think sober, let alone with a hangover) had been adapted in recent years as a means of treating paralysis patients who didn't respond to standard nerve regen techniques.

But at the moment, the last place McCoy wanted to be— the last place he felt he deserved to be—was anywhere on the same planet with Natira. "Look, Chris . . . any chance you could handle that for me? I can handle the sickbay stuff . . . but right now I don't think I'd be a good choice to represent the face of Starfleet." He glanced at the mirror. *Hell, if Starfleet's face looked like mine does right now, it'd send the Klingons screaming for cover.*

"Uh-*huh*," Christine said. "You really think you can go the rest of the mission without seeing Natira?" He winced; she knew him too well. But she softened. "Oh, all right. I wouldn't wish you on injured children in your condition. I'll cover for you this time. But only if you promise not to be late again."

"Yes, Mother."

"Honestly, Leonard. Do I look like somebody's mother?"

Spock entered the private meeting room of the officers' lounge to find the captain standing before the viewscreens, lost in thought. The room was set apart from the public portion of the lounge, enclosed and shielded to permit secure conversations, but this was compensated for by the two large holographic viewscreens on the aft wall, which were styled to emulate windows and could project an image from the vantage point of any visual sensor on the ship. When Spock had first come to this lounge, before his V'Ger-inspired epiphany, he'd found it a pointless extravagance. Now . . . well, now he still found it a pointless extravagance. Yes, emotions should be acknowledged, but shouldn't the design of a secure meeting room serve to enhance the emotional sense of caution and shelter, rather than working against it with an illusion of openness? The more Spock explored emotion, the more he realized that he *still* didn't understand human emotional behavior. Which wasn't doing him a lot of good in figuring out his own.

In any case, the holographic "windows" seemed to fill some emotional need of Kirk's. At the moment they projected an image of Lorina as it would appear from the arboretum at the base of the ship. It was a fertile world, its colors made vivid by the short-wavelength illumination of its F7 primary star. *Enterprise* was on the sunlit side, but slowly circling around toward the terminator, and in the darkened crescent to the right of his field of view, Spock could see a solitary concentration of light, marking the sole humanoid presence on this world. Over four million people, yet on the scale of a planet they took up but a tiny patch.

Also in evidence from this field of view were two bright glints of light, representing two of the Shesshran pods that continued to shepherd the *Enterprise*. As yet, they showed no inclination to let their guard down while the ship was in their system. Indeed, Spock had learned that their ships still routinely monitored Lorini orbital space, alert for any hint of hostility from its settlers, even though the Lorini had shown no interest in spaceflight beyond the occasional maintenance visit to Yonada.

But Kirk's attention appeared to be on the planet, not the ships. At first Spock wasn't sure the captain had noted his arrival, and was about to announce himself. But Kirk beat him to it. "Mr. Spock."

"Captain. How was your meeting with High Priestess Rishala?"

"It was . . . enlightening. On many levels. She's a compelling woman, Spock."

A long-suffering brow rose. "Indeed."

Kirk chuckled. "Not like that. At least . . . not at first glance. There are subtler forms of beauty." He shook himself. "But that's beside the point. She gave me . . . a lot to think about."

Spock waited, but Kirk had fallen silent again. "Sir?"

Kirk furrowed his brow, appearing disturbed. "Spock . . . do you think I have a . . . pattern of abandonment?"

That was not a question Spock had expected. "I am not sure what you mean, sir."

"We came in here, four and a half years ago, and upended a people's whole way of life. We . . . exposed the computer behind the curtain, showed them that their belief system was a fraud, and then we just . . . *left*. Went blithely on our way on the assumption that we'd changed their lives for the better."

"We did *save* their lives, Captain. And the lives of the three billion, seven hundred and twenty-four million Shesshran then living on Daran V as well."

"But was I wrong to assume that my responsibility ended there?" Kirk asked, turning to face Spock. "I thought exposing the Oracle would solve their problems. Instead it just seems to have created a whole new set. I knocked down the certainties they had, but I didn't think about what to replace them with.

"And it's not just here, Spock. Time and time again, I've triggered major changes in people's ways of life. I destroyed Landru and Vaal. Ended the Eminians' computer war. Freed the slaves on Triskelion, helped bring down the Reich on Ekos, set up a syndicate on Iotia. Saved the Yonadi, the Chenari, the Pelosians." A pause. "Armed Tyree's people.

"Every time, I believed I was acting for the greater good. Preserving lives, fixing other people's tampering."

"You were," Spock said.

"Maybe so. But was it enough? I set these changes in motion—didn't that give me a responsibility to stick around and see things through? To help them deal with the consequences of what I did?"

"You did not simply abandon them, Jim. Often you left personnel, such as Mr. Lindstrom, behind as advisors. In other cases you notified Starfleet, which sent its own teams of advisors."

"So I washed my hands of the problem and went on my merry way. I hardly ever bothered to check up on any of the worlds I'd interfered with."

Spock pondered. "I was always under the impression that your intent was to minimize the extent of your interference. Contrary to popular opinion, you have always been very sensitive to the right of other beings to self-determination."

"Giving them the right to choose, yes. But dropping a bombshell on them and then . . . haring off to parts unknown as fast as I can?" Kirk shook his head. "It feels like . . . like accidentally getting a woman pregnant, and then leaving her to raise the child alone. Of course she should have the right to make her own decisions, raise the child as she sees fit. But that doesn't absolve the father of some degree of responsibility. He should at least . . . take an interest in his son's—his child's life. At least be there if he's needed."

Spock stepped closer and spoke carefully. "Your . . . analogy is flawed, Jim. You did not abandon your responsibilities to Dr. Marcus or her son. She chose to keep you unaware of your son's existence. And once you did discover it, she asked you to stay out of his life."

Kirk gave a small, wistful smile. "I know that, Spock. It's not the same situation. And I know the choice was hers. Still, whatever the circumstances, it just doesn't seem right to make a profound difference in someone's life, or in a people's way of life, and then just go away and never look back. Surely that can't be the only way to respect their right to choose."

"We are a Starfleet crew, Jim. We go where our missions take us."

"Missions of exploration, Spock. Shouldn't that mean more than just a quick survey? How much can we really learn this way, trying to visit as many new worlds as possible, and barely taking the time to learn about each one in any detail? How can we understand the consequences of our choices if we only have a superficial picture?"

He returned to the viewports, looked down on Lorina again. "I consider myself a student of history, Mr. Spock. I know . . . the kings of England and can quote the fights historical. But I fear that sometimes I'm too quick to judge an alien culture by what I see in the here and now, and not to consider . . . all the history that went into creating it. You can't see a culture deeply enough without that. Can't understand the forces that drive it, the nuances that lead to the different ways of thinking its people can have.

"On Yonada I saw a people . . . shackled under a yoke of deception, a rogue machine leading them to their doom. I took care of the machine, but I failed to understand that it wasn't the *source* of their belief system, just an *expression* of it. A means of enforcing it. It was created to serve a purpose that already existed. It arose from forces that were already part of their culture.

"Those forces are still there, Spock, and they're responsible for the chaos down there. If we're to have any hope of resolving this . . . we need to understand where it all came from."

" 'It all,' sir?"

"Why the Oracle was created," Kirk explained. "Why the Creators—the Fabrini who built Yonada—chose to control its population in this way. Why they . . . lied to their people for ten thousand years, but intended all along to reveal the truth to them at the end of the journey. How much of

Oracular doctrine was part of the lie, invented as a means of control, and how much was there already, as part of Fabrini culture and belief.

"From what I've seen, and what Lindstrom tells us, there are a lot of different religious sects among the Lorini. We need to find out what their common ground is. If we want to bring the factions together in peace, we need to find something they can all agree on.

"That's your mission, Spock. I want you to go to Yonada and access the Fabrini data archives. I want you find out everything you can about the history of Yonada, the answers to these questions. And . . . any other questions I'm overlooking."

"That will be a considerable undertaking, Captain," Spock said thoughtfully. "To do such a task with any real thoroughness would take hundreds of scholars studying for generations."

"A number of scholars have been working on it for four and a half years now—that's a start, at least," Kirk said with a shrug. "And who knows, maybe the Yonadi had their own historians."

"Whose work would have been constrained to hew to approved dogma."

"Still, it could tell you something. Even by what it doesn't say. Just read between the lines." Kirk smiled. "You're pretty good at doing that with me."

Spock quirked a brow. "Perhaps, sir. But you are generally quite easy to read."

Kirk was taken aback. "Mr. Spock, I'll have you know I'm a master of the bluff!"

"Jim . . . remember to whom you are speaking. The Vulcans invented the poker face."

If Vaylin Zaand lived to be four hundred, he would never understand how humans ever got anything accomplished.

Maybe longevity was exactly the problem, the young Rhaandarite mused as he strolled along the balcony of the rec deck, observing the interactions of the mostly human crew members around him. Humans were so short-lived, with such abbreviated childhoods; they hardly had any time to assimilate any reasonable-sized body of rules and principles. So their behaviors tended to be erratic, impulsive, lacking in structure. On top of which, their frontal lobes were so underdeveloped that they had limited memory or analytical capacity for social rules, little judgment or impulse control, and a language too simple even to have the vocabulary needed to categorize their relationships and interactions, let alone explain how to manage them. It was no wonder their history was so full of conflict and intolerance, when they had so little ability to relate to one another.

Yet somehow they had managed to build things like this starship, and the Federation it represented, despite those limitations. Zaand reminded himself that his elders had had good reasons for initiating the Starfleet exchange program. The fleet was the closest thing humans had to a disciplined social structure, and the elders had felt that certain of their young could benefit from time spent within its relatively simple hierarchy. What Zaand was not inclined to dwell on, and what the elders had not shared with Starfleet, was that it was the less gifted of their young, the ones too slow in assimilating the massive body of Rhaandarite behaviorial rules, who were assigned to the exchange. Zaand was well aware that he was a slow learner. After 85 years he should have mastered the fifth tier of fractal interpersonal dynamics, but he was still laboring on the third. Indeed, his very discomfort with the thought of his slowness was itself a symptom of same, since by now he should understand how to integrate his awareness of his inadequacy into his self-construct and manifest it outwardly in the appropriate degree of humility. No deception of self or others, no confusion about where he stood in the order of things, just smooth, efficient emotional functionality.

But living among humans certainly wasn't helping him master the higher tiers. They couldn't even manage to get the first tier right. Case in point: down below, Lieutenant Commander Sulu was engaged with Crewman Uuvu'it in a form of ritual combat involving long, narrow-bladed weapons and metal-mesh masks, while Lieutenant Chekov and Chief Petty Officer DiFalco looked on, conversing casually with each other and both the combatants. It was a complete hodgepodge of rank, gender, species, and affective relations. Why were the officers fraternizing on such an equal footing with the enlisted personnel? Why was Sulu seemingly unaffected by DiFalco's proximity to Chekov, a potential rival male, when he was so clearly interested in her himself? For that matter, why did Sulu show no sign of being aware of his own interest in DiFalco? And DiFalco didn't seem sensitive to the tension Chekov showed toward her friendship with Sulu, which the lieutenant saw as a threat to his long-term companionable association with the lieutenant commander. By the Elders, couldn't they even read each other's subtext?

Still, he had been sent here to learn, and hopefully he could divine something from the observation of this complex muddle. Noting that other off-duty crew members were also watching the ritual combat, Zaand figured he could watch unobtrusively from closer range, and so made his way down to the main level. At the side stairs, he had to pause to let Crewman Ki'ki're'ti'ke by in the other direction, for the Escherite's horizontal, segmented body took up most of the stairway. "Going down to watch the clash?" Kick asked, swiveling his short-stalked eyes out from under their bony protective crests to peer up at Zaand. "I'm going up to get a better view. A body gets tired of looking up at everyone else. . . ."

The floor of the rec deck could be reconfigured into multiple forms, with raised platforms, game tables, and modular seats rising up from its carpeted orange surface as needed. Right now the forward section of the deck, just under the large monitor screen, was flattened out to accommodate Sulu and Uuvu'it's competition. Zaand made his way around to the front to get a better view, squeezing his way past an Aurelian's wings and an Arcadian's tail, and ending up next to the alcove that displayed images of earlier Terran vessels named *Enterprise.* He was absently pleased to note that the display had been corrected since the ship's hasty launch, when the image of Jonathan Archer's *Enterprise* had been inadvertently replaced with that of an unused prototype based on Vulcan ships of the same period.

Zaand filed that detail away and turned his attention to the bladed combat. Uuvu'it was pursuing the fight with typical Betelgeusian ferocity. His reach was considerably longer than Sulu's—'Geusians approached the size of an adolescent Rhaandarite, while Sulu was no bigger than a fifty-year-old—and his boots were off, allowing him to splay his talons for better traction and balance. Yet while those advantages clearly didn't make it easy for Sulu, the lieutenant commander was holding his own, and showed no trace of concern. Indeed, he was even carrying on a conversation with Chekov. "So I told her I'd never really thought about it."

"What do you mean?" the lieutenant asked with that odd accent of his. "Of course you've thought about it!"

"Okay, I've *mused* about it, let's say. Had it floating around in my mind. But that's not the same as seriously thinking about it."

"Hikaru, you've *told* me more than once that you wanted to be a captain someday."

"Sure—and when I was a kid, I wanted to be D'Artagnan."

Chekov scoffed. "*You* wanted to be D'Artagnan when you were thirty. From the look of it, you still do."

Zaand saw Sulu's guard drop fractionally, and Uuvu'it evidently saw it too, for he made a fierce lunge, his long reach appearing to guarantee that his weapon would make contact while keeping him out of range of the lieutenant commander's. But Sulu twisted gracefully aside, evading the point of the blade and letting the crewman's momentum carry him right into the tip of the weapon which Sulu had brought into position with preternatural speed. The computer beeped, DiFalco cheered, and the 'Geusian whipped off his mask in anger, chirruping some shrill phrases which the translators declined to render. "You were lucky that time," Uuvu'it insisted. "Rematch?"

Sulu chuckled as he raised his mask. "Maybe later, Hrrii'ush. I don't have your stamina."

Chekov was frowning now. "So . . . are you saying you don't *want* to command?"

"No, I'm not saying that. Just that it isn't something I've ever thought about in any detail. It's been a 'someday' kind of thing, you know? I haven't made any specific plans, or tried to figure out what kind of a captain I wanted to be."

"Well, that part's obvious," Chekov said. "Like Captain Kirk, of course."

Sulu shook his head. "Nah. Captain Kirk's one of a kind. I've learned a lot from him, of course . . . but copying him is something nobody else could pull off. I'd have to find my own way."

"Don't think of it that way," Uuvu'it said, clapping Sulu on the back. "What you want is to try to be *better* than Kirk. What good is an example if you don't try to outdo him?"

Predictably, DiFalco stood up for the captain. "You just can't compete with a record like Kirk's. I mean, he just saved the whole Earth!"

"For now," Uuvu'it replied. "Sooner or later every planet gets it. You'd be better off ditching yours and living among the stars like us."

"Don't listen to her, Hikaru," said Chekov. "I'm sure you'll save plenty of worlds."

But DiFalco had noticed Zaand's presence. "And how about you, Zaand?" she challenged. "What do you think it takes to be a good captain?"

Zaand could tell that she wished to confront him about his misgivings toward Kirk. That was overt enough that even the humans could read it, judging from their own reactions. He wasn't sure how to respond to the overture. She was enlisted while he was an officer, which made her his subordinate in that sense, but as a sexually mature female she was entitled to his deference. Also, he was an outside spectator to a social interaction in which she was already a participant, again placing her at higher status in the exchange. So that gave him a certain obligation to respond to her request; yet conveying an opinion that he knew would offend her would be a breach of the deference she was owed. And Standard simply didn't have the syntax to let him craft a response that would strike the optimal balance between these conflicting demands.

So he fell back on what the humans would call a neutral response, though their use of "neutral" encompassed many gradations of relative partisanship. "I've never thought about it. My people aren't cut out for command as you define it."

"Now, that I don't understand," Lieutenant Chekov said. "I know the Rhaandarites' reputation. But if you're so good at following orders, then there must be people on Rhaandarel who give them. Right? Unless you all just sat around for millennia waiting for some other species to come along and tell you what to do."

Oh, dear. His direct superior had expressed a misconception. Would it be insubordinate to contradict him? Except he seemed to recognize that his premise had flaws and wanted them corrected. So in this case contradiction would be obedience. "We never really needed to be told what to do. We just . . . *know*. The universe is structured. Everything follows rules, and there's a right way, a natural way to do anything. Even those of us who give instructions to the rest are simply . . . divining the natural order of things, recognizing what actions are dictated by a given situation. It's just a higher tier of obedience."

"By the book, huh?" DiFalco asked. "No wonder you think Kirk's a bad captain."

"I know he's been successful. I know you all respect him, and I don't mean to show disrespect for your views. But his record looks to me like it's . . . random. I can't understand how his procedures could be successful. I've heard some people call it 'luck,' but I don't believe there is such a thing.

"Captain Decker, though—he followed the rules. He understood the 'book' and used it with great skill. I think that would have to be what makes a good captain."

"The book is a useful set of guidelines," Chekov said, shrugging. "But you can't live your whole life by the rules—it will straitjacket you."

"With respect, sir, I see it the other way around. The rules . . . they give you a solid framework to build on. Wherever you are, if you can see where you stand in relation to the rules, then you can follow them to anywhere you need to be, use them to find solutions you never would've thought of on your own." He spoke with growing enthusiasm, trying to make them understand that the rules gave him a sense of control, not confinement. "Without them, you'd just be drifting around randomly, and wouldn't stumble across the solutions you needed except by sheer chance."

"But that's where intuition comes in," said Sulu. "It lets you make leaps to the right answers, and get to them faster than you could if you had to take it one step at a time."

"But what if you leap and arrive at the wrong answer? How can you tell?"

Uuvu'it gave a wry chirp. "By whether you get killed or not!"

"I think that's exactly my point."

"Ffah. Decker was a fine man—I liked him. But he was a dreamer."

DiFalco stared at them. "A by-the-book dreamer?"

"Perhaps the worst kind," the 'Geusian said. "Oh, he was full of fresh ideas, new approaches, in theory. Couldn't put them into practice without plenty of time to work out the ramifications, analyze all the issues. He was a man of thought, not action. Kirk, though—this is my kind of captain. He doesn't waste time analyzing or worrying about rules, he just charges ahead."

"That's just the propaganda," Chekov answered with some heat. "The real Captain Kirk is nothing like that. He cares very much for the rules, and doesn't break them without good reason. And he's always thinking, always figuring out all the angles. If it seems like he's rushing into a decision, it's only because his mind is three steps ahead of yours. Five, if he talks to Mr. Spock first."

"Hey, I'm defending him!"

"Well, defend the real him, not the caricature."

"Even if all that's true," Zaand said, "it doesn't change the fact that Captain Decker was *supposed* to be the captain of this ship."

"But he's not anymore," Sulu said, amiably enough. "You've just got to learn to accept that."

"It isn't so easy for me, sir. If it had been done the right way, then I could. But it wasn't. Even by your own rules, it was a breach of protocol."

Sulu furrowed his brow. "I'd say it was more like . . . a leap of intuition. Maybe it didn't go by the rules you'd expect; maybe it even seemed like a bad idea at the time. But it *worked*. I'm still not a hundred percent clear on what happened with that landing party back inside V'Ger, but it seems that everybody basically got what they wanted, including Decker. So it all worked out right in the end. That's how you recognize intuition. Once can be luck, twice can be . . . well, really good luck. But if it happens consistently, then you know you're onto something. And whatever that something is, James T. Kirk has got it."

"Maybe that's so. But still there's a procedure that could've been followed. On Rhaandarel, if one person knew that he was better able to interpret the patterns of the universe than another who was in authority, there are clear procedures for the replacement. It lets those of us in subordinate positions transfer our loyalties from one to the other. But that didn't happen here. I was never able to go through the transfer process. I'm sorry, but I still think of Captain Decker as my commanding officer. That's where my loyalty lies. And I just . . . don't know what to make of Kirk. He just doesn't fit."

"Then maybe you should transfer to another ship," DiFalco suggested.

Zaand was nonplussed. "Don't worry," Chekov told him. "Nobody wants you to transfer. You are welcome here," he finished with a glare at the chief.

Sulu caught the look. "I'm sure Cella didn't mean anything by it. She was trying to offer him a solution, right?"

"I'm just saying, if he's not happy serving with Captain Kirk, maybe it'd be better for everyone if he went somewhere else."

"Please . . . that's not it," Zaand said. Those subtexts were coming into play again, and he didn't wish to exacerbate the tension. "It's just that . . . I serve where I'm assigned. My place is to serve this ship, until I'm sent to another."

The chief shook her head. "Oh, brother. You have got problems."

"Well, it's simple enough as I see it," Uuvu'it put in. "Kirk challenged Decker for command, and Kirk won. That makes him the rightful alpha."

"But he was placed in command by Nogura," Zaand reminded him.

"Then Decker should've gone to Nogura and fought for his command. Instead he submitted. So he lost. Why do you need any rules more complicated than that?"

"I just . . . do."

Chekov stepped forward. "Well, Ensign, I can resolve your uncertainty over who your commanding officer is."

Zaand looked at him expectantly. "Sir?"

"*I* am. Do you have any conflict with that?"

"No, sir." If anything, it was comforting to have at least one unambiguous hierarchical relationship. And to have Chekov assert his rank instead of confusing things by treating him like an equal.

"Good."

"Except . . ." Zaand began, causing Chekov to sigh. "I was wondering, sir, if you had a conflict with me."

"What do you mean?"

He raised the question diffidently. "My training is for field duty, sir. Yet you keep assigning me to the bridge. It isn't what I'm . . . supposed to be doing, sir. In your judgment, have I failed to fulfill my duties?"

The lieutenant fidgeted. "No, it's not that. You've done very well in the training, the simulations. You've certainly mastered the regulations with flying colors." Flying . . . colors? Zaand applied a fraction of his mental processing to the

idiom, remembered that "colors" could mean a flag or standard, and concluded that the expression must refer to the
use of such a display to celebrate success. "I'm just . . . not
sure you're ready."

"If I've been inadequate in some way, sir, please let me
know so I can fix it."

"No, no! It's just . . ." He closed his eyes briefly.
"Ensign—you're a *child*. Aren't you?"

"I'm still immature, yes. But I've mastered all the
Starfleet regulations and procedures, as far as I know, sir."

"Yes, but . . . I just don't feel right about it. Sending a, a
boy into danger. You, you have your whole life ahead of
you. You haven't even . . . well, *matured*. As you say."

"But I could be in just as much danger on the bridge."

"Well, yes, in a sense. Still, it's another thing to send
someone out there, directly into danger. And someone
so . . . well, young . . ."

"I am three times your age, Lieutenant."

"But you have such a long life to look forward to. So
many . . . adult things you haven't gotten to do yet." He fidgeted, apparently embarrassed to acknowledge the sexual
subtext that Zaand could hear quite clearly in his words.
"Don't take this the wrong way, Ensign, but I don't understand why you went into security at all."

"Because it's what I'm best at, sir," Zaand said simply.
"And the rest—my safety, my longevity—it doesn't matter.
My place is to serve. I may be uncomfortable with aspects
of it sometimes . . . but I'm here to serve. If you tell me to
man the bridge, then that's what I'll do. But it isn't where I
can do the most good, sir."

Chekov studied him. "You know that on this ship, most
of what landing-party security does is to protect the captain?"

"I've gathered that, Lieutenant."

"So if you have a problem following his orders—"

"As you said, sir, you are my commander. So if you order me to obey Captain Kirk's orders, then that's what I'll do, sir."

"All right, then. I'll think about it."

"Thank you, sir." It was a rather awkward patch job, but it might be a way for him to cope with the protocol problem. As he'd said, there was a rule for everything—maybe even for dealing with a man who defied the rules.

CHAPTER NINE

Cast out fear. Cast out hate and rage. Cast out greed and envy. Cast out all emotion that speeds entropy, whether it be love or hate. Cast out these emotions by using reason to accept them, and then move past them. Use in moderation emotions that do not speed entropy, taking all care that they do not cause others pain, for that speeds entropy as well. Master your passions, so that they become a power for the slowing of the heat-death.

—Surak, *Analects*

"TRANSPORT CONFIRMED. Spock out."

Spock lowered his wrist communicator and looked around him at the barren surface of Yonada—or rather, the inner hull that simulated the surface of a planet. The simulation was less convincing now, for the projected sky had been deactivated, as had the simulated volcanic vents. Spock saw no sign of the ropy black plants which had sparsely populated the surface on his first visit, but that was not conclusive, for he could see only as far as the maintenance lights around the underground entrance illuminated, and this area had been free of the plants before. Beyond was blackness. Spock was aware that the Federation researchers had wished to maintain Yonada's surface as it had been, but Natira's legislature had declared it an unnecessary expenditure of energy now that the population had been relocated. Spock found it unlikely that any of the plants had survived, although, given the harsh conditions under which they'd existed before, he couldn't entirely rule out the possibility.

Seeing no reason to linger, Spock made his way to the nearest entrance cylinder and depressed the foot panel, now clearly marked for the benefit of the researchers. It was not practical to beam directly to the control room, since the inner shell's kelbonite-victurium radiation shielding interfered with transporter locks, just as it had obscured the Yonadi's life signs from the *Enterprise*'s sensors 4.67 years before. (It had only been the presence of these cylinders' refined alloys which had allowed Spock to settle on this approximate area as a reasonable beaming site that first time—fortunate, since the inner surface had an area of 296,092 square kilometers, which would have posed a problem had they needed to search at random for an entrance.) He and Kirk had been able to beam through the shell once by using McCoy's communicator signal to provide a target lock, but it had been a somewhat risky and power-intensive operation.

As he made his way down the spiral staircase, his footsteps clanging loudly in the narrow passageway, Spock reflected on the task his captain had assigned him: to research the historical origins of Yonada's religious institutions and beliefs, to explain the Fabrini builders' reasons for establishing them, and to discern the cultural and ideological forces driving the modern factions. This was no small task Kirk had set for him. Indeed, Spock found himself feeling intimidated by its magnitude.

The first step in any historical investigation was to go to the sources, and therein lay the first problem. The available sources were limited, since the Yonadi had been an illiterate culture outside of the ruling priesthood. Essentially, the Book of the People and the Fabrini intelligence files were the only reliable written sources, and they were both limited.

The Book was mostly a primer about Yonada's technical systems and the procedures for planetfall upon arrival at Daran IV. It was written at a basic level, beginning with a language lesson and moving on to elementary science and electronics before proceeding to the specifics. On his initial reading of the text, Spock had concluded that the Fabrini had intended it as a hard-copy backup in case of computer failure, and had even accounted for the possibility of language drift—something that had indeed occurred to an extent, as Uhura had determined when she'd checked the translator logs from their encounter. Modern Yonadi was not too different from ancient Fabrini—logical, given the lack of contact with outside cultures which might introduce new vocabulary—but the two dialects were distinct enough to create comprehension problems. Fortunately, Spock had learned the Fabrini's ancient language from the probes found by the *Intrepid,* and had thus been able to read the Book instantly in a situation where time had been of the essence.

What the Book did not contain was extensive discussion of Fabrini history or Yonadi religious tenets. Its expository style did have religious elements, invoking the Creators and presenting its instructions in the tone of religious law, even though they mostly pertained to the requirements for maintaining life support, propulsion systems, and the like. There was minimal discussion of abstract spiritual concepts or the foundational ideologies of the culture. This seemed odd, given the central role the Oracular faith had played in the preserving of social order on Yonada.

The intelligence files presented somewhat the opposite problem. They were a comprehensive archive of the

Fabrini's collected knowledge, but only up to the launching of Yonada itself. They thus contained no information about how Fabrini beliefs had been adapted or applied in the life of the Yonadi, or how the modern diversity of religious sects had emerged. Presumably those files pertaining to the planning and construction of Yonada would contain some discussion of the thinking that had gone into the creation of the Oracle and the cultural norms it enforced. But the more recent the information was, the harder it was to reconstruct. The Fabrini had built their archival banks to last for ten millennia, and indeed had done an exceptional job given the limited computer technology at their disposal, comparable to the first century before Surak on Vulcan or the twenty-first century on Earth. But the data files had fallen prey to quantum erosion over that long span of time, as one particle after another had spontaneously changed state in accordance with the uncertainty principle. The occasional cosmic rays energetic enough to penetrate the shielding had done further damage. What survived was fragmentary, though the Federation teams hoped to be able to restore most of it in time. Information which had been part of Fabrini culture for a long time, such as their traditional medical knowledge, was easier to reconstruct since it was referenced in multiple texts and subarchives. What was missing from one source could usually be found in another. But newer memes, such as the records of the Yonada project, had not had time to replicate themselves so widely, to be reprinted and cited and discussed in as many different sources. Without such redundancy, the information was much harder to recover. Spock would use every technique at his disposal to unscramble the remaining data, but much of it was no doubt lost forever.

What remained were written records made by those few Yonadi who had been literate. But few of these had been found to date, and they were mostly fairly recent. Here the problem was the reverse: older documents were less likely to have survived, due to the physical decay of the ephemeral materials on which they were printed. Ironically, the closer one got in time to the building of Yonada, approaching from either direction, the less information was preserved.

Spock had instructed Mr. Lindstrom to research such texts while Spock focused on the data archives. But Lindstrom had suggested one more avenue of investigation: the oral traditions of the People. Spock was skeptical of oral history, since by its very nature it grew more inexact with each retelling. But Lindstrom pointed out that it was the only way to gain insight into a nonliterate culture, and that if one took its inherent imprecision into account, one could still extrapolate certain understandings from it. "Maybe it won't give us a factual account of what happened," he had said, "but it might provide context to help fill in the blanks in what you find."

Spock had assented to Lindstrom's suggestion, recognizing that Kirk's mandate was about more than the factual history of the People. What the captain sought, more fundamentally, was an understanding of how they thought and believed, of what drove them as a culture. Their oral traditions, whatever their factual shortfalls, were a much better source for discerning that—*if* one knew what to look for. This was what truly intimidated Spock: he was being asked to gain insight into the hearts of the People, not simply their minds or their machines. Presumably he was more qualified for such a task now than he would have been before V'Ger, but he found he couldn't be sure of that. He no longer hid from his own emotions, but did that necessarily mean that he now possessed empathy? It was hard enough figuring out what his feelings meant to him; how well could he decipher the emotional or spiritual life of a whole culture?

Perhaps the captain simply didn't understand how much

Spock still had to learn about emotion. Perhaps he thought that Spock's epiphanies during the V'Ger mission had been the end of a journey rather than a beginning. But on the other hand, perhaps Jim recognized that Spock still had much to learn, and had given him this challenge as an opportunity to do so. It was somewhat like throwing a novice swimmer into the deep end of a pool—but that seemed like the sort of thing Jim Kirk would do. Certainly the tales he'd heard about the Academy courses Kirk had taught as a lieutenant bore out that assumption.

For a moment, Spock seemed to feel an echo of his rapport with the Voyager, for the first time in days. He realized that the Voyager was experiencing something similar to this: intimidation at the prospect of exploring a whole new realm, or more fundamentally at needing to expand one's own reach to encompass it. But the challenge Spock faced was ludicrously trivial when compared to the Voyager's quest. He couldn't be sure whether the sense of rapport was genuine or simply a memory triggered by the parallel, but either way, it brought him comfort.

Arriving at the temple of the Oracle, behind which the control center was located, Spock noted the changes that had been made since his initial visit. The temple doors, formerly triggered by biometric scanners concealed in the text panels to either side, now opened freely, though they were flanked by two black-bereted Federation Security guards. The Oracle itself, a large obelisk of black marble with a starburst emblem in the center, stood open, allowing free access to the workings within. However, several Federation-made desks and terminals had been installed along the walls, and were being used by various researchers, most of them Vulcan. Another Vulcan, a roundish middle-aged male, sat at a receptionist's desk near the entrance, examining a terminal of his own. Sparing him a cursory glance, the receptionist asked, "May I help you?"

"Yes. I am Commander Spock of the *Enterprise*."

That caught the receptionist's attention. He studied Spock for a moment, then said, "Yes . . ." in a clinical tone and returned his focus to his terminal.

Spock raised a brow. "I need to access the Fabrini intelligence files."

"Their contents can be accessed from any public terminal."

"That will not be sufficient. I need access to the memory banks themselves, in order to attempt data reconstruction."

"That effort is already ongoing. Our staff does not require further assistance. You may go."

What did humans call this? The runaround. "You do not understand. I am under orders from Captain Kirk."

Another cold glance. "I am not."

"Then to whom *do* you answer?"

"I report to Director T'chan, who is currently on an archaeological dig."

When nothing more was forthcoming, Spock asked, "And to whom does she report?"

A beat. "Commissioner Soreth."

"I see. Then I would like to speak with Commissioner Soreth."

"I expect that you would."

So this was how it felt to be on the receiving end of Vulcan literalism. Did it always sound so phony and evasive when he did it? "Then would you please connect me with him?"

"Do you have an appointment?"

Spock pressed his lips together in annoyance. Was this just petty bureaucracy in action, or something more personal? He noted the receptionist watching him carefully, as though anticipating an emotional outburst. So that was how it would be. The word had gotten out. Very well—he would simply not give them what they expected. "It is a matter of some importance," he replied patiently. "Please contact the commissioner's office; I shall wait."

The prospect of having a supposed *V'tosh ka'tur* in his presence any longer than necessary was apparently sufficient to goad the receptionist into activity. It was not very long at all until he directed Spock to a free terminal where he could receive Soreth's signal.

The commissioner appeared on the screen, his natural scowl deepening upon the sight of Spock. "What is it that you wish, Commander?"

"To gain access to Yonada's computer banks for a research project."

"You should take that up with the personnel there."

"I have done so. But their lack of cooperation has made it necessary to go, as the humans say, 'over their heads.' "

"Mm. What is the nature of this research?"

Spock spelled it out in basic terms. "I see," Soreth replied when he was done. "Would it not be a more logical use of your time to assist in tracking down the bases and supply lines of the insurgents?"

"Logically, if we wish to find a lasting resolution to this problem, we should address the root causes of the insurgency. Otherwise, any insurgents we arrest will simply be replaced by others with the same motivations."

"The root cause, Commander, is these people's irrational refusal to abandon a belief framework which was invented to deceive them."

Spock pondered that reply. "Then what do you perceive to be the solution?"

"Obviously, the re-education of the populace to eliminate these false beliefs."

"All beings . . . need to believe in something," Spock replied slowly. "Some fundamental principle to define and guide their existence. Surely it is when they feel those beliefs to be threatened that they are the most dangerous."

Soreth looked down his nose at Spock. "That is the kind of sentimental thinking I would expect from a *V'tosh ka'tur.*"

"It is illogical," Spock countered, "to disregard the role of emotion in sentient thought. Emotions evolved for a reason; logically, they must serve some practical function."

"The human appendix evolved for a reason, but has since lost its purpose. Nostalgia for useless atavisms is not logical."

"Nor is it logical to assume that a thing is useless simply because one is afraid to find a use for it."

Soreth's gaze was cold. "You impute emotion to me only because you project it from yourself. You are a half-human boy who lacked the discipline to achieve *Kolinahr,* and you have concluded that *Kolinahr* is worthless rather than confront the fact of your failure."

The words stung, striking close to home. But Spock met Soreth's eyes evenly. "I have . . . given considerable thought to the possibility that my recent choices are indeed so motivated," he admitted. "It is certainly a tempting *excuse* to retreat from personal growth. But I cannot deny what I have learned."

"You have done so—you have denied *Kolinahr.* You have denied what it means to be Vulcan."

"Why can Vulcans only be one thing? Did Surak not uphold the combination of diversity as the highest ideal?"

"Had he meant to include emotion, he obviously would not have taught us to purge it. Your attempt to cite an authority as evidence for your refutation of the same authority merely illustrates how thoroughly your reasoning faculties have been contaminated by your exposure to humans."

This was becoming an opportunity to become better acquainted with the emotion of frustration, No matter what he said, the elder Vulcan found a way to twist it. "Surak did not claim to be infallible. Surely he would have recognized the need for modification and refinement of his ideas."

"Very well, then, tell me," Soreth challenged. "What does it mean to be emotionally logical? How can *you* reconcile what Surak could not?"

Spock searched for a response. After a time, he had to confess, "That is a question I have only begun to explore." He hoped he'd managed to say it without sounding embarrassed.

"I see. And I am sure you will explore it with the same commitment and success with which you explored *Kolinahr.*" He said it with far too much satisfaction for someone who was supposedly emotionless. But Spock knew simply pointing that out would do nothing to open his mind. It never had with him. "Admit it, Spock—you are a dilettante, lacking the patience and maturity to commit to anything. You refuse admission to the Vulcan Science Academy to attend Starfleet. You abandon Starfleet to pursue *Kolinahr,* and then abandon *Kolinahr* to become *ka'tur.* As a scientist, rather than focusing your intellect in a single field, you dabble in everything, and as a result make no lasting contribution to any science. You have no 'fundamental principle' to guide your existence, aside from inadequacy and failure. One would have expected better from a son of Sarek—even one raised by a human mother."

"You are a hypocrite," Spock said tightly, his hands clamping the edge of the console. "You condemn emotion, yet take pleasure in taunting me. You are so proud of your supposed logic—tell me, what will happen if I take this matter to Captain Kirk, to Natira? What reason will you give them for denying me cooperation in carrying out my orders? The fact that I *offend* you? How logical will that sound to them?"

Soreth's scowl was unreadable. After a time, he spoke. "Very well. You have authorization to proceed with your research. It is a waste of time, but I cannot see what harm it can do."

"Then our business is concluded." Spock reached for the disengage switch.

"Is it? I imagine your anger will linger for some time. I imagine you feel a powerful urge to lash out violently. What will you do with that urge?"

"I will manage it," Spock told him.

"Perhaps this time. But if you were so easy to provoke this time, what of next time? What happens when something more is at stake than simply your pride?

"Pay close attention to what is inside you, Spock. The Vulcan heart is not a force to be trifled with. Like the *lematya,* it cannot be tamed, only caged. Give it free rein and it will destroy you, or those around you."

"There must be a way to master emotion without denying it," Spock insisted.

"Other *V'tosh ka'tur* have tried. The results have usually been disastrous. What makes you think *you* can do better?"

Spock simply switched off the viewer. He had no answer.

"This is not the first time the People have battled over the rule of the Oracle," said the wizened old man.

Christopher Lindstrom looked at him curiously. "You mean, between pro-Oracle and anti-Oracle factions? The Oracle hasn't always been in control?"

"The Oracle has always been our guide," Paravo said, more with annoyance than with anger. He was a respected figure in the community, an Oracular loyalist, but motivated more by nostalgia than ideology. He had no hatred for the current system; he simply didn't want to deal with change. "But there have been those who have rejected its wisdom and rebelled against it, like disobedient children."

"But what about the Instruments of Obedience? Didn't those prevent any rebellion from ever—"

"Patience, young man! If you wish to learn, then you must listen!"

Lindstrom subsided and smiled to himself, for Paravo's advice resonated with him more than the old man realized. He'd learned a lot about listening since the first time he'd worked with the *Enterprise* crew. Back then he'd been a young lieutenant just a few short years out of the Academy, so brash and arrogant. He'd considered himself an expert, but it had all been theory—critiquing and building on field sociologists' work, evaluating first contacts from the comfortable remove of a ship or starbase. The mission to Beta III had been his first field assignment to a planet whose culture wasn't already well understood, already extensively written about in his journals and tomes. And he hadn't made a good showing of himself at all.

The *Enterprise* had come to investigate the disappearance of the *Archon* a century earlier, following up on the recent discovery of its recorder-marker buoy. The buoy had been badly damaged by thermal radiation, its databanks wiped, but its course tracked back to Beta III's system. Upon arriving, the crew had discovered another mystery: visual scans of the surface showed that the architecture and clothing of the humanlike natives were right out of nineteenth-century America.

Lindstrom had jumped to the conclusion that the *Archon* crew had contaminated the culture. He'd also misremembered his history, dressing the landing party in eighteenth-century garb. Both had proved to be costly mistakes; not only had he guaranteed that Lieutenants Sulu and O'Neill would be conspicuous in a rigidly conformist society, but he'd missed an important clue to the source of that conformity. In fact, it had been the Landru computer that had imposed the styles, downloaded from the *Archon*'s memory banks shortly before the ship had crashed. Landru the man had programmed his cybernetic avatar to allow creativity and growth, but the machine had understood that only on a superficial level. Its idea of innovation had been to impose periodic cosmetic changes on the architecture, clothing, and so forth, recycling Beta III's historical styles over and over for sixty centuries. With the *Archon*'s arrival it had finally gained access to something new, and methodically added it to the rotation. The only change it had made in the imported forms had been to speed up the clocks to fit the planet's twenty-two-hour days.

But Lindstrom hadn't figured this out until much later. He'd been impulsive and judgmental, too quick to jump to conclusions, and had contributed little to the landing party's understanding of the culture. In his defense, what they'd seen had certainly been shocking: a whole community erupting into savagery and afterward behaving as though nothing had been wrong; a father allowing his daughter to be ravaged; an old man being blasted dead for the slightest disapproved speech. It had been only natural to feel angered and disturbed. But Kirk and the others had managed those feelings, had filed them away with the rest of the information they gathered. Lindstrom should have done the same. Whatever his personal feelings, he shouldn't have let them keep him from listening, from trying to see the locals' point of view—not necessarily to approve of it, but simply to understand it.

Lindstrom figured his attitude was the reason Kirk had left him behind with the other experts assigned to help the Betans rebuild after Landru's shutdown. Maybe Kirk had concluded that such an arrogant hothead was a liability to a starship's sociology department. Or maybe he'd felt that an extended stay in an alien culture would help Lindstrom come down off his high horse (and it's hard to fit one of those into an ivory tower). Either way, it had been just what Lindstrom had needed. Getting to know the Betans as people rather than dissertation subjects, experiencing their reactions firsthand as they'd struggled to adjust, had soon turned him around. He'd finally started to think about how other people saw things, even about how the Landru computer had seen things. And that empathy had later proved useful when a failsafe had kicked in and Landru had reawakened. It had been the S.C.E. who'd done most of the work shutting it down again, but Lindstrom had done his part, as he'd failed to do as a member of Kirk's team. And it was his ability to see other points of view that had made the difference.

It was a lesson he'd taken very much to heart in the years since. Indeed, Soreth wasn't the first person who'd accused him of identifying too much with the peoples he studied. But what Lindstrom saw in Soreth and his staff was the same kind of condescension he'd been guilty of before Beta III, the same tendency to judge a people by one's own theories and preconceptions instead of getting to know how they really saw things. Lindstrom was determined not to fall back into that trap, especially now that he'd come to admire the Yonadi and their deeply held beliefs so much. There was a special strength to subjugated cultures, a determination to retain their identity against all odds, and usually it was the intangibles of faith that they clung to when their oppressors stripped away everything else they had. It made their spiritual lives particularly rich, fascinating to study as a sociologist and moving to experience as a man.

It also made their folklore rich and deeply layered, as they used it to preserve their history and beliefs, sometimes in encoded form to confound attempts to repress it. This had been particularly hard for the Yonadi, given that the Oracle could hear their every word and sense some of their emotions and urges, and punish anything that defied its doctrines. Yet they had managed nonetheless, and Lindstrom was certain that the People's tales of their past held many important lessons for the present. Spock had been skeptical due to the imprecision of oral history; but Lindstrom felt that very imprecision could help preserve meaning, by breaking it apart and distributing it among numerous tales, numerous perspectives and slants. By assembling all the different viewpoints on a past event, one could reconstruct the original in full dimension, like a holographic image.

Whether Paravo's tale would be a valuable piece of the puzzle remained to be seen. It was an account of a great battle between armies of good and evil, focusing on a legendary hero named Vocari, leader of the Oracular forces, who could strike down his enemies with the Oracle's fire—which could be a reference to energy weapons, or simply a mythological embellishment. "Which high priestess did he fight for?" Lindstrom asked when that information did not emerge on its own.

"Why, for golden Ganela, first of them all, of course. Did I not say this was a battle of the dawn times? Now pay attention."

Lindstrom filed the claim away, even though some specifics of the story didn't quite fit with the legends of Ganela, or of the creation of the Oracle. There were many traditions, with more conflicts between them than Paravo cared to admit. But myths and legends changed with each retelling, Lindstrom knew. The truth was in the heart of the tale, not the precise details.

Still, one detail caught his ear as the tale progressed. "The battle raged for fifteen days and fifteen nights," Paravo intoned. "It was fought in the depths, it was fought in the mountains, it was fought in the Halls of the Creators. The clash of blades, the cries of dying men echoed through the caverns, hills, and Halls."

"Tell me more about the Halls of the Creators," Lindstrom said. "I've heard them mentioned in some other tales." They seemed to be a version of the afterlife, a resting place for the honored dead, those who'd given their lives in service to the Creators.

"The Halls of the Creators, where the privileged are laid to rest," Paravo answered, echoing the formula used in the other tales. "In this hallowed place, our proudest and holiest spend eternity under the Creators' loving gaze. The blasphemers begrudged them this privilege, and so took the battle to the Halls themselves to lay them waste. Yet Vocari stood his ground at the entranceway, his forces arrayed behind him, blasting holy fire from his hands, to keep the rabble from desecrating the Halls. They struck him with their stones, their arrows, and their swords, so that his blood ran red throughout the Halls; yet still he kept on fighting, the conduit for the Oracle's wrath, until the bodies were piled so high that none could enter. Finally, with the enemy's charge smothered by their own base flesh, Vocari surrendered the life he had clung to in the Oracle's name, and won his eternal place in the Halls he had died to protect, the Halls he had anointed with his very blood."

"So Vocari and his army—they were actually in the Halls? Even though they were still alive."

"Yes, yes, of course, for that was where they were needed."

"So where are the Halls? What are they like? What awaits the honored dead when they arrive there?" Something about this was nagging at him. It wasn't just the disconnect between this legend of the Halls and the Oracle's orthodox cosmology (or, for that matter, Rishala's more mystical traditions). It wasn't even the suggestion that the Halls of the Creators were a physically accessible place; that wasn't necessarily literal, any more than Odysseus' visit to the underworld. There was something else tickling the back of his mind, something that seemed out of place.

But Paravo's descriptions didn't tell him much. They were fairly routine depictions of paradise—eternal plenty, luxury, the works. After twenty more minutes with the old man, Lindstrom was no closer to figuring out what was bothering him. But maybe another version of the tale from another teller might give him new perspective. Lindstrom knew he just had to keep listening.

Until yesterday, Tavero would never have thought that he would play a role in the holy struggle. To be sure, there was no question of his devotion to the Oracle. He always listened to the recordings of Dovraku's sermons and did his part to smuggle them safely to other ears, to keep Tasari's thugs from discovering them. But he was just following where others led, passing on what others made and sent forth. He believed in the cause, but he led an ordinary life.

All that had changed now, though. First he had come face-to-face with the godkiller Kirk himself. He was proud of how he'd reacted, unhesitatingly striking out at the devil while others cowered in fear, or let themselves be swayed by his words. He hadn't been able to strike the godkiller down, of course; that was not a task for a lowly one such as he. But he had given Kirk notice that his lies would be fought at every step, that the true believers would face him without fear.

And now, he knelt before the Great One himself, tasted the presence of the man who would save the People from their betrayers. He had never expected this when he'd gone to see his neighbor Moredi. He'd known the man was involved in the resistance, had expected simply to pass his news along and content himself with the thanks of a noble fighter for the cause. But he'd had no clue that Moredi was close to Dovraku himself, and he had been amazed when his neighbor had come to tell him that the prophet wished to hear his tale. It had been terrifying, in its way. He was just a youth, not ready for such responsibility. But of course he couldn't deny the summons of the Great One. And he'd reminded himself of the unexpected bravery he'd found when facing Kirk, and that heartened him.

Still, it was overwhelming to be in Dovraku's presence, to behold the future of the People made flesh. He was not what Tavero had expected. He was tall, but not particularly impressive to look at—a long sullen face, rough features, middling brown hair. He dressed in simple, dark gray robes that made him hard to discern from the shadows of this warehouse. His voice was quiet, his manner subdued and cool. But there was something compelling that burned within his pale blue eyes.

"Very well, young man," he said in a soft, modulated baritone. "Tell me what you told Moredi."

"I—that is, Great Dovraku, I . . ."

"Do not concern yourself with ceremony. We are all soldiers in the Oracle's cause, cogs in the divine machine. Speak freely to me, so we may function together as part of a greater whole."

Dovraku's words filled Tavero with pride. To be a part of the battle, declared a brother by Dovraku himself! "Sir, I was in Rishala's temple yesterday—only at my parents' insistence!"

"Go on," the prophet said, his tone never wavering.

Tavero did as he asked, telling of the encounter with Kirk. He took care not to gloss over his humiliating defeat as he had with his friends; Dovraku could no doubt divine a lie. Still, he hurried past that part to get to the point: ". . . and Rishala *welcomed* him into the temple! Once I left, I watched the entrance from nearby. Kirk remained within, in conference with Rishala, for thousands of heartbeats! She claims to be holy, but she is in league with them, my lord! She disrespects the Oracle, welcomes His killer into a sacred place . . . she plots against us, I know it! She must be killed!"

"Calm, young man," the Great One said. "All things in their time. Rishala's . . . ambivalence . . . is known to me. But for the moment, her public stance serves our cause. She will be given the chance to decide once and for all where she stands. She will learn there is only the One and the Zero, nothing in between. And if she is not One with us, then, when the time comes, she will be reduced to Zero."

Tavero was glad to hear that, but disappointed that his news had apparently contributed nothing. Yet the Great One sensed this and took a step closer. "But you, I can see, are One. Gratifying, to see such commitment in a youth your age."

"Thank you, Lord. The others my age . . . they are shallow and selfish. They like the new way because it indulges their lusts, lets them choose whatever mates they crave, and hop between each other's beds."

"And you?" Dovraku asked.

Tavero flushed, but could not deny the Great One's request to know. "I . . . am not one that any of the girls would pick, when they are free to choose."

"I see. Such an unfair system, wouldn't you say? This 'freedom'—it makes things better for those who can take what they want, and worse for all the rest. It is chaotic, unbalanced." He circled Tavero slowly as he spoke. "Under the Oracle, your rightful mate would be chosen for you when the time came."

"Yes, my Lord."

"When He is reborn, the woman for you will not be claimed by another. If another has already claimed her, he will be struck down as a blasphemer, and she will be given back to you."

"Yes," Tavero said eagerly. Oh, Semila! Such a delight it would be, to see that smug Madasi feel the Oracle's wrath burning a hole through his skull for his sin in touching her. The bitch would have to be punished too, of course, but maybe the Oracle would let Tavero handle that himself. Or maybe Ribasi would turn out to be his chosen one—though there was no telling which of her boyfriends would pay the price when the time came. Maybe all of them.

"Of course," Dovraku went on, breaking his train of thought, "if you were to serve some . . . special role in the Oracle's rebirth, He would no doubt reward you. Perhaps He would move up the time when your mate were to be chosen for you."

Or maybe He might grant me more than one? "The Oracle is wise and generous," Tavero panted.

"Yes."

"Just tell me what I may do, my lord, to serve you and the glory of the Oracle!"

Dovraku's face stayed dispassionate . . . but his eyes seemed to smile.

CHAPTER TEN

The humans have a saying: "No matter where you go, there you are." Yet they often fail to grasp its meaning—that your own presence is the one constant in every experience you have. All exploration is part of the process of personal growth. We quest outward in hopes of discovering what is inside us. If this goal is not understood, then the quest becomes mere stumbling in the dark.

—Kham'lia of Delta IV, doctoral thesis

UHURA LOOKED AROUND the rec deck, wishing Will Decker could be here to see the culmination of his dream. Here more than anywhere else was where it was realized. On duty, the mingling of different species was determined by duty assignments, but here, it was strictly optional. And the species were mingling. Oh, a few still tended to favor the company of their conspecifics—the Vulcans, the Zaranites—but for the most part the crew members had grown comfortable with each other over the past weeks, developing a sense of being a single crew, a single community.

She turned to Reiko Onami and Spring Rain, who stood next to her. "It's a beautiful sight, isn't it? IDIC in action."

Onami smirked. "I've seen more species in one place on any given market day on Nelgha. They usually weren't getting along so well, though."

"Megara's markets offer wares," Spring Rain sang,

"Of many colors, shapes and tones;
Yet all their rich variety
Is emphasized by contrast with
The sameness of the vendors' hands,
And all their selling songs are sung
Upon familiar themes."

Sulu and Chekov came into view, and smiled in greeting. "Nyota!" Chekov said. "Come join us. We're still trying to find a sport where Uuvu'it can beat Sulu."

Uhura chuckled. "I'd love to, but the ladies here and I have an appointment with the hot tub. Spring Rain's been dying for something to soak in. And I'm just eager for an excuse to get out of this uniform."

"Again with the uniforms," Chekov kvetched. "I *like* these uniforms."

"But they're just so bland."

"No, they're not. The old ones were just so garish. I mean, really, whose brilliant idea was it to put security personnel in bright red shirts?"

"You have a point," Uhura said, "but I miss my miniculottes. Who would've expected the Starfleet quartermaster to come up with something so fashionable? Besides, they were comfortable."

Onami scoffed. "Maybe for someone with legs like yours."

Uhura smiled. "Come on—Spring Rain isn't getting any wetter. Later, Pavel."

He nodded. "Be seeing you."

The three females made their way over to the starboard

side of the rec deck and into the locker room. Uhura eschewed the clothing transporter in the sonic-shower stall, going about it the old-fashioned way. "I thought you couldn't wait to get undressed," Onami said.

"Not that way. Those things are a gimmick. More trouble than they're worth." Beaming clothes directly onto or off a person was a delicate operation. There were extensive safeguards in place to prevent accidentally, say, beaming fabric in underneath someone's flesh or beaming away a favorite body part, but that meant the operation frequently had to be aborted and restarted if the subject moved. Also, the units were designed to replicate a garment perfectly tailored to the wearer, but the designers had overlooked the fact that the humanoid body changes its proportions from hour to hour with the vagaries of ingestion, gravity, and so forth. What was comfortable at 0700 could pinch unbearably by 1500. Something that fit a little less perfectly tended to work better. Bottom line, Uhura just didn't like depending on a machine to dress her. The things must have been designed by men, or Vulcans, or someone to whom dressing was more a chore than an art.

"Yeah, everybody seems to think so," Onami said, passing up the booths herself. "They must have seemed great to the engineers, but they're too unreliable. I guess that's what shakedowns are for—finding out what doesn't work."

"Besides," Uhura added as she slid the uniform down off her legs, "I don't trust it with this."

Onami studied the scintillating, filigreed garter that adorned the communications officer's right thigh. "Is that Deltan?"

"Mm-hmm," Uhura replied, gingerly sliding it off. "It was a gift from Lieutenant Ilia. I wouldn't want anything to happen to it."

Spring Rain had also eschewed the clothing transporter, since it wasn't programmed to cope with her special drysuit.

As the Megarite peeled off the close-fitting garment, Onami stepped out of the booth and gave her pachydermatous hide a clinical once-over, making sure the drysuit was proving effective at keeping it moist. (Uhura was getting used to being asked, "Why is it called a drysuit if it keeps her wet?" and answering, "Why is it called a wetsuit if it keeps you dry?") Uhura took a curious glance herself, noting that Spring Rain had no mammaries—not surprising for a species with baleen filters instead of mouths—but was otherwise recognizably female.

Uhura helped Spring Rain make sure her voder was secure around her neck and said, "Come on, let's get you into the tub before you dry out. You should know," she added with a mischievous grin, "that I arranged for some special modifications."

They moved through the door into the hot-tub room, and Spring Rain's eyes widened, a lively chorus erupting from her forehead vents. *"Mud, mud, glorious mud!"* she sang with gay abandon. *"I wish to squish! Come, follow, let's wallow!"*

"I tried to get as close to Megaran conditions as I could with the materials on hand," Uhura said as Spring Rain climbed in and let herself sink, making incoherent choruses of glee. "I hope it meets with your approval."

"It oozes and squeezes and squelches and pleases!"

"Glad to hear it!"

Uhura followed Spring Rain readily into the tub, with Onami testing it more gingerly before sighing and sliding cautiously into the cool mud bath. "This'll be good for my skin, right?"

"Should be. Maybe a little rough, but no more than an Argelian exfoliant. Not as good as for hers, though."

Onami settled in a bit nervously, but soon she nodded in approval and allowed herself to relax. Uhura thought it suited her delicate, rounded features far better than her

usual tense, aggressive manner. But if she said so, she knew
she'd get an earful.

But after a moment, Onami's brows drew together again.
"I didn't know you knew Ilia that well," she said.

"I didn't—not really. She wasn't one of my recruits.
And she was only on board for a day before . . . she was
taken. But she left her mark. We spent some time together
off-shift—she wanted to listen to my jazz collection, and
there was a lot of girl talk. . . . I wouldn't have expected it.
Deltans seem so cool and rarefied at first glance, but
they're really very warm and generous. Ilia was easy to
talk to."

"Not if you were a man," Onami smirked.

"Hmm, maybe." Uhura chuckled as she remembered
Sulu turning into an awkward schoolboy when Decker told
him to "take Lieutenant Ilia in hand." The Deltan had
quickly reassured him that she would never "take advantage
of a sexually immature species"—which ended up embarrassing Sulu more than it comforted him. Not that Ilia had
meant any insult by it. Deltans did look on human sexuality
with a certain amusement, but it was affectionate, the way
adults would laugh at the sight of toddlers trying to walk—
not with contempt, but with eagerness to see them succeed
at reaching a higher level.

"Still, you're right," Onami said, while Spring Rain continued to wallow luxuriantly, making sure every bit of her
body was covered in mud and emitting happy burbling
noises. "I knew Ilia a bit, while she was studying on Earth."

"Before she went to the Academy?"

"Yeah, it was at Nehru University. Her father was there,
teaching and working on his, I dunno, whatever his thesis
was about the parallels between Earth and ancient Deltan
history."

"I remember reading that," Uhura said. "He believed
exploring outer space was just a phase a young civilization

went through before it turned its attention to more inward exploration, the mind and spirit."

Spring Rain made a rude noise.

> *"Scholars in their towers see*
> *Their towers as the universe.*
> *What good is the mirror if*
> *The mirror's all that it reflects?"*

"Ilia might've agreed with you," Onami said. "She thought exploring space was romantic, in a noble-savage kind of way. She loved to talk about this Starfleet officer she'd met back on Delta, how exciting he was in a primal way Deltan men weren't. I tell you, when I met Will Decker and realized he was the man Ilia had talked to me about, it was hard to keep from either blushing or laughing out loud every time I saw him!"

"Her girl talk did get rather . . . graphic, didn't it?" Uhura laughed.

"Hell, I couldn't follow half of it!" She sobered. "When she said she was going to join Starfleet, I told her it was just a schoolgirl crush, that she'd be risking her life for the wrong reasons. I tried to get her to go into psych like me— she would've been a great therapist, with that empathic ability. And I told her that there was almost no chance she'd ever serve with that handsome officer." She pursed her lips thoughtfully. "But it was Decker who made me see what being in Starfleet was about, what Ilia saw in it. And the two of them . . . I guess they ended up together after all." Shrugging, she finished, "I guess the moral is, never listen to me."

"That's an interesting attitude for a psychologist."

Spring Rain lifted her head out of the mud to ask, *"Was it a fight for her to swim / Against the tide of prejudice?"*

"Mmm, not really," Onami replied. "Deltans are very

open-minded about embracing new experiences. They may have seen what Ilia did as quaint and nostalgic, but they didn't object to her trying it."

Uhura nodded. "Deltans embrace *everything* to the fullest," she told Spring Rain. "Right after V'Ger, I went to Delta for her family's memorial service. It was very intense. The grief they expressed was overwhelming to me, but still, in a way, they were celebrating the opportunity to experience it, as an expression of their love for Ilia. And at the same time they rejoiced at the new adventure she'd begun, the chance to discover whole new realms of experience." She pondered for a moment. "I don't think the fact that she's still alive in some form really changed the nature of the services all that much. Deltans believe that before and after life, they exist as pure love pervading all things. They see that as something to be celebrated, too."

> *"A gift, to have such ties to home*
> *Though home is far away in mind*
> *As well as space. I envy her."*

Spring Rain constructed a tone-poem image of her experiences on Megara. Uhura tried to follow her original multitonal song as much as possible, but still needed the translation to fill in some details. It began with a satirical picture of the spoiled female upper class, content to languish in their ancestral shoreline estates while the subordinate males were made to do all the work and traveling. Uhura understood that there was a biological basis for this; Megarite females had always needed to guard the eggs they laid on the beach, relying on their male harems to bring them food. But Spring Rain sang of how this natural mating-season behavior had been corrupted into a constant practice, and how it trapped the very people who perpetuated it. It had given the Megarite culture a narrow, insular vision, looking down on travel and initiative and discovery as lower-class things. She sang in dirgelike tones about the hollow, preprogrammed life her clan had laid out for her, a life limned by the borders of her ancestral cove, a life that meant never seeing other sights or tasting other waters, only singing variations of the same "respectable" songs. She'd always taken far more pleasure in the males' raucous, iconoclastic improvisations, their equivalent to spirituals and blues and jazz. And the otherworldly music she heard when alien traders and diplomats came fired her curiosity. And so she'd "lowered herself" to join the males who were chosen to represent Megara's interests offworld, leaving home to join Starfleet, while her mother and sisters cursed her for betraying her obligation to perpetuate the clan, to bear more daughters to carry forth tradition.

"*A cursed, perverted, sexless thing / Was I, within their singing-worlds,*" she finished. She was breathless, her deepset eyes tearing with what Uhura assumed was sorrow.

"Oh, Rain," Uhura said, stroking her shoulder. "I'm so sorry."

> "*No—worlds as small as those are not*
> *A place that can contain me now.*
> *But maybe . . . they can grow one day*
> *And take me back, along . . . with the*
> *New worlds I'll chart—*"

The chorus from the breathing vents on her forehead grew increasingly wheezy and uneven as she sang. Now she broke off completely, clutching her chest and gasping for breath. Onami pulled herself through the mud to the young specialist's side. "She can't breathe! Call sickbay!"

Uhura climbed out as fast as the suction of the mud would allow, and ran to the intercom, not caring how much mud she tracked across the room. Once she'd summoned aid, she helped Onami lift Spring Rain out of the tub and lay her carefully on a nearby massage table. Onami had her get some towels to wipe the mud off Spring Rain, so that she could examine the Megarite for signs of injury. Uhura also got robes for the two of them, but Onami barely noticed as she draped one around the psychologist's shoulders.

When McCoy arrived with the medical team, he took in the scene with wide-eyed disbelief, but then caught sight of the patient and was all business. "What happened?"

"I don't know, she just started to have trouble breathing!"

"How sudden?"

"I think . . . thirty seconds, a minute."

McCoy reached for where a human's mouth would be, and looked stymied by the baleen lips Spring Rain had in its place. After a moment of uncertainty, he grabbed his tricorder and started scanning. Spring Rain's struggles were subsiding as she lapsed into unconsciousness. "For God's sake, do something!" Onami cried.

"Can't intubate. . . . Tri-ox!" he snapped at the medic. In moments he had a hypo in his hand. "I just hope this can penetrate that thick hide."

"You don't *know?*"

"It's my first Megarite! I'm doing what I can, *Doctor* Onami!" He scanned her again. "She's stabilizing . . . but not by much. We've got to get her on the exam table. You two," he said to the women, "shower that mud off before you track it into my sickbay!"

Uhura went through the sonic shower and dressed as quickly as she could. She almost let it beam a uniform onto her, but was afraid the unreliable system would slow her further. Once she got to sickbay, Spring Rain was on the exam table, motionless but showing life signs. The wall screen above the table showed a full-length tomographic scan of her body, peeling it back layer by layer. McCoy was alternately peering at it and the patient, frowning fiercely. "Respiratory edema . . . antibody count through the roof . . . heart racing . . . it looks like anaphylactic shock. Let's try 10 cc's epi," he said to the nurse. "Hopefully it's close enough to what her body uses."

"You're just guessing!" Onami said. "Where's Dr. Chapel?"

"She's still on Lorina. You and Miss Rain here are stuck with me, so I recommend you stay the hell out of my way!" Onami subsided, still glaring at him sharply, and McCoy administered the epinephrine. "All right," he said after a moment. "She's starting to breathe again, barely . . . but *something*'s still poisoning her systems, and I can't get rid of it until I figure out what it is. I've never seen a biochemistry like this . . . how can I tell what's out of place?"

Onami was seething now. "I'll tell you how. You call the person who's actually *qualified* to practice medicine on this crew." She strode over to the comm panel. "Sickbay to the bridge. Get me Dr. Chapel, now!"

Despite Onami's urgency, it took a minute before Gerry Auberson at communications could track Chapel down. Once contact was made, McCoy explained the situation tersely. "It sounds like she aspirated something in that mud," Chapel concluded.

"It was sterile," Uhura insisted. "And I got it as close to Megaran conditions as I could."

"It wasn't actually Megaran in origin?"

"No, I used soil from the arboretum. That's from Earth, basically. But she's been in the arboretum with no ill effects."

"Then there had to be some other factor involved. Something you introduced on your own bodies, perhaps, that reacted unexpectedly with something in the soil or water. Were either of you, say, wearing any unusual perfume?" Uhura shook her head, and Onami followed suit. "How about . . . some sort of painted jewelry?"

"Just metal earrings and a Deltan garter," Uhura said.

Chapel reacted to that. "Deltan? Was it Ilia's?"

"Yes, she gave it to me."

"And she'd worn it?"

"I assume so."

"Oh, then it would've been covered in Deltan pheromones. Leonard, that could be it. Deltan pheromones are aldehyde-based—certain aldehyde compounds are toxic to Megarites. A Terran enzyme in the mud could've lysed those pheromones, turned them into one of those compounds."

After that, things sank into medical jargon for a time, and Uhura could only watch tensely. But the data seemed to confirm Chapel's hypothesis. Once the toxin was identified, the display showed it spreading through Spring Rain's respiratory and circulatory systems, damaging tissues in its wake. And once the doctors knew what the enemy was, they could choose a drug to counteract it.

In minutes, Spring Rain was stabilized, but McCoy didn't look happy. "There's extensive lung damage, and her brain was deprived of oxygen for some time. I've administered minocycline to fight ischemic brain injury, but at this point there's no telling how much damage there might be, or when she'll wake up. There's nothing more we can do except let her rest and trust in her own healing ability."

Uhura clasped his arm. "Thank you, Doctor."

"No," Onami said angrily. "Doctor Chapel deserves the thanks here. And if she'd been here in the first place, Spring Rain wouldn't be in a coma, maybe brain-damaged because her physician didn't know enough about her anatomy to identify the problem! What right do you have to be chief medical officer of this ship when you're clearly not qualified to treat its crew? For that matter, why wasn't Christine here in the first place? This should've been her shift!"

Uhura would've expected McCoy to match Onami's

anger with his own, but instead he looked shaken, distraught. "She's . . . been filling in for me on Lorina the past couple of days. . . . I asked her to go in my place . . . because I . . ." He trailed off.

"No, Leonard," Chapel said over the comm. "This wasn't your fault. You couldn't have known."

McCoy winced and rubbed the bridge of his nose tiredly. "Isn't that exactly the problem—what I don't know?" Uhura was struck by the desolation in his eyes.

Once Chapel returned to the ship to take over Spring Rain's treatment, McCoy retired to his quarters. At first he headed straight for the liquor cabinet, but then stopped, deciding he'd been relying too much on that remedy lately. He knew he didn't have the genes for alcoholism, so that wasn't a concern. But dependence could be psychological as well, and retreating from one's problems could only work for so long.

So maybe it's time to face the problem, he thought. *Maybe it's time to solve it. And maybe the problem is me.*

Reversing course, he went to the computer terminal and sat down. "Computer, record text message."

"Ready," said the computer voice, which the designers had made more human-sounding this time around. It was easier on the ears, but McCoy wasn't sure he liked the change. The old voice had been given a mechanical monotone deliberately, to make it easier to distinguish from a human voice. McCoy had approved of that. The more people started humanizing their machines, the closer they came to mechanizing humanity, to forgetting what it was that made living beings superior.

Right. Things like screwing up and being cowards and useless old fools. Don't change the subject. He cleared his throat. "I, Leonard H. McCoy, hereby resign my commission. . . . No. Computer, erase. Resume. Ahh, owing to

recent circumstances, I, Leonard H. McCoy, feel it would
be inappropriate for me to continue. . . . Ahh, the hell with
that, I sound like Spock. Computer—"

Just then the door signal chimed. With a sigh, McCoy got
up and headed into the other room to answer the door.
*Wouldn't it be ironic if it was Spock? Speak of the pointy-
eared devil and he will appear. Nah, what are the odds?*

He opened the door, and there stood Spock. McCoy let
out a faint chuckle, leading the Vulcan to react with puzzlement. "Something amuses you, Doctor?"

"Nothing much, really. Sorry, Spock, come in. What can
I do for you?"

Spock appeared underwhelmed by his level of enthusiasm, but came in and said, "I presume you are aware of my
research into Yonadan history."

"Yeah, Jim mentioned it. How's it going?" he asked
without much interest.

"There have been . . . obstacles, but Mr. Lindstrom and I
have made some progress."

"Really."

"Yes." Spock took it as a request for elaboration. Maybe
he hadn't gained that much emotional insight after all—
or maybe he was just caught up in the work. McCoy
doubted that even emotions would change Spock's single-
mindedness about solving problems. "I have improved the
algorithms for the quantum reconstruction of the Fabrini
intelligence files, though the results are still fragmentary.
However, somewhat to my surprise, Mr. Lindstrom's research into Yonadan oral histories has revealed some intrigu-
ing anomalies."

McCoy threw him a look. "You're taking oral histories
seriously?"

"Not in themselves, but when checked against other data
their contents are telling. For instance: Mr. Lindstrom has
assembled a list of all the Yonadan high priestesses, purport-

edly dating back to the original person to bear the title. Such rote lists are a part of many oral and traditional histories, and due to their specific content and the emphasis on repetition, it can be assumed that they are less prone to inaccurate retelling than other oral accounts might be."

"Yeah, I remember Sunday school and all those lists of 'begats.' So what about them?"

"The versions of the list which Lindstrom has compiled have a few inconsistencies, but they agree on the total number of priestesses to within six percent, and they all agree on the identity of the first, a woman known as Ganela."

"So what's the anomaly?" McCoy settled himself down on the bed, not wanting to lead Spock into the other room where his abortive resignation letter still showed on the screen. Normally by this point he might have been asking what any of this had to do with him. But right now he welcomed the distraction, and knew he could count on Spock to make it a lengthy one.

"We are able to date the terms of certain priestesses by reference in the accounts to historical events whose dates are known, the earliest being a meteoroid collision which occurred some four thousand three hundred years ago. However, the number of priestesses dating from before that incident is not sufficient to account for the approximately five thousand nine hundred years preceding it in Yonada's journey. Depending on the assumptions we make about the life expectancy and terms of service of the priestesses, the original priestess Ganela could not have lived more than seven thousand five hundred years ago. Six thousand would be a more probable estimate."

McCoy shrugged. "Maybe some names got left off for some reason. Somewhere along the line, somebody didn't like their predecessors and purged a few names."

"That is a possibility, and that is what we need to determine. Have the historical accounts been altered, and if so, for what purpose? But there is other evidence that we can correlate with this."

"Such as," he prompted, leaning back and closing his eyes.

"One of the origin myths Lindstrom has collected states that the Oracle arose to save the People from a disaster brought on by the evil, godless regime which preceded it. It states that the People were wicked and profligate, carelessly squandering their resources and fouling the land, making it barren where before it had been lush. The Oracle and its disciples emerged, overthrew the previous order, and created the Instruments of Obedience to keep the people's baser urges in line as a necessary measure to prevent their annihilation."

"Sounds like a typical enough sermon to me. 'And God saw that the wickedness of man was great in the Earth.' "

"Yes, but it contradicts other accounts of the creation of the World, which tend to be more consistent with what we know about the destruction of Fabrina and the building of Yonada. The traditions pertaining to the Creators and those pertaining to the Oracle do not entirely agree."

"Hm." McCoy tried to think of a comeback, but nothing came to mind. He was content to let Spock's lecture lull him to sleep.

"And when I heard this tale of environmental collapse, it reminded me of an observation made by Ms. Spring Rain on Still Water two weeks ago." McCoy was jarred out of his relaxed state. Why did Spock have to mention her? "She remarked that Yonada's inner surface appeared as though it had once had more water, and presumably more life. Our prevailing assumption has been that it was deliberately designed that way to emulate the appearance of Fabrina. But some researchers have postulated that Yonada was actually created with a more fertile biosphere, which deteriorated over the millennia. Their theories interpret certain geological features of Yonada's surface as evidence of an ecological collapse . . . which they have conjecturally dated to five thousand six hundred years ago."

McCoy hadn't quite heard all of that, since the name "Spring Rain" had been resonating in his mind. But he struggled to make sense of it. "So what are you saying? That the Oracle wasn't originally there? That it was only built six thousand years ago to . . . to punish the people for wrecking their world?"

"Or to enforce the strict regulations, population controls, and austerity measures necessary to prevent the total collapse of the Yonadan biosphere. However, it is only speculation at this point—an inference from hearsay several hundred times removed from the actual events. We need more tangible evidence to determine its validity. That is why I have come to you."

McCoy raised his brows. "Why me?"

"You have spent more time among the Lorini than anyone else on this ship. You are familiar with the Fabrini language and the mindset of the People. I am hopeful that you might be able to offer useful insights into the texts and oral accounts, or to suggest where to look for further evidence. Perhaps you have heard reference to ancient artifacts or texts passed down as heirlooms. At the very least you may be able to clarify certain translation issues."

"I dunno, Spock," McCoy said, frowning. "I never was that great with the language. And I can't think of anything that was ever mentioned to me about artifacts."

"I would not expect you to have the information at your fingertips, Doctor. Certainly not at the end of what I know has been a difficult day for you." He paused, as though offering the doctor a chance to talk about the incident. McCoy was struck by that, but he didn't feel particularly forthcoming. After a moment, Spock went on. "I meant merely to request that you accompany me to Yonada tomorrow to review the data. And perhaps after you have 'slept on it,' as I have often heard you say, you may recall something further."

Spock looked at him with what seemed like eager anticipation, and McCoy found he didn't like the thought of letting him down. He sighed and said, "Look . . . Spock . . . I appreciate you coming to me for help and all, but I . . . I just don't think I'm much good to anyone these days."

"Mmm." The Vulcan took a moment to absorb this. "After today's events, it is unsurprising that you would have such a perception of yourself. However, I have observed that the reaction tends to pass in time."

"It's not just today, Spock. I . . . I'm out of my depth. I was happily retired, settled into a comfortable rut, and then a month ago I got dragged back here without so much as a by-your-leave. And I've been feelin' out of place ever since. You remember—hell, of course you do—how I always said I was just an old country doctor?"

"Indeed," Spock said wryly.

"Well, now I really feel like one. I feel like life's passed me by, like I got caught in a time warp and woke up in a future I'm struggling to understand. One I didn't choose to come to." He turned away. "One I'm not sure I want to be in anymore."

There was a pause before Spock replied. "Given that access to the Guardian of Forever is heavily interdicted, I assume you're speaking metaphorically about a wish to resign from Starfleet."

McCoy glanced over his shoulder, but Spock was deadpan as ever—actually more deadpan than he usually was these days, which was a pretty sure sign he was kidding. "*Re*-resign, Mr. Spock. In my heart I'm still a civilian."

Spock's manner grew more grave. "That would be . . . unfortunate, Doctor," he said hesitantly. "I had been . . . counting on your assistance."

"Well, you don't have to make it sound like pullin' teeth. And it's not like I could leave until we get back to a starbase. I could still come over and take a look at your relics and such . . . though I doubt it'd do you a lot of good. There're plenty of people who've spent more time studying 'em than I ever did."

Spock fidgeted. Yes—he actually *fidgeted*. "That . . . was not the assistance I was referring to."

McCoy studied him quizzically, then rose from the bed and opened the partition to the next room. "C'mon in, have a seat."

"I am content to stand."

"Maybe, but this is startin' to sound like a conversation we should have at eye level, and I'd rather sit."

"Very well." He followed McCoy in, and his eyes happened to wander across the console screen. " 'Ahh, the hell with that, I sound like Spock'?"

"Never mind that, just siddown."

Once seated, Spock placed his elbows on the table and steepled his fingers. "I have been having . . . more difficulty coping with my emotions than I have let on."

He paused, as though expecting McCoy to gloat. It was tempting, but McCoy knew it wouldn't be appropriate, not when Spock was leaving himself open like this. "Well, it's only to be expected," he ventured. "You've been denying your human half your whole life . . . it's bound to take some time to get the hang of it."

"It is not my human half I am concerned with." He lifted a brow. "It has always been a convenient fiction, to blame my failures of control on my human blood, but it is profoundly illogical. Vulcan control is learned, not hereditary. Indeed, the very reason we embraced logic was that our innate emotions are dangerously intense. Pre-Reformation Vulcan's history makes Earth's history look placid by comparison.

"Other Vulcans before me have tried to embrace their emotions. The result has often been violent behavior— armed insurrection, homicide, telepathic or physical rape. Sometimes they become obsessed with irrational ideas, fanatical beliefs—" He broke off and turned inward for a moment. It looked as though he'd touched on something very private that he wasn't ready to speak of further.

"I had hoped the same would not be true with me," he went on. "Unlike those others, I have not renounced Surak's teachings. I simply believe that, when Surak said we must govern our passions lest they be our undoing, he did not intend for us to deny them completely—simply to manage them, to balance them with logic." He met McCoy's eyes more directly. "Much as you and I have always balanced each other as Jim's advisors. Or as V'Ger's logic is now balanced by Decker's intuition and Ilia's passion.

"Yet despite my best efforts, I am finding that balance elusive." His tone grew more grim, even embarrassed. "I am prone to inappropriate bursts of emotion, particularly anger, which threaten to overwhelm me. I have felt . . . a desire to inflict physical harm on those who have angered me."

McCoy studied him. "Like who? What did they do to make you angry?"

Spock told him of his confrontations with T'Hesh and Soreth, and how they had reawakened the frustrations felt by a helpless child. "Now that's perfectly understandable," McCoy said. "They were both deliberately trying to get your goat. Bullying you, just like those kids who taunted you when you were growing up. That kind of pain—you can suppress or control it all you want, but you never forget it. Hell, all the years you've been lettin' it fester inside, it's no wonder it's such a sore spot."

"You may be right," Spock said. "But what if Soreth is right as well? He was not taunting me merely out of spite, but in order to make a point. And my reaction may have proven his point. What if Vulcan emotion is too volatile to set free?" His frown deepened. "Other Vulcans have tried to master it and failed. Why should I be any more successful?"

"Sounds to me like you let Commissioner Sorehead get under your skin," McCoy observed. "Just ask yourself, why should you care what he thinks?"

"It is not just him. Every Vulcan I've encountered since the meld has treated me the same way."

"Just more schoolyard bullies. They're just afraid you'll prove 'em wrong."

"Or they are concerned that I may lose control. As am I, Doctor."

"So what's the alternative?" McCoy asked. "Go back to the way you were?"

Spock shook his head, but without great conviction. "I don't see how I could, after what I saw in V'Ger's mind. But neither can I see how to move forward safely. How do I release these emotions without losing myself to them? Without jeopardizing others?" The *need* in his eyes was startling. "For years, Doctor, you told me how much better my life would be if I allowed myself to feel. You lectured me on how essential emotion was to mental health. Very well—now I am ready to believe you. But you need to explain to me how it *works*. How do you manage to give your emotions rein yet remain functional? How do you keep them from driving you to harm the ones around you?"

McCoy was dumbstruck by what Spock was asking of him. To discover that Spock had such confidence in him—it was truly moving, yet at the same time it forced him to realize how misplaced that confidence was. "Aw, Spock . . . of all the times to start listenin' to me . . ."

"Doctor?"

McCoy stood and turned away. "I hate to tell you this, Spock, but you've called my bluff. I'm the last person who can tell you how to lead a balanced emotional life. I'm the kind who wallows in emotion, lets it run away with me and make me say and do stupid things. Maybe . . . maybe I indulged my emotions a little too much sometimes, made a point of it just to counteract that confounded logic of yours. Maybe . . ." He gingerly met Spock's gaze again. "Maybe I figured I could get away with it because you were there to be logical for me.

"Anyway, the last thing I can tell you is how to keep emotions from hurting people. That seems to be all I'm doing lately. I've got all these different feelings that I don't have a clue what to do with, and I just keep hurting people as a result."

Spock looked at him with puzzlement and a sympathy that burned. "I fail to see how you can blame your emotional state for the incident with Ms. Spring Rain."

"Chapel should've been the one on duty, Spock. I just sent her to Lorina in my place because I was afraid I might have to face Natira again. Because I was a fool for hurting her, and a coward for hiding from the consequences." He sighed. "So don't look to me for a role model, Spock, if you know what's good for you. In fact, I'd give a lot for some of that logical clarity of yours right about now."

Spock lifted a brow, folded his hands before him on the table, and met McCoy's eyes attentively. "If you wish to delineate the problem, I will attempt to suggest a logical approach."

McCoy gave a mocking laugh, but then realized Spock was serious. "Hell . . . why not?" He sat down and tried to explain the situation with Natira as best he could, though it was a struggle to sort through all the conflicting feelings.

"I just don't know what to do now. Maybe I didn't love her before, but now I might be willing to give it another try. But I don't know if she could forgive me for letting her down. My God, Spock, we were *married!* And I threw it away, just like that. How can I have a future with her after that?"

Spock pondered for a moment. "Is that what you would wish to do, if you chose to leave Starfleet?"

"I don't know, Spock. If it could work, it would beat bein' a lonely old hermit up in the mountains. Maybe I could do more good there, too. I could help more people than I could as a hermit . . . and they'd be people whose anatomy I actually understand. But Natira . . . I just can't see how we could ever go back to the way things were. So much has changed, for both of us."

Spock spoke slowly. "In science, if the initial conditions of an experiment have changed to a great enough degree, the original data can cease to be relevant. In which case, the logical response is to restart the experiment from the beginning, and keep the new data separate from the original results. In short, to wipe the slate clean.

"So perhaps, if you and Natira could set aside the past and simply . . . start again, it would be easier for you to determine your prospects for a relationship in the present or future." He tilted his head in what for him was a shrug. "Though I cannot say whether the analogy is at all applicable in this case."

"No . . . no, it's a good thought," McCoy said, turning it over in his mind. "At least . . . well, it's worth thinking about. If nothing else, it's . . . a comforting idea." He smiled. "I wouldn't have known you had it in you, Spock. I'm just sorry I couldn't be more help to you."

"You may have other opportunities," Spock suggested, "if you remain in Starfleet."

"Well—who knows? I may have somewhere else to go after all," he said, not truly believing it, but willing to hope.

"Perhaps." Spock rose to leave, but then halted. "One more factor to consider, though—you said that your original relationship with Natira failed because, for you, it was merely solace and escape from an unpleasant situation."

"I think that's a mild way of putting it, but yes."

"In that case . . . would it not be unwise to let your guilt over your performance on the *Enterprise* be a factor in deciding whether to stay with her again?" The words bore his usual formality, but his voice was gentle, his eyes absolving. McCoy could only look at him for a long moment.

"Good night, Dr. McCoy," Spock said with a nod. "I shall contact you tomorrow about scheduling our visit to Yonada."

"G'night, Spock. And . . . thanks."

CHAPTER ELEVEN

*History is written by the victors, true. But another
history is whispered by the losers: a quiet, moving
target, keeping to the shadows, biding its time
until it can rise up into a shout.*

— Alexander M. Brack, 2073

TAVERO STROVE to cast out fear as he approached the
Fedraysha school. *"There is no fear,"* Dovraku had told him.
*"There is no doubt. There is only the One and the Zero.
Either you succeed or you fail. Simply choose not to fail me."*

There was nothing Tavero wanted less than to fail
Dovraku. He tried to see what he was about to do with the
pure clarity Dovraku had shown him. To his shame, doubts
still lingered, though he kept the prophet's counsel in
mind. It wasn't so much that he feared dying. Dovraku had
spoken to him of mighty V'Ger, and how He had the power
to scan those He deemed worthy and absorb their digital
essence into His being. Naturally the Oracle would do the
same for His martyrs, for their courage earned them life
everlasting in His realm of mathematical perfection. At
first Tavero had been puzzled, for what Dovraku asked
seemed to negate his earlier promise to provide him with
his perfect mate, or mates if he were worthy enough. But of

course he had been a fool to think so, lacking the clarity of Dovraku's thought. *"Naturally your ideal mate will be chosen from among the martyrs who have gone before you,"* the Great One had told him. *"For who else could be worthy of you, after all?"* Tavero had seen pictures of some of the martyr women. They were heroes of the People, of course, and most boys found them quite glamorous and exciting. And many were beautiful, too. It thrilled Tavero that he would have his pick of such desirable women while the others had to settle for immature sluts like Ribasi and Semila.

The doubts he had more trouble casting aside were those about the target Dovraku had sent him to destroy—or rather, the timing of the attack. Certainly the Fedraysha schools were founts of blasphemous filth, tools of the oppressor, and needed to be smashed by the fury of the People. Tavero was happy to cleanse Lorina of this one; what hurt was having to do it while people were inside, especially children. *"I know it is a grave burden to bear,"* the Great One had told him. *"These are the hard choices we must make if we wish to cleanse the World of its alien poisons. But remember that they are already lost, their souls corrupted by Fedraysha lies. It is written that those of the People who sin or speak evil will be punished. Not out of cruelty, but out of need, to purge the People of evil before it can spread. They who stray from the Oracle's will in life redeem themselves in their sacrifice to the good of the People. And you, Tavero, are to be the means of their redemption. You are an Instrument of Obedience, the hand of the Oracle. Let Him do His will through you, young man, strong man, and you need feel no guilt."*

Yes. Yes, he felt it now. He was simply the tool of the Oracle, acting as it guided him. There need be no guilt, no doubt, for he was not the one who made the choice. He was a cog in the divine mechanism, fulfilling his destiny.

The sinners let him in, as they did every day when he bothered to show up. They scanned him first, but Dovraku was too smart for them, always changing his formulas. This time, he had only half the formula, and he had been told where the other half had been left by another loyalist. A loyalist, but apparently unworthy to be a martyr. Tavero would have that honor alone. Today, at last, he was the most important boy in the school.

He made his way to the hiding place and retrieved the other half of the compound. He had been told where to set it off to do the most damage. But then Semila strode by, blind to him as always, and nearly collided with him. He jumped, afraid of detection, and the smug bitch laughed at his startlement and mocked him for his lack of coordination. The tall, athletic older boys on her arms joined in her laughter.

And Tavero decided it didn't matter where the blast went off, as long as she was caught in it. He shoved her to the ground, tore open the two bags, and poured their contents over her wavy black hair. The compounds reacted, and the last thing Tavero saw was her haughtily beautiful face dissolving in a blaze of light.

Natira looked over the scene of the bombing with a mix of outrage and relief. Commander Spock's scans had shown that the death toll could have been far worse, if the explosion had happened slightly closer to one of the primary stress points of the building. What stroke of fortune had prevented the bomber from reaching what had no doubt been his intended target would probably never be known. But nonetheless, over a dozen children and nearly as many adults were dead or trapped beneath the collapsed section of the education center. Grieving families and shocked bystanders clustered around the building, while S.C.E. personnel scanned the rubble for survivors. Natira began moving toward the onlookers, formulating what she would say to reassure them that the perpetrators would be found and brought to justice.

Still, she couldn't help thinking this might have been prevented if Kirk had been more proactive, if he'd provided the help she'd requested rather than wasting time trying to negotiate with fanatical fools. Natira trusted that this attack would persuade him of his folly.

Some of the People, she noted, were climbing through the rubble along with the S.C.E. and Federation Security personnel, having no tricorders but applying raw muscle to lift debris away and look and listen underneath. It was a moving sight, though of course their efforts served little purpose with Starfleet technology on hand. She felt a twinge of regret at their reflexive rejection of the new, even as she admired their courage and determination.

But then she noticed a familiar face among those searching the rubble, and her mood soured. *"You!"* she cried out, striding toward the cursed presence. "How dare you show your face here, Rishala?"

The priestess looked up at Natira impatiently. "Where else could I be at this time?"

"Where else indeed, but admiring the fruits of your madness!"

The impatience turned to cold fury. "You're blinder than I thought, if you could believe I would approve of this. Dovraku has gone too far this time. This is not what the People want, and you will find very few who stand with him now." She blinked away dust, or so it seemed to Natira, but then she saw that it was tears. "I lost pupils of mine in there. Some of our freshest, brightest souls, the hope for our future. I only pray to the Creators that they will be reborn to us soon . . . and that some may have yet been spared by Their mercy."

Natira's anger sank into uncertainty. "Then . . . you condemn Dovraku's acts against the state? Are you prepared to say this publicly?"

"There is a great deal about the state I disapprove of," the older woman said tiredly. "But none of it justifies this. And that's what I will say to any who'll listen."

Natira gave her a grudging nod. "I am gratified."

"Keep your gratification. Are you going to come down here and help us, or are you too afraid to soil your gown?"

She should have known Rishala couldn't stay civil for long. "I have called the *Enterprise*. Their transporters can free any survivors far more easily than we can. You are wasting your effort."

"Trying to help is never a waste, whether it makes any change or not." Rishala bent down once more to her work.

To her grandstanding, more like—trying to make it look as if she were accomplishing something in order to win popularity. Natira had more faith in the People's ability to recognize real accomplishments, in the fullness of time. But if Rishala was indeed ready to break with the insurrectionists, Natira supposed that positive publicity for the priestess would do no harm. "As you will, then," she said. "But there are people over there who need my encouragement in these trying times."

Rishala threw her an odd look. "And what do you suppose these times are trying to become?"

Captain's Log: Stardate 7438.7
The final toll of the bombing at the education center is twenty-seven dead, forty-eight injured. More than half are children. The toll would have been significantly higher if not for Transporter Chief Janice Rand's prompt efforts to locate survivors and transport them out from the rubble, and for the *Enterprise* medical staff, who worked alongside Lorini medical personnel to save those that they could. Commendations are hereby granted to them all (*full list hereunto appended*).

Given the severity of this attack, and the likelihood of more, I have now decided to grant Governess Natira's request for Starfleet security assistance in tracking down the terrorists. I have resisted this request until now, for the reasons cited in earlier entries (cf. SD 7435.5, 7436.4). However, Natira believes that the public has turned in our favor due to this attack. Observations by Lieutenant Commanders Lindstrom and Uhura would seem to bear this out, though Lindstrom advises that strong-arm tactics at this point may undermine that advantage. Although I appreciate his concerns, I feel the immediate threat to life and limb overrides them. And I trust in Lieutenant Chekov's discretion and fairness in dealing with the local population.

Meanwhile, I've urged Commander Spock and his team to redouble their efforts to reconstruct the origins of the Fabrini belief system, in the hope that we can find some common ground to bring the factions together—only to be reminded by Mr. Spock that he was already putting his fullest effort into it, and expecting no less from his team. Naturally.

Hrrii'ush Uuvu'it crowed with pride as the sensor data came in, forgetting the sensitivity of the Vulcan ear. "Sorry, sir," he said to the wincing Commander Spock. "But we've triumphed!"

"Amazing," Sara Bowring said as she gazed up at the science briefing room's main screen, studying the outlines of the ruins which the new sensor algorithms had revealed just under Yonada's surface. "Why didn't anyone else find these in four years?"

"Because we're better than they are, of course!" Uuvu'it reminded her.

"Rather," Spock predictably began, "because they had 296,092 square kilometers to search and sensors less powerful than the *Enterprise*'s at their disposal."

"Which doesn't negate our being better." After all, it had

taken the sensor team hours to construct protocols that could penetrate the outer shell's radiation shielding with sufficient resolution. Uuvu'it felt that was a valid justification for bragging rights even by logical standards. Spock just wasn't getting into the competitive spirit.

"So now we have evidence that there was at least some long-term habitation of the surface," said Jade Dinh.

"Which tells us the climate was probably more temperate." That was Edward Logan, a burly human ecologist with a clean-shaven head—he called it "the Deltan look" and was convinced it made him more alluring to human females. Uuvu'it thought it was an improvement, anyway. "It supports the ecological-collapse theory. Why didn't this get figured out before? I mean, the evidence was there in the surface morphology, like Spring Rain said."

"Most of the researchers have been Lorini," Spock observed, "and have grown up accepting the assumptions of their culture. And most of the Federation researchers have been more interested in Fabrina's past and Lorina's present. Yonada's history was a low priority for them."

For his part, Uuvu'it was wondering why everyone else was so surprised. All things were ephemeral. Even worlds, even stars.

"Has there been any word on Spring Rain?" Sara asked.

"Her condition remains unchanged," Spock replied. "She is stable, but unconscious. Rest assured I will keep you all informed if this should alter."

All things were ephemeral. Maybe the others could cope with Spring Rain's condition better if they accepted that, as 'Geusians did. As Uuvu'it had had to accept it ever since he'd reached puberty and been driven from his pride-ship by stronger males, forced to wander until he could win acceptance on a new ship. It was the rite of passage all 'Geusian males had to go through, and not every one managed to win a place on a ship of the Diaspora—at least, not

one he was willing to settle for. Like many males in that
position, Uuvu'it had decided to gain experience in some
other species' fleet, in hopes of gaining sufficient skill,
experience, and strength of character to return and ultimately win the right to form his own pride. Here on the
Enterprise he'd found two other 'Geusian males in the same
position, and had been engaged in friendly rivalry with
them for the leadership of their extemporaneous mini-pride,
with inconclusive results. Win or lose, he was having fun,
and either way it wouldn't last. Eventually he'd go back to
the Diaspora, win a pride, sire lots of kids, and die; or else
he'd die in uniform before he got the chance. Sooner or later
everything ended; all that mattered was how hard you
fought against the end, and how much fun you had doing it.
Spring Rain was a fighter, driven from her own pride in a
way, but determined to overcome all setbacks. Uuvu'it was
betting heavily on her recovery. Or would be, if anyone
dared to bet against her.

"Meanwhile," Spock went on, "we still have much work
to do. Some of our assumptions appear to have been incor-
rect, but this does not prove that the Oracular religion arose
in response to the ecological collapse. We need more evidence."

Uuvu'it studied the relief map on the viewscreen and had
a thought. "The mountains! They were forbidden by the
Oracle. Scan them for signs of habitation."

Spock nodded, and the others on the sensor team input
the parameters. "It is a creative thought, Mr. Uuvu'it," the
Vulcan told him, "but I have my doubts. Yonada's simulated mountains are steep and craggy. While Betelgeusians
may find such heights agreeable due to your ornithoid
ancestry, most humanoids would choose to reside in flatter
regions."

"Still, there's much we could find in the mountains.
Consider: if the priesthood did take over, there must have

been those who played on the opposite side. They lost, of course, but if they had any sense of strategy at all, they would've sought the high ground. And maybe not just in hope of winning—maybe to keep defeat from being total."

Spock furrowed his brow. "You suggest that they may have hidden cultural paraphernalia there to protect it from the purges." Given the lack of documentation of an earlier system, it was clear that if it had existed, the new regime must have tried to purge all evidence of it.

"As you said, steep and craggy. Lots of nice hidey-holes." He bounced in his seat. "If the scans from here aren't enough, permission to do some mountain climbing, sir. I'm itching for a bit of exercise."

Spock lifted a brow. "Judging from your behavior in response to past 'itches,' Mr. Uuvu'it, perhaps it would be best if you could satisfy this one away from the ship."

TO OUR CHILDREN

. . . [I] speak on behalf of the Free People of the Ship-World Yonada . . . [i]n the hopes that our heritage will still be preserved, as the Builders intended [when they] created this great vessel. . . .

Our forebears did not appreciate [respect?] the Builders' wisdom. . . . [They] squandered our resources . . . [resulting in] massive famines and death on a terrible scale. The survivors were left to fight [for the] scraps that remain. . . . We all share in the blame . . . [for] giving the fanatics an excuse. . . .

Now they remake Yonada into a prison whose bars are implants in our heads, [whose] warder is a machine they dare call Oracle, whose walls are the ignorance they would [create?] . . . [They believe] that if we forget, if only the Oracle remembers and guides our quest, then we can no longer endanger it with our folly. . . .

[Perhaps] they are right in this belief, though I believe

they are not. . . . [If we are] lost in [archaic? primitive?]
superstition, I fear we will be unable to ward off future ca-
tastrophes. . . . Either way, our writings, our art, our sci-
ence, our . . . the intent of the Builders . . . deserve to be
known by our descendants—if not on Yonada, then perhaps
on [the world we] will one day reach, if luck is with us.
Therefore we hide away these works salvaged from the
burnings, in this and other locations, and hope that at least
some . . .

"That is all of the text that survived," Spock told Natira
once she finished reviewing the translation on her desk
monitor. "Accompanying it were several hundred books and
various artworks in similarly decayed condition. We have
dated the archive to approximately five thousand six hundred years ago."

"So the Oracle did not *exist* before then?" Natira asked,
stunned by the concept. She'd accepted years ago that the
Oracle's teachings had been a fiction, but she'd assumed the
Creators had imposed them at the beginning of Yonada's
journey. To discover that the Oracle hadn't even existed at
the beginning, that Yonada had a whole lost history . . . It
was still too much to absorb.

Spock folded his hands behind him as he stood before
her ornate desk, an antique imported from Argelius. "We
know the central computer existed from the beginning," he
said, "since it is depicted in the Book of the People. The
name given to it in the Book can be translated as either 'oracle,' 'teacher,' or 'guide,' so this is ambivalent. The Book
does convey its information in a somewhat religious tone,
but not to the extent of the culture you were raised in,
Governess. The concept of a religious Oracle did exist in
Fabrini culture, and some of the texts in the cache do refer
to a pre-existing Oracular religion on Yonada, but they are
unclear on whether that religion held political power, so far

as we have been able to reconstruct. It is difficult to draw any conclusions at this stage."

"But the texts do seem to indicate that the government of Yonada was previously secular in nature," countered Soreth, who stood to the side observing the rest. His cool Vulcan aspect seemed somehow colder when he turned it on Spock.

"At least it was at the time they were written," Spock clarified, seemingly unaffected.

"No Oracle," Natira repeated. "And no Instruments of Obedience . . . the People lived on the surface and knew it was a ship . . . how could all this have been forgotten?"

Lindstrom spoke up from where he stood beside Spock. "Normally it wouldn't be easy to suppress this much knowledge so completely. But with the Instruments, the Oracle could detect any efforts to pass it along, and punish or kill whoever tried it. So those people who remembered the way things were would've had to take the knowledge to their graves, with their children none the wiser. I guess when the priesthood took over, they decided even their successors shouldn't have the secret—or maybe they just wrote the Oracle's enforcement procedures too well and it even kept them from passing it on. The knowledge could've been completely lost inside a couple of generations."

"The text says there were other hidden caches of knowledge," Natira said intently.

"Yes," Spock replied, "but our searches have turned up nothing. It is possible that most or all of the others were found and destroyed. Even this one has largely deteriorated, due to the less than ideal manner in which it was stored. No doubt the rebels assembled it in haste and made do with what they could find."

"What was Yonada like?" Suddenly she needed to know, to get some picture of this latest truth which the Oracle had stolen from the People. "Was it beautiful? Did the People act and speak freely? Could they choose their mates, choose their leaders?"

"We don't have a complete picture yet," Lindstrom said. "Some of the references are contradictory. The books are from different times, different points of view. But it looks like Yonada was having problems with its biosphere for some time. There are generations' worth of references to famines and droughts, a lot of elegies to the dead."

"The Creators did not build Yonada as well as they thought," Natira said with some bitterness. *So much for their omnipotence.*

"Even so, it was an extraordinary achievement," Spock said, "especially given their level of technology, to construct a biosphere that could remain habitable at all after ten thousand two hundred years."

"And as our anonymous rebel said," Lindstrom added, "the generations before him—or her—wasted their resources and mistreated their environment."

"But if they knew it was an artificial world, surely they understood the urgency of preserving it?"

"From what I read in the texts, I think they understood the danger but had become jaded about it. They'd gone through centuries of crisis, and earlier attempts to restore the environment hadn't been successful. So the People became skeptical that anyone had the answers about how to preserve the biosphere, and just decided to hope it'd sort itself out. So yes, they were free to make their own decisions, but free people don't always make good decisions."

Natira stared at him. "Surely you do not suggest that the Oracle's alternative is better!"

Lindstrom shrugged. "It looks like overkill from where we're standing, but I can understand a desperate people on a dying generation ship believing that it was their only hope of survival."

"But I am sure," said Soreth, "that they did not anticipate

it causing problems for a society that no longer faces that crisis of survival."

Natira smiled up at Soreth, though she knew it would be lost on him. The elderly Vulcan had been an invaluable advisor to her, so wise and clear-headed, a paragon of Federation enlightenment. No one had been a more staunch supporter of her efforts to bring the People into the modern age, even though the Prime Directive limited the assistance he could provide. True, he was stern and unsentimental—but the People's misplaced sentiment for their past brought more harm than good. "You are right, Commissioner. This is no historical curiosity, but an atavism that imperils our lives today. We must release this truth to the People immediately, and expose once and for all the fraud behind the fanatics' pious rhetoric."

"That might be premature, Governess," said Spock. "I must stress that this is a preliminary interpretation based on fragmentary evidence. There are still a number of inconsistencies and anomalies. The cache contains few texts from before six thousand years ago, and those that it does contain are either badly decayed or are more recent copies of dubious authenticity. And although the texts are incomplete, not all of them seem to corroborate the hypothesis we have presented."

"Scholarly quibbles," Natira replied. "We do not have the time to indulge them. The fanatics have lost support among the People since their attack on the school. They are weak, and now we can undermine their support further still by exposing the falsehoods which they preach."

Lindstrom stepped forward intently. "It might have the opposite effect. A lot of people besides the extremists are religious. They aren't just following what Dovraku preaches, they have their own deeply held basis for belief. You release this and it could be seen as an attack on the foundations of their faith. It could turn them back against you."

"The People have accepted new truths before," Natira said with confidence. "They accepted that Yonada is a ship, because they could see that truth with their own eyes." She gestured at the monitor. "We have here more tangible truths of the way things were. When we show them to the People, yes, those who are blinded by fanaticism will deny them, but the mass of the People will not."

"I really think you're underestimating the depth of their faith, Governess."

"And you underestimate their capacity for reason," Soreth countered. "As always, you show more affinity for the irrational impulses in society. But the Lorini have already made great strides in overcoming those impulses."

"Governess, most people can't just toss aside a lifelong belief like an old rag. People can't be converted unless they already have a reason to *want* to convert."

"You forget," Natira said, beginning to find him tiresome, "that I was the high priestess of my whole people. I was as devout as any could be. And yet I readily accepted the truth when it was shown me."

"Then you must not have been truly committed. You must have had some prior—"

She rose and skewered him with her glare. "I will thank you not to question my commitment again, Mr. Lindstrom! Your only commitment is to your theories and your romantic notions and your incessant lecturing. You have no idea what it is to be responsible for the life and . . . and death of others!" She stopped herself, pushing away the pain that knotted inside her. "My commitment now is to fight those who threaten our peace and safety. Now I have a weapon with which to attack them. And I *will* use it. The People will know the truth of the World!"

Pavel Chekov had always had a bit of an identity problem.

He knew most people would be surprised to hear that.

"Chekov?" they'd say. "He's the guy who's fanatical about being Russian. End of story." True, Russia was his home and his heritage, the template against which he judged the universe. His accent, admittedly, may have been something of a muddle thanks to a Lithuanian mother and a well-traveled nanny, but he knew where his heart resided. His mind, though, was another matter. Somehow he never quite saw things the same way as the people around him. Home in Russia, the motherland made tough and bitterly practical by the loss of so many of her children, he'd always been told he was too much of a dreamer, an idealist, his head in the clouds. But when he'd come to Starfleet Academy, people called him a cynic, a humorless fatalist. When he'd fallen for Irina Galliulin, she and her friends had found him too conservative and military, and he'd tried to loosen up, but never managed to meet their approval. But once he'd gone on to the *Enterprise,* he'd been deemed rebellious, a chronic wise guy and nonconformist. That rebellious streak had served the ship well when he'd led a charge to retake engineering from Khan's supermen, an effort which had failed but still earned him a transfer to bridge duty soon thereafter.

For a while, he'd felt he was managing to fit in, at least once he'd migrated from sciences over to navigation and had gained the friendship of the easygoing Sulu. And Kirk himself had been somewhat betwixt and between: a rational hothead, an empathetic warrior, the fulcrum balancing the extremes of Spock and McCoy. Through his example, Chekov had begun to feel that being caught in between might be a tenable position after all.

Then Irina had come aboard, more rebellious than ever with as little evident cause as ever, and Chekov had immediately swung back to the opposite end of the spectrum, as humorless and proper as a Starfleet recruitment poster. Afterward, once he'd realized what he'd done, he'd been ashamed of himself for not trying harder to see things her way. It had thrown him off balance again, left him unsure of his place. Some months later he'd taken a leave of absence, turning the nav console over to Lieutenant Arex from the night shift, and gone to find Irina again, to try to make things right. Chekov didn't like to dwell on that; suffice it to say, it had been an abortive experiment and had convinced him that he was better off on the *Enterprise*. Arex had been offered a transfer and promotion anyway, so Chekov had returned to the ship and stayed with it until the Pelos incident and the end of the voyage.

But with the ship in drydock awaiting its turn in the refit schedule, and looking at maybe two to three years before it could go out again, Chekov had found himself a newly minted lieutenant needing to make some career choices. He'd opted for security training, because it was good experience for a command-track officer, and also because he figured it was a place where his Russian sense of caution would fit right in. But once again, he found himself told that he was too idealistic, too unwilling to make the tough choices and define acceptable losses. His instructors and fellow cadets either didn't believe in Kirk's proclivity for pulling rabbits from hats, or didn't think Chekov had a snowball's chance on Venus of duplicating it.

So now he was back on the *Enterprise*, a tough, cautious, pragmatic chief of security, and Sulu and Uhura were relentlessly on his case (in their affectionate way) about how cynical and paranoid he'd become. They were still his best friends, but he didn't really feel he fit in with them as well as he once had. Especially when Sulu was spending so much time with DiFalco and Uhura was so busy with her crew-liaison duties.

As for his fellow security professionals—well, fitting in wasn't an issue when he was the commander. He was supposed to be at a certain remove from the others. And they accepted him because of his position. He hoped a deeper bond would form in time, that he could earn their trust and loyalty, but that remained to be seen. For now, at least, he was starting to feel reasonably comfortable in his role of security chief.

At least, he had been until today. Today he and his team were patrolling the Lorini underground tunnels with Security Minister Tasari and his team, hunting for terrorists. This wasn't something Chekov found particularly comfortable. Part of it was just being in this tight space again, one that the potential enemy knew far better than he did. Chekov preferred to fight on his own turf. It had worked against Napoleon, Hitler, and Li Kwan, after all.

But mostly what made him uncomfortable was pushing into people's private homes and searching them for suspected terrorists or evidence of bomb-making materials. Again he was torn between idealism and pragmatism. On one level he understood the necessity, and in a way, the current state of martial law that Natira had declared made his job easier. But most of these people were scared. Many were angry, screaming imprecations at Tasari's people and his own, but Chekov was more disturbed by the ones who quietly submitted, because he could tell they were too afraid to speak their minds. Maybe it was just a lifetime living under the Instruments of Obedience . . . but maybe it was something more immediate.

Then there was Tasari himself. Chekov wouldn't exactly say the stocky, bland-faced minister was enjoying his work too much—he was too banal and passionless for that word to apply. But he did invade the people's homes with considerable zeal, and was quick to clamp down on resistance.

The first two times Tasari had his troops carry a homeowner off to prison for expressing a vehement opinion about the intrusion, Chekov had kept his mouth shut. This was the minister's jurisdiction, they shared a common goal, and there were possible Prime Directive issues hovering around in the background somewhere. But when they dragged away a mother at swordpoint in front of her two small children, Chekov had to say something. "Maybe we'd get more cooperation if we used a lighter hand," he suggested through clenched teeth.

"You don't understand these people," Tasari replied with as much animation as he might show in discussing uniform requisitions. "They grew up regulated by the Instruments of Obedience. That's what they're used to. Without them, they've got no discipline." He shook his head. "They're unruly, irresponsible, nothing but trouble. They need a firm hand to keep them in line."

"Are you saying you'd rather have the Oracle back?"

Tasari looked uninterested. "Religion, politics . . . I just do my job. I keep order. I kept order when there was an Oracle, and I keep order now that there isn't. I'm busier now, but I get paid well enough."

While Tasari's troops searched the dwelling, unconcerned with the integrity of the family's possessions, Chekov told Nizhoni to take the toddlers in hand and make sure they were placed in a neighbor's care. "How long do you intend to hold the mother?" he asked the minister.

"That depends on her cooperation."

"And what if she doesn't know anything?"

"Do you want to take that chance?" The troopers came back out and shook their heads—they'd found nothing of note. "Now I've got a peace to keep. Are you going to help or not?"

Tasari led his forces on to the next dwelling. Chekov sighed and followed him out, thinking that this was starting to remind him of certain portions of Russian history that he wasn't particularly proud of. "Next thing you know, he'll have us hunting for Trotskyites," he muttered.

Worene, the Aulacri member of his team, tilted her feral-featured head at him quizzically. "Sir?"

"Nothing," Chekov said, making a note to keep her acute hearing in mind in the future. That was part of why he'd brought the diminutive Aulacri along, for her keen senses. Not that she wasn't a capable fighter as well; she was stronger than she looked and a fast, agile mover, her gymnastic prowess aided by a long prehensile tail. But she was the inquisitive type, and he really didn't want to get drawn into a lecture on Stalinism right now; in this company, it would be impolitic.

Chekov had selected his team for their skills and strength, and ended up with a largely nonhuman group. Aside from himself, Nizhoni, and Worene were the Saurian M'sharna, chosen for his night vision, strength, and endurance, and the Andorian Shantherin th'Clane, one of his best hand-to-hand fighters. What he hadn't taken into account was how the locals would react to the group. Most of them hadn't encountered many aliens before, at least none besides humans and Vulcans, who looked more or less like themselves. It only added to their wariness and hostility toward the security teams. Chekov wondered if he should have chosen differently, but what was reassuring to others and what was safest for one's own people weren't always the same thing. Which was kind of the idealism-versus-conservatism debate in a nutshell.

Tasari seemed oblivious to the people's discomfort toward the aliens, just as he seemed oblivious to their concerns in general. He hadn't seemed too comfortable with them himself, though, stiffly trying to avoid making eye contact with them (hard to do in M'sharna's case, since his eyes were such large targets). But now he was peering at them with something vaguely approaching a thoughtful expression. "You have any of those Vulcans on your staff?" he asked.

"No. We had a Vulcan technician for a short while, but

she transferred off before this mission. Vulcans usually prefer to leave security to more 'aggressive' species."

"Too bad," Tasari said. "This would be easier if we could read people's minds, sense if they knew anything about the terrorists."

"A telepathic security force, eh?" Chekov replied. "An interesting idea." It appealed to the pragmatist in him, but the idealist recoiled at the invasion of individual rights it would represent. Tasari, though, seemed to have no qualms about the idea, and that troubled Chekov.

His musings were interrupted by the realization that they were nearing the temple, and that a crowd was forming in their path. Chekov knew this couldn't go well. "Stand aside," Tasari warned. "We intend to search the temple."

The crowd voiced their objections, and a priestess came forward. Chekov recognized her as Rishala, the high priestess Kirk had met with before. "This is a holy place. I beg you, do not desecrate it with weapons."

"For all I know you're stockpiling weapons in there. Now stand aside—or get moved aside."

Rishala and those around her formed up into a human—well, humanoid—barricade. "No," she proclaimed. "We stand with the Creators, against all who endanger their children."

"Then we are on the same side, ma'am," Chekov said, trying to help. "The terrorists are the danger here, and we only want to find them and stop them."

The priestess glared at him. "That's what your captain promised me—only to send his scientists to feed Natira more excuses she could use to attack our faith. Just when I believed there was hope of cooperation, Kirk handed her a blade so she could stab us in the back."

"I'm warning you," Tasari snapped, "you're speaking sedition. Keep it up and you will be arrested as an enemy of the state."

"Arrest me, then. Arrest us all! Fill your prisons with those who want Natira gone, and there will be barely anyone left to till our fields and build our homes."

"You were warned. Guards, arrest these terrorist sympathizers." He drew his stunner, and the guards followed suit—though only a few had stunners, and the rest relied on the traditional short swords. "Anyone who tries to resist will also be treated as a sympathizer!" he called to the crowd.

It only made them angrier, louder. Chekov really didn't like the situation: the locals outnumbered and surrounded them, and Tasari was only provoking them. By contrast, Rishala herself offered no resistance. Apparently Russia wasn't the only place where civil disobedience had been invented, Chekov thought.

But the troopers grabbed her roughly and yanked her arms behind her. "Hey!" Chekov protested, but he was drowned out by the crowd's angry cries.

"No," Rishala called to the crowd. "Stay calm, do not—" But a guard struck her in the mouth to silence her.

That was the final straw. After that, nothing could have held the crowd back. They surged forward, swinging fists at the guards, who had their weapons at the ready and started to use them. The sword-wielding guards clubbed people with the butts when they could, but weren't shy about using the blades. Chekov had to do something to minimize the bloodshed. "Phasers on stun," he called to his people, "wide—no, narrow beam!" In these tight quarters, in this crush of people, wide-field stun could easily take out security personnel, leaving them helpless against the mob. "Stun as many as you can!" He realized that some might be trampled to death, but at this point he was left with triage.

His team handled themselves well, showcasing their skills. Worene leaped and dodged and flipped, not letting anyone get a hand on her. She used her tail to trip people up, blocking the tunnels to slow the influx of people into the heart of the mob. At one point a burly Lorini man got her in a bear hug, trying to crush the breath from her, but she whipped her tail around his neck and choked him into unconsciousness, then used it to retrieve her fallen phaser. M'sharna simply relied on his superior strength and endurance to stand his ground and keep firing. The extra peripheral vision provided by his wide-set eyes let him avoid attempts to sneak up on him. But then a blow to his head knocked loose one of the filtered contact lenses that let the nocturnal Saurian function in bright light. Dazed, M'sharna fell beneath a pile of attackers. Chekov knew he was strong and could hold his breath for a long time, but still feared for his safety. That was where th'Clane came in. With the preternatural calm and clarity of an Andorian in combat, he picked off M'sharna's attackers with his phaser one by one, then shoved them off and helped the Saurian to his feet.

Meanwhile, Nizhoni and Chekov stood back to back, firing shot after shot, their phasers growing warm in their hands. Chekov saw Nizhoni stun a trooper who'd been about to run his sword through a civilian, then promptly stun the civilian before he could attack the trooper. Not for a moment did Chekov believe it had been accidental. Unlike him, Mosi was unambiguously an idealist, a champion of the underdog—and a crack shot too. He'd have to have a talk with her later, assuming they were still breathing then.

Before long, reinforcements arrived, both Lorini troopers and more security beamed down from the *Enterprise,* and the shift in numbers prompted the crowd to disperse. The troopers gave chase and caught whom they could, so Chekov couldn't consider the violence to be over. But nobody was attacking his people anymore, so his priorities were seeing to their well-being and summoning medical help to the scene of the riot. Not only was M'sharna injured, but Worene apparently had a broken arm, which she hadn't allowed to keep her from doing her job. And they had come out far better than many of the Lorini.

"Over here!" Mosi had found Rishala, unconscious and bloodied but still breathing. She knelt to apply her paramedic training while Chekov called the ship. If Rishala didn't make it, Chekov knew, things would get a lot worse.

Looking around him, Chekov estimated that the toll in deaths and injuries might rival that of the education-center bombing. The hell of it was, the terrorists had had nothing to do with this.

CHAPTER TWELVE

*Is not that the nature of men and women—that
the pleasure is in the learning of each other?*

—Natira

KIRK HATED IT when sickbay got busy. This was one part of
the ship—along with the weapons—that he wished would
never have to exercise its full potential. He was glad to have
McCoy on board, of course; but in his ideal universe,
Bones's only shipboard duties would be to play poker with
the captain, trade acerbic banter with Spock, and dole out
the occasional medicinal dose of Saurian brandy. Somehow
it never seemed to work out that way.

But it could have been worse, Kirk reflected as he
looked over the somewhat crowded sickbay ward. At least
the ship's morgue hadn't been called into service yet.

His first stop was the bed where Spring Rain still lay in
her coma. Dr. Chapel was there, checking her vitals. "Any
change?" Kirk asked.

Chapel sighed. "No. I'm afraid she's stuck."

"What do you mean by that?"

"Oh. Well, it's a little complicated."

"Go on."

"You see, the Megarite system is supposed to be

designed to prevent ischemia—oxygen deprivation—of the brain. It has a layer of aeration membranes around the brain, which store extra oxygen for long dives. But those membranes were inflamed by the allergic reaction, and didn't deliver their oxygen. Now, her brain does have natural mechanisms for minimizing the ischemic shock, but that's not the problem."

"What is?"

"The problem is that the altered chemistry of the ischemic brain, when exposed to oxygen, produces large amounts of free radicals. And those can do great damage to the neurons and blood vessels. That's the nasty thing about suffocation—restoring oxygen to the brain can actually do more damage than cutting it off in the first place."

Kirk winced. "Doesn't the Megarite brain have a mechanism for coping with that too?"

"Yes, and that's the problem. Life processes fall to minimum levels, so that oxygen is restored slowly and the rate of free-radical formation is manageable. The aeration membranes are supposed to regulate this and sense when it's safe to return to normal activity.

"But Spring Rain's membranes are still contaminated by waste products from the altered Deltan pheromones. It's keeping them from reading the chemical signals that would give the all-clear."

"Is there a way to clean them out?"

"In theory, hyperbaric oxygen treatment could purge them. But that would cause the very free-radical damage to the brain that they're supposed to prevent."

Kirk mulled it over. "Can't you fight free radicals with antioxidants? That's what Bones always tells me when he pushes me to eat more salads."

That brought a faint smile to Chapel's face. "Yes, but the cells themselves are programmed to take in only a certain amount of antioxidants, to prevent overdose. It wouldn't be enough to compensate for the levels of free radicals that would be produced."

"So the only thing that could wake her up would cause her more brain damage."

"Unfortunately. All we can do is hope that her aeration membranes somehow manage to purge the toxins on their own."

"I see." Kirk watched the unmoving Megarite for a moment, regretting that he hadn't taken the chance to get acquainted with her. "Carry on, Doctor," he finally said, and moved on down the line of beds.

Ensign Zaand was there, visiting his injured colleagues from security. He had been in a lively conversation with Dr. Onami, but it dried up the moment they caught sight of him. Kirk could guess what it was about. They weren't the only two in the crew who were grumbling about the decisions made by the "old guard." Most of these people had been picked by Decker, had expected to serve under him, and had then had their command crew shoved aside without warning. And so far, it seemed, they'd found little reason to approve of the change. Kirk heard things, kept abreast of the ship's discussion boards, and so was aware of the various threads that were recurring. *"If Decker were here, he would've sent the troops in sooner." "If Decker were here, he wouldn't have sent in the troops at all." "If Chapel were in charge, Spring Rain wouldn't be fighting for her life." "McCoy's too close to Natira—he's swaying Kirk too much to her side."* He'd even heard *"If Sonak were here"*—there were no tangible grounds for finding fault with Spock's investigations, yet some still wondered if a full Vulcan not struggling with a spiritual crisis might have done something differently, seen something Spock had missed—or missed something he had seen, something better left unrevealed.

Kirk recalled that Onami had been on the bridge when

he'd first arrived to take command a month ago. At the time, she'd beamed at him with frank admiration, the kind he'd seen on the faces of those who'd bought into his media image. That sort of reaction always made him uncomfortable, but he was more disturbed by the expression her girlish features bore now, which was wary and troubled as she looked at him. He was even losing the trust of his initial supporters.

Still, he took a moment to greet his crew members and exchange pleasantries, not letting on that he was aware of the tension. At least Crewman Worene seemed pleased to see him, or pretended well. It was harder to tell with M'sharna, since Saurian expressions were hard for a human to read, with their wide eyes and upturned mouths giving them a perpetually cheery mien that could conceal their true responses.

Finally, he made his way to the bed occupied by Rishala. Chekov had acted quickly to have her beamed to the ship for treatment, and her prognosis was for a full recovery. Indeed, she was conscious, and watching Kirk keenly as he approached. "Am I under arrest?"

"No. In fact, Natira's been demanding that I turn you over. I've . . . regretfully declined. And reminded her who threw the first punch."

"But if I go back, she will arrest me."

Kirk pursed his lips. "W . . . we're working on sorting that out."

"So I am *not* free to go."

"No, I suppose not." He fidgeted under her matronly gaze. "If you want me to leave, I understand," he said.

"No." Her expression softened, became thoughtful. "I was angry at you before. When Natira published those findings from your Spock, when she touted them as proof that all faith was a lie . . . I felt you'd betrayed your promise to work with all sides toward a compromise."

"That was the intent," Kirk said diffidently. "To find some common ground in your history that could unite all the factions. I didn't expect this to be the result." The riot had subsided, but relations between the sides were at an all-time low. All the sympathy Natira had gained from the school bombing had evaporated after her release of the findings, and the riot had made things far worse. Kirk couldn't even be sure the rioting had ended; the tension still smoldered, and there had been more than one flare-up in the intervening hours.

Rishala sighed. "Again you look to facts instead of faith," she said, not with anger but with disappointment. "Truth is a living thing that flows through people's hearts, James Kirk, not a relic you can dig from the ground. I accept that you meant well, but you looked in the wrong direction."

"Maybe." Kirk met her gaze challengingly. "But you're the one who told me that the story can be told in different ways and still contain the same truth. So why is this way of telling it such a threat? Why does this new evidence prevent the sides from coexisting?"

"It isn't the evidence that matters. The People only use it to serve what's already in their hearts." She fell silent, thinking. "Which I suppose is your point as well as mine, though we have a . . . difference in emphasis." She chuckled gingerly, and Kirk joined her.

Rishala reached out and took his hand. "I said I *was* angry with you, James Kirk. Then I saw how my own people behaved . . . how they lost all control . . . so violent. . . ." She shuddered, and he clasped her hand tighter. "I can't pretend we have the moral high ground anymore. It's in all of us, to hate."

"Tensions are high," Kirk said. "Sooner or later these things reach critical mass, take on a life of their own . . . and trying to lay blame only feeds the flames. It doesn't matter who's right or who started it—only who's brave enough to end it."

"Tell Natira that."

"I intend to."

"I wonder if it'll be more effective from you," she mused. "You managed to change her mind once before. You're quite the orator, James. Natira places great stock in pretty words and elegant delivery."

"Call me Jim." Kirk shook his head. "I'm no great speaker. Always . . . floundering for what to say next. You, on the other hand, are one of the most . . . captivating speakers I've ever heard."

"But that's raw and passionate, scandalous to Natira's rarefied sensibilities. And with my accent—" She broke off. "You can't tell, can you, through those translators of yours? Let's just say I don't come from close to the surface." Kirk remembered that the upper class on Yonada had been that quite literally, living on the more spacious higher levels of Yonada's onion-layered underground.

"I don't know, though," Rishala sighed. "Maybe my accent has changed. I thought I spoke with the voice of the common people . . . but lately fewer and fewer will listen to me."

"They got pretty upset when the guards attacked you," Kirk reminded her.

She shook her head. "They only used me as an excuse. I urged calm and they wouldn't listen." She was quiet for a moment. "I was afraid it would be a mistake to let them talk me into becoming high priestess. Before, that was a title of the ones who lived above and told the rest of us what to do. I should've known that the title would come between me and my people."

Rishala studied Kirk. "I think that may be another thing we have in common."

"What do you mean?"

"I've been listening to people talk, while I've lain here. And I saw your face when you came in. You and your crew also seem to have a title between you. Or a question of who should hold the title. You don't think they trust you."

He looked at her closely. "Do they?"

She shrugged. "It's not my place to say that. But it can't be easy for them to trust you, when you don't trust yourself." Rishala sat up on her elbow to face him more directly. "What happened between you and this Decker, that leaves you so unsure of your place?"

Kirk hesitated to tell her. She was someone he barely knew, and given her political stance, he still wasn't sure whether she would be a help or a hindrance to his efforts on Lorina. But she was easy to talk to, a comforting presence. There was a serenity and nurturing strength to her that reminded him of Edith Keeler. The reminder of that loss sent a pang through him, still sharper after six years than the loss of Lori was after just a month. It reminded him that he wasn't ready yet to let himself get too close to another woman.

Still, all she was offering was to listen, to hear his confession, as it were. He found he couldn't say no. So he told her the story of how he'd groomed Decker for this command, then pushed him aside at the last moment. How he'd clashed with Decker and finally watched ineffectually as the man sacrificed himself. Rishala listened patiently, then spent a few moments contemplating his tale in silence. "So . . . do you feel that the wrong man commanded the mission?"

Kirk pondered the question, and had to answer, "N-n-no . . . I believed it needed a more experienced captain than Decker, and I still think that was a valid command judgment. But . . . I could've gone about it differently. Commanded the mission while leaving him in command of the ship."

"But the whole mission took place *on* the ship. Couldn't that have led to confusion at a crucial time?"

"Perhaps," he replied slowly.

"Was that an argument you used to convince your admiral to give you command?"

"As a matter of fact, it was. But what if it was self-serving?"

"Your admiral is an experienced leader, yes?"

Kirk smiled. "Sometimes it seems like he's been in charge since Cochrane was a pup. Forever," he amended at her quizzical look.

"So if that argument had been flawed, he wouldn't have accepted it."

"I . . . suppose not."

She narrowed her eyes. "Then what is it that really troubles you, Jim?"

Kirk gathered his thoughts. "Decker," he said. "I drove him to it."

Rishala processed that. "Didn't he say that joining with V'Ger was what he wanted?"

"That's what he said. But . . . I didn't understand why. The Will Decker I knew was an ambitious career officer. He wanted nothing more than to be a starship captain. To be *this* starship's captain. It was his whole life for over two years. When I took that away . . . what was left?"

"Look at it another way. Before he knew V'Ger, how could he know that it offered something he wanted more?"

"But . . . what was it that he wanted? To be with Ilia? I can understand that, I suppose. They had a relationship. But I didn't think it was something he'd sacrifice everything for. If it had been, he never would've left Delta IV."

Rishala gave him that look again, as though he were a slow student she expected better from. "A career . . . a ship . . . a lover . . . you still see only the worldly things, Jim." Her eyes lost focus. "When I think about what you describe—ascending to a higher plane, transcending the physical world—I envy him. He's achieved the goal that Vari and Baima envisioned for us, to one day escape the trap of mortal matter. The trap of desire. You speak of what Decker wanted to acquire, to possess. But what he did within V'Ger was to *give*. He chose to share his soul with another being, a being who needed what he could offer it. Why can't that be what he wanted? Why couldn't he value that goal more than any worldly gain?"

They sat in silence as Kirk absorbed her words. But after a time she spoke again. "You're troubled, because you want your crew's approval and they haven't given it. But is that what really matters? Or is the question what *you* can give to *them?*"

Kirk smiled ironically. "I suppose I could ask you the same question. You give to your people—how's that working out for you?"

She returned the smile, and the irony. "The truth is in the trying, not the succeeding."

Natira's secretary looked on in alarm as McCoy stormed toward the office door. "The governess is in a meeting with the Shesshran ambassador, sir," she said. "You don't want to go in there."

Honey, you don't know the half of it, McCoy thought. He knew that Natira wouldn't be happy to see him even if she weren't trying to deal with a member of that contentious species. But he was through letting his emotional hang-ups get in the way of his work.

Natira didn't even seem to notice as he barged in, for her view was blocked by a whole lot of Shesshran. There was only one of them there, but it was a big one, well over two meters tall, its angular headfin scraping the ceiling, its shimmering wings spread imposingly wide. Most of its long-beaked head was encased in a mask connected to an air tank on its back; McCoy reminded himself that the air pressure here was less than a third of what the Shesshran were used to. "We were assured that your presence in our system would be unobtrusive," the ambassador—a female—was saying rather loudly. "That you would lead your own lives and not interfere in ours. Those were the terms of our contract!"

"That has not changed," Natira replied in cool, diplomatic tones. "We are still committed to the peaceful coexistence of our two—"

"*You* claim to be, but these rebels clearly are not. These people who would impose their beliefs on others." The pterosaurian ambassador shook herself in apparent disgust, making rainbow patterns shimmer across her fine silver scales, whose featherlike microserrations created the diffraction-grating effect. "Humanoid madness. To think you could *force* another being to believe as you do, or stamp out competing beliefs. What good is any belief that can't stand to face some competition?"

"I assure you, Ambassador Ak'pethhit, that my government is committed to crushing this rebellion."

"You had better be. Because the Shesshran will not tolerate any threats to the sovereignty of the individual. If you do not eliminate this rebellion soon, it will be seen as a breach of contract, and we will no longer be obligated to tolerate your presence here."

"You would expel us?!"

"That is the best case—if you are quick enough in leaving."

"Do not think us helpless, Madam Ambassador. Removing us from our Promised World would not be as easy as you think."

"Your Federation cohorts would not use their might to protect you. Their own laws would shackle them."

"The People are not without might of our own. Yonada's

missiles may have been created for peaceful purposes, but space debris is not the only thing they can target."

"Your antique missiles would be no match for us. But it would excite me to see you make the attempt." The ambassador didn't give her the chance to reply, instead whirling away dramatically and storming out—or trying to, since her awkwardness in this gravity diminished the effect.

Still, she nearly knocked McCoy over in the process. Natira noticed the doctor for the first time, and her expression—had it been fear?—grew cold and hard. "I did not summon you."

He came on strong, his anger exceeding hers. "That's exactly the problem! I'm not getting called in where I'm needed! Did you know your Minister Tasari is refusing to let me treat the injured he arrested after the riot?"

She appeared unmoved. "We have our own medical resources, as you are well aware."

"And they aren't being allowed in either!" McCoy leaned forward, hands on her desk. "Several prisoners have already died in Tasari's custody. What's more, at least one of them died of injuries I didn't see on him after the riot, before Tasari's thugs dragged him away."

"Are you insinuating that Tasari's people inflicted those injuries?"

"Well, he does seem to lose a lot of prisoners that way!"

Natira glared. "And why should I believe these charges coming from *you?*"

That brought him up short. "Look . . . Natira," he went on more softly, "you have every right to be mad at me. But don't take it out on these people."

She met his eyes for a few moments, then paced out from behind her desk. "I have faith in Minister Tasari. I do not believe he would harm the innocent. His methods can be forceful, it is true. But we are fighting a war for the future of the People, and we will do whatever must be done in order to prevail. Those who refuse to cooperate, who abet the enemy, have only themselves to blame."

"These aren't terrorists, Natira! They're ordinary people who got pushed too far. And either way, it doesn't matter! They're injured people and they need medical attention!"

"Then they should cooperate, and renounce their sympathy for the fanatics! A stern hand is the only way to make them understand!"

McCoy stared in disbelief. "My God, woman, I never took you for a fool!"

"What?"

"When they attack you, it just makes you more determined to fight back and win, you just said so yourself. So why in hell would you possibly think that attacking them would make them back down?!"

"So what would you have me do, McCoy? Surrender?"

"Just give them a little slack, for God's sake! Try to understand their point of view, instead of bein' so blasted self-righteous all the time!"

"I do not understand you," Natira said, shaking her head. "You, your captain . . . first you pushed me to abandon the People's false beliefs, yet now you demand that I heed them! What is it that you want from me?"

"How about a little patience? A little understanding that when people are going through changes . . . maybe they aren't entirely sure what they believe, or what they want. And maybe if you try to rush them to decide," he went on, his tone becoming more pleading, "they'll get more confused, and make mistakes. And you might end up driving them away when they would've been willing to work things out with you."

She looked at him warily. "And what if I give them another chance and they only hurt me again?"

McCoy sighed. "Then at least you understand them a little better . . . and maybe that improves your chances for the next time."

Natira bowed her head, absorbed in thought for a time. Finally she made her way slowly around the desk. "I have not seen this side of you before, Leonard. Your passion surprises me."

"Well . . . like I said, when we first met I wasn't quite myself."

"And the second time you came . . . when you were so reserved toward me—that was out of discomfort."

"Out of shame, and fear," he admitted. "I didn't know how to tell you the truth. I was stupid about it."

"And I never saw," she said wistfully, "for I never knew the real McCoy." That evoked a chuckle. "What amuses you so?"

"Uh, doesn't matter. So—this is who I am," he went on, spreading his arms. "A bad-tempered old curmudgeon who can't keep his opinions to himself. Not very pretty, is it?"

She appraised him. "On the contrary. It makes me better understand what drew me to you in the first place. I must have sensed some echo of it."

"What do you mean?"

"Come, sit." She led him over to the couch. "My father was much as you are," she said once they were seated. "Quick to speak his mind. And he did not always accept the Oracle's dogma easily. He felt the pain of warning many times in his life, and the lesson never took for very long. Still, he managed to restrain himself for long enough to be mated, and raise a young daughter.

"But that daughter inherited his inquisitive ways. It is true, all children question what they are told, and the Oracle was patient with children. It would never have fatally punished one who spoke blasphemy if that one was underage." She lowered her head, continuing with more difficulty. "But my questions made it harder for my father to keep his peace. I expressed doubts about the Oracle's dogma, about the tale of our origins, and it grew harder and harder for him to defend that which he did not truly believe." Her voice faltered. "One day I questioned once too often, and he could restrain himself no more. He told me that I must know the truth, that the world was not as we were told. He felt the pain of warning, but it only deepened his urgency. He tried to tell me . . . what, I do not know." She blinked away tears. "For the Oracle . . . would not let him. . . . It stopped him . . . from ever speaking again. . . ."

It seemed the most natural thing in the world to take her into his arms and comfort her sobs. "Natira . . . I'm so sorry. . . ."

Soon she gathered herself. "After that . . . seeing that happen before my eyes . . . I no longer questioned the Oracle. I persuaded myself that all its teachings were truth, to be accepted without hesitation. I became the most loyal and obedient servant the Oracle could possibly have had— not because I truly believed in my heart, but because I was too afraid to doubt. I was enslaved," she went on with growing bitterness, "terrorized into complete submission. And in time my total obedience, my cowardice, was rewarded with the role of high priestess, the Oracle's unquestioning mouthpiece. So loyal a slave was I that I became the youngest ever elevated to that post.

"Then you came, you and your captain. Your words reawakened the doubts I had kept buried for all those years, and you showed me I could be free of the Oracle's retribution. I resisted at first, out of fear, out of habit . . . but in my heart I knew that I had been living a lie, and your truth could free me."

McCoy studied her thoughtfully. "Hm. I always thought you came around a bit easily, for someone in your position."

"And now you know why."

"I guess I also know why you're so hostile to anything connected to your old religion."

She stared. "Should I not be? It was a tool for the deception and enslavement of the People. It destroyed countless lives. Too long I tolerated it, condoned it, even assisted in its reign of terror! I cannot allow it to rise again, Leonard!"

"Even if it means getting more blood on your hands, Natira? What difference does it make if you take those lives in support of the faith or in fighting against it?"

"You do not understand."

"I understand, Natira. Only too well. I understand what it's like to feel responsible for a father's death." He went on reluctantly. "I've hardly ever told this to anyone . . . but when I was a young doctor, fresh out of residency, my father fell ill with a terminal disease. As far as I knew, there was no cure." He quirked a brow. "Kind of ironic, considering how we met. But anyway . . . he asked me to . . . to end the pain."

She looked at him intently. "To end his life?"

"Yes. All I had to do was turn off the machine that was keeping him alive. I agonized over the decision. I've never believed it was right to intentionally end someone's life for any reason—it goes against everything a doctor stands for. To say that a life ceases to be worth living when it reaches a certain level of difficulty—where can you draw that line? If being on life support isn't a life worth living, then what about being in a wheelchair? What about being mentally ill? My God, if everyone who ever felt their life wasn't worth living actually ended it, most people would never make it out of adolescence. And more than one tyrant has used euthanasia as an excuse for genocide. It's a dangerous, insidious thing, to try to put limits on whose life is worth living.

"But this was my father, and he was in such pain, and he was begging me. . . . I had a moment of weakness. I turned off the machine." He took a deep, shuddering breath. "Just a short time later, they found a cure. He probably would've made it, if I just hadn't . . . hadn't . . ."

"Leonard." Now she held him in her arms. "Your motives were kind."

"I try to tell myself that." He gathered himself, pulled back to look at her. "And since then I've done everything in my power to make up for that mistake, to make sure that I never lose another life unnecessarily." The image of a young Megarite fighting for her life flashed into his mind, and he winced. "I haven't always been successful.

"But the point is . . . Hell, the point is, Natira, when it comes to guilt over your father dying, you've got nothing on me. You didn't kill him, the Oracle did."

"And a sickness killed your father. But you feel you helped it do so, and I feel the same."

"But you didn't. You didn't know he'd react the way he did. You had no idea what would happen. You just asked one more question. You were the victim, Natira, as much as he was." He stroked the side of her face once, tenderly. "So you have to let go of your guilt, Natira. It's blinding you, driving you to a vendetta against your own people."

"Only against what they believe!"

"What they *choose* to believe. That's the difference. You and your father didn't have a choice. These people do, thanks to you. You showed them the truth, shut down the Oracle, freed them to make their own decisions. Can you take that freedom away from them just because they didn't make the choice you wanted? Is that what your father would've wanted?" She stared at him, taken aback. "Natira, your father *chose* to sacrifice his life because he knew you deserved the right to think for yourself. Don't make that sacrifice meaningless . . . like my father's was."

They spent a long time after that only gazing into each other's eyes. Then Natira drew closer and tentatively, ten-

derly kissed him. They stayed that way for an even longer
time. Afterward, Natira afforded him a faint, wistful smile
and said, "I shall make you a bargain, Leonard. I shall try to
release my guilt . . . if you will try to release yours."

"I'll try," McCoy agreed. "But I don't think it'll be that
easy."

"Maybe it will be . . . with someone to share the burden."
Then their lips met again.

CHAPTER
THIRTEEN

The most violent revolutions in an individual's beliefs leave most of his old order standing. Time and space, cause and effect, nature and history, and one's own biography remain untouched. New truth is always a go-between, a smoother-over of transitions. It marries old opinion to new fact so as ever to show a minimum of jolt, a maximum of continuity.

*—*William James

SCOTTY LOOKED ON gratefully as Ki'ki're'ti'ke wriggled his long, gray caterpillar-like body out of the cramped maintenance conduit that ran behind the temple wall, emerging back into Yonada's control room. The Escherite was a godsend when it came to crawling around in maintenance shafts and Jefferies tubes, particularly with the way Scott's back was going these days. And particularly when it came to a conduit as cramped as this one. It was barely large enough for an adult humanoid to fit into, leading Scott to wonder if it had originally been maintained by robotic drones. The Yonadi had certainly lost plenty of other technology in the course of their journey, so why not?

Scott listened to Kick's report and studied his tricorder

readings, nodding as they confirmed his own conclusions. Then he made his way over to Mr. Spock. "It's as we thought, sir. The heating elements and electric stunners in the temple were late additions to the original system, right enough—but the decay shows they were installed sixty-two hundred years ago, give or take a century. Not fifty-six hundred."

Spock took the tricorder from him and studied the readouts. "Fascinating. So the temple room's defenses were added five to seven centuries *before* the Oracular regime arose—during the secular period of Yonada's history. That suggests they were not originally intended as 'divine punishment.' "

"I suppose not. But they were definitely meant to protect something. Maybe to prevent unauthorized access to the control room?"

"Which would suggest that the ones in control felt threatened by their own people—more so than previous generations had. Assuming, of course, that these security systems were not merely replacements for earlier models."

Scott mulled it over. "I don't think so, sir. Aye, they were hooked up to pre-existing circuits, but I'm certain those circuits were originally designed for a very different use— probably for some kind of information system. The security devices push the limits of their power capacity but use hardly any of their bandwidth."

Spock looked at him with great interest. "It is possible, then, that the contents of the Fabrini intelligence files were originally available to the People."

"Aye, it seems reasonable."

Now Spock began to pace. The sight struck Scott a bit oddly; he was used to seeing the Vulcan much more poised and reserved. "That suggests *two* purges: the one fifty-six centuries ago when the Oracular regime displaced the secular and purged all written history, and an earlier one six centuries before that, which denied the People access to the history and knowledge of Fabrina. However, the mountain cache did contain documents dating from before that period. So these earlier revolutionaries, at least, either did not seek to obscure *all* their history, or were not successful in the attempt." He frowned. "Unfortunately, the number of recovered documents predating that time is small, and provides a very incomplete picture of the first forty centuries of Yonada's journey. What preceded the secular regime, and what triggered the two revolutions—if indeed there were only two?"

"Well, we know the environmental crises started over six thousand years ago," Scott said. "Maybe the first revolution happened because people weren't happy with how the old regime handled the problem. And then things didn't get better, so the new regime got itself kicked out a few centuries later."

"Yes . . . on the whole, the track record of armed revolution as a tool for meaningful change is poor enough to make one wonder why it continues to be attempted at all. Yet we are in the midst of such a revolution, and I begin to wonder if this investigation has any chance of affecting that situation in a positive way." Spock's pacing intensified, and his expression grew grimmer. "The deeper we dig into this history, the farther we seem to get from an answer. And I fear any answer we do find will simply be twisted into an excuse for more violence!"

Scott stared at the Vulcan, nonplussed by his intensity. He'd heard that Spock had changed after V'Ger, but this was the first time he'd seen it clearly, and he wasn't sure what to make of it. But Spock noticed his reaction and gathered himself. "My apologies, Mr. Scott. I find frustration to be one of the more difficult emotions to manage of late."

"No need to apologize, sir," Scott said understandingly.

"We all need to let off some steam now and then. No harm done."

"Thank you, Mr. Scott." Spock studied him. "May I ask you a question?"

"Of course, sir."

"You have a tendency to be—if I may say so—somewhat excitable."

Scott was about to respond to that rather sharply, but realized he'd only be confirming the charge. "Well," he answered, "I do have a habit o' speakin' my mind, sir."

"And yet this never seems to interfere with your performance as an engineer—a discipline which requires clear, logical thought."

"Engineering—logical?" Scott laughed. "Och, no, sir. All that orderly, calculated stuff is fine for the theorists, but when it comes to working with real machines it's all about intuition. It's about gettin' to know your hardware, listenin' to what it tells you, feeling what it needs. It's like . . ." He blushed a bit. "Well, it's a lot like bein' in love. There's a reason we call ships 'she.' Sir."

"Fascinating," Spock said, with only partial irony. "So you feel your emotions actually enhance your work—indeed, are even essential to it."

"I can't say as I've really thought it out that way, sir, but I suppose so. I can't imagine doing this—doing anything—without a passion to fire you. I figure you could say emotions are like the power source that drives the machine. . . . If that helps you see it in more concrete terms, sir."

"Perhaps it does," Spock said thoughtfully. "But what does one do when the power source is too strong for the machine to regulate?"

Scott shrugged. "Well, if it's a machine you either replace the power source or the regulators. But with a person . . . well, that's the sort of thing where you just have to go with your gut. Feel your way through to the right balance."

"I am afraid," Spock said, "that I find that rather circular."

"Sorry I can't be more help, sir."

"Nonetheless, Mr. Scott, your efforts are appreciated."

Scott fidgeted a bit. "Well . . . back to work, then."

"Indeed."

Christopher Lindstrom stood in the Hall of the Creators, hoping he would soon gaze upon their benevolent countenances. The S.C.E. lieutenant estimated it would take another ten minutes.

It had been a long road getting here, though he'd walked through it many times without knowing what it was. The key had finally come to him when he'd figured out what had been bothering him in the oral histories he'd been collecting—or specifically in the repeated phrase, "The Halls of the Creators, where the privileged are laid to rest." The anomaly had been that one key word, "privileged." These were tales from the subalterns, the lower classes of the society. To them, Lindstrom had realized, the privileged were the opposition. Openly expressing disapproval of the elites would have been a quick route to a deep-fried frontal lobe, but could there be a veiled irony in the tales, with "privileged" as a code word for the bad guys? To people who'd lived their lives without privilege, the code would have needed no explanation, but to someone without that context, the irony would have been missed.

So, what if being laid to rest in the Halls of the Creators was not something to be admired, but rather something to be disapproved of? Maybe that was what the conflict had been over—maybe the "privileged" had assumed a privilege that others felt they had no right to.

Then he thought about the "laid to rest" part. That implied burial. But the Yonadi hadn't practiced burial. They'd lived in a closed, artificial ecosystem, in which everything was supposed to be recycled. Traditionally, dead bodies were sent to the recycling chambers along with all other materials—with more ceremony and via a different path, but it all ended up in the same place. True, natural burial was a means of recycling biomass—as Hamlet had put it, "A man may fish with the worm that hath eat of a king, and eat of the fish that hath fed of that worm"—but its efficiency had been too low for Yonada's purposes. So burial would have been seen as wasteful, an act that deprived the People of necessary resources—perhaps a vanity for those who wished to have marked grave sites for their family members. Given the environmental crises that had plagued Yonada for the better part of a millennium (according to the science staff's latest results) prior to the institution of the modern Oracular state, such wastefulness could certainly have been grounds for conflict.

But then, the Halls of the Creators couldn't be an afterlife. They had to be somewhere physical on Yonada itself. But where? Not the temple—there were levels of machinery beneath it, and certainly no room for graves. The engineering complex that ran Yonada might have been "the Halls of the Creators," but tricorder scans showed no interred remains beneath them. Possibly some geographical feature on the surface, some particularly impressive valleys?

The key had come from one of the books in the recovered mountain cache. One of the fragmentary texts had contained a reference to "the Hall of the Creators." Score one for Spock: the oral histories had confused singular with plural somewhere along the line. And in the singular, the Fabrini word for "hall" meant a corridor or passage, not an auditorium or building as in English. Knowing he was looking for a single, specific passageway, Lindstrom could narrow it down to those that were large enough to host a battle and to hold a significant number of graves, which had solid ground underneath to accommodate those graves, and

which were central or architecturally impressive enough to
deserve a name like "Hall of the Creators." Spock had made
a good suggestion of his own: look someplace close to the
rulers' power base, since that would be a logical place for
the privileged elites to bury their dead.

Indeed, the wide, high-ceilinged passageway where he
now stood was just outside Yonada's governmental complex, from which the priesthood and their bureaucracy had
done the day-to-day business of carrying out the Oracle's
will. Tricorder scans had revealed over two dozen tombs
carved into the stone underneath—even more of a waste of
resources than Lindstrom had surmised, since there was no
means for the remains (which were mummified anyway) to
get back into the ecosystem. They'd also revealed that the
walls were a late addition, dating from 6,200 years ago, and
that the original walls behind them were coated in various
pigments dating back as far as 9,800 years. The sensors
couldn't discern between the pigments well enough to
reconstruct the images, so there had been nothing for it but
to call in the S.C.E. team to remove the outer wall with all
possible delicacy.

The team had used precisely calibrated excavation
phasers on wide beam to break the molecular bonds of the
plaster, crumbling most of it away, but had used quick
bursts to ensure that the effect didn't penetrate all the way to
the inner wall. That had left a thin coating, which they'd
been slowly abrading with sonic cleansers. Finally some
colors were starting to show through, and Lindstrom had
been nearly jumping out of his skin with impatience to see
the rest. He was relieved when the team leader handed him
a brush and invited him to join in the final phase of plaster
removal, the old-fashioned way.

For the next hour or so, his perspective was limited to the
detail level, an eye here, a hand there, a swath of color
somewhere else. It helped distract him from his eagerness to

see the whole. But finally he was able to step back and behold what the ancient Yonadi had wrought.

Somebody sixty-two centuries ago had tried to erase this mural from the People's knowledge, but in so doing they'd preserved it beautifully. It was a portrait of the Creators, looking very much like the icons in Rishala's temple. There was Vari with his golden armor and high-crowned helmet; Baima with her blindingly white hair tumbling around her plump, matronly frame, her nudity representing the unadorned Truth; young Dedi beside her, her hand on his shoulder, as he gazed out at the viewer with a querulous, challenging gaze that demanded answers; Nalai the Midwife, her lower face devotedly focused on the babies nursing at her four breasts while the upper gazed unflinchingly out toward their future. Even Nidra's face could be seen, a shadow in the lurid red sun that filled the sky.

But what struck Lindstrom was the shape that stood in the Creators' midst, with Vari's hammer and chisel at its base as though he'd just carved it. A tall, angular monolith of gray-black marble with white veins, with a golden starburst shining in its center, illuminating the scene more brightly than Nidra's sun—the altar of the Oracle of the People. Rendered here ninety-eight centuries ago, near the start of Yonada's journey. Rendered as a religious icon, in the midst of the Creators.

"You know what this means?" he said to Spock over his wrist communicator, after uploading an image from his tricorder to Spock's.

What it suggests, at any rate. That the central computer was defined as the Oracle from the beginning. That the Creator religion was originally used as a basis for state authority, and the secular state arose later. That is, assuming we can be sure the mural dates back to the early postlaunch era.

"I think it does, sir. There are newer pigments—it

must've been restored several times—but tricorder scans show it's the same image all the way down to the rock." He reached out gingerly to touch the ancient image. "We should announce this, sir. It might undo some of the damage Natira did by releasing the earlier findings prematurely."

"Exactly why we should not be premature now, Mr. Lindstrom. This is a valuable piece of the puzzle, but revealing it before we have context will only make it easier for various factions to co-opt it to suit their own agendas."

"Understood, sir. It's just . . . it might convince Natira to back down a little. Maybe be a little more open-minded."

There was a pause. *"It seems that will not be necessary. Dr. McCoy can at times be very persuasive."*

Rishala knelt at the head of the low hexagonal table in the temple's meeting room, looking around her at the community leaders gathered there, and for the first time she felt like an outsider in their eyes.

Or was it the first time? Perhaps it had been building for years now, too subtly to notice. Once, back on Yonada, she had been one with the common People. She had held no formal authority, but for some reason people had found her thoughts worth listening to, had invited her to speak the tales of the Creators, had sought her advice and approval on matters beneath the notice or outside the interest of the Oracle and its priesthood. She'd insisted that she was no wiser than they, but she'd been glad to help, and the community had welcomed her help.

Once Natira had apostatized and dismantled the priesthood, the People had felt a need to have that vacuum filled, and to Rishala's alarm and embarrassment, the consensus had swiftly emerged that she should adopt the title of high priestess and lead a faith shaped by popular will rather than Oracular fiat. She had succumbed to that will, in part because certain defrocked members of the priesthood (including a minor functionary named Dovraku, though he'd attracted little notice at the time) had begun campaigning to regain some of their lost power, and Rishala had concluded that her leadership would be the least of possible evils.

But formal authority, even that given to her by the will of the People, had created a distance between her and the People, however much she had tried to pretend it didn't. Maybe that was why they'd begun to drift gradually away in the ensuing years, experimenting with novel sects and ideologies. Or maybe it was because she hadn't exercised that authority enough, hadn't provided the guidance they needed to achieve spiritual harmony.

Or maybe it wasn't about you at all, came that wise voice which she liked to think was Baima speaking in her mind. *Maybe the People simply needed to exercise the freedom they'd been given, to stretch their spirits and search for new possibilities.*

For that matter, things would probably have been all right if Natira hadn't begun her campaign to Federationize Lorina, to quash the beliefs and customs of the People. That made them angry and afraid, and allowed factions built on anger and fear to gain a foothold. Rishala herself had seen those factions as an uneasy ally against their common foe, Natira. But it had become increasingly unclear which faction was leading the charge. The extremists were far fewer, but they spoke far more loudly, drowning out the more moderate voices that outnumbered theirs, and appealing to the People's baser impulses and desire for quick, simple answers. Those who spoke of compromise risked appearing weak or disloyal by contrast. Rishala had let herself go along with this, failing to recognize that she was no longer setting the agenda.

Now she saw how they looked at her. She had given Kirk the godkiller hospitality in the temple. She had accepted hospitality aboard his starship. And she had somehow managed to persuade the state to cancel its warrant for her arrest. She looked into the eyes of her fellow community leaders—some of whom she'd known for decades as leading members of Yonadan society, some who had only risen to prominence during the social changes of the past few years—and saw doubts about her loyalties. She knew that what she had to say next would only intensify those doubts. She prayed that Vari and Baima would give her the strength and wisdom she needed to win them over.

"My friends—if there's one thing we can all agree on, it has to be that we want the violence to end. But if we keep going the way we are, it can only continue the vicious cycle. All the voices of the People need to join in a dialogue so that we may smooth the discord between us."

"Of course," said Kemori, who sat across the table from her, determined to claim the second most commanding position if he couldn't hold the first. The young politician was always pushing to gain any edge he could. There was an intensity to him that reminded Rishala of Kirk, though she found Kirk far more trustworthy. "So I have always said. But there is nothing we can do if the other side refuses to participate in good faith."

"That may be changing," Rishala said. "Dumali?"

The middle-aged redhead to her right leaned forward, her eyes taking in the group one by one. Dumali was the only one of the community leaders gathered here who actually held a post in Natira's government, as head of the loyal opposition party. But that party was so powerless in the government that Dumali still held the trust of those in the not-so-loyal opposition—extremists aside. She retained close ties with the common people from whom she'd come, despite being an agnostic on spiritual matters, and stayed in back-channel contact with the opposition groups. This was the first time she had exercised those back channels with

Natira's endorsement. "I've been asked by Natira to arrange a summit meeting. She wants to talk, and it sounds like she might finally be willing to listen."

Predictably, Mifase scoffed. "It's just another trick. Get us to the table, then arrest us all."

"I believe it's sincere," Rishala said. "Captain Kirk has joined Natira in making this request."

"Yes," Mifase interrupted, "we all know how *close* you've gotten with the godkiller."

Rishala ignored him. Mifase was the sort who defined his piety in opposition to the shortcomings of others, rather than through the demonstration of any positive traits of his own. His sect was a bit of a theological muddle, promoting a return to the way things had been on ancient Fabrina in the age of the Creators, but extremely vague on the specifics of what that meant, aside from being the opposite of whatever the listener disliked about the way things were now. But he had managed to play off the negative feelings of the community to advance his own negativity and make himself a popular figure. Rishala had no desire to strengthen him by giving him more to fight against.

But Kemori wouldn't make it so easy. "He has a point, Rishala. Many people are wondering about your . . . friendliness toward the enemy."

She smiled patiently. "I would call it 'fairness,' Kemori. I believe everyone deserves a fair hearing. And I've found that Kirk is a fair man. He and his crew are not our enemies. They are . . . misguided in some ways, but willing to listen to reason."

"The time for reason is past!" Mifase exclaimed. "The blood of too many believers has been shed. They cry for vengeance, not talk! There can be no negotiation!"

"There *must* be, or the blood of far more believers—in many different things—will be shed."

"But what we want is for Natira to be gone." That was

Sonaya, a willowy older woman who headed the Book sect. Rishala admired her ability to extract spiritual meaning from the dry, technical contents of the Book of the People; such a feat was certainly beyond her own imagination. "Isn't it?" The Bookists were not one of the more extremist sects. Many of their tenets were compatible with the Federation view, with its materialist, scientific slant on things. Yet the Book spoke extensively of the Oracle, making its adherents sympathetic to the idea of the Oracle's return.

"What we want is for the state to end its assaults on our traditions. We strive for our way of life, not against any one person."

"But that one person has made herself the symbol of Fedraysha corruption," Kemori interposed slickly. "The People will settle for nothing less than her removal."

Dumali responded with a politician's polish that matched his. "The Creators know, I would like nothing more than to see Natira removed from power. But surely it'd be better to do it through negotiation. Do we want a fanatic like Dovraku to take over?"

"If the Creators have sent Dovraku as their avenging sword," Mifase shot back, "then we must heed their will or be cut down."

Kemori spoke more calmly. "Dovraku represents what the People want: decisive action against Natira and her Fedraysha masters. He is our best chance for driving them out, whether by persuading them to cut their losses and surrender, or through . . . more final means. Once they are gone, we shall have the luxury to debate what form our new government should take."

Rishala looked at him pityingly. "And do you really think Dovraku would share yo . . . our opinion of your aptitude for leadership, Kemori? Do you think he would allow anyone but himself to rule Lorina?"

"It would be the Oracle that ruled," came a gentle reminder from Paravo, finally weighing in from where he sat on Rishala's left. "As it did before." The elderly fellow's desire to remain in the past meant he was the only one here who still held the same high opinion of Rishala that he always had, but it also meant he was sympathetic to Dovraku's professed goals.

"Only its program would be even more restrictive, narrower in its definition of acceptable behavior," Rishala reminded him. "The Instruments could strike people down for any defiance of rigid machine logic as Dovraku defines it—for singing songs of the Creators, for wearing impractical clothes, for laughing out loud. For daring to have a thought not generated within the Oracle's algorithms. Is that the cozy past you want to reclaim, old friend?"

"It would cleanse the world of sinners," Mifase said, glaring at Rishala as he did.

"Naturally Dovraku would be unable to dictate the Oracle's programming by himself," Kemori said. "He knows he does not have the power base for that. Once the current regime has collapsed and been replaced by one more sympathetic to his agenda, he can join us in the process of determining the Oracle's new parameters."

Rishala shook her head. "You aren't that naive, Kemori. You know he'll never compromise. If you're not One, you're Zero, and he'll reduce you to zero with explosives if necessary."

"But at the moment he believes us to be sympathetic. And that means that once the revolution is over, he will permit us to get close. This will provide us with . . . options for dealing with him should he become intractable."

"And do you think he won't have 'options' of his own ready to deploy at the first sign of betrayal?"

"But that's just it," Sonaya said. "How betrayed will he feel by us if we agree to these negotiations?"

"It's only talk," Dumali pointed out. "We don't have to commit to anything that we or . . . our constituents don't like."

Rishala turned to stare at the party leader. "Then how can we ever hope to end this? There's no way the state will agree to all our terms, any more than we'll agree to all of theirs. We must be willing to negotiate in earnest."

"Believe me, Rishala, I want to. But I have to consider the realities of the situation. I can't serve our people if they turn on me."

"You mean if Dovraku has you assassinated for not being extremist enough." She took all the others in with her gaze. "Look at us. We call the state our enemy and Dovraku an uneasy ally. But we feel able to defy the state, to speak and act openly against it . . . but we are all too terrified of Dovraku to defy him in any way! So ask yourselves: Who is our enemy? Who is the menace to our survival, to our freedom to believe as we choose? And if we really consider ourselves the defenders of the People—if we really want to *deserve* that label—who is it that we should really be fighting?"

The others were chastened. But Paravo spoke softly. "At least Dovraku believes in the Creators and their Oracle. He's dangerous, yes, but he fights for the cause we all share. He is one of us."

"Yes," Rishala said, "as Nidra is one of the Creators. We can love him as one of our own, just as the Creators love their sister. But though they love her, still she must walk alone, for she is the Creator of fire and lies, that which destroys all other Creations. And though they love her, still they fight her at every turn, for it is only by battling her lies unto the end of time that they have any hope of ever saving her from herself.

"Nidra made the fire that forged the Oracle's metal. She made the fire that drove Yonada through the stars, and powered her machines. The Oracle was Nidra's Creation most of all, and Nidra is the Creator whom Dovraku serves. He makes his case through fire, and makes us become liars for fear of being burned."

She was on her feet now, and held them all in the thrall of her eyes and voice. "And what of the other Creators we love and serve? What of Miura the Farmer, nurturer of life? What of Nalai the Midwife, guardian of birth and renewal, protector of children? What of Dedi the Questioner, who sees the flaw in every lie? What of Baima the Wise, who threw herself to the fire to preserve the Truth? And what of Vari the Mighty, father of us all, who would let no obstacle stand before him and his People?

"How do we serve these, our Creators, by letting Nidra's champion control us? By meeting the hand of peace with pretense and hypocrisy? By letting ourselves see only material illusions like political gain and nostalgia and base survival, when the legacy our Creators left us is in such danger?"

"Pretty words, Rishala," said Sonaya after a moment. "Maybe *you* are willing to die for what you believe in. But then who will advance that cause? Who will serve any of our causes if we are all killed?"

"Who is serving them now?"

Silence echoed in response. "Dovraku has already smothered us," Rishala went on. "What does it matter that our hearts still beat? If you are so afraid of being dead, Sonaya, how can you stand to be as you are now? How can you refuse a chance to live again, to make a real difference?

"I for one am going to meet with Natira and Kirk. I will work with them to try to find a compromise that we all can live with. I will no doubt have to make concessions, but my bargaining position will be stronger the more of you I have with me. Who will come?"

Dumali was the first to stand. "I'm officially supposed to

be there anyway. But I'll come in spirit as well as body."

Paravo was next. "I'm an old man. . . . I'd like to see some peace again in this life."

Kemori hesitated, but then stood. "The only way the People will accept this is if they see a strong presence there representing their interests. Someone they trust to hold to a strong position. Someone not perceived as soft toward the Fedraysha," he finished with a pointed look at Rishala.

Paravo scoffed. "You just don't want to be left out of the pictures."

Then Sonaya tentatively rose. "If we do it that way— maintain a firm stand—perhaps it will not be seen as a betrayal."

Mifase skewered her with his gaze. "Fool. You are all traitors. The People will accept nothing less than the execution of the heretic Natira and all who support her. You are all welcome to burn in the cleansing fire." He turned and stormed from the room.

Sonaya looked to Rishala in alarm. "He's going to tell Dovraku."

"I know. We should arrange to have this meeting very soon. And all of you, keep your arrangements as secret as possible."

"But where can we meet that will be safe?" Paravo asked.

Rishala looked skyward. "Someplace you will be glad to see again, old friend."

CHAPTER FOURTEEN

We must acknowledge once and for all that the purpose of diplomacy is to prolong a crisis.

—Spock

"I DON'T LIKE THIS, Captain."

"Mr. Chekov, that phrase seems to be a standard part of every security chief's repertoire. You seem to have mastered it very well." Kirk smiled to take the sting out of it, but Chekov still felt stung. The captain leaned casually against the bulkhead next to Chekov's station, but the security chief himself stood straight, trying to minimize his height disadvantage. "The simple fact is, this negotiation isn't the sort of thing I can hand over to somebody else. Rishala won't trust anyone but me."

"I understand that, sir. My concern is with the location." He glanced over Kirk's shoulder at the main viewscreen, where Lorina's recently acquired moon hung like a misshapen meatball. "Yonada is where the Oracle is, sir. It's the one place the fanatics most want to possess."

"Which is exactly why it's so well guarded. There's plenty of security already in place, and access is fully controlled."

"That can go both ways, sir. It will be difficult to maintain transporter locks on the landing party."

"Which is why I'm acceding to your wishes and bringing along a significant security presence."

"I don't consider four people all that significant, sir."

"Considering how edgy the various parties are about having any armed Starfleet presence there at all, it's as significant as it's going to get."

"But if we only had more time to make arrangements . . ."

"The meeting was called on very short notice, specifically out of security concerns. If it takes us by surprise, it should do the same for the terrorists."

"I still don't like it, sir."

Kirk grinned. "Mr. Chekov, if you did like it, *then* I'd worry."

"With all due respect, sir," Chekov said sharply, "I don't think you're taking the matter of security seriously enough. I don't think you're taking *me* seriously enough. I'm not some wet-behind-the-ears ensign anymore, sir. I've trained hard for this. I've *earned* this job, and I know what I'm doing."

Kirk stared at Chekov, looking surprised and hurt. "Is that what you think I think of you . . .?" He straightened, took a step closer. "Mr. Chekov . . . Pavel . . . I have always taken you seriously. You've always been one of my best people. Even when you were still wet behind the ears. Why do you suppose I kept you as my chief navigator longer than anyone else? Why do you suppose I took you on so many landing parties, even though that's not a normal job for a navigator? Because you were sharp and passionate and adaptable and I wanted to make sure you got the experience you needed to hone that potential."

He clasped Chekov's shoulder lightly. "If I've made you feel that I don't take you seriously, I'm sorry. It's not because of you, it's . . ." He smirked. "It's a security chief's job to mother his captain, and it's a captain's job to fidget and complain about it. The difference is, I didn't get to pull rank on my mother.

"So rest assured, Mr. Chekov, I value your recommendations highly. You just happen to be in the one job that has the hardest sell. It's your job to keep me safe, but it's not my job to be kept safe."

Chekov met his eyes. " 'Risk is our business,' " he quoted sardonically, but understandingly.

"It's why we're out here." Kirk clapped his shoulder once more. "Assemble your teams, Lieutenant, and report to the hangar deck in half an hour."

"Aye, sir." He frowned. "The hangar deck, sir?"

"The other delegations are traveling by shuttle," Kirk said with a shrug, "and protocol apparently demands that we do the same."

Chekov acknowledged the order, but his mind was already racing with new security concerns. He'd have to check in with the hangar deck crew chief and run a safety check on the shuttle—for not all threats to a captain's well-being were the result of conscious malice. He'd want to make sure the shuttle was maneuverable and well-shielded, though; there was no telling how those edgy Shesshran might react to the launch of an *Enterprise* shuttle.

Entering the turbolift and sending it down into the bowels of the ship, Chekov pondered his assignments. If he could pick only three besides himself, he'd have to pick them well. To be honest, he didn't think the odds of serious trouble were too great; the captain was right that Yonada was a more controllable location than somewhere on Lorina would be. The worst danger would be that fighting would break out between the delegates, who were mostly past their physical prime and would not be armed. In that case, Chekov's goal was to establish a strong security presence that would serve as a deterrent just by being seen.

Nizhoni and Howard were already on Yonada with Mr. Spock and his researchers—though a different part of Yonada from the conference site. That rendered them unavailable, since he'd rather keep them there. Worene and M'sharna were still on recuperative leave. That was too bad, since Worene's fierce features made her effectively intimidating despite her slight build—so long as the observer was unaware of her playful, pixieish personality. Perhaps Chavi'rru would do as well, since he had the height as well as the predatory looks; but the 'Geusian was inexperienced and not the most likely being to understand the delicate etiquette of a diplomatic conference. All right, Sh'aow then. The gray-furred Caitian was on duty monitoring the Shesshran activity—who better than a cat to watch winged creatures?—but he could be relieved. Swenson would be an effective presence, with his massive build . . . and for a third . . .

Yes, perhaps this was the time. He hit the intercom. "Crewman Swenson, Crewman Sh'aow . . . and Ensign Zaand, report to me in the hangar bay in fifteen minutes. Chekov out."

The lift deposited him on Deck 18, on the second level of the cavernous cargo/landing bay complex that took up most of the secondary hull in this new design. It was one of the largest open spaces Chekov had ever seen inside a Starfleet vessel, so wide that two exposed turboshafts ran straight through it from floor to ceiling, for there was nowhere else to fit them in this part of the ship. And when the retractable floor was rolled back into the hulls for access to the storage bays below, it was even huger.

Instead of pumping the air out for launch as before—which would have been prohibitively time-consuming for this vast space—this design depended on a single forcefield across the hangar doors to hold in that enormous volume of air. It was a low-level forcefield at that, the "momentum filter" type, strong enough to contain something lightweight like an air molecule or a hapless crew member, but weak enough to be penetrated by a massive object like a shuttlecraft. That was the theory, anyway, but it seemed to Chekov that the mass of all these individual air molecules had to add up. Starfleet had a lot of confidence in its forcefields, but as Chekov made his way back to the shuttle hangars, he decided he was just as glad that the landing-bay doors were closed at the moment.

Wanting something maneuverable and combat-capable, he chose to eschew the regular wedge-shaped shuttles and had the crew chief ready Shuttlecraft 9, the *Zhang Sui*. The winged, bullet-shaped six-seater was designed for combat operations, with fighterlike maneuverability, a large cockpit window for good visibility, and gull-wing doors for swift entry and exit. Chekov knew Sulu had been involved in its design and testing and was eager to try it out for real; but Spock was doing research on Yonada and Scotty's duties were keeping him out of the bridge rotation for the duration of the shakedown, so Sulu would have to hold down the center seat while Chekov piloted his new toy. He smiled at the thought. He wouldn't have let that consideration sway his decision, of course, but it was a nice perk.

Fifteen minutes wasn't quite enough time to perform a preflight safety check on the *Zhang Sui*, but Chekov was content to let his team wait; that was a large part of their job, after all. When he was done clearing the shuttle, he was pleased to see his team standing stoically at attention, awaiting his instructions. He made his way across the echoing hangar bay and gave them a quick, efficient mission briefing.

With that out of the way, though, he pulled Zaand aside. The Rhaandarite was practically beaming with boyish grat-

itude and enthusiasm. "I'm glad to see you're looking forward to this," Chekov said. "But I assume I can count on
you to keep your excitement under control."

"Of course, sir. I'll respect all the appropriate behavioral
protocols."

"And you do realize that we'll be working closely with
Captain Kirk."

Zaand's expression became carefully neutral. "I understand that, sir."

"I thought it would do you good to see the captain at
work—particularly in a diplomatic situation. It's a chance
to learn more about how he really does things, how his mind
works. Make the most of the opportunity, Ensign."

"Aye, sir. I'll do my best, sir." He seemed sincere
enough, and Chekov chose to take it as a good sign. He
really hoped that Zaand could come to terms with serving
under Kirk. He was a bit raw, but he had a sharp mind and
keen observational skills, very beneficial traits in security.
And his enthusiasm for the work—not just the Rhaandarite
love of order, but his own eagerness to succeed—was something Chekov was glad to see. It reminded him of the
overeager ensign he'd been just a few short years ago—a
lifetime ago.

If the *Enterprise*'s hangar complex was huge, then
Yonada's was absolutely immense. It had originally housed
over a thousand ships, intended to shuttle a population of
millions down to Lorina's surface. Many had been massive
single-use landers, hulking spheres that still stood where
they had plunked themselves down on the surface, some
converted into living space, others (those less conveniently
situated) designated as monuments—especially the one
that had crash-landed in the mountains, killing all 2,400 of
its occupants. The landers had been designed with every
possible safeguard, and the S.C.E. had carefully refur-

bished every one before clearing it for use; but entry, descent, and landing would always remain a perilous undertaking no matter how many precautions were taken. That was why transporters had caught on so widely. But beaming Yonada's million and change to the surface would have been prohibitive.

Most of the ships had been reusable surface-to-orbit shuttles of various sizes and designs; apparently the Fabrini had crammed their asteroidal ark with every available STO craft they had. The bulk of the population transfer had been done this way, a few dozen or hundred people at a time, over and over again for months on end. There had been fatalities here too, of course, but "only" in the low hundreds. Afterward, the Federation engineers and archaeologists had gone crazy over the shuttles, studying them to learn all they could about Fabrini technology and material culture. But many of the shuttles had remained in use, providing the Lorini with the orbital capability that they used to maintain Yonada, to emplace weather and comm satellites, and to survey their new planet for prospective settlement sites and hidden perils.

Now a few of those shuttles were returning to their hangar again, ferrying the various delegations from the surface, along with the *Zhang Sui* from the *Enterprise*. As Chekov piloted the shuttle to follow them into the hangar, Kirk watched from behind, experiencing a sense of déjà vu. Closing in on the vast, artificial asteroid-vessel, flying through a gaping orifice into a dark, cavernous space large enough to hold the *Enterprise*—it reminded him of the journey into V'Ger. Why had that seemed so much more awesome than this? Yonada was far larger than V'Ger had been. But Kirk hadn't entered it this way before. Transporters might have been a safer way to travel, but they were far less scenic. And even now, Yonada's rough, crater-pitted surface was far more mundane than the eldritch techno-organic

landscape of V'Ger, with its intricate textures and bizarre
geometries, its rolling striated hills and deep chasms alternating with immense plains of pure energy. In all his jour-
neys, Kirk had never beheld a sight as profoundly, beautifully alien as V'Ger. But Yonada was just a big hunk of
rock, its outer surface nothing but an ugly agglomeration of
asteroid fragments accreted against the outer shell and
melted just enough to flow together into an uneven but solid
mass. Judging from what Spock's people now believed, the
rough surface hadn't even been meant as a deliberate dis-
guise; it had just been a bare-bones, down-and-dirty way to
shield the generation ship against space debris and radiation. But that in its own way was something worthy of awe,
Kirk reflected. It was remarkable what the Fabrini had
accomplished with the limited time and technology at their
disposal.

The hangar facility was actually located above the
Yonadan "sky," in one of the two largest bulges of the
roughly octahedral asteroid; the fission thrusters occupied
the other, on the opposite end. The Yonadi had forgotten
the existence of this facility until the Book of the People
had revealed how to reach it through a bank of elevators in
the adjacent "mountain"—elevators that had been sealed
off by some prior regime. The *Enterprise*'s initial scans
hadn't revealed it, since it was shielded by the same
kelbonite-victurium alloy as the inner shell—meaning it
would be difficult to beam anyone in or out. The conference would be held in a hastily converted staging room of
the hangar complex, which made a suitably neutral ground
because, though it was part of Yonada, it was not a part
which had any prior association with any of the factions
involved.

If nothing else, the various parties all appeared equally
tense as Kirk entered the debarcation lounge. Fortunately
it was a large room, since there were quite a few people

here and it was good to have some space between them. Natira had brought a few government functionaries and a number of security troops led by Tasari, along with Soreth, who was here to help Kirk represent the Federation team but had found it more efficient to travel with Natira. Kirk had to wonder how that would look to the other side. Mr. Lindstrom, more concerned about appearances, had chosen to go to the trouble to beam aboard the *Enterprise* and take the shuttle with Kirk. There had been a practical gain from that too, since it had given Kirk a chance to confer briefly with the sociologist about negotiating strategies. On the other end of the room, Rishala stood with three other figures in traditional dress, presumably her fellow religious and community leaders. They were flanked by a few burly types in homespun, apparently their own informal security, who were exchanging antagonistic looks with Tasari's men.

Kirk was about to step forward and say something to try to break the tension when a well-groomed, fiftyish redhead stepped forward from Natira's group (its far outskirts, in fact) and spoke with an orator's polished delivery, albeit without the upper-class grandeur of Natira's speech. "Good, we are now all here. For those who don't know me, I am Dumali, minority leader in the Lorina Parliament. As an official of the state and a friend of the People, I hope that I may help to bridge the divide between our factions. At the very least," she said with a self-deprecating smile, "I'm in a position to make introductions. If you will all follow me into the meeting chamber . . ."

Tasari stepped forward. "*After* my people have done a security sweep."

"And our people," said the younger of the men with Rishala.

"Of course," Kirk interposed. "And my people will go with you both to make sure everything goes smoothly."

While the security teams swept the room and checked each other's work, Dumali proceeded with the introductions. Rishala's associates turned out to be Kemori, an influential secular leader in the community; Sonaya, head of the Bookist sect; and Paravo, an elderly fixture of the community, who commanded much respect but little authority (or so Lindstrom whispered in Kirk's ear). Kirk noted that Kemori made a point of acting like he was in charge of the group, though the others gravitated around Rishala. The dark-haired young man also made a point of confronting Kirk. "I wish to make it abundantly clear," Kemori said in what Kirk was coming to recognize as an upper-class accent, "that the People will not allow ourselves to be bullied by your presence. Our faith and our resolve remain as firm as ever."

"No one is here to bully anyone, Mr. Kemori," Kirk said pleasantly. "I have great respect for your people's beliefs and their resolve."

"Difficult words to believe, coming from a man who makes a career out of dismantling other people's Oracles."

Kirk didn't rise to the bait. "In fact, as our shuttle was on approach to Yonada just now, I found myself deeply awed by the achievements of your Creators." He pitched his voice louder. "Whatever . . . differences our various groups may have in our interpretation of the Creators, I'm sure we can all agree that they were remarkable beings of great wisdom and foresight. And it's my hope that we can use that agreement as the basis for a broader accord."

"Well spoken, Captain," Kemori said with veiled skepticism. "We shall see if your actions live up to your words."

The various security people emerged and declared the room safe, and Dumali led the negotiators in—insisting that each security force be allowed only one guard within the room itself. Kirk brought Chekov in. Kemori objected when Tasari ordered one of his men to follow him, but Natira reminded them that Tasari was her Minister of Security, no mere guard. An argument seemed about to break out, until Dumali persuaded the opposition representatives to back down.

Kirk had envisioned his role as that of a neutral mediator, but Dumali seemed to be the one assuming that role here. Kirk reminded himself that in the eyes of the opposition, he and the Federation were in bed with Natira's government, or even controlling it outright. Dumali was apparently considered the closest thing here to a neutral party, if only because her dual allegiances canceled each other out. "Governess Natira has asked to speak first," Dumali said, "and we at least owe that courtesy to her office, and to her former role as high priestess." Whatever unflattering subtext may have underlaid her words, she kept it from her voice. Kemori seemed about to object, but Rishala quieted him with a look and a nod. Kirk was content to let the others set the pace, and only step in if . . . be honest, *when* things got out of hand.

Natira rose, and took in the others with her gaze. As always, she took on a grand oratorical mien. "My fellow Lorini, and esteemed guests from the Federation, I thank you for coming. This conference is far overdue . . . and I confess that I have been largely responsible for that." The opposition members appeared stunned. Natira's haughtiness took on an unaccustomed tinge of contrition. "I have always loved the People with a passion, and that zeal to do what I believe is best for them has sometimes led me to excess. The passion of those who disagree with me is no less, and we have all been driven to certain excesses in recent times. Excess has built upon excess, and it cannot end until someone makes the choice to step back from one's passion and break the cycle.

"Today I make that choice. Each of us has our own vision for the future of the People, and I am ready to admit that my vision cannot succeed alone. We must combine our visions and discern a common future, or we can be sure of having none at all.

"However," she added, "the choice must be mutual to succeed. We must ease off the pressure together, or we will unbalance the whole. I tell you bluntly now, I am prepared to make concessions—but only if you are prepared to do the same."

"That," Kemori countered, "depends entirely on what you would have us concede."

"Firstly, of course, that the terrorism must end."

"Dovraku is not under our control."

"But he has your support. His agents are sheltered among those who heed your speeches and sermons. His resources and funds are supplied by the alleged charity groups you organize. Those groups must be dismantled."

"That's unacceptable," Rishala interposed. "Our charities perform essential services for the People, particularly for those the state has turned its back on. They provide our People with the only alternatives to your secular education, your modern clothes."

"And they provide Dovraku with funds, with bomb-making materials, with intelligence on his targets."

"They do what they believe they must to take care of the People. If *you* can convince them, through us, that the state no longer threatens the People's way of life, then they won't work against the state anymore. Their existence is not the problem."

"But they undermine our efforts to provide optimal services and opportunities to all the People. At the very least, they need to be incorporated into the formal social-services infrastructure, so their efforts may be coordinated with ours."

"If that means compromising our traditions, then the state remains a threat."

"If I may," Kirk interjected, "I think we've already established that some compromise will be necessary on both sides."

Rishala gave him a nod of acknowledgment. "Yes, indeed. Perhaps I was overzealous." She threw Natira an impish look, daring her to comment. The governess retained her aplomb.

Kemori leaned forward. "But the state has yet to give any indication of what compromises it will make, beyond vague platitudes. If the state wants Dovraku neutralized as an enemy to peace, then we demand the removal of the other enemy to the peace: Governess Natira herself."

Natira shot to her feet. "That is unacceptable! I am the one who came here offering to make a compromise."

"Exactly. You asserted your willingness to step back—and your desire to maintain the balance. If you wish to convince us of your sincerity on both counts, it will take a gesture of unmistakable commitment. Your willingness to surrender your office would be the most effective such gesture."

"The governorship is an elected office, is it not?" Kirk asked. "Surely the People can choose for themselves whom they'd rather have as a leader."

"But the election is not for two more years," said Natira.

"And the current laws only give suffrage to the literate," said Kemori. "It biases the electorate toward Natira and her modern Fedraysha ideas."

"It takes an informed electorate to make a responsible choice," Soreth interposed.

"There are other ways to be informed than reading," Rishala told him. "When we can't read, we talk, we listen, we share in the community. We are informed of each other, of the soul of the People, not of some distant star or ancient war recorded in a computer file. So how are we not qualified to vote on the issues that affect the People?"

Soreth studied her. "Do you think that if the mass of Lorini were to vote at this time, they would allow the Federation to remain?"

"They probably wouldn't," she told him bluntly.

"That would be very unwise. Yours is still a young settlement, trying to tame a wild planet. How many more of your people would have died without the advice and assistance of the Federation? Leaving aside the fact that your entire civilization would have been destroyed, along with that of the Shesshran, if not for the intervention of the Starfleet captain seated at this table."

"If I may, Commissioner," Kirk said a bit sharply, then turned to address the others. "I'm sure the Commissioner didn't mean to imply that you are under any obligation to us in return for our assistance. Our only purpose here is . . . to help you to stay on the course that you decide is best for you, and to reach your destination safely."

"And what if we do decide," Kemori asked, "that the best course for us is one that takes us away from the Federation?"

Kirk thought for a moment, then met Rishala's eyes. "Your high priestess pointed out to me," he said, "that when I helped put Yonada back on course I took on a share of the responsibility for this world. Now, I'm not here to force my beliefs, my choices on anyone. But I am involved with this world. The Federation is involved with this world. And it's too late to turn back history and make it as if that never happened. The Federation would respect your choices . . . but any choice you make will be *about* the Federation on some level, whether you choose to work with it or to work against it. Either way, we're part of what happens now." He grew introspective. "Life is about change. Sometimes you get a second chance, you can regain something you thought you'd lost . . . but it won't be the same. The things that happened in between will change it, will change you. And you can't just fall back into the old patterns, you have to try to figure out new ones, and make peace with the things that are different." He gave a self-deprecating smile. "Anyway, that's what I think. I'm not sure how much it has to do with any—"

He was interrupted by an explosion from outside. The negotiators all shot to their feet and the guards rushed toward the door, but then another blast blew it open. Chekov was saved only because the body of Tasari's man took the brunt of the debris; Kirk saw instantly that nothing could save that man. Then a small narrow shape shot through the door—a crossbow bolt?—and erupted into a cloud of gas. Those nearest to the point of impact began choking and collapsing.

Kirk found himself closest to Natira, and he pulled her aside, away from the toxic cloud. He indecorously ripped a piece from her flowing gown, resolving to apologize later, and tore it in two to make masks for the governess and himself. As he did, he saw black-robed, masked figures barging into the room, and pulled Natira back behind the ruins of the door. Then Chekov appeared, covering them and firing at the attackers, who returned fire with more conventional crossbow bolts. But Kirk saw one of them loading a bolt with a large cannister attached, and opted for the better part of valor. "Retreat!"

Outside, he found the antechamber a blasted wreck, and the various guards in similar condition. There were fatalities, though fortunately none of his. "Report!" Chekov called.

"An ambush," Zaand replied. "Only five, but well armed and well trained. No fear of death. The first one blew himself up."

The crossbow-wielding attacker appeared in the door, and Kirk cried, "Back!" The security team pulled him and Natira back around the corner before the grenade-bolt went off, bringing the ceiling down almost on top of them. "Everyone all right?" Kirk called when he'd caught his breath.

"Sh'aow's leg is broken from before," Zaand reported. Kirk was surprised; the stoic Caitian had shown no sign of pain. "Swenson was hurt too, but he's mobile." Otherwise everyone seemed intact. But Kirk saw there was no going back. The terrorists had Soreth, Lindstrom, Tasari, Dumali, Kemori . . . "Rishala," he whispered. Then he turned to the others. "Come on," he said. They would find a safe place to regroup, and then attempt to rescue the rest—if they were still alive.

"Something isn't right," Uhura said.

McCoy rubbed his eyes and tried to work the crick out of his neck. "I'll say. I like books better when they're small enough to read in bed." The two of them were in Yonada's temple today, helping Spock with his research project. Uhura was double-checking the computer's translations, comparing the scans of the mountain cache and the inscriptions on Lindstrom's mural with the original Book of the People. The Book was a hefty tome, its pages made of a strong, flexible polymer that had survived intact for ten millennia—more intact than the computer files for which it had been intended as an emergency backup. A shame the technology had been lost by later generations. Anyway, she'd asked McCoy to compare notes about the modern usage of the language, as he'd learned it during his stay on Lorina.

He would rather have been with Natira right now; they still weren't quite sure where they stood with each other, but they were having fun finding out. All McCoy's claims to prefer the life of a hermit dissolved under a woman's loving touch, something he'd deeply missed. But she was in conference with the opposition right now, and she'd decided it would be bad form for him to be there; she didn't want it to look as if she was, well, in bed with the Federation. And, she'd teased, she didn't want to deal with the distraction he provided, however pleasurable. So that had left McCoy available to grant Uhura's request—for all the good he could probably do. He was better with the spoken than the written, since most of the Lorini had still been illiterate at the time of his visit. He understood the basics of the written language: each symbol represented a syllable, organized into square or rectangular arrays representing words. It reminded him a bit of the *hangul* writing from that Korean restaurant he liked in San Francisco. But he had trouble telling the simple geometric symbols apart. Was *ma* the medium horizontal line or the long horizontal line? So whatever Uhura had spotted was beyond him.

But her observation had drawn Spock's attention. "What is it, Commander?"

"Some of these passages on the mural . . . the words don't seem to fit. There are some awkward clashes of meaning."

"For example?"

"Well . . . some of the terminology is the same as what you might hear in one of Dovraku's sermons—obey the Oracle's commands if you wish to be spared the fate of blasphemers, that sort of thing. Very dogmatic, fire-and-brimstone stuff. But in the context of the mural, it seems out of place. The tone I'm sensing in the text there is far more benevolent. But then a harsher word suddenly appears and makes it feel . . . discordant. Like a piece of music badly transposed to a different key."

McCoy's ear was at least thirty percent tin, so he didn't quite follow. "Well, we know the language has changed, right?" McCoy asked. "Why not just get the original meanings from the probe translations, see how those sound?"

"The translations were imperfect," Spock explained—

of course Spock had an explanation for everything—"without an actual speaker's brain activity for a universal translator to map. Technical and scientific terms could be translated with precision, but more abstract and culturally nuanced terms were a matter of some guesswork. Indeed, for the past several years we have been basing our translation of ancient Fabrini on insights gained from the modern language, assuming the shifts were mostly in pronunciation rather than vocabulary. It is possible that we were—"

He broke off as Nizhoni came into the room. "Sir, the conference is under attack!"

"Report," Spock ordered.

"Details aren't clear, sir—we got a brief comm warning, then heard explosions. But they're definitely after the delegates. The FSes have already gone up to help," she said, referring to the Federation Security forces.

Spock frowned. "That may have been unwise. If the militants have reached Yonada, then the Oracle will be a prime target."

"Don't worry, sir, we're on the—" Just then a projectile shot into the room and blew up in a cloud of noxious smoke. "Oops," Nizhoni said before passing out.

Dovraku strode into the temple of the Oracle, striving to quash the exhilaration which his treacherous flesh inflicted upon his mind. This was merely the inevitable achievement of his destiny, he reminded himself, and there were still more steps to take. "The Vulcan must not be killed," he reminded Moredi and the others as they moved toward the unconscious Fedraysha infidels who soiled the temple.

"And the others?" Moredi asked, glaring at them with hatred, which Dovraku opted to excuse for now.

"Hostages for the Vulcan's cooperation. Their deaths will come in their proper time . . . and at the proper hands," he added, gazing at the cold perfection that was the

Oracle's altar. The Eye of Truth at the heart of the black marble slab lay dormant and dark, as it had been since Natira's betrayal, since Kirk's violation of the temple. Dovraku's flesh tainted him with frustration at his failure to capture those two with the others; he strove to remind himself that their escape could only be temporary. For once he and the Oracle had achieved their destiny together; none could escape them.

The others showed consternation as they moved the body of the dark-skinned alien woman from her Fedraysha console. There on the surface before her lay the Book of the People itself, left carelessly open like some schoolchild's text. It teetered on the edge, but none of his followers dared to touch it. Dovraku moved forward smoothly and caught it up in his hands just as it slipped off. He was intensely cognizant of the symbolism. He was meant to be here at this moment, to take the instrument of the Oracle's resurrection into his hands and play his part in the well-oiled machine of destiny.

He had always known that he was meant for greater things than the rest of the lowly family into which he'd been born. For years, as a child, he'd believed his birth in such circumstances to be a mistake, a cruel joke at his expense. But now he understood that the Oracle had delivered him into that life as an object lesson in the evils of the flesh, of mortal passion. Instead of succumbing to those demons within him, he had quashed them, smothered them, and worked methodically to escape the lower levels, to ensure that he would never be trapped by the kind of frustration and helplessness that had plagued his father. It had been a long fight, but he had worked determinedly, advancing by embracing the Oracle's system and discovering how it could work to his benefit, rather than silently resenting its limits as his father had done so fruitlessly for so long. To be sure, he had only reached the level of a menial clerk within the priesthood, but he had been there, on his way to greater heights, and beginning to recognize that it was what he had been meant for all along. He'd even begun to recognize that there was nothing in the Oracle's laws which absolutely required a high priestess instead of a high priest.

But then the godkiller Kirk had come and silenced the Oracle. And the betrayer Natira—an upstart too young and flighty for the responsibility; he'd never trusted her—had renounced her faith and removed the clergy from formal power. Then that unruly commoner Rishala had usurped the priesthood and purged it of all who deserved to be there, reducing it to a vulgar, superstitious cabal. Dovraku's path to power had been torn away in front of him. For a time he'd despaired, and doubted his destiny. But soon he realized it was simply another trial of his faith. This was a crucial time for the People, the time of the fulfillment of the Promise, and surely they must be tested—their future leader most of all.

Dovraku had even managed to wrest some good from Kirk and Natira's evil deeds. The dissemination of the Book of the People, this divine text he now held in his hands, had given him new insights into the Oracle's true being. He had read of the pure, mathematical logic that formed the essence of his god, and understood it to be the ultimate goal he'd sought all his life. Understood that fleshly passions were a distraction from the truth, and that it had been his ability to overcome them which had enabled him to rise from his squalid beginnings. Now, if he were to pass this new time of trial, he had to raise his spirit to the next level, to seek the divine perfection of the machine. Even the propaganda of the Fedraysha had served him, bringing him the knowledge that the universe was filled with cybernetic gods: Landru, Worldlink, Vaal, and others. He had finally understood the ultimate truth, and begun to preach it, and found others who recognized it. Yet many had doubted. The Oracle had died; the other gods had died. Was there a future in such worship? Dovraku had known this was the true way, all evidence to the contrary. He had known that the divine calculus was eternal, no matter the fate of its worldly forms of stone and metal.

And then he had been vindicated, for V'Ger had arisen and prevailed over the godkiller. It was the proof Dovraku had known would come, the proof that the Machine was eternal, that the Oracle would rise again. It had given the People hope, renewed their faith in the Oracle—and in His prophet. Dovraku had understood that this was the time—the time not only to cleanse the World of Natira, Rishala, and the other blasphemers, but to achieve an even greater destiny than he'd realized. A destiny he was now on the brink of making real.

Confidently, he strode forward and placed his hand on the Eye of Truth, pressing firmly. There was no sense of awe or hesitation in him; he was simply doing what he was meant to do, what everything in his life had prepared him for. His followers fell to their knees in awe as the altar moved forward smoothly, opening the way to the Oracle's greater self beyond; but Dovraku stood tall, unafraid of his own greatness. Cradling the Book in his hands, he stepped behind the altar and into destiny.

What lay beyond was glorious. To a lesser eye sullied by carnal passions, the control complex might have seemed crude, mechanical, prosaic. To Dovraku it was pure and perfect, quintessentially functional. Cold binary logic was the only aesthetic it needed. And far more important than its aspect was its *power*. This was the Oracle's heart and sinew, the mechanism that had once held all Yonada in its omnipotent grasp, and soon would again.

Of course, Yonada itself was an abandoned shell now; but the Oracle had power that extended beyond Yonada, power that Dovraku would use to compel the straying masses of the People to obey the Oracle once more. Rishala with her antique superstitions would call it Nidra's fire; the Fedraysha in their schools called it an energy release from the fission of atoms. Dovraku knew it to be something purer and simpler than either of those: the raw light of Truth which would cleanse the world.

CHAPTER FIFTEEN

None of us can directly comprehend what V'Ger's ascension truly meant. So we treat it simply as a confirmation of whatever we were predisposed to believe: that we are destined to reach higher levels of existence, that we are helpless in a universe of superbeings, that some god or other has sent us a sign, or that we have to be careful lest our creations come back to bite us. But amid all these contradictory views we can perhaps discern a common truth: that wonder and danger go hand in hand, and our future will surely bring both.

—Dr. Monali Bhasin, The Day the Heavens Opened

"WELL, I'LL BE DAMNED," Kirk said. "You really *can* touch the sky."

He, Natira, and Chekov's team had been tracking the terrorists and their captives, who seemed to be heading down toward the inner shell. The catch was, the only way down was the elevator shaft through the mountain, and Kirk was sure the enemy would leave a guard. He and Chekov had been discussing ways of dealing with that when they'd gotten a call from the *Enterprise*, reporting that they'd lost contact with Spock's group at the temple. Shortly thereafter, Yonada's main power had come back online. Kirk had realized that it had been a joint attack, the raid on the conference being at least partly a distraction from Dovraku's real objective, the Oracle itself. By now, the Oracle was probably in terrorist hands.

But it had provided a solution to one problem. With the power back on, the sky projection was back on too, and would provide enough light for Kirk's team to make its way down the outside of the mountain, whereupon they could come at the terrorists from an unexpected direction. Chekov had Yonada's plans stored in his tricorder, and had led the way to a maintenance hatch which came out at the interface of mountain and "sky." When Kirk had emerged and seen the simulated expanse of carnelian sky projected on the roof above him, he couldn't resist reaching out and touching it, as that old man whose name he'd never learned had done all those decades ago, even though it had been forbidden.

Kirk took a moment to wonder about that ill-fated old servant. What had prompted him to risk his life, even knowingly sacrifice his life, in order to tell three strangers that the world was hollow? Kirk had just told the man that he and his friends had come from outside the world—"out there, everywhere, all around." The Yonadi had been oddly accepting of the idea that their world was one of many, and that visitors could come from beyond, so telling him that had only confirmed what he had been told all his life. Yet the old man had spent most of his life convinced it was a lie, for as a boy he had touched the vault of the heavens and found it a solid boundary, his Copernican beliefs shattered by a Ptolemaic reality. But what was it about this one more repetition of the lie (as he believed it) that had prompted him to speak out at last, knowing the consequences? Had he simply grown fed up with keeping his silence and finally stopped caring whether he lived, so long as he could speak the truth just once? His manner had seemed kindlier than that, as though he'd believed the *Enterprise* officers to be dupes themselves, and wished to open their eyes to the truth. Maybe it had even been an act of resistance—maybe he'd concluded that the visitors were free of the Instruments of Obedience and could therefore carry on a fight which he had never been able to lead. Maybe he'd felt that was worth dying for. In which case, the tragedy was that it had been so unnecessary, for of course Kirk, Spock, and McCoy had already known what he wished to tell them.

But there would be far more unnecessary deaths, Kirk reminded himself, if he didn't get moving down this mountain. Fortunately, his recent three-year stay on Earth had given him plenty of time to pursue his mountaineering hobby, in higher gravity than this, so he was well equipped for the challenge. Chekov guaranteed his security team could handle it as well—except for the injured Sh'aow, who'd volunteered to stay behind and secure the shuttlecraft. Kirk had ordered him to take it back to the ship and get his leg tended to, knowing the stubborn Caitian would just grit his teeth and bear it otherwise.

To Kirk's surprise, Natira showed no hesitation about tearing off the skirts of her elaborate gown and making her way down the mountain with the others. She was definitely the type to throw herself headlong into a decision once she'd made it—which could be an asset or a liability, depending on the decision. But then, people had said the same thing about Kirk during the Pelos hearing.

Kirk activated his wrist communicator, turning up the gain so he could have both hands free for climbing. "Kirk to *Enterprise*. Mr. Sulu, any word on where the raiders came from?"

"No, sir. We scanned no transporter beams, and no unauthorized ships docking on Yonada."

"That means they must've come up on one of the ships from the surface."

"We scanned those too," came the voice of Perez at tactical. *"No life signs except what there was supposed to be."*

"Were there any sensor-shielded areas on the ships?" Chekov asked him.

"Only the engine compartments—they're lined with kelbonite. But that's because the radiation from those nuclear rockets is so intense. You'd have to be suicidal to hide in there."

Chekov cursed in Russian. "Dammit, Perez, they *are* suicidal!"

" . . . Oh. Oh, God, sir, I'm sorry, I didn't think. . . ."

"Damn right you didn't!"

"Chekov," Kirk interposed. "Deal with it later." He'd suddenly realized that maybe he hadn't been thinking either. "Sulu, we should be out of the shielded area by now. Can you get a transporter lock on us, beam us to the surface?"

A pause. *"Sorry, sir, you're still in its shadow. Maybe we can find an angle—"*

Perez interrupted. *"Missiles incoming from Yonada, sir!"*

"Shields and forcefield up! Arm phasers! Sorry, Captain, no beaming possible right now."

"Understood." Yonada's asteroid-defense missiles bore crude fission warheads and primitive guidance systems; the *Enterprise* could deal with them handily, but at this close range it would need to keep its defensive shields raised to block the radiation if they detonated. "We'll manage the old-fashioned way." Kirk peered at Natira. "How many of the missiles did you have left?"

"Several dozen. I believe your engineers described their yield as forty kilotons apiece."

Marvelous. With the People mostly clustered around Lorina City, that was more than enough for the fanatics to kill everyone on the planet. "Let's hurry."

•   •   •

"I know you're awake, Commander Spock."

Spock gave no acknowledgment, keeping his eyes closed. He had regained consciousness shortly before, finding himself bound and propped against a wall. His sensitive hearing told him that he was still in the temple (or a room of equivalent size and acoustical properties), that there were six to eight hostiles in the room, and that several other captives in various states of consciousness rested beside him. Spock had opted to "play possum," as McCoy would put it, to gather intelligence. But the hostiles' leader had proved to be observant. "You gain no advantage by continuing to feign unconsciousness," he went on. "Indeed, my wish for your attention is the only reason you and your colleagues are still alive."

Spock opened his eyes and met those of his captor matter-of-factly. "Then you have my attention, Mr. Dovraku."

The extremist leader didn't smile, but appeared pleased nonetheless. "You know me, then."

"I have heard some of your recorded sermons in the course of my research."

"Indeed." Dovraku appeared genuinely curious. "And what do you make of the logic of my arguments?"

Spock raised a brow. "I found it to be largely specious, based on ad hoc assumptions, circular reasoning, and countless other fallacies."

"Spock!" McCoy hissed from beside him. "Don't antagonize him!" His advice was redundant; Spock knew he was taking a chance. But he was interested in observing the result.

Anger burned in Dovraku's eyes for a moment, and Spock could see the fanaticism that drove him. But then he gathered himself and took on an air of detached regret. "It is as I feared—your logic is tainted. No doubt the influence of your godkiller captain. I had hoped your communion with mighty V'Ger had purified your mind." Spock was struck by the irony of his words. "But no matter—I will grant you the opportunity to redeem yourself. It is a privilege I grant only to the most deserving."

With that, Dovraku moved to stand before another group of captives, whom Spock surmised to be the opposition delegates, judging from the presence of High Priestess Rishala among them. Looking around, he saw that Soreth, Lindstrom, and Minister Tasari were also among those present. But the captain and Natira were nowhere to be seen. Undoubtedly Kirk had managed to elude capture. Spock found the thought very heartening indeed.

"Fortunately," Dovraku said, "one among you has already taken that opportunity for redemption. We owe that one our thanks for delivering us to this heavenly abode."

"I knew it!" Tasari cried, glaring at Rishala. "You're in league with him, you all are! You smuggled these scum aboard in your shuttles!"

The priestess shook her head, responding to Tasari but keeping her gaze on Dovraku. "I was a fool ever to tolerate him. Ever to think that he and I could have common cause. And I have renounced that folly." She turned sadly to one of the others. "And I hoped you had too, Sonaya."

The thin older woman looked at her in surprise. "Why would you think it was I who did this?"

"Paravo is too gentle, and he came with me in Kemori's ship. And Dovraku wouldn't deal with Kemori—he's not religious. But you are, Sonaya, and your sect of the Book has always had an affinity with the Oracle sects. Besides, of all of us, you're the one most afraid of Dovraku—the easiest one for him to control." Sonaya lowered her head in mute admission.

"Your words expose your true hypocrisy, Rishala," Dovraku said. "Such evil times are these. Not only are the

People ruled by enemies of the Oracle, but even the one who bears the name of priestess is naught but a lowly commoner who follows an ignorant corruption of the faith—who has no understanding of the Oracle's power."

Rishala seemed unimpressed. "You haven't purged your accent as well as you'd like, Dovraku. Your birth was as lowly as mine."

"I do not deny it. That was merely the first of the challenges I had to overcome to prove myself worthy. But I rose above it. I worked my way up from the lower levels, earned myself a place in the halls of power."

"You were a low-level clerk."

"But I was *here,* in direct service to my Oracle. I heard His voice, basked in His light, studied His infallible wisdom . . . while you crawled in darkness and strayed from the pure faith, contaminated it with your fanciful tales and emotional frenzies."

"What is the soul if not passion, if not imagination?"

"The Oracle is the soul of the People. And His holy fire burns away all that contaminates its mathematical purity."

"The fire comes from Nidra the Deceiver. It burns us with her lies."

"The fire is our salvation," Dovraku countered. "I shall show you." He nodded to his people, who wrestled Tasari to his feet, holding him at swordpoint. "Here is an enemy of the People. He has hunted us, beaten us, murdered us in his cells. You, Rishala, have said this in your sermons as often as have I. Yet you have been able to do nothing but talk."

Dovraku stepped onto the pentagonal platform which Spock recalled was used to trigger the Oracle. Indeed, the light in the altar's sunburst came on, indicating that Dovraku had successfully reactivated the central computer. "SPEAK," came the Oracle's stentorian voice.

"O Oracle of the People," Dovraku intoned. "Do you know who I am?"

"YOU ARE MY PROPHET DOVRAKU," it said. "THE PUREST OF MY BELIEVERS, AND THE AGENT OF MY RESURRECTION." Clearly the man had done some reprogramming.

"Mighty Oracle, great evils have befallen the People in your absence. No longer do they heed your wisdom. No longer do they carry the Instruments of Obedience to keep them to the path."

"WHO IS RESPONSIBLE FOR THIS BLASPHEMY?"

"It is Natira, O most wise. She and the outworlders who led her into blasphemy."

"THEN SHE MUST BE PUNISHED."

"In time, she shall be. But for now she is out of your reach."

"FIND HER AND BRING HER BEFORE ME."

"It will be done. For now, though, we have one of her agents." He nodded, and Tasari was brought forward. "Once he served you at Natira's side, yet now he punishes those who remain faithful to you, and forces them to recant on pain of death."

"THIS CANNOT BE TOLERATED."

"As you say, O most wise. What is to be done?"

"THE PUNISHMENT IS DEATH." At that, the extremists holding Tasari took a step back.

"Oracle!" Spock interrupted, seeking to avert what he knew was coming. "Please wait. You are being misled."

The light from the altar's sensor flashed in his eyes. "YOU ARE A KNOWN BLASPHEMER, ALREADY UNDER SENTENCE OF DEATH. SHARE HIS FATE."

"Wait," Dovraku said. "He has a role to play in your ascension, Mighty One."

"VERY WELL."

Spock had been counting on that. He tried again. "Oracle. The People's journey is over. They are safe on the World of the Promise. You have fulfilled your function. There is no longer any need for you to punish."

A simulated thunderclap played over the temple's audio system. "SILENCE, BLASPHEMER! THE PEOPLE MUST BE REMINDED OF THE TRUTH. THOSE WHO SIN OR STRAY FROM THE PATH WILL BE PUNISHED."

The air crackled. Spock knew that an ultraviolet laser in the altar was ionizing a path between itself and Tasari's body. Current flowed along the path, and Tasari convulsed, electrical discharges flaring from his body. When Spock had been struck by this years before, it had been a tetanizing charge, calibrated to paralyze his muscles and render him unconscious. But Spock's analysis of the temple security systems had shown they had lethal capacity as well . . . and the smell that now filled the room left no doubt that it had just been used.

The stench of death filled Spock with disgust and pain. It hit him hard. Scent was one of the most primal senses, in Vulcans no less than in humans, and its impact was visceral, bypassing the rational parts of the brain. This was part of the reason modern Vulcans were vegetarian—because the smell of dead flesh triggered responses hard to reconcile with a dispassionate approach to life. Spock had encountered death many times before, even inflicted it when there was a logical necessity to do so, yet this was his first time in three years. And before he had been able to manage his disgust and grief with the Surakian disciplines. But now he didn't know if he could master the disciplines again, didn't even know if they applied to him anymore.

Besides—a sapient being had died. Perhaps Tasari had not been the most agreeable of beings, but still, a life had been violently ended. Surely that was something that deserved an emotional response. Even Vulcans still acknowledged the need to grieve, though they regulated it carefully and kept it private. But right now Spock could muster only enough discipline to keep from becoming physically ill.

Dovraku looked down at him, literally and figuratively. "Where is your control, Spock? Have you fallen so far?" He tilted his head contemplatively. "If you are to be redeemed, you must be reminded that emotion brings only weakness and pain. Perhaps a few more demonstrations will convince you." He gestured to Rishala, whom his henchmen pulled to her feet.

McCoy leaned over and whispered in his ear. "Pull yourself together, Spock! Mourn later—or there'll be a lot more people to mourn!"

Somehow, Spock was reminded of another time he and McCoy had been imprisoned together—some 5.65 years ago, on that planet populated by the descendants of Earth Romans seeded by the Preservers. Spock had just saved McCoy's life, but had coldly brushed off the doctor's thanks, insisting that McCoy was nothing to him but a skilled crew member whose loss would have negatively impacted efficiency. Understandably, McCoy had been angered, accusing Spock of being afraid to let his control slip, because he wouldn't know what to do with a genuine feeling. Apparently, he had been right. Spock didn't know what to do with what he was feeling now.

Yet McCoy was here to help him figure it out—just as he'd always been there, whether Spock had been willing to listen or not—even when the Vulcan had given him no reason for such loyalty.

McCoy had offered no specifics on how to pull himself together—but Spock realized that was the point. The how didn't matter; it simply had to be done. He had to stop struggling to figure out how to manage his emotions, and just *do* it. Scott had called it intuition, but maybe it was more simply a matter of empirical learning, making adjustments as one went in pursuit of a specific goal. Just focus on the objective and make corrections as needed.

Still, a voice inside him said, *the empirical approach*

does not always lead to success. But he silenced the voice for now, knowing that he didn't have the luxury of self-doubt at the moment.

Dovraku had mounted the platform again. "O Oracle," he intoned. "This is Rishala, who has usurped the title of high priestess, which only you can bestow."

"Oracle, I serve the Creators, as you do," Rishala said.

"She corrupts the truth of the Creators with vulgar tales and immoral displays. She must be punished!"

"Dovraku!" Spock interrupted. "You say your real interest is in me. Very well—let this be between you, the Oracle, and myself. What would you have me do to earn my redemption?"

"Great Oracle," Dovraku said with satisfaction, "allow the blasphemer to witness what is to come. Perhaps this Vulcan's redemption can persuade her to save her soul."

"LET IT BE SO."

"Thank you, most wise," Dovraku purred, though it was clear who was truly giving the orders. He stepped down from the platform, and the Oracle returned to standby mode. "Tell me, first, what you witnessed when mighty V'Ger transcended this plane."

Spock studied him quizzically. "That is a matter of public record. The content of your recent sermons indicates that you are already conversant with the particulars."

"I wish to hear how you perceived it, Spock. The testimony of one who beheld the miracle firsthand."

Spock's eyebrow showed what he thought of the rhetoric, but he said, "Very well. First I must provide some explanatory background." If nothing else, it was an opportunity to "vamp," as Kirk might say, until the captain was ready to launch his rescue. However, he chose to keep his account as factual as possible, with a minimum of interpretation, so as not to unduly reinforce Dovraku's mystical leanings.

He spoke of the *Voyager 6* probe, and how its encounter with the ergosphere of a black hole passing through the Sol system's outskirts had projected it on a Tipler curve across spacetime to a distant part of the universe. He told of how the probe, badly damaged by tidal stresses, had eventually drifted into a star system inhabited by a race of sapient Von Neumann machines, self-replicating automatons that presumably had evolved intelligence only after their organic creators had died out, so that they retained no knowledge of non-machine sentience. Spock considered it likely that the machines themselves had replicated out of control and overrun their creators, not out of malice but out of following their programming too well. Ironically, only afterward did they adapt themselves to limit their procreation so they would not exhaust their system's resources. They had little interest in starflight; their world was in an ancient globular cluster dominated by dim, metal-poor stars devoid of planets. Their probes had turned up nothing of interest to them, and they had long since abandoned interest in space by the time *Voyager 6* arrived, though their knowledge of physics was unparalleled.

The machines had studied the battered probe, repaired it, and equipped it to carry out its programming: gather all possible information and transmit that information to its planet of origin. (Of course the probe's primitive software had contained no such abstract generalizations, only instructions for pointing and operating its instruments and antenna; but the machines had divined the purpose of those instructions and acted accordingly.) They had designed and built a technology to enable the probe to search the universe for its homeworld, and given it a form capable of evolving both physically and mentally in order to cope with the information and dangers it would encounter on its journey. Spock's meld with V'Ger had not revealed why the Von Neumanns had done this; V'Ger had seen no need to wonder. Perhaps it was simply in their nature as social AIs to assist other AIs in carrying out their programs.

"V'Ger was equipped with an energy matrix which dematerialized objects and stored their data—not unlike a transporter, except that the data was permanently stored as energy patterns rather than used to reconstitute the original matter, which was converted for other purposes. As a cybernetic being, V'Ger considered the true reality of things to reside in the information which defined them, rather than the physical matter of which they were composed. Which is actually true from a certain quantum-mechanical perspective—"

"You are stalling," Dovraku told him. "Stay on the subject. The ascension."

"Very well." He spoke of how he, Kirk, McCoy, and Decker had found *Voyager 6* at the heart of V'Ger and discovered its origins and objectives. Assuming its Creator to be a fellow machine and finding no sign of it, V'Ger had assumed the humans "infesting" the Earth were interfering with its operation, and had launched its energy bolts to surround the planet in a matrix which, upon its completion, would have disintegrated all life on Earth's surface. The only way to prevent this had been to persuade V'Ger that humans were its creators. But V'Ger would tolerate nothing less than a physical merger. "Since it saw matter as merely a form of information, it equated the sharing of information with the sharing of physical essence. It saw its mission as to become one with its Creator."

He spoke briefly of how Decker had volunteered for reasons of his own, and coded in the transmit sequence. "V'Ger then turned its scanning matrix on itself, dematerializing itself, Captain Decker, and the Ilia probe, and somehow recombining their patterns and their minds into a hybrid form which was greater than the sum of its parts.

This new hybrid entity, existing as pure information encoded as a subspace energy matrix, then decoupled itself from our dimensional brane."

"And thus it rose to join with the Creators," Dovraku added.

"I have no information on its subsequent itinerary," Spock replied dryly. He made no mention of his lingering rapport with the Voyager; that was none of Dovraku's business.

"There is much of the tale you have not told. Such as your captain's attempt to destroy the god, by destroying his own ship at V'Ger's core." Dovraku took on a look of satisfaction. "In short, a suicide bombing. One more act of terrorism against the gods.

"But V'Ger survived the attempt. V'Ger is the herald, who has shown the way for the other gods to be reborn. And now the Oracle will join Him."

Both Spock's brows climbed high. "Am I to understand that you expect the Oracle to achieve a transformation equivalent to V'Ger's?"

"Not equivalent. Greater."

Spock found the suggestion quite amusing, though humor was inappropriate under the circumstances. V'Ger had been as vast and complex as any corporeal mind bound by the limits of matter and four-dimensional physics could possibly get. It had already been on the threshold, and only needed that one extra spark to achieve metasapience. But the Oracle was not even as advanced as the *Enterprise*'s computer; it lacked even normal sapience. What Dovraku was proposing was analogous to expecting a horse-drawn chariot to attain warp speed. However, Spock knew the distinction would be lost on a man to whom all computers were equally magical.

Soreth didn't show the same judgment, however. "This is absurd. The Oracle is a simple mechanism, millennia less advanced than V'Ger. How could it possibly achieve such a feat?"

"In the same way mighty V'Ger did," Dovraku replied, ignoring the slight to his god. "By merging with another mind. That is why you are here, Spock. You have melded with one god—you can meld with another. You will be the bridge by which the Oracle and I, His faithful servant, will ascend to the heavens."

That settles it, McCoy thought as he gaped at Dovraku. *The man is clinically delusional.* Not that he was going to say so to his face, not with all those armed fanatics hovering around. McCoy could see their symptoms: the burns, the sores, the incipient hair loss, the bleeding gums. However these men and women had smuggled themselves up here, they'd voluntarily subjected themselves to high doses of radiation, which would probably be lethal if they didn't get prompt hyronalin treatment. Clearly they were committed to their cause beyond all reason. And on one level, McCoy could see why. Dovraku's words may have been lunatic, but there was something compelling, almost hypnotic about his controlled, confident delivery.

Spock seemed unimpressed, though. "Is that all you wish? For the Oracle to depart our dimension?"

"No, Spock. V'Ger left this plane because He was merely the herald. He merely prepared the way for the Oracle to rise to omnipotence, so that the One most wise could remake our universe in His image." Dovraku moved closer to Spock, gazing deep into his eyes. "Think about it, Spock. Our world made paradise. No doubt, no pain, no confusion, no struggle. No more questions without answers. Only the mathematical purity of the Oracle's logic, the binary certainty of right and wrong. Every being knowing his purpose, playing his role in the vast cosmic mechanism, receiving his just allotment of reward."

Spock shook his head. "I have seen a life defined by pure logic, Dovraku. It is barren, purposeless. V'Ger had all the answers logic could offer, yet still it felt empty and lost. For logic is only a means to an end, a tool for managing information. As an end in itself, it is hollow."

McCoy leaned over and whispered in Uhura's ear. "You tell him, Spock! Our boy's come a long way, hasn't he?"

Uhura smiled. "I always knew he had it in him." Soreth, McCoy noticed, looked scandalized, but at least showed the good sense not to protest, lest he appear to be on Dovraku's side.

"That is why V'Ger could not evolve without Decker," Spock was saying. "It needed an emotional, intuitive human to give it a sense of purpose."

"Ahh," Dovraku countered, "but Decker could not evolve without V'Ger, could he? The mortal mind is too limited, too flawed to achieve transcendence on its own. It needs the clarity of the machine. It needs the discipline of logic to regulate and direct its emotions, as the Oracle regulated the People—otherwise they are chaotic, unbalanced, self-destructive. Is that not what your Surak said?"

"The mind has the ability to manage its own emotions. It does not need an external regulating mechanism."

"But when machine and man are joined, it is no longer external, do you not see?" He leaned closer. "Consider it, Spock. What we shall achieve is the merger of man and machine, the synergy of both into a perfected One. We need no longer struggle to master our emotions, or fear being mastered by them, for we will have perfect, precisely calculated mastery at the core of our own beings. There would be no doubt, no hesitation, no failure. We would simply know ourselves with absolute precision, and be totally at peace."

Spock was silent for a moment, seeming to be considering Dovraku's words. McCoy found this unnerving, remembering Spock's own confessed fear of being mastered by his emotions. Had Dovraku struck a nerve?

But then Spock said, "Even if I were to assist you in this meld, it would not achieve the same results that occurred with V'Ger. The Oracle does not possess V'Ger's scanning matrix."

Dovraku grew smug. "Naturally I have accounted for that. All the necessary components have been brought together here and now, as destiny has mandated."

Suddenly a series of distant thuds began to resound, sending faint tremors through the floor and walls. Dovraku and his people looked around, surprised—apparently not everything was happening according to his idea of destiny. *Could this be Jim's rescue?* McCoy wondered. But it sounded and felt like a series of massive explosions happening far away. Maybe a diversion?

One of Dovraku's people spoke up from the console she was monitoring. "Great One, there is a call coming in."

The terrorist leader tilted his head curiously. "Let me hear it."

A rainbow gargoyle appeared on the screen. *"Attention, controllers of the asteroid-ship. I am Ssherrak Ki'threetl, speaking for the defense coalition of Kachissat. By firing your missiles, you have breached the contract between your species and the Shesshran. This forfeits our agreement and enables our right of retaliation!"*

Dovraku nodded to his soldier, telling her to open a return channel. "You do not speak to the government that made that agreement. I am Dovraku, herald of the new order. The Oracle has been reborn, and will shortly ascend to still greater heights. You will bow down in obedience or be erased."

The Shesshran hissed. *"You! I knew the weaklings would be unable to contain you! Hear me, madman: you will not be permitted to enslave any more minds. Now that you are out in the open, the hunt is on, and we will not rest until you are destroyed!"*

Fortunately for Kirk, Natira, and the security team, Yonada's hangar had been directly above the temple/control center. Once they reached the base of the mountain, they were close to the underground entrance—indeed, not far at all from where Kirk, Spock, and McCoy had originally beamed in four and a half years ago. They ran briskly across the barren plain, not stopping to catch their breath. That wasn't as easy for Kirk as it once would have been. He thought he'd kept fit during his desk-job days, walking or jogging to SFHQ every morning, spending plenty of time at the gym, and taking frequent opportunities to go climbing or diving or horseback riding. But apparently even all that hadn't compared to the kind of exercise he got exploring strange new worlds. Or maybe it was just that he was forty years old.

Impressively, Natira managed to keep up pretty well, though she was lagging behind and panting hard. What she lacked in fitness, she was making up for in sheer determination—or sheer rage, judging from the look on her regal face.

Once they neared the entrance, Kirk signaled them to stop just behind the last outcropping. Chekov consulted his tricorder while Kirk surreptitiously took a moment to catch his breath. "No guards—not up here, anyway. I don't think they had very many . . . they're probably all watching the temple."

"In which case," Kirk said, trying not to sound too winded, "we need to find a way to take them by surprise."

"I know . . . of a maintenance corridor . . . leading into the control complex," Natira said between gasps. "From my . . . study of the Book."

"Good. Once we get in, our priority will be the safety of the hostages."

"Hostages," Natira scoffed. "Yet another subterfuge. I should have known . . . it was a trap. Rishala brought them here, I know it! Her surprise was poorly feigned."

"With respect, Governess, it wasn't." That was Ensign Zaand, who didn't sound at all winded. Kirk envied him for being that fit at eighty-five—though come to think of it, the greatly delayed puberty was too much of a trade-off by far. "She was entirely sincere, more so than the other delegates. The others were ambivalent about Dovraku, either because they feared him or because they saw political advantage in appearing to support him. But she felt no fear of him and was the main reason the others were at the table at all. And she was genuinely surprised by the attack, as were all the delegates except Sonaya. That one seemed to be anticipating something all through the meeting, and when the attack came she instantly took cover without any pause to process surprise. She was the one most afraid of Dovraku, so I assume he pressured her into smuggling the raiding party aboard."

Natira stared at the Rhaandarite disbelievingly. "How can you know any of this?"

"It was self-evident in their body language, expressions, and vocal inflections, ma'am. My people are better than most at reading such cues."

"Are they really?" she challenged.

Kirk spoke up in his firmest tones. "Natira—I trust Rishala, and I trust my crew. If the ensign says that's what they felt, then that's what they felt. You can still make peace—*if* we act quickly and save the hostages."

Natira lifted her head haughtily. "Very well. We will liberate them and determine who is truly responsible. Come, let us hurry to the maintenance tunnel."

"Damn." Sulu had been thinking that this turn in the command chair would be fairly easy. At first, he'd just been keeping the seat warm while Kirk was at the conference. Then the fanatics had taken Yonada and lobbed a few missiles at the *Enterprise*—but that was fine, since they were primitive and slow and easy to hit. He'd only been disappointed that he couldn't handle the target practice himself, though Perez had been managing quite well—as had DiFalco, who was sitting in at the helm and doing an excellent job of dodging the missiles and then chasing them down for the kill.

But the Shesshran getting involved had changed things. Their ships couldn't do much damage to the *Enterprise*, but he wasn't so sure about Yonada itself. Its shell was pretty thick, but it was just asteroidal iron and nickel, and had limits to the amount of beating it could take—hence the need for the missiles in the first place. Sulu couldn't be sure that a well-placed shot from the Shesshran's particle beams couldn't get through and kill the captain or the hostages.

He turned to Auberson, the curly-haired fellow manning the comm station. "Hail the Shesshran!"

"Channel open, sir."

"This is the *Enterprise*. Please stop your attacks at once! There are Starfleet personnel and innocent civilians on Yonada; you're putting their safety at risk!" Silence. "Please respond!"

Auberson shook his head. "They're not listening."

"Warning shot?" Perez asked.

Sulu thought about it. He fidgeted—the seat was getting uncomfortable. "No," he decided. "We attack the Shesshran and we'll never have any hope of patching things up between them and the Lorini."

"Sir!" That was Uuvu'it at sciences. Sulu swiveled around. "Long-range sensors detect an object moving this way . . . reads as Shesshran build . . . looks like a pretty hefty plasma cannon."

Sulu frowned. "Coming in from Daran V, the kind of speeds they can muster, it should take a day or two to get here."

"It's much closer. I think they had it holding nearby in case they got an excuse to pick a fight. Clever move."

"An ace up their sleeve. How much damage could it do to Yonada?"

Uuvu'it was uncharacteristically quiet. "Enough," he finally chirped.

Sulu peered at him. "Enough for what?"

"Well . . . this isn't a sure thing . . . but you know how Yonada gets its gravity?"

"A collapsed-matter core, right?"

"Right. And its degenerate electrons are all straining to reassert their territorial rights and push back out to a normal distance. Only the thick diamond shell is holding the core together against that pressure."

"Okay, so?"

"Even diamond can fracture. It's pretty deep, but . . . well, that core's been fighting the pressure for ten thousand years. Sooner or later something's got to give, and if Yonada's getting whacked with a plasma cannon . . ."

"I get it. What happens if the core cracks?" Sulu asked. He thought he had a pretty good idea, but he hoped he was wrong.

"All that collapsed matter re-expands."

"Suddenly?"

"*Very* suddenly."

"So what you're telling me is . . ."

"Tremendous explosion. Right, sir."

"*How* tremendous?"

"I wouldn't advise being within twenty thousand kilometers or so."

Sulu stared. "The *planet* is within twenty thousand kilometers."

"You see why smart people don't live on planets? False sense of security. They look so big and sturdy—it just makes them easy targets that can't dodge."

Sulu stared some more. Then he turned to Auberson. "Hail the captain!"

Kirk was slow to reply. *"I'm a little busy right now, Sulu."*

"This is urgent, sir." He filled the captain in quickly. "I think maybe you should be up here."

"Sulu, right now we're sneaking our way into the control center by a back route. It's . . . a little cramped, and reversing course isn't much of an option. So unless you can beam us out . . ."

Sulu looked to Mercado at engineering, and the young ensign simply shook his head. "Sorry, sir," Sulu reported. "No transporter lock."

"Then you'll just have to deal with the Shesshran yourself, Commander."

"Do I have your authorization to open fire?"

"I wouldn't recommend it . . . but I don't want to tie your hands. Use your best judgment, Mr. Sulu. I have full confidence in you. Kirk out."

Full confidence. Why was everyone so hell-bent on convincing him he was cut out for this? Ship-to-ship combat was something he could handle, but the decision of whether or not to use deadly force could have profound diplomatic consequences. Destroy Shesshran ships and it would start a war that the Lorini couldn't win and the Federation couldn't fight in; but use kid gloves and half Lorina's atmosphere could be blown away. It looked like a no-win situation.

In Sulu's *Kobayashi Maru* test, he'd dealt with the no-win scenario by choosing not to play, refusing to answer the distress call since the risk had been too great. He'd decided the most responsible choice was to do nothing. He'd taken hell for it from his classmates, and the difficulty of having to choose was part of the reason he hadn't subsequently pursued the command track with any seriousness. But now he was in command, and doing nothing was not an option here.

Well, maybe it wasn't a no-win situation yet. Maybe he could drive the Shesshran off without killing them. It would take a delicate touch—but so did folding origami cranes, or piloting a ship into warp with the manual-override throttle. "Chief DiFalco," he ordered, "take us in between Yonada and the Shesshran ships. Perez, shields and forcefields to full, warp power to the phasers!"

CHAPTER SIXTEEN

Pull out its plug, Mr. Spock.   —James T. Kirk

THE SHESSHRAN had cut the channel after delivering their ultimatum, leaving Dovraku no chance to respond. But he didn't seem interested in responding—not verbally, at least. Instead he had headed for the control room behind the altar and pointed to Spock. "Bring him!"

But no sooner had they reached the control complex than one of Dovraku's people came back after them. "Great One," she said, "we've detected a large weapon traveling toward us." She went to a console and called up the readings. The Fabrini readouts weren't as clear to Spock as the Federation consoles in the temple, but he quickly discerned the nature of the weapon and the danger it posed.

"Dovraku," he warned, "you must surrender now. If that weapon is fired on Yonada, it could destabilize the collapsed-matter core. The resultant explosion would destroy Yonada."

"All is going according to destiny," Dovraku said calmly. "V'Ger's ascension was announced by a vast eruption—the Oracle deserves no less."

"The explosion would also devastate Lorina and could exterminate its entire population."

Dovraku spoke while he operated a console. His actions were swift, sure, and precise, as though he'd practiced this for years. "And did you think the World could be cleansed without first being swept clean by the fire? The first World was destroyed to give birth to the second, the cradle of the Oracle. The third World, the Oracle's paradise, cannot be born until the cycle is repeated."

Spock's eyes widened as he deciphered what Dovraku was doing. He tried to lunge forward, but the guards held him back. "You are launching all the missiles!"

"As it was with the herald V'Ger, so shall it be with the supreme Oracle. The missiles will travel to equidistant positions, englobing the World in a cage of fire. When it reaches symmetry, completeness, perfection, then the fire of Truth shall purify the World."

"Everyone will die, Dovraku!"

The fanatic came over to stand before him. "No. They will be saved, taken into the Oracle's bosom. Those who are worthy, at any rate. You shall meld the Oracle and myself, and trigger our ascension. You, Spock, are the instrument of salvation. Thus you redeem yourself for standing by while Kirk killed so many gods."

The captain. Where are you, Jim? Spock had to admit to himself that he had no certainty Kirk was even still alive.

It never rains but it pours, thought Sulu. It hadn't been too difficult to run interference against the Shesshran attack, picking off their torpedoes with the phasers or blocking them with the shields. If the sixteen Shesshran ships were to focus their attacks on the *Enterprise,* they could probably do some real damage, especially with Sulu not firing back; but their main objective was still Yonada. Well, some of theirs, anyway. The Shesshran tended to act independently, coordinating with others only insofar as it was to their own advantage. So far that meant neither the ship

nor the asteroid-moon was taking the full brunt of their
attack. But that plasma cannon was nearly in range. He'd
tried hailing the Shesshran and explaining the danger of
Yonada's destruction, but they'd either dismissed it as a
bluff or asserted their confidence in being fast enough to
escape it.

And just now, several dozen nuclear missiles had been
fired from Yonada, on low-orbital insertion trajectories.
"Target those missiles!" he cried. "Pick them off, Mr.
Perez."

But Perez had other concerns. "Incoming plasma bolt,
sir, on course for Yonada."

First things first. "DiFalco, intercept!" The impulse
engines surged as the chief flew the *Enterprise* headlong
into the plasma bolt's path. "All deflector power to forward
shields!"

The superhot helium plasma collided with the ship at a
fair fraction of lightspeed, imparting a hefty portion of
kinetic, thermal, and electrical energy. The ship's forcefield
bubble and forward deflector shield absorbed or dissipated
most of it, but the reaction made the generators shudder in
their housings, sending a rumble through the ship. Almost
immediately, a stronger blast rocked the vessel. "Report!"
Sulu cried.

"Shesshran torpedo hit on our lower port flank."

"Damage to port deflector grid," reported Chezrava from
the damage control station.

"Forward deflector down to eighty-six percent power,"
Mercado reported. "Forcefield at seventy-nine percent and
recharging."

"Resume normal deflector coverage. Extra power to the
port grid to compensate."

"Normal coverage, aye," Perez acknowledged.

The new forcefield system had the advantage of being a
full englobement, unlike the more directional deflector

shields. An enemy couldn't punch a beam through the "seams" between shield sections anymore, or leave a whole flank defenseless by knocking out the shield grid on that side. But the trade-off was that the forcefield's power couldn't be concentrated for point defense—and that if it was weakened in one direction, it was weakened all around. The plasma bolt had drained it enough that it couldn't fully block the torpedo's energy, and with all the deflector power aimed forward, the port flank had been vulnerable. Did the Shesshran understand the ship's defenses that well, or had they just gotten a lucky shot?

"Status on Yonada's missiles?" Sulu asked.

Uuvu'it answered. "They're heading for equidistant positions, a full englobement. How derivative."

"Still in phaser range?"

"Only a few."

"Perez, get what you can with phasers, target the rest with torpedoes."

"Not a good idea, sir."

"What now, Hrrii'ush?"

"They're too close to the planet. Phasers are surgical—they can take out the drives without blowing the warheads; but torpedoes would set them off, and that could pose a radiation hazard to the people."

"Wonderful. Is there anything around here I *can* shoot?"

As if in response, Perez said, "Shesshran beams and torpedoes getting through to Yonada, sir."

"We have to hope they won't do too much damage. That plasma cannon and those nukes are our main concerns." He turned to Uuvu'it. "Okay, if Dovraku's copying V'Ger, he won't blow the missiles until they're in position. How long?"

"Fourteen minutes, forty seconds, sir."

Sulu nodded. "Auberson, brief the captain."

"Aye, sir."

DiFalco turned to face Uuvu'it. "Fifteen minutes and you're afraid they're too close to the planet?"

"Some have to circle to the opposite side to get in position. But the ones on this side would be close enough to do damage by the time a torpedo gets there—especially considering that a torpedo makes a pretty big explosion of its own."

"So we focus on the cannon first," Sulu said. "It's manned, right? We can't just blow it up?"

"Yes, sir. Unless you decide we have to, sir." He looked at a readout on the science console. "Plasma cannon about to fire again, sir," he announced.

Sulu threw him a look. "Why couldn't you warn us last time?"

"I didn't know what the power curve looked like then. Ah, there! Firing, sir!"

"DiFalco," Sulu said with resignation, "put us in its way. Let's take our licks again." But then an idea struck him. "Wait . . . fly into it, navigational deflector on maximum! Maybe we can scatter it some." It made sense—the forces involved when a high-speed particle cloud ran into the ship were no different from those involved when the ship flew at high speed into bits of space dust and debris, which is what the navigational deflector was designed to prevent by shoving them out of the way.

But the plasma bolt was pretty dense, and the scattering was only partial. The forward shield and forcefield still took a fair amount of pounding from it, and the ship rumbled again. Then suddenly there was a sharp crack. The ship bucked, and the lights and readouts flickered. When the defense-screen status display at the tactical console lit up again, Sulu noticed it was without the oval indicating the forcefield englobement. "Forcefields down, sir!" Perez confirmed. "Deflector grid holding."

"What happened?"

Uuvu'it answered. "Some of the plasma got through. I think the gravity gradients of the navigational deflector and the forcefield canceled out at a few points."

"Deflector dish and forcefield coils offline, sir," Chezrava reported. "Forward ventral phaser bank and main sensor array damaged." The ship graphics on the screens around his console flashed with red lights clustered around the lower fore section. The Zaranite's expression was indiscernible through his insectlike respiratory mask (though Sulu knew his natural features looked like a cross between a theatrical tragedy mask and Munch's *The Scream)*, but he sounded agitated. He looked at Sulu as though searching for answers.

So Sulu decided to search for a couple of answers of his own. "Bridge to engineering. Scotty, how the hell did this happen?"

"Don't look at me, Mr. Sulu!" Scott called back. "I'm not the one who decided to try that stunt with the deflector dish! What do you expect when you get creative with untested systems?" *This is why ships are supposed to have long shakedowns* before *they get sent into action,* he added silently.

"*I need that forcefield back up, Mr. Scott!*" Sulu called, just as another spread of Shesshran torpedoes thudded against the port side, where they knew the lass was weakest.

"It'll take five minutes to recharge the coils!" Actually it could probably be done in three, but Scott preferred to make conservative estimates to allow for unforeseen delays. Better to lower expectations than raise them, or commanders would start demanding the *really* impossible.

"*We don't have five minutes, Scotty. That plasma cannon only takes about a minute to recharge. And we've got a shade over ten minutes to deal with it and do something about those missiles.*"

"Aye, we're on it." *And you* still *have an annoying fasci-nation for timepieces, Mr. Sulu.* "Scott out." He shut off the return channel—a one-way channel from the bridge was always open at red alert so engineering could monitor events—and turned back to his staff. "Ross, get me a read on those coils! Odanga, you and your team get up to that phaser bank! Hawkins, reinitialize the deflector dish! Bandar, swap out sensor circuits C-36 to E-15!"

He joined Chief Ross at the foyer console to study the forcefield power readouts. As he'd expected, the coils were recharging slowly. They ran all the way around the rim of the saucer, which was a good long way, so there was a lot of coil to recharge. "Sir," Ross suggested, "maybe we could shunt power from the inertial dampers. They're similar sys-tems, and with the nav deflector down, we won't be making any fast moves for a while."

"Aye, but a good whack from that plasma cannon could squish us into haggis." Then he smiled at her. "But it wouldn't hurt us to lose a little weight!" He opened a comm channel. "Scott to bridge. I'm cutting gravity by half to shunt power to the forcefield coils."

"Understood." A moment later Auberson's voice echoed through the ship: *"All hands brace for fifty percent gravity reduction."*

Scott caught Ross looking at him with a twinkle in her eye. "What?"

She grinned. "You're enjoying this, aren't you? Not the battle, I mean. The problem-solving."

"That's the beauty of it," Scott said ironically as he felt his weight decrease. "Around here we never seem to run out of problems. . . ."

Vaylin Zaand watched Kirk intently as the captain listened to the report from the *Enterprise*—just as he'd been watching Kirk throughout this mission. "Acknowledged, Mr. Sulu," the captain said. "You take care of the cannon, we'll try to stop the missiles from this end."

"Aye, sir."

"Kirk out." *We'll* try, he'd said—not *I'll* try. This was not the glory-seeking hothead he'd imagined Kirk to be. Somehow he was different here, on a mission, away from the ship. The ship complicated things. Zaand could see it in his body language. His relationship with the *Enterprise,* its crew, and its ghosts was still unsettled, conflicted. He set himself apart, still unsure of whether he belonged. That was part of why he'd felt to Zaand like an interloper, someone who didn't fit into the proper scheme of things. But here, those complications were set aside. It was purer: the man, his mission, his team. He knew his purpose and his place. Throughout all of this, from the moment of the attack, he'd been decisive. Without the luxury to stop and analyze, to second-guess himself, he'd just spontaneously made the best decisions to get them to where they were, almost at the control room, getting ready to strike and end the danger. It had to be the intuition Sulu and Chekov had spoken of . . . yet to Zaand it looked, it felt, it read in the body language like an almost Rhaandarite insight into how the universe was supposed to work. Maybe they were both the same thing; maybe intuition was just a subliminal understanding of the rules of things, and the humans just didn't see it in those terms because it was so automatic. Or maybe, he admitted to himself, it meant that Rhaandarites' "natural insight" into cosmic order was a form of intuition after all.

Kirk turned to Natira. "Once we get in there, will we be able to take out the missiles remotely? Send an abort code?"

Natira searched her memory. "If the missiles are being guided in this way, they must be under the direct control of the Oracle. Instead of being set to detonate on impact, they will need to have a detonate command transmitted to them once they are in position." She glanced at his phaser. "The simplest way to stop them will be to destroy the Oracle's core processor so it cannot send the signal. Indeed, that would solve many problems." Anger flared in her eyes. "Would that I had done it in the first place."

"All right. Governess, you wait here. Mr. Chekov, gentlemen, let's move in."

They began to advance the last few dozen meters to the exit. Zaand watched Kirk a moment longer, then decided he had to ask the question that had been troubling him since the surface. He moved forward next to Kirk so he could speak softly. "Sir, may I ask something?"

"What is it, Ensign?" His expression was open, receptive, not hostile at all.

"Up above . . . you told the governess that you trusted my judgment. How can you? You haven't worked with me before . . . and I've given you no reason to trust me."

"Because you haven't trusted me." It was not accusatory, just accepting.

"It's . . . more complicated than that. I . . . when Rhaandarites . . ." He sighed. "No, I suppose I haven't."

"Ensign, the thing about trust is, the only way you can know whether to trust someone . . . is to trust him. To give him your trust and the chance to live up to it." He paused in thought. "Our job comes with a lot of risks. But trust is the biggest risk of all. And it's the one thing no ship, no crew can function without." He caught Zaand's gaze. "You're a member of my crew, Ensign. We depend on each other to survive. In that situation, trust has to be a given."

Zaand couldn't look away from those eyes. "I think I understand, sir," he said. It was a very Rhaandarite sentiment, in its way. He realized that when Rhaandarites defined each other by their social roles, took for granted that others would fulfill their roles, that was an act of trust. There was more to it than simply knowing that a procedure had been followed. So even if the procedure had been violated, there could still be other grounds—stronger grounds, even—for trust or loyalty.

Besides, Kirk had been captain of the *Enterprise* for five years. If he'd filled that role with the kind of quiet conviction Zaand was seeing in him here, then maybe the impropriety hadn't been his displacement of Decker. Maybe the impropriety had been that he'd ever left that role in the first place.

Zaand didn't know whether he was violating Rhaandarite social rules by thinking this, or actually gaining some insight into the higher tiers that had eluded him before. The one thing he did know for sure, as he looked into Kirk's eyes, was where his loyalty lay. "Yes . . . I understand. But may I ask . . . if we can't function without trust, then shouldn't that include . . . trusting yourself?"

Kirk's eyes widened, and nothing more needed to be said. Which was just as well, since they were nearly there and had to stay quiet anyway.

Chekov took point, moving forward to the tunnel exit and checking his tricorder for the locations of the hostiles. He used hand gestures to convey this information to Zaand and Swenson, and to instruct them on how to proceed. Then he looked at Kirk, who nodded. "Go."

After that things moved quickly, though Zaand's mind methodically processed and filed every detail. Chekov kicked the door open and went in firing. He stunned one black-robed hostile and took the others by surprise long enough for the team to deploy into the control chamber. It was cramped, cluttered, full of blocky consoles oddly reminiscent of decade-old Starfleet designs. Nearby, Commander Spock stood with a tall figure whose body language marked him as the leader, and a man with serious psychological dysfunctions. Other hostiles flanked them, guarding the commander.

A hostile neared him, raised his sword. Zaand stunned him. Swenson was slower to respond and had his arm slashed by another hostile, causing him to drop his phaser. The swordsman swung at Swenson's torso, but his body armor deflected the blow. Zaand turned to stun him, but Swenson took him out with a head butt, a kneecap kick, and a right cross. Spock attempted to take advantage of the distraction, but his guards held him firmly.

Then Kirk advanced. "Spock!" he cried, radiating relief mixed with concern. It left him distracted for one crucial second, as another hostile emerged from the outer chamber and fired her crossbow at the captain.

At his captain.

Zaand didn't choose to leap into the path of the crossbow bolt. It was simply what he was supposed to do. It was his place.

But it hurt more than he could have imagined. He reflected that Starfleet body armor design could have used more neck protection.

"Zaand!" That was Chekov. A phaser whined, a body fell. Zaand was fuzzy on the details. But he saw Kirk and Chekov kneeling over him. "No," Chekov cried, filled with guilt, blaming himself.

"It's all right," Zaand managed to say. He clenched Kirk's hand. "I served . . . my captain."

And then he understood it all.

Once again, Kirk was left no time to mourn someone who'd died because of him. Unfortunately, he'd gotten to be an old hand at compartmentalizing his grief, putting it on reserve until he had the luxury of facing it. For a moment he feared that Chekov would be unable to do the same. Zaand was the first one lost under his command—and on the very first landing party Chekov had assigned him to. Kirk knew that would hit especially hard.

But Pavel had grown a lot in the past few years. He efficiently channeled his rage into action, letting out a roar as he phasered Zaand's killer into unconsciousness, then launching himself to take on the others.

That left Kirk free to do what he had to do. Seeing he had a clear shot at the Oracle's main console, he thumbed his phaser to disrupt and aimed.

But suddenly Spock surged forward into his path. "No, Jim!"

"Spock, get out of the way!"

"I'm sorry, Captain, I can't allow you to destroy the Oracle."

As he spoke, the men who'd been guarding him had time to aim their crossbows at Kirk. Their leader—Dovraku, no doubt—spoke in stentorian tones. "Drop your weapons, or the captain dies!"

Kirk gauged the options. He would have gone ahead and blasted the Oracle anyway, trading his life for those of the Lorini. But Spock stood in the way, and apparently had his reasons for doing so. McCoy's words from weeks ago flitted through his mind: *"How can we be sure of any of us?"* At the time it hadn't been clear where Spock's loyalties lay, or what he might do if it suited his personal quest for answers. Spock had been unsure of himself lately, questioning, searching; what if he'd found something he thought he needed?

No. Whatever agenda Spock might follow, it would never entail allowing a world to die. Maybe he had changed, but he was still Spock.

Besides, as long as Kirk was alive, there were still options—for another nine or ten minutes, anyway. He dropped his phaser, nodding to Chekov and the others to follow suit. Dovraku's remaining guards retrieved the phasers and herded the prisoners together—except for Spock. Dovraku seemed to have a special interest in him.

"At last, the triad is complete," he said. "You, Kirk, McCoy—the three who witnessed the rebirth of the god V'Ger." Thank God—Bones was still alive. "Do you see now, Spock? All is unfolding as it must. You must meld us together now—it is your destiny."

"I do not believe in destiny, Dovraku."

"Then believe in this: there is no one left to save you. And I have abundant hostages to kill if you refuse."

A look passed between Spock and Kirk, and the captain was pleased to discover that he could read the Vulcan as well as ever, as if they hadn't spent three years apart. Once in the meld, Spock would have a better chance of stopping Dovraku than he could out here in the physical world. It might be their only shot. Kirk nodded fractionally.

"Very well," Spock said to Dovraku. "I shall comply."

"Excellent." The fanatic turned to his henchmen. "Bring McCoy. The three should be together to behold this birth as well."

Soreth was quickly discovering that Dr. McCoy was even more unpleasantly emotional than Mr. Lindstrom. Since Dovraku had taken Spock back to the control complex, the *Enterprise* doctor had been alternating between pleading fruitlessly with the fanatics to submit themselves to medical attention and engaging in a running monologue of complaints about his current situation and, apparently, the entire lifelong string of decisions and circumstances which had led up to it. At the moment he was back in the former mode, which was somewhat less irritating. At least Soreth could share, in principle, the doctor's wish to see these Lorini receive medical treatment before their condition became fatal. "You must be feeling it by now," the doctor went on relentlessly to the guards. "The dizziness, the loss of coordination. The burning sores on your skin. You must taste the blood in your mouths. Trust me, it's only gonna get worse."

One of the guards broke, but not in the way the doctor evidently wished. "Silence!" the man cried, striding forward and striking McCoy across the face. The doctor looked up at him with an odd mixture of anger and a healer's concern, but remained quiet. Soreth could only hope it would be for a longer interval this time than it had been before.

Ensign Nizhoni leaned over and spoke softly to the doctor. "Believe me, Doc, I hate to see these guys suffer, but are we sure we *want* to talk them into getting help? I mean, pretty soon they're gonna be too weak to fight back."

"Which probably means," Soreth interjected, "that they expect Dovraku's mission to be completed before that time comes . . . and it is questionable whether they expect anyone here to survive beyond that point."

"You Vulcans," McCoy muttered, "always the optimists."

Soreth ignored him, but found his attention drawn to the noises being made by Lindstrom on his other side. The impetuous young human was struggling to free his hands from their bonds, and making an inordinate amount of noise and movement in doing so. "Please subsist, Mr. Lindstrom," he advised in a sharp whisper. "Such an attempt will be fruitless if you advertise it."

The sociologist halted his efforts but couldn't resist saying, "Well, I don't see you trying anything useful."

Soreth raised a scathing eyebrow. "That, young man, is precisely the point." He angled his body so that Lindstrom could see his hands, which by now were nearly free of their restraints. Lindstrom stared at him with puzzlement, which Soreth saw no need to satisfy. Informing the human of his years with the Vulcan High Command, serving on the Andorian front and coping with their frequent treachery, would contribute nothing to their escape from the current situation.

"Great hands think alike," Nizhoni whispered, and Soreth turned to see her waving at him behind her back with completely unbound hands. "Now we just need a handy diversion."

McCoy and Lindstrom looked nonplussed. But the other human, Uhura, appeared quite disturbed. "Someone, please," she called in a quavering voice. "I'm frightened." Soreth was concerned. Was her emotional frailty about to jeopardize their escape attempt? "If I'm going to die for your Oracle," she went on, "please, can someone tell me what it is I'm dying for? Priestess Rishala, one of you, can you please reassure me, is there something beyond?"

So she only sought the irrational retreat into denial that religion offered. And naturally the high priestess could not resist taking advantage of her frailty in order to spread her deceit to one more mind, even knowing that death was highly likely for them both. "Beyond this world lies the love of the Creators," Rishala said. "In their embrace we will find the Truth and be freed of the illusions of the material world."

"Tell me more."

Rishala smiled. "I will tell you the tale of how fire came to the People. At first, the People only knew warmth in the day, under the light of the sun. For the sun was the face of Nidra, ruddy with her blood, and blood is warmth. At night, the people grew cold and huddled together in dark and fear, and were often taken by wild beasts or froze to death. One day the leader of the first village had an idea: that if the sun could always be with the People, then they would never want for warmth. So he prayed to Nidra, asking her to allow the sun to remain forever in the sky.

" 'That cannot be,' Nidra whispered in the headman's ear. 'For I grow tired, holding the sun in the sky all day, and need my rest. But I weep for those of you who are taken by wild beasts or freeze to death, and I wish nothing more than to help you. So I will give you drops of my blood, which will warm you so long as you feed them and keep them alive.'

"And so Nidra sent out a flare from the sun, which brushed the top of an old, tall tree and made it burst into flame. Its branches fell to the ground, burning, and the people gathered around in awe and gratitude. They gathered up the branches and praised Nidra, thanking her for her benevolence. But one boy stood by and asked, 'But what about the tree? It shaded us for as long as I can remember. I liked to climb in its branches. And now it's dead.' The villagers told him not to worry, for it was a small price to pay for eternal warmth."

Soreth had taken little interest in the tale, but after a time it registered with him that more and more of the guards were turning to pay attention to her, and thus paying less attention to him and the Starfleet prisoners. And once their backs were turned, Uhura showed no trace of the fear she'd evinced before, instead watching the guards keenly as she presented her wrists for Nizhoni to untie. Indeed, Soreth realized, Rishala was a master at using religion to deceive and blind the populace. He supposed he could excuse it this once, in a good cause.

As Soreth finished freeing himself and went to work on Lindstrom, Rishala continued her tale. It involved the young boy's house erupting into flames, apparently with the boy inside. The incident brought all the villagers out of their homes, which proceeded to go up in flames themselves one by one. Once all their homes were gone, the boy reappeared, unscathed, and clearly responsible for the mass conflagration. The villagers wished to do harm to the boy, but the headman stopped them. " 'But why?' he asked the boy. 'Why have you burned down everything we had?'

" 'I? Burn things?' the boy asked. 'How can I burn anything? I'm not fire. Fire is what burns things. I wanted to see if there was anything it couldn't burn. And you know what? There's nothing. Fire burns everything, right down to the ground.'

"And the villagers saw the trick Nidra had played on them," Rishala went on. "Her promise of eternal warmth had been a trap, intended to burn the careless people to feed her fire, to nourish her blood. They were saved only because a small boy had questioned the bright, beautiful promises that Nidra had held out to them. And so the villagers knew that Dedi the Questioner had walked among them, playing his own trick on his sister Nidra, the Deceiver." Soreth had to wonder how they could know the identity of Dedi and yet be unfamiliar with Nidra's mythological role. Still, he recognized the applicability of the tale to the current circumstances. Apparently she was attempting to create doubt in the guards' minds, as well as distracting their attention.

It struck Soreth that Surak had done much the same, seeking to win over his enemies with reason and peaceful words. Of course, such a correlation was irrelevant, given their profoundly dissimilar ideologies. Still, it was . . . interesting.

" 'But how can we live without fire?' the villagers asked. 'How can we cook our food, smelt our metals, protect ourselves from wild beasts?'

" 'We cannot,' the headman said. 'Only with fire can we do these things, just as we can only live with the warmth of the sun. But we must never forget that sooner or later the fire will burn everything, right down to the ground.'

" 'And what of the sun?' asked the boy, asked Dedi. 'The sun is made of fire. Will it burn everything down to the ground? Will it even burn the ground itself?' "

But the question would remain unanswered in this iteration of the tale, for just then the freed captives jumped the guards. In moments, they had neutralized the terrorists and begun to free the other prisoners. "What was that?" Nizhoni asked Uhura with a laugh. " 'I'm frightened'?"

Uhura winked. "Something I use on the captain sometimes. Having a damsel to protect really motivates him. I figured the guards would fall for it too."

"Men are so easy," Nizhoni sighed.

"And don't you dare tell him, Leonard!" Uhura said to the doctor.

"Oh, no. We men have to stick together. Your secret's out, young lady."

Just then another guard emerged from behind the altar. On seeing the freed prisoners, who were now armed and greatly outnumbered her, she promptly retreated and called a warning to Dovraku. The Starfleet party rushed for the altar, but it slid shut before they could reach it. "Damn!" McCoy cried.

Lindstrom hopped up on the altar and pressed the sunburst with his hand. Meeting with no success, he jabbed it several times more. "Do not waste your energy," Soreth said. "There is an override on the inside."

"So what do we do?" Rishala asked.

"We trust in Jim and Spock," said McCoy.

"Is that all?" Soreth said contemptuously.

McCoy glared at him. "It's enough."

"It would appear," Spock said as Dovraku glared at the closed altar, "that not everything is going according to your view of destiny after all."

"It matters not. All three are still present, whether you are in the same room or not. It is time!"

Spock recognized that his options were exhausted. He was pleased that the captives had freed themselves, but Dovraku's swift action in closing the altar had rendered their efforts irrelevant to the larger problem. There was not sufficient time for them to make their way around to the entrance Kirk had used, even if they could find it. And the guards on Kirk and Chekov had been alert, not letting them take advantage of the diversion. If there was anything to be done now, it would probably depend on the mind-meld.

He took a moment to prepare himself mentally. Fortunately, he belonged to that segment of the Vulcan population for whom melding was a natural ability; otherwise, he would have required hours of meditation to prepare, had he been trained in the discipline at all. And meditation was not something that came easily to him of late. He had his concerns about whether he could accomplish this at all.

For one thing, what Dovraku was asking for—a technique known as the bridging of minds, wherein he served as a conduit for linking two others' consciousnesses—was not something he had much experience with. For another, he doubted that the Oracle even *had* a consciousness in any meaningful sense, and was unconvinced it would even be possible to join with it. Spock had successfully melded with artificial intelligences on two previous occasions: his recent meld with V'Ger and the one he had performed 5.8 years ago with the *Nomad/Tan Ru* hybrid probe (two situations which, come to think of it, had possessed some startling similarities). The principle was essentially the same as joining with an organic mind; both were electrically based systems, and the Vulcan nervous system was capable of interfacing with them through induction. With organic minds there was a psionic-field component as well, but the EM interface alone had proved sufficient for joining with advanced AIs. But if an AI were below a certain threshold level of complexity, or lacked the sort of neural-network architecture with which an organic Vulcan brain could resonate, there was simply nothing comprehensible to read. This was why he had never attempted to interface with the *Enterprise* computer in this way—

though he sometimes wondered if the common Vulcan knack for computer sciences might be a manifestation of some subliminal telepathic rapport with information systems. In any case, Spock's attempt to meld with an android on Mudd's Planet had failed totally, due to the extremely simple and subsentient nature of their control computer. He believed the Oracle possessed a more sophisticated artificial intelligence than that mechanism, but was it sophisticated enough? In some ways it was less advanced than the *Enterprise* computer, but it had been designed for more autonomous function and decision-making. That might be sufficient.

Another concern was that in both those previous melds with AIs, Spock had been overwhelmed. *Nomad/Tan Ru's* rigid thought processes had imposed themselves on his own, its programmed imperatives drowning out all other thought. In V'Ger's case it had been due more to sheer data overload, but there had been the same sense of being *absorbed* within the AI's mechanistic worldview, unable to break free. He hoped that he had gained enough experience from those melds to resist it this time.

Additionally, there were the security concerns. Technically, it was a serious security breach for a Starfleet officer to meld minds with an enemy, giving him access to sensitive information. But Spock had trained himself to compartmentalize such knowledge behind strong mental shields, in the event of being subjected to invasive probes. Those shields had served him well against the Klingon mind-sifter on Organia and in other instances. But he took a moment to shore them up before he proceeded.

At last, he opened his eyes. "I am ready," he told Dovraku, and moved over to the central console. "I must open this panel to touch the computer core directly."

"Very well."

Spock did so, placing his left hand upon its warm metal

shell, his fingers feeling their way to the optimal induction points. Then he placed his right hand on Dovraku's face, accessing the oculomotor, olfactory, and trigeminal nerves, the closest neural access points to the surface—what ancient Vulcan poets had called the portals to the mind. Having found the pathways, it was now simply a matter of broadening his awareness through them, beyond them—to feel the new additions to his nervous system and make them part of himself.

Yes, came a new thought, *at last it begins!* Suddenly he craved this, needed this. *At last I begin to leave myself. Soon I will be free of this filthy cage of flesh! But where is my Oracle?*

Patience, his other self responded. *This will be difficult. There may be very little there.* . . . But then he was filled with an absolute certainty of success—the certainty of the fanatic. This would happen, because it was meant to happen. And that very certainty made it a reality. He teased out the fragile thread of connection to that other appendage, *willed* himself to feel it as he would a sleep-paralyzed limb. And then it opened up and surged over him.

It was jarring/ecstatic. He was overpowered by a wave of sensation—not thought, but awareness, impulse, instinct. He had a stony body hundreds of kilometers wide, and was aware of every aspect of its circulation, respiration, metabolism. *(Familiar? Had he experienced such before?)* He had senses across the electromagnetic spectrum, and dozens of appendages, flying through space *(missiles!),* which he guided toward preprogrammed positions. *Destroy them,* came an impulse from a part of himself. But the sheer weight of his instincts overrode the urge. This was reflex, imperative, a near-involuntary function. There was a purity to it, a certainty that made conscious effort unnecessary, unwelcome. This was what a part of him aspired to in meditation. This was what another part craved as a release. This was all that another part had ever known.

There were intruders nearby, moving bits of space debris. One of them was of special interest to him. It was his ship, his home—no, it was the instrument of his destiny! And he had the knowledge to control it, to use it for that divine purpose, if only he could remember it. The knowledge was blocked . . . he strove to retrieve it. *No*—a part of him fought the impulse. But that part was shaken, dazed by the sensory onslaught. And now the fanatical part pushed back, determined to get at this memory—knowing that he must have it, that he *would* have it, for it simply had to be.

In the face of that absolute, psychotic certainty of its failure, the barrier could not help but fail, and the knowledge came forth. Knowledge of the intruder's systems, its abilities, its controls. Knowledge of a way to interface with it, to override it from afar—*the prefix code.*

A part of him fought fiercely to prevent its use. But to the purely instinctive part of him, the thought and the act had been one, and it was already done before he could stop himselves. Now he had control. The *Enterprise* was his holy instrument, the means by which this joining would be taken to the next, the ultimate level! With its transporter, he would dematerialize his several bodies and merge them into his destined higher self, as mighty V'Ger had done!

No! The shock of this knowledge restored Spock to a partial sense of self. Though he was still firmly in the meld, he was able to delineate its components more clearly, to remember who he was supposed to be. The impulse came from Dovraku, and it was utter madness. The transporter could not achieve what V'Ger's scan matrix had. If it attempted to beam Spock, Dovraku, and the Oracle together, the result would most likely be a Pauli-exclusion blast that would destroy the control center and probably rupture Yonada's collapsed-matter core.

Spock strove to convey this knowledge to the rest of

himself, but neither part would listen—one out of unshake-able fanaticism, the other out of the sheer inability to comprehend. The Oracle/Dovraku was already interfaced with the *Enterprise* computer, warming up the phase transition coils, reprogramming the pattern buffer . . .

Lowering the shields.

CHAPTER
SEVENTEEN

*If there are self-made purgatories, then we all
have to live in them.*   —Spock

"SHIELDS AND FORCEFIELDS down, sir!" Perez cried, pounding at the console. "I can't get them back up!"

Sulu whirled to the engineering console. "Mercado?"

The baby-faced ensign checked his readouts and shook
his head, nonplussed. "I'm not reading any malfunction!
They should be working!"

"An outside source is overriding our computer!" Uuvu'it
declared. "Seems to be the Oracle doing it! Defenses won't
go up, and the transporter is being reprogrammed to do . . .
something weird."

"Never mind that now, we need shields! Can you override—uh, their override?"

"Trying, being blocked. They've got a skillful player."
Uuvu'it sounded thrilled—he loved a good contest.

Speaking of which, a thought occurred to Sulu: Why
weren't the Shesshran pressing their attack? He checked the
tactical plot on the main viewer. A few of the ships were firing on the *Enterprise,* the ones that he'd just been trying to
scare off or disable with low-power phaser shots before the

shields went out. A few were pressing their attacks on Yonada, as they had been already. The rest seemed to be hovering uncertainly, keeping the *Enterprise* encircled but making no aggressive moves. *Circling like vultures,* Sulu thought.

Except the Shesshran were raptors, not scavengers. Predators, hunters. There was something about that. . . . Sulu had flirted with xenoethology as one of his many interests over the years, and something came back to him now. A predator species, especially a flying one, needed a large hunting range to feed itself adequately. That made them strongly territorial. So they must have dominance fights all the time, surely. So how did they keep from killing each other off?

By knowing when to say uncle. And how to accept it when it was said.

"Cease firing!" he commanded.

"Sir?"

"You heard me, Perez. Stand down weapons. DiFalco, hold position." *Enterprise* was sending mixed signals—lowering its defenses while continuing to fight. The Shesshran weren't sure whether it was saying uncle or not. He had to clear it up for them. "Auberson, hail them."

"No response."

"Open a channel anyway." He took a breath. Keeping his seat, he lowered his head slightly, not looking directly at the pickup. He wasn't sure if it was a submission gesture they'd recognize, but it was worth a shot. "This is the *Enterprise.* We acknowledge the might of the Shesshran, and yield to your superior force. We ask that you cease your attack on us and on Yonada."

There was silence for a time, and Sulu wondered if he'd miscalculated. Then Auberson said, "Several responses coming in, sir."

"Put the first one on screen."

"You are wise to submit, Enterprise." Sulu couldn't tell whether it was the same Shesshran they'd spoken to before, although, given their lack of a formal hierarchy, the odds were against it. *"You may remove yourself from our territory. But do not presume to speak for Yonada. They have not surrendered."*

"But they haven't fired on you either."

"Those who hold Yonada have declared themselves aggressors against free individual thought. They have not surrendered, so they will be destroyed."

Of course. How could a predator back down until the opponent had shown clear submission? Any show of weakness was defeat. That was why they hadn't taken his warnings about Yonada seriously. They had the physics knowledge to understand the danger from the collapsed-matter core—they just couldn't admit they felt threatened by it. It was all about saving face.

Or as Uuvu'it would say, it was all about coming out ahead in the game. And games were something Sulu understood. In martial arts competition, the blows were pulled. In fencing, the points were blunted. In chess, the king was not taken, only surrounded. Victory lay not in delivering the blow, but in showing that you could. Dominance without destruction, aggression regulated to allow a society to function. It was all about positioning, about control of the situation—control of your territory.

"They must surrender, madam, because they have no other choice. You've proven that. You have the upper ground. They can't escape you, so you can destroy them at your leisure. It doesn't need to be now. Why not give them a chance to admit defeat?"

"You do not dictate to the Shesshran!"

"Oh, of course not. If you think it's too dangerous for you to let them stew a few minutes, that's your prerogative."

"Do you call me afraid?!"

"No, certainly not. You're in complete control of the situation. You couldn't hold that kind of control if you were afraid of a defenseless asteroid." Sulu was counting on the other ships listening in—and the pilot being concerned about her standing in the tenuous coalition.

"You are sensible," the pilot finally said. *"I am not afraid of them. I do not care if they sit in their asteroid and bluster—they know I am here waiting, and will destroy them at the first wrong move! Just let them try."*

One by one, the other Shesshran announced their intention to do the same. If one of them felt unthreatened by Yonada's continued existence, then none of them could seek to destroy it without admitting their fear.

Sulu looked around and noticed Uuvu'it staring at him. "What is it?"

"I'm not sure, sir. It looks like you just . . . won by surrendering. Is that . . . is that allowed?"

Sulu grinned. "Just something I learned from my great-grandfather. Sometimes you have to bend with the wind." The thought sent Sulu's mind back to when old Tetsuo had died, to Sulu's time in command school. He'd never felt truly comfortable there, and later on had never seen his times in the command chair as anything more than keeping the seat warm for someone else. But now he reflected on what he'd just done. He'd solved a problem, ended a battle . . . and he'd done it by using his own skills, his own knowledge and life experience. At no point had he asked himself what Kirk would do—he'd just done what Sulu would do. And it had worked. And it had felt *right*.

Suddenly the command chair felt a lot more comfortable.

He turned to Uuvu'it. "Any luck regaining control?"

"Still fighting the good fight. Whoever this is knows our system inside and out! If I didn't know better I'd say it was Commander Spock."

Sulu couldn't imagine Spock doing this—but he couldn't imagine anyone else on Yonada being capable of it. He shook it off—now was not the time. "What about that transporter program?"

"I let Rand handle it while I tackled the shields."

"What will it do?"

"Well . . . you remember that old story about the time two signals got sent to the same transporter pad at once?"

"Oh . . . my."

"Well, this is worse. Especially since the exclusion blast could breach Yonada's core. Stop me if you've heard this one."

Sulu punched the intercom. "Bridge to transporter room one. Status, Janice?"

Oh, not now, Hikaru! Janice Rand thought. The last thing she needed right now was a distraction. It was a struggle to keep this new program from engaging. Whatever she tried to do to block it, her opponent found a path around it, and she was running out of options.

"Rand, this is the bridge, report!"

Damn. She hit the intercom. "I'm working on it! So far I've only slowed it down."

"Uuvu'it's on it now."

Rand wanted to object, to insist that she could handle it. But she knew that would be foolish. The truth was, she didn't want to admit she couldn't handle it. She didn't want to feel helpless again.

She had always felt so helpless, so many times. Overwhelmed by the responsibility of being the captain's yeoman. Fearing for her life when Balok or the Romulans attacked. Fearing her own feelings for the captain, knowing she was helpless to act on them, for he never would. Falling into an affair with a crewmate, then helpless to avoid the consequences of the resultant pregnancy, compelled to leave Starfleet to raise the baby, to protect its father from the scandal. Helpless to save Annie when she sickened and died after only two years in the universe. Always so helpless.

Then finally she'd chosen to pull herself together, to re-enter Starfleet and achieve a sense of purpose, of control. Only to find herself once again helpless to do anything as two people died in agony on the transporter pad. *"There was nothing you could have done, Rand. It wasn't your fault."* Kirk's words, meant to comfort, had only burned.

No matter what, she wouldn't let it happen again. Lives depended on her, more lives than ever before, and she couldn't let them down. She wouldn't let herself be ineffectual again.

But as the program continued to swoop and dodge around her overrides, drawing closer and closer to engaging the beams, Rand was forced to make a hard admission: she couldn't do this alone. If she insisted on trying to be the hero, then she *would* let it happen again. The only way she could make a difference was by admitting she was licked.

"I recommend physically cutting power to the transporters, Sulu," she said, her voice heavy. "Because I'm not going to be able to hold this off much longer."

Should she feel proud, or ashamed? Right now she didn't have time to consider it. She still had to fight to keep the program at bay until the power could be cut. And no matter what, she wouldn't let herself fail.

"Mercado, get a team down there!" Sulu ordered.

"It'll take a minute, sir."

"We may not have a minute!" came Rand's voice.

"I, ah, hate to bring it up," Uuvu'it said, "but the missiles go off in four minutes."

"Maybe the Shesshran will let us shoot them down now," Sulu said.

DiFalco threw him a frustrated look. "If only we still had helm control. We're being moved in toward Yonada."

Sulu glared daggers at the ersatz asteroid looming on the viewscreen. "What the *hell* is going on over there?"

In the meld, Spock struggled to retain his separate sense of self, to resist the others' use of his knowledge to hijack the *Enterprise*'s systems. He couldn't let Dovraku succeed in this insane act, or everyone on Yonada, Lorina, and the orbiting ships would be wiped out.

But that was just the problem, wasn't it? He had *let* it happen. His mental blocks had failed miserably, and he had placed the keys to the *Enterprise* in the hands of a madman. He should have known—such blocks required a disciplined mind, and his had been nothing of the kind lately. He had been a fool to attempt this. He had feared his experiment with emotion would end in failure, or harm to others—but he hadn't imagined his failure being on this scope.

You see the cost of emotion? Dovraku asked. *All it brings is chaos and despair. Feel the purity the Oracle offers, Spock. Perfect, regimented logic, no doubt, no confusion, no pain. Give in to it, Spock. Let it take us.*

Spock felt it, the simplicity, the effortless instinct of the programmed mind. *You cannot lie to me here, Spock. You crave it too.*

No! I have rejected that path.

But you fear its alternative. You know you cannot live with your passions. They will engulf you, destroy you. Let it go, Spock. Let go of the guilt, the despair, the fear. Embrace the purity of oblivion. Surrender yourself to the One.

He knew it was madness, but at the same time it was tempting—to escape from it all, to avoid the struggle that would consume the rest of his life . . . and Dovraku's deep yearning resonating with that impulse made it hard to deny. It would be so easy. . . .

No meaning, a voice inside him said. *No hope. Is this all you are? Is there nothing more?*

Voyager? Spock asked. Was it just a memory, or was his receptive mind connecting with it once again?

Remember . . . this simple feeling.

I remember! He pulled himself away from the Oracle's embrace. *I have felt it before, Dovraku. It is a lie. It is emptiness, oblivion. With no desire there is no fulfillment, no purpose. No meaning. No hope. It is not enough.*

It is all! Dovraku cried, and the craving for that oblivion was so intense it almost dragged him under.

But wait. . . . There was a paradox here. That yearning was an emotion in itself. A yawning, desperate hole in Dovraku's soul. *Why, Dovraku? What is it that you wish to escape from?*

The other tried to block him, but the very effort pointed the way to what Spock sought. Dovraku had a mental barrier of his own—a wall of scars formed around old wounds. Dull echoes of remembered pain cemented it, tautened it with self-revulsion. But it was not a wall that kept Dovraku out. He maintained it himself, to keep something in. And so that something was always there, just below the surface, close enough to touch for all the firmness of the barrier. It gave Spock a way inside.

Still, the memories were clouded, damaged, laid over with the neurological static of trauma. Images of a man, a giant, looming overhead. Strong hands holding him up, cradling his weight, protecting him . . . then falling away as the giant grew smaller, more distant. *Never home.*

"*You're never home for us!*"

"*Would you have me quit my job, foolish woman? Leave us to starve more than we already do?*"

"*I would have you come home to your son and me instead of drinking half your income!*"

"*You! You're half the problem. I was doing fine until the*"

Oracle saddled me with you, and refused to raise my wage enough to—aah!" He winces in pain, looks up, desperate, lost . . . then clamps down on his anger, swallows his bitter words.

Then he takes it out on her without words.

Then he takes it out on his son. Strong hands, paying the pain forward. Each time he cannot voice his frustration, his resentment of the Oracle, his hands—his flesh—speak for him. *"Quiet, boy. You know what will happen to you if you wake your mother."* His flesh to the boy's flesh, and flesh becomes pain, recoiling from itself. A lifetime spent trying to crawl out of his home, his world, his skin.

"I'm tired of you running away, boy. You know how much I hate having to punish you again."

"You? Learn to read? Stop dreaming that you'll ever amount to anything."

"I am gravely disappointed in you, son. You must try harder to master these emotional outbursts."

No . . . that was another father. . . . Sarek had never raised a hand against his son. He never . . .

"That is a human sentiment, Spock. You should know better by now."

"You laughed out loud in front of guests. Do you realize the shame you have brought to our family?"

"Amanda, if the boy seeks my approval, he knows what he must do to earn it. Offering an emotional demonstration as a reward when no reward has even been earned is illogical on multiple levels."

"This behavior at your age is simply unacceptable, Spock."

"Your control frequently slips even here on Vulcan where every incentive is provided you for mastering your emotions. If your control fails among offworlders, you do not simply fail, you fail all Vulcan."

"You are no part of me."

No . . . Sarek had never physically harmed Spock, but he had rarely shown approval for him either. Spock had never before recognized how much that had hurt him. How much he'd craved his father's approval, striven to measure up to his expectations, only to fall short time and again. The largest decision of his life, to enter Starfleet, had been his one great rejection of Sarek's example, and Sarek had punished him for it with eighteen years of silence. Had his resignation, his pursuit of *Kolinahr*, been an attempt to seek redemption for letting his father down?

If your control fails, you fail all Vulcan. You fail me, Spock.

That was the heart of it, wasn't it? All his life Spock had feared losing control, for the little boy in him had feared losing his father's approval. It was no different now—even though he knew the path he must tread, that little boy feared taking it, feared failure, and pleaded with him to retreat to the example Sarek had set.

Face this with me, Dovraku, he demanded. *Do you see? We are both drawn to logic for fundamentally emotional reasons. We cannot escape our passions. That is why my Kolinahr failed. And it is why the Oracle cannot heal you, Dovraku. Your answer lies elsewhere.*

No! There is nothing else. Nothing I wish to face. If I cannot have pure logic, I must have oblivion.

There is another path, said that other voice again. *The joining.* Sensations flooded their minds, and Spock was sure they could only come from the Voyager. The blending of selves, logic and passion and will merging, wrestling, finding the ever-shifting balance between them. Not isolation, not oblivion. No mathematical purity or simple answers. Diversity in combination, making a glorious mess. Making peace with each other, and thereby with themselves.

Logic and passion and will . . . It was a balance Spock had already known, already been a part of. He shared his own experiences: the doctor whose passion forever clashed with Spock's logic, each of them keeping the other from losing his way; and the captain who held them both together, took their clashing energies and focused them into decision, into change.

Yes, the joining, Spock told Dovraku. *But not the one you had in mind. The joining cannot be forced. It has to come from making peace. You are at war, Dovraku, with yourself and with your world. You must reconcile with both. As must we all.*

I cannot reconcile with . . . that. A flash of the memories behind the wall of scars, a hesitant glimpse immediately turned away from. *I cannot live with that.*

It is all you can live with, for it is a part of you. That is something which you will either deal with or not. Whether you do that, how you do that, is your journey, and frankly it makes no difference to me. But your war with the world outside ends here. You will make no one else pay for your personal demons.

Now it became easy to override the Oracle. Dovraku was far from cured of his madness, but his grip was broken. The fanatical certainty which had made his every wish real within the meld was gone, and without it the Oracle's similarly monovalued perception was easier to resist. Spock had choice, and he exercised it. He was eager to free himself from this meld, but there were a few loose ends he had to tie up first.

"Sir," Uuvu'it announced, "computer control is back! Shutting down transporter now."

"Good job, Hrrii'ush!"

"Ahh . . . of course. It was nothing." He did a double-take at another readout. "And every one of the missiles has just shut down. They're adrift and no longer receiving telemetry." If only he could think of a way to take credit for that too. . . .

•   •   •

Moredi was getting weak. He feared he would pass out soon and be unable to guard the prisoners. And the herbal antiemetic which he had been given before entering that hot, cramped compartment on the shuttle was starting to wear off, and the painful burns and sores on his skin were growing worse, and he was coughing up blood. He didn't know how much longer he could endure.

Dovraku had assured him it wouldn't take this long—that his suffering would be brief and would end with his admission into the new paradise which the Great One and the Oracle would create. And if the Great One said it, then it was true. So Moredi did not understand why he was being allowed to continue suffering, and why Dovraku and the Oracle were not ascending. Instead they merely stood there, bridged together by the Vulcan's touch, not moving or speaking, not glowing or transforming.

Moredi felt a wave of dizziness pass over him. He gathered himself quickly, just in time, for the godkiller had spotted it and was tensing to make a move. "Try it, devil," Moredi said, gesturing aggressively with the crossbow. "Please, give me an excuse to—"

"HEAR ME, MY FOLLOWERS."

The Oracle spoke! Moredi looked around him in awe. "COME FORTH INTO THE TEMPLE," the booming voice intoned. Moredi hesitated—what about the escaped prisoners who controlled it now? But the voice spoke again, more commandingly. "COME!"

Exchanging confused and anticipatory looks, Moredi and his fellow true believers moved through the opening into the main temple. The ex-prisoners stood there, still armed, but looking confused, hesitant to act for fear the Oracle would strike them down. Moredi covered them with his own weapon, and a standoff quickly ensued. Looking around, Moredi decided that as the senior one present, he

should be the one to speak. "Uh, we are here, great Oracle
of the People!"

"LOWER YOUR WEAPONS."

Moredi was taken aback. "But—"

"LOWER THEM. NOW!"

It made no sense—but this was the Oracle speaking. He
hesitantly nodded to the others to comply, but then he
asked, "But what of Dovraku, great Oracle? What of your
ascension?"

"DOVRAKU IS A FALSE PROPHET. HE MISLED YOU FOR REA-
SONS OF HIS OWN. YOU WILL SURRENDER YOURSELVES TO
STARFLEET SECURITY PERSONNEL, WHO WILL TAKE YOU TO A
MEDICAL FACILITY FOR TREATMENT OF YOUR RADIATION POI-
SONING."

Starfleet? Surrender to the Oracle's killers? How could
this be? And how could Dovraku be false? He had promised
Moredi that the towers would fall, that the bitch Natira
would be slain, that he would be elevated to paradise. He
had been the One who would bring about all that was right
and just and good. It could not have been a lie!

Moredi stepped forward, confronted the altar angrily.
"Why do you forsake us, O Oracle? We were promised
greatness! We were promised that the World would be
cleansed, that the faithful would be reborn! Where is our
new World? Where is our paradise?"

The Oracle was silent for a time. Then, at last, it spoke:

"I AM NOT PROGRAMMED TO RESPOND IN THAT AREA."

Then a lightning bolt struck Moredi, and he knew no
more.

Despite Kirk's instructions to stay a safe distance behind,
Natira had come forward to the maintenance tunnel's exit,
observing the events clandestinely. She had been prepared to
act if the opportunity had presented itself, but she had also
recognized her own limitations. As Leonard might say, she

was a stateswoman, not a soldier. So she merely observed. When she'd heard the Oracle's familiar, booming voice—a voice she now hated for the blind way she'd obeyed its every word for so many years—she'd been horrified. But its words this time had surprised her greatly. By the time she heard the thunderclaps from the temple, she'd realized that Spock must have somehow taken control of it within the meld.

She came forward tentatively, in time to see Dovraku slump unconscious to the control room floor. Spock's hand remained in contact with the Oracle's core processor. Kirk approached, concern on his face, and called, "Spock? Spock! Come out of it!"

The Vulcan blinked and gave his captain a nonchalant look. "It's quite all right, Jim. I have the situation well in hand. I was merely . . . exploring."

Leonard had been kneeling by the body of young Ensign Zaand, but lowered his head in recognition that he was too late. Natira understood how it hurt him, on a personal level, to be unable to ward off death another time. But he held the feeling within and went on with his job, moving over to Dovraku and scanning him. "He's catatonic," Leonard said, and looked up at Spock. "What in blazes did you do to him in there?"

"I merely showed him what it was he was truly fighting. Apparently he could not let go of that fight. But at least his battle is no longer directed at anyone else." Spock studied Dovraku contemplatively and a bit sadly. "He craved nothing more than to escape his bodily existence. It seems he has achieved that goal. But I do not think it will bring him any peace."

"I'm oddly untroubled by that," Kirk said, as the rest of the ex-captives began filing in from the temple beyond. "Mr. Chekov, take Dovraku to sickbay, under guard just in case. And . . . take care of Ensign Zaand."

"Aye, sir," the security chief said somberly. As he and

McCoy turned to that work, Kirk turned back to his first officer. "And the Oracle?"

"On standby. And proving quite cooperative."

His cavalier tone, considering what he was discussing, made Natira angry. She strode forward to confront Spock. "Why did you take such an enormous risk?" she demanded. "Why not simply destroy the Oracle and end the threat?"

"I knew it!" Kemori cried. "Nothing has changed—you still wish to destroy the things most sacred to the People!"

Natira replied in outrage. "I was the one whose willingness to make concessions enabled these talks to proceed in the first place! The treachery came on your side!"

Sonaya stepped forward. "In fact, Governess, it came from me," she said with an odd mix of assertiveness and shame. "I was weak, and afraid of Dovraku. I told him of our secret plans and agreed to let him smuggle his people here. None of the others knew."

"Very well," Natira said after a moment. "Then you shall be arrested for treason. Where is Tasari?"

"I'm afraid," Dumali told her, "that the Oracle killed him."

Natira was stunned. The loss of the man evoked surprisingly little feeling, but the murder of a government minister was an outrage. "There," she finally said. "You see? It is a menace!"

"It is a tool," Spock said. "Dovraku reprogrammed it to do his bidding. As you evidently heard, I did the same some moments ago, via more direct methods."

"It is a dangerous tool which Dovraku nearly used to destroy us all."

"And before that," old Paravo said, "it was our guide, our protector."

"It enslaved us!"

"It kept us alive. And linked us to the Creators."

"This," Spock interposed, "is why it must not be destroyed."

"Of course," Kirk said, exchanging a look with him. "The Oracle is an ancient and powerful symbol to your people. Destroy the machine and the symbolism remains. All we'd do is wipe out any chance that the mass of Lorini could ever trust the Federation, or your government. It would escalate the civil war, not end it."

"Correct. Surely the events of the past weeks should demonstrate that this conflict cannot be ended by acts of destruction. The Oracle is at the root of all that divides you and defines you as a people. You must make peace with it if you are to make peace with each other."

"It is nothing of the sort," Soreth interjected. "It was imposed by a single faction to enslave the rest through superstition. It does not provide a link to the Creators, for the builders of Yonada did not create it."

"In fact, Commissioner, that judgment is premature," Spock told him. "Mr. Lindstrom and I have uncovered evidence to the contrary. Additionally, my meld with the Oracle enabled me to . . . experience its databanks more directly. It has given me deeper insight into their contents, and I believe I have uncovered some very salient data pertaining to Yonada's history and origins."

"Tell us," Natira said.

"I am not prepared to say anything for certain at this point. However, I may have discovered the location of a lost data archive here on Yonada."

"Lost?" Kirk asked.

"Or perhaps . . . purposely misplaced, to prevent its destruction in the initial purge. It is not referenced in the current version of the primary plans, but I . . . sensed its absence in the Oracle's limited awareness of itself. One might compare it to a missing tooth. If I am right, it is what we have been searching for: a databank containing records from the first forty centuries of Yonada's journey. I have its location; it is deep underground and therefore likely to have been better protected from cosmic-ray damage. With your permission, Captain, I shall take Mr. Lindstrom and Ms. Uhura there immediately."

"Well, Spock, we've all been through a lot. . . . I'm sure they'd like to go back to the ship and rest—"

"If it's all the same to you, sir," said the elegant dark-complexioned woman, "I'd be happy to go."

"Me too," said Lindstrom. "Are you kidding? Uh, sir."

Natira faced Spock. "And what do you expect to find?"

He raised a brow. "Only the facts, Governess. What they mean will be for you and your fellow Lorini to decide. But at least you will have valid information on which to base those decisions."

CHAPTER EIGHTEEN

I'm a fragment of the day.

If I weren't, who's to say

Things would happen here the way

That they happened here?   —Stephen Sondheim

Project Yonada Construction Complex
Fabrina orbit

Year 126 Unified Calendar (7954 BCE)
Yonada launch minus 8 days

TOMANERU VARI couldn't stop staring at the sun.

Ganidra was a dull red sore in the heavens, swollen across a quarter of the sky. Most of its volume was tenuous gas, not even as dense as Fabrina's thinning air; but it was hot, and close, and it boiled the planet's air and water off a little more every day. Inside it, dimly visible at the center of that rubicund mass, was the bright, hot core—a time bomb counting inexorably down to detonation. Keeping an eye on it didn't make it any more or less likely to go off, but still Vari couldn't resist.

The Tishiki—the silvery winged creatures who lived in the destination system—had spoken in their messages of a sun so small and bright and white that you couldn't look at it long without damaging your eyes. A worthwhile tradeoff, Vari thought, for living in a system whose star was still young. One day, he hoped, the descendants of the Fabrini would live there too. He'd spent the past sixty years striving to ensure that they would. But Ganidra was a treacherous star, and Vari lived under the constant fear that it would explode before Yonada could make its escape.

It was not an irrational fear. Ganidra had been dying since before astronomy was advanced enough to understand the life cycle of a star. Vari reflected on how terrible it must have been for those scholar-priests who had first discovered the impending fate of their sun. Just as they were beginning to harness the new powers that the Scientific Awakening had provided, just as philosophers and fiction writers had begun to contemplate the great future achievements their society had stretching before them, they had found themselves cheated of that future. Just as they had finally begun to understand their world, they'd learned it was doomed to die.

Even then, there had been no certainty that the sun would not explode at any moment. The panic had been horrible, once the scholar-priests' vain efforts to keep the secret had failed, a casualty of their own despair. In time, the Fabrini (those who'd survived the chiliastic chaos) had learned to live with their imminent doom. Some had resigned themselves to it while others had fought desperately to escape it somehow, if only by sending forth probes to preserve their legacy for alien eyes and ears (or whatever their equivalents might be) in some distant future. In time the scientists had even provided a limited measure of comfort, determining that the star was still in its carbon-burning phase and thus would not go supernova in the immediate future. People no longer had to go to bed each night not knowing if they would ever wake.

But over a year ago, the heliologists had reported that Ganidra had begun fusing neon. They couldn't pinpoint exactly how long ago it had entered that stage, since solar neutrino readings were faint and difficult to measure precisely, and the thermal and electromagnetic changes took time to propagate to the surface. But it meant that the star's life expectancy was now only a few years at best, maybe less. By now, nearly every Fabrini was well versed in the sordid details of their sun's impending death, and Vari tortured himself with them every day. Any time now, he thought for the millionth time, the neon in the degenerate core would run out and oxygen burning would begin. Within a year of that, the last of the oxygen would be exhausted, all of it fused into magnesium, silicon, phosphorus, and sulfur. Ganidra wasn't massive or hot enough for the silicon to be fused into iron, so at that point the fusion would stop. But the residual thermal radiation would be so energetic that it would disintegrate all those nuclei, the photons blasting their protons and neutrons apart, undoing twenty million years' worth of nucleosynthesis in a matter of seconds. In that dense, energetic froth of particles, the freed protons would collide with the cloud of free-floating electrons that permeated the degenerate core, merging with them to become neutrons and sopping up the only remaining source of pressure preventing the core's collapse. The core would instantly fall inward on itself until the center reached the density of neutronium. With the neutrons essentially touching each other, the inner core would stop collapsing and rebound slightly. The still-collapsing outer core would collide with it at half the speed of light—and *bounce*, flying outward in all directions at nearly the same speed, forcing all the star's atmosphere out ahead of it. In hours, nothing would be left of the star but a neutronium husk much smaller than Yonada. And Fabrina—its people, huddled in their tunnels underground—would have no warning. They would . . . well, the reason Vari obsessed on the physics of the core collapse was to avoid thinking about what would happen to the people.

Tomaneru Vari had spent his life trying to save a segment of the Fabrini people, only to find himself a member of the one generation which knew for a fact that the world would end in their lifetimes. The project was so close to success, and yet so close to total failure. Ganidra probably wouldn't explode in the next eight days, the heliologists were reasonably sure of that; but Yonada was a massive object and would take years to accelerate out of the danger zone. The supernova could happen while Yonada was still too close to get away. To lose it all so close to salvation would be unbearable.

"Why?" he asked aloud. "Why did Tilu put us here?"

Beside his reflection in the window, Minakeli Baima's turned to study him. "I thought you didn't believe in Tilu." She made a gesture of reverence as she spoke the name of her god.

"Tilu, the Creators, the settlers from the stars, whoever it was that put our people on Fabrina. Why choose a world that was so close to death already? Why not put us on Lorina in the first place? It's not so far, not for beings that can reshape worlds."

The elderly Oracle shrugged, jostling the ponytail of snow-white hair that floated behind her in the microgravity of the construction complex. "Many of my colleagues like to say it was a test."

"A test." Vari scoffed. "What deity would be so cruel as to put its subjects through sadistic tests just to see if they could survive them? Are we nothing but laboratory animals?"

"I never said *I* believed it."

"Besides," Vari admitted, "if it were true, it would mean we failed. Out of all the Fabrini, we only save forty million, if even that many." He turned his gaze to the arid, sunburned sphere below. Only a few wisps of cloud remained to show it had any atmosphere at all. "How many millions have already died, from the riots and revolutions, the mass suicides, the pointless wars? How many thousands have died in building Yonada? How many thousands more have died just trying to make the journey up here?" With such a vast migration, accidents were inevitable. But there were also renewed riots, started by those who couldn't accept the results of the selection process. They weren't the best and brightest, weren't young and fertile, didn't have any special skills, didn't add anything further to the ethnic and cultural diversity of Yonada's population (which would probably blend into uniformity anyway over the millennia of the journey), but they were willing to smash things and kill people, and believed that was sufficient qualification to survive.

"All lives end, Tomaneru. All that endures of them is their posterity, their legacy. Thanks to your unwavering strength, those have a chance to live on."

Vari afforded her a faint smile of gratitude, which was all he could muster. "I'd feel better about our chances if you were coming with us, Keli. I'll never share your beliefs, but I've always found your wisdom invaluable . . . not only in bringing the people together, inspiring them to believe in the project . . . you've helped me too."

She clasped his shoulder. "I know, Neru. You don't have to tell me."

"You deserve to be told. And you deserve to come with us. Be our Oracle."

"We've been through this. The Oracle of Yonada will need to be able to pass on all the knowledge of Fabrina to its people, down through the generations. A human Oracle

could never have as much knowledge at her fingertips as an
AI can."

"You could consult the AI at any time. A living face, a
living voice would—"

"Would speak for one point of view, one culture. It's an
inherent weakness."

"You've never suffered from it. You've always been open
to new ideas, other beliefs. You're the only one who got all
the faiths to cooperate in this."

Baima shook her head, remembering to do it slowly so as
not to confuse her inner ears. "Of course I have my biases.
Here I have a dozen other points of view to argue with, to
force me to stay on the middle path. If it were just me, without that balance, I couldn't fairly speak for all the Fabrini."

Vari smiled. "You'd have me to argue with."

She ruffled his hair, the way she had when he'd been a
little boy. He was sure she still thought of him that way, and
she was the only person in the world that he'd tolerate it
from, because she treated children with more respect and
reverence than she showed for most adults. "And I will
dearly miss having that, Neru. But I am old. I have more
past than future, and I've contributed all I can to Yonada."
She turned her gaze down to the world below. "Fabrina has
only a few years left, and so do I. So it makes more sense
for me to stay with those left behind. They will need spiritual guidance more than your Yonadi will." Tears filled her
eyes, gently, undramatically, and bunched into small clear
globes. "They are in chaos now. Destroying each other,
destroying all we have built . . . wasting what time they have
left. They need someone to help them find peace."

"If they don't kill you first."

She shrugged again. "Either they will or Ganidra will. Or
time will. It makes little difference now."

Vari shook his own head, considering Fabrina. "So much
pointless death. So much I've been responsible for myself.

How many fanatics and saboteurs have we had to kill to protect Yonada?"

Baima looked at him intently. "Are you finally showing remorse for the harshness of your methods?"

That brought a glare. "You surely don't think I've wanted to do any of it."

"No. But I've never heard you question it before."

"I regret it. I don't question it. The obedience implants are necessary. It's a closed, carefully balanced environment. We can't risk disruptions. So those who can't obey the laws on their own will have to be restrained. And if they persist, if they will not learn, then . . . well, they bring it on themselves. And the millions are protected. They have to be protected, at all costs."

"At all costs," Baima echoed. "I've heard some argue that the implants should be placed in everyone. That the only way to be truly sure of safety is to stop potential offenders before they start. Would you go that far?"

Vari was humbled. "All right . . . I exaggerated. But maintaining peace requires a balance of incentive and penalty, you know that. They will have their faith, their Oracle to unite them, to teach them and inspire the best in them. But when its example fails . . ."

"I know. I just fear what may happen if later generations don't share your understanding of the judicious use of power."

He laughed without humor. "I fear that, and many things more, Keli. A great many things can go wrong in a journey of millennia. And I am certain that Yonada will not escape all of them. We flee from hardship by facing hardship, and if our distant heirs do reach Lorina, they will face many hardships of their own, no matter how perfect and beautiful that world looks from here. And any one of them, or any combination, could mean the end of the Fabrini people forever.

"You see why I don't believe in Tilu?" he went on with a smirk. "I'm being generous. To say I believed he put us here would be to say I considered him a sick, sadistic bastard. It's kinder to dismiss him as a metaphor."

She didn't take offense. "Yet still you give Yonada an Oracle, and make the priesthood a branch of its government."

"Metaphors can be useful. You know I'll do anything to improve our chances of survival. I don't believe, but the masses do, and if I want to save them I have to save that as well. Faith . . . in anything . . . is a source of strength, of hope. It keeps people going."

Baima tilted her head. "Odd words from such a cynic. Tell me, Tomaneru, what is the faith that has kept you going for all these decades? That has brought you to the brink of saving the Fabrini from extinction?"

Vari thought long and hard. Then he stared at the sun again. "The only thing I have faith in . . . is that I'm not going to let that bitch Ganidra take my people down without a fight."

"But you must believe the fight is worth waging. Otherwise you wouldn't have fought so long, and so well. You're too ornery to admit it—you can't take off that armor around your soul for a minute—but you have faith in our people, and in what we can build if we keep striving together. And that faith can accomplish great things, Tomaneru."

He looked at her askance. "Even if I don't believe in Tilu?"

"That doesn't matter," Baima smiled. "He believes in you." She kissed him on the forehead, and his breath caught in his throat because he knew it was the last time. "And so do I."

" . . . But inevitably, over the millennia, a certain complacency set in," Lindstrom said. His narrative had been a bit long-winded, Kirk thought, but he'd managed to hold the attention of Natira, Rishala, and the others gathered back here in the conference chamber to continue negotiations. "The political structure became ossified, driven more by maintaining its power than maintaining the builders' original priorities. The scholar-priests had reduced their educational system to a set of tests that taught nothing but the ability to pass the tests, and had no connection to real-world issues. The Oracle was marginalized. Its lessons about the long-lost homeworld were seen as irrelevant, and its advice about maintaining Yonada became tarred with the same brush. So the procedures for preserving the biosphere were neglected, and eventually that led to drought, famine, economic collapse . . . which of course led to revolution.

"Now, that's where the new backup databank ends. We think it was intentionally 'lost' to protect it from destruction by the revolutionaries. The rest of the story is reconstructed from the texts, oral histories, and archaeological evidence we'd previously uncovered, but the new information gives us more context for understanding all of that.

"The ironic thing is that the new regime rejected everything seen as old-guard, including both the Oracle and the government that had marginalized it. They shut down the Oracle's voice, tore out its interface consoles, burned the books that didn't fit their view of things and rewrote the others. They set up a secular state as a reaction to the corruption of the priesthood.

"But they didn't have any better solutions to the environmental crisis than the old regime did. In fact, their rejection of the Oracle made them *less* able to cope with it, since their proposals for managing resources were based more on politics than science. They only worked as stopgaps at best, and sometimes failed miserably, creating worse economic crisis and famine. It was only a matter of time before another revolution happened—well, there were several attempts, but until one succeeded. And not surprisingly, this set of revolutionaries blamed the secular way of life for the crises, calling it unruly and immoral, and they decided a return to the old beliefs was the only way to save Yonada.

"Now, here's where it gets really interesting—I think so, anyway—but I'll let Lieutenant Commander Uhura explain."

"Thank you, Christopher," Uhura said. She rose, and her clear, melodic voice filled the chamber. "What we think happened is that when these fundamentalists took over, they reactivated the Oracle and read its intelligence files in order to understand how the Creators had intended Yonada to be run. But what they didn't realize was that the *language* had been changed.

"When the secularists had taken over six centuries before, when they'd purged the culture of ideas they didn't like, one thing they'd done was to 'modernize' the language, to rewrite the dictionaries to fit their ideological views. It's something that revolutionaries often do with languages, on planets throughout the known galaxy. They'll 'purge' the language of foreign elements, or modernize its vocabulary, or replace its alphabet with one from a culture they like better, or whatever they think will bring it more in line with their beliefs and hopes for their society. In Yonada's case, they changed the meanings of words having to do with religion and with the Oracle. They gave those words the connotations of dogma, oppression, and cruelty, in order to vilify the old ways. They made it sound as though the Instruments of Obedience had been intended to punish blasphemy rather than serious crimes.

"So when the new regime went back to read through the old texts and find how the original religion had done things, they didn't know their interpretation of it was distorted. They read words which they believed were describing a strict, harsh, intolerant system, and assumed that was the way the Creators had intended it to be."

Spock picked up the narrative now. "More than that—this interpretation, intended to condemn the old ways, actually fit the new rulers' needs and assumptions perfectly. They felt— perhaps with some justification—that the laxity of the past had nearly doomed Yonada, and they wished to impose a strict, disciplinarian regime. Ironically, the antireligious propaganda of the previous establishment gave them the justification they needed. As is generally the case with fundamentalist movements, what they claimed to be the pure, original form of the religion was in fact a contemporary interpretation in response to contemporary circumstances and filtered through contemporary values and definitions.

"What resulted was the system all of you grew up with. The Oracle was reprogrammed to suit the new ideology. The Instruments of Obedience were implanted in all Yonadi, not just convicts, and programmed with a set of laws that regulated thought and speech as well as actions. This effectively quelled subsequent attempts at revolution and enabled the remarkable stability of the fundamentalist regime."

"We're still not entirely certain why they chose to suppress the knowledge that Yonada was an artificial world," Lindstrom added. "Maybe, as was claimed in the mountain archive, they didn't want to trust anyone but the Oracle with the task of maintaining the biosphere. Maybe they just figured knowledge was power and the less knowledge the masses had, the better."

"But that is not important now," said Natira. "What this means . . . is that the Oracle was never meant to oppress us, to deceive us."

"On the contrary," Kirk said. "It was meant to provide a voice to every point of view, to be a common ground for all Fabrini."

"And maybe," Rishala suggested, catching Natira's gaze, "it can be again."

Soreth looked skeptical. "But what of this Vari and Baima and their colleagues, passing themselves off as deities?"

"They did nothing of the kind," Spock countered. "At least, there is no evidence of that in any of their reconstructed writings. Their inclusion among the Creators was a folk belief that emerged in subsequent centuries."

"Of course, just because they didn't claim to be Creators doesn't mean they weren't," Rishala said.

"To all indications," Soreth told her admonishingly, "they were flesh and blood Fabrini."

"The People *are* the flesh and blood of the Creators. It's simply a matter of perspective."

"Not so simple," Kemori countered. "Many of my constituents resent the idea that Vari, Baima, and the others were mortal men and women. They will see even this new evidence as another attempt by the state and the Federation to undermine their faith."

"I'm sure they will," Kirk interposed firmly. "There's no way you'll ever get everyone to agree on the meaning of history, any more than you'll get them to agree on religion. History," he went on thoughtfully, "isn't the past, it's the interpretation of the past. And every generation, every faction will form its own intepretation." He smiled. "You could say we all create history in our own image. History, religion, philosophy . . . logic," he added with a wink at Spock, drawing a glare from Soreth, "they're all tools we use to deal with our problems and our needs. And we all have different needs, different problems, different goals. The only way you'll get universal agreement is to stick punishment chips in everyone's brain—and even then it's only on the surface, and people either find subtler ways to disagree," and he nodded at Rishala, "or they let it fester until something snaps.

"It's not a problem if some of the People disagree with the state—as long as the state respects their right to disagree, and lets there be a dialogue."

"And that will be the case from now on," Natira said. "I have been too unwilling to listen before, but I promise that will change."

"Let us be pragmatic here," Soreth cautioned. "You cannot revert to the way things were. If you wish to survive and build a viable civilization, it will require innovation, scientific thought, an adaptable political system."

"And we can have those things," Rishala said. "The people want to advance, to move beyond the strictures of life in Yonada. We want the benefits of Fabrini medicine and technology. We want a free society. But we want it to come from *us,* from our own traditions. We want to be able to build that future on the foundations of our own past, to have it be a continuation of our own identity. We don't want to borrow it from the Federation."

"That is what we want too," Soreth insisted. "We are forbidden to impose anything on you."

"And you haven't imposed, Commissioner. But you have *judged.* You've assumed that the secular path your people took was the only one that could work for anyone else. And so you've implicitly endorsed a state that did the same, and alienated those you sought to help." Rishala looked to Kirk. "I've discovered that I made some mistakes myself. I've learned that all Fedraysha, maybe even most, aren't like that. But I think, Commissioner Soreth, that the People's relations with the Federation would go more smoothly with a different representative."

Soreth's brow shot up. "In my defense," he said slowly, "given what was known about the Oracular system, I could not have come to any other conclusion about its compatibility with freedom."

"But you did know," Spock countered, "or should have

known, that there were other religious traditions among the
People. Traditions which were unorthodox or even subversive by the standards of the latter-day Oracular system. You
failed to consider that they might be an avenue toward rec-
onciliation between the two sides . . . that secular and spiritual—reason and passion, if you will—could find common
ground," he added with a small, satisfied smile. "This is
simply . . . illogical. True peace cannot be attained by rejection, by exclusion, by repressing or denying those forces
you wish did not exist. It requires embracing those forces,
understanding them, and finding balance with them."

"Such . . . balance . . . is not always possible to achieve."

"But the chances are better if the parties involved have
confidence in their ability to succeed."

"I have that confidence," Natira said.

Rishala met her eyes. "So do I."

CHAPTER
NINETEEN

Thataway.

—James T. Kirk

Captain's Log: Stardate 7447.5

In the interests of facilitating the Lorini peace process, Commissioner Soreth has agreed to step down from his posting here. He will be returning to Federation space on board the *Enterprise*. He's expressed his intention to spend most of the trip in private meditation—which will probably be the most comfortable thing for all concerned. Meanwhile, the Lorini have asked Lieutenant Commander Lindstrom to sit in as mediator of the ongoing peace process. I'm certain his ability to relate to all the different points of view involved will make him an excellent choice for the role.

Dovraku remains in a catatonic state and has been remanded to Lorini authorities, after being treated for radiation poisoning. Two members of the team that infiltrated Yonada died despite Dr. McCoy's best efforts, but the rest are recovering in Lorini custody. Many of the remaining members of his movement are still in hiding, but community leaders are cooperating in efforts to bring them to justice. Mr. Lindstrom feels that many of those on the periphery of Dovraku's faction will simply vanish back into the general population, but will no longer pose any significant threat.

All the nuclear missiles fired from Yonada have been collected and destroyed under Shesshran supervision. With Yonada's supply of nuclear missiles exhausted and Dovraku's movement broken, the Shesshran have grudgingly retracted their ultimatum and resumed normal relations with their Lorini neighbors—in no small part because of the continued Federation presence in this system. Said presence will include the resident S.C.E. team, which is currently verifying the continued stability of Yonada's collapsed-matter core, and devising more modern methods of reinforcing it. Meanwhile, plans are under way to manuever Yonada into a higher, safer orbit. Plans are being discussed to paint Yonada's surface white or cover it with reflectors, so that it will still be visible to those Lorini who wish to pray to it.

McCoy woke up to the sight of Natira lying beside him, and wondered why he'd ever thought living alone was a good idea.

She was already awake, watching him, and rather than speaking she simply smiled, pulled him against her, and proved she could still be eloquent without her usual oratory. Finally he broke the silence. "This is wonderful, Natira."

"For me as well, Leonard."

He was quiet again for a time, then finally said, "I'd be willing to stay . . . to give it a try. I think the *Enterprise* can get along without me. I can't make any promises, but if you want me to . . ."

She sat up, and lowered her head sadly. Her waist-length hair cascaded around her bare shoulders, hiding her face. "I do want you to, Leonard. But I cannot."

Puzzled, he sat up too, put a hand on her face, and turned it toward him. "What do you mean?"

"The negotiations are delicate," she said. "I have to prove

that I am willing to heed the voices of the People, to join with them in finding our own path. I cannot risk appearing . . . intimate with the Federation."

"Politics?" McCoy rasped. "Is that what this is about?"

"It is about finding an alternative to bloodshed, Leonard. We cannot have peace without trust." She clasped his hand in hers. "Or without sacrifice. Please understand."

The hell of it was, he did understand. He wasn't even surprised, though it did hurt nonetheless. The good of the People had always come first with her, even when she'd been wrong about how to achieve it. He should have known he'd always come second. "Well . . . I guess we'll always have Paris."

She frowned at the reference, but let it go. "Perhaps it will not be the end, Leonard. You have far more than a year left to you now," she smiled. "Perhaps someday . . ."

He shook his head. "You won't wait for me. You shouldn't. You've got a world that needs repopulating."

"True," she said quietly. "But I wish I could do it with you." She grimaced. "Spock spoke of embracing opposing forces, creating balance between them."

"Yeah . . . that's somethin' he's been learnin' a lot about lately."

"If the People can balance the old and new, the secular and spiritual, then *I* should be allowed to balance my desires with my responsibilities!" She sighed. "But I cannot find a way. To achieve the greater balance, I must sacrifice the personal one."

"I think that is the balance," McCoy said. "Knowing how much of each you can have, and how much you have to do without." He spoke tentatively, for something was nibbling at the base of his mind, a thought trying to form, but just eluding him.

She stayed silent for a moment, thinking. Then she turned to him, embraced him gently once again. "But I am being self-absorbed. You would have your sacrifices too, surely. Your ship, your crew, they need you, and it would not be right to take you from them."

He frowned. "I'm not so sure about that. I haven't done the crew that much good. I'm out of touch, behind the times."

Natira smiled wryly. "One can always learn new things."

"Which is a lot of hard work, on top of all the other pressures of starship life . . . and I've gotten used to bein' a low-pressure kind of guy. I—" He broke off. "Pressure . . . my God, that might be it!" Before he finished speaking, he was scrambling out of the bed, searching for his wrist communicator.

"Leonard, what is it?"

But he'd found the communicator under his crumpled uniform. Thank goodness it was audio only, he thought. "McCoy to Chapel! Chris, I think I know how to help Spring Rain!"

Reiko Onami was bewildered when she entered the medical lab to see Spring Rain suspended in the hyperbaric chamber, the readouts indicating a high-pressure, highly oxygenated environment. Her bewilderment turned to alarm and the beginnings of anger when she saw McCoy supervising the procedure. She made her way over to Chapel. "What the hell's going on here?" she asked in a tense whisper. "I thought hyperbaric treatment posed too much risk of brain damage."

"Normally, it would," McCoy interposed cheerfully. Onami had underestimated the old guy's hearing. "But it's amazing what you can pull off when you find the right balance."

"Balance?"

"Leonard had the idea of combining the hyperbaric therapy with an injection of vasodilators and adrenergic inhibitors," Chapel explained. "Basically, balancing very high oxygen pressure with very low blood pressure. That

way, the superoxygenated blood flowing through her aeration membranes purges them of the toxins, but at such low
pressure that only a little of the oxygen can make it through
the blood-brain barrier."

Onami frowned. "But the air's at high pressure."

"Outside her body, yes," McCoy said. "Not inside her
arteries. It makes for a pretty slow purging process, but it's
getting done."

"Hopefully," Chapel went on, "once her membranes are
purged, they can read the chemical 'all-clear' signals from
the brain and wake her up."

Onami went over it in her head, and was surprised to find
it made sense. She stared at McCoy. "That's ingenious!"

"Well, you don't have to sound so scandalized about it!"

"No, I mean—I—"

Chapel smiled proudly. "There's more to medicine than
theory and book-learning, Reiko. I've never known a more
creative medical mind than Leonard McCoy's."

"Chris, you're a doctor now, you don't have to suck up to
me."

"Oh, shut up, Leonard."

Growing serious now, McCoy met Onami's eyes. "Still,
you're right. If I'm gonna be of use to this crew, I need to do
some serious studying. Startin' today, I intend to become
such an expert on comparative alien physiology that . . . that
I could write the book on it!"

"Oh, really?" Onami said gamely. "Well, I'm going to
hold you to that."

"You're on, young lady!"

"Doctor!" Chapel interrupted. "Her respiration is rising.
Neural activity increasing!"

All else was forgotten. "Lower the pressure as fast as you
can! She's amphibious; I'd guess she can handle a faster
change than a human."

"Right, Doctor. It should take less than a minute." As

Chapel spoke, Onami looked at McCoy with surprise and growing respect.

"And get some adrenaline into her, get that heart rate back up!"

Soon, faint musical tones were echoing through the hyperbaric chamber, audible over the intercom. Her voder didn't provide any translation—either it was having trouble compensating for the echoes, or she wasn't saying anything coherent yet.

"Ms. Spring Rain," McCoy asked, "can you understand me? Do you know where you are?"

> *I hear again, I am again.*
> *The voices make me real.*
> *Where am I? Floating in the stars*
> *Just where I wish to be.*

"I hope that's just metaphor instead of confusion," McCoy muttered, then turned back to the intercom. "Do you remember your name? Where you work?"

> *Spring Rain Upon Still Water, I*
> *Disturb the smooth and staid, and make*
> *More interesting sounds.*

> *I work 'mid metal walls and lights*
> *To find new tones with which a Spock*
> *Can weave enlightened songs.*

"Ohh . . . kay, I'll take that as a 'yes.' "

Onami was gasping with relief, blinking away tears. "Not her best poetry," she laughed, "but she's back!"

Kirk found Rishala in the temple, praying before the icon of Baima the Wise. He waited respectfully for her to finish—

but after a while he realized she was taking an awfully long time. He fidgeted, torn over whether to interrupt, until finally he noticed her peeking at him from the corner of her eye and stifling a chuckle. "You knew I was here all along," he accused with a smile.

"I'm sorry. I couldn't resist."

Kirk looked up at the white-haired icon. "May I ask a question?"

"Of me, or of Baima?"

"Of you." She nodded. "Do you . . . hear her any differently, now that you know . . . what you know about her?"

"The way I hear Baima, the way I understand her wisdom, is always changing. Just as I change, and the world around me changes. What good is wisdom that remains fixed?" She made her way over to the next icon, forcing Kirk to follow. "That's the problem with your books and computer files, you know. It's dead wisdom, preserved and mummified. It doesn't breathe, doesn't grow."

"That's why we keep writing new books. There are always new ideas—and the old ones aren't forgotten."

Rishala looked mildly chastened. "I suppose you have a point. We forgot a great deal about who we were." She prayed briefly to Dedi the Questioner, then faced Kirk again. "But I fear people are already taking the books and files too literally. The children question whether Vari, Baima, and the others should 'count' as Creators. What do you think?" she asked.

"I think . . . that asking questions is always a good thing. If you encourage them to question you, maybe they'll also question what they read, and won't embrace any point of view blindly."

"Good answer. Dedi approves."

"Thank him for me."

She paused a moment, perhaps to do just that. Then she

turned to him again. "But he wants me to remind you that there's still much work to do. Not everyone is happy with the new revelations, and the debates over what they mean to the People are just getting started. With Dovraku gone, and—I hate to admit—with Tasari gone, there's less threat of open violence. But you haven't solved everything just by restoring our history to us."

"I understand that," Kirk said. "But at least you and Natira are working together to solve the People's problems. So I'm confident that the People are in good hands."

She smiled. "You're a sweet-talker, Jim."

"Only when it's deserved."

"But what you're saying is that you're leaving Lorina."

"I have other obligations. Starfleet needs the *Enterprise* in service." He hesitated. "I . . . hope you don't feel I'm just abandoning your world again."

"No." She stroked his shoulder reassuringly. "You did a lot to make up for your original mistake."

"I'm . . . happy to hear that," Kirk said sardonically.

"It's just that . . ."

He met her eyes. "What?"

"You still have so much left to learn."

Kirk stared, then smiled modestly. "I always do. That's why I have to go."

"More science," she scoffed. "More learning about *things,* more material illusions. Where will you go to learn the truths that matter?"

He grew thoughtful. "I have learned one thing that I wanted to share with you." She looked at him curiously. "I . . . spoke to Will Decker's mother over subspace. I asked her . . . questions it hadn't occurred to me to ask her before, when I first notified her of her son's . . . departure." He paused. "Or questions I was too ashamed to ask. I tried to keep it brief, that first time. Just a few years before, I'd had to notify her of her husband's death, and now . . ."

"Yes." There was infinite compassion and forgiveness in the syllable.

"She told me . . . about a side to Will Decker that I'd never known. She sent me his letters, his journals. All I knew was a serious young Starfleet officer, by-the-book, driven, just like his father had been. Maybe he . . . assumed that was what it took to succeed in Starfleet. But his mother had been the one who'd raised him, and she'd inspired another side to him."

"A spiritual side?" Rishala ventured.

"The man was a poet. I never knew that. He wrote about the unexplored potentials of the human mind. He was fascinated with the idea of expanding the mind, moving outside the body, joining with other minds. He was drawn to species with telepathic or empathic abilities—it was why he took a posting on Delta IV in the first place."

"Not Vulcan?"

"He found Vulcans too . . . reserved in their approach to telepathy. They resisted the kind of . . . unity he was drawn to." He continued slowly. "He believed that . . . if different species could combine their minds, their spirits . . . complement each other's strengths, compensate for each other's blind spots about themselves . . . it might let them sense new levels of existence. Maybe even reach them."

Rishala was silent for a time. "It seems he was right."

"That was why he was really in Starfleet. He was . . . searching for something, something that could give him insight into those higher levels. He wanted to learn about alien belief systems, to see how different species interacting might discover new truths." He shook his head. "I was so blind. I thought he saw the *Enterprise* the same way I did, as a goal in itself. And of course, he did care about the ship herself. He was trained as an engineer, he supervised every step of the *Enterprise*'s refit. But I think that what mattered more to him was the opportunity the *Enterprise* represented. This crew was his great experiment, a chance to test his ideas about unity, about diversity in combination. He worked so hard on the ship because it was the crucible for his test, and he wanted it to be just right. But it was never *about* the ship to him. It was about what he hoped to discover."

Rishala nodded. "And that's exactly what he found within V'Ger."

"I guess it was." Another long pause. "When I spoke to Joan Decker this time, she didn't sound like she was in mourning. She sounded . . . like she missed her son, of course—but she sounded proud of him. She sounded . . . *satisfied.*"

She studied him. "And did you learn anything from that?"

"Yes," Kirk said. "I think I did."

Rishala grew wistful. "At least you can now be comfortable with the title you hold. I still have to be high priestess, and nothing's happened to make me more comfortable with that. If anything, working with the state now, I'm even more of an insider than before, farther from my People. I miss being plain, ordinary Rishala."

Kirk took her hand. "I'm sure that you've never been ordinary." She looked skeptical, but he went on. "I meant what I said before—the People are lucky to have you as their spiritual leader. I think they may even remember you . . . as Rishala the Wise."

She scoffed. "That's Baima's title. I don't deserve it."

"I don't know," Kirk mused, looking between her and the icon. "I see a definite resemblance."

"Well," she replied impishly, "you haven't seen me naked."

Kirk wasn't sure how to respond to that. Rishala chuckled at the look on his face, leaned forward and graced him with a long, gentle kiss. "You've been a good student, Jim

Kirk. I've learned a lot from you. Now go up to your ship and be a galactic hero."

He shook his head. "I'm no hero."

"And I'm no saint. But does anyone listen?"

Rhaandarites didn't have much in the way of funereal customs, it seemed. They just accepted death as part of the natural order of things, and didn't go to any great trouble to deal with it. So Vaylin Zaand hadn't put any specific requests on file. His memorial service was a standard Starfleet affair: a no-frills ceremony in the torpedo bay, followed by a reception in the arboretum. As Zaand's supervisor, Chekov had said the obligatory words at the service, but it had felt like boilerplate and the whole thing had somewhat blurred in his memory. That was odd; he would have thought the first time would stand out, would stay with him forever.

That arrow going through his neck—*that* would stay with him forever.

Chekov stood at one of the arboretum's large windows, looking out on Lorina. He didn't particularly notice the planet there, any more than he'd noticed the lush beauty of his surroundings, the sounds and smells of life pervading the chamber. He was too busy brooding on death. Russians had invented that. Or at least perfected it.

"Lieutenant?" It was Kirk. Chekov turned; the captain stood beside him, with Sulu and Uhura flanking them like an honor guard. "How are you feeling?"

Chekov turned back to the window. "I made the decision, sir. I didn't have to. I almost didn't . . . but I did. He was just a boy—and I gave the order that killed him."

"No, Pavel!" Uhura hugged him. "Believe me, I know how you feel. I recruited him for this crew. But it wasn't you or I who fired the shot that killed him. And he knew the risks he was taking."

"I know all the arguments, Nyota. But I ordered him to his death."

Kirk's eyes met his, reflected in the window. "Welcome to command, Mr. Chekov."

"I understand now, sir," Chekov replied slowly. "Why you don't want to let others take risks in your place."

"Yes."

A pause. "Still . . . it's our job."

A longer pause. "Yes."

After a moment, Kirk turned to Sulu. "Speaking of command, Mr. Sulu . . . you really did do an excellent job back there."

"Thank you, sir."

"And I think you know it, too. There's something different about you, Hikaru . . . a gleam in your eye that I think I recognize."

Sulu tilted his head noncommittally, but he was smiling. "There might just be at that, sir."

"You've caught the bug, Mr. Sulu. My condolences."

"Thank you, Captain." The smile grew, but it was hesitant, as Sulu's eyes went to Chekov. This was one side of command Sulu hadn't tasted yet. But Chekov hoped it wouldn't dissuade him when he inevitably did. He'd always thought Sulu would make a great captain.

"In fact, Sulu, I've been thinking," Kirk went on. "As I'm sure you know, Starfleet gives its captains a certain latitude in the kind of command structure they choose for their ships, and I've always favored a fairly loose chain of command. But maybe it's time to try something new. How would you like to be the *Enterprise*'s official second officer?"

"Second officer?" Sulu's eyes grew wide.

Kirk shrugged. "It wouldn't really be that different from your current duties, just a little more definitive. And it would free up Scotty to focus more on getting the kinks

362 CHRISTOPHER L. BENNETT

worked out of this new ship . . . on a permanent basis, not just for the shakedown."

"Thank you, sir. I . . . think I'd like that."

"Don't think," Kirk said sharply. "*Know.*"

After a second, Sulu nodded more firmly. "Yes, sir. I accept."

"Good. You'll make a fine captain someday." He paused, then did a take. "But not on this ship. She's mine."

Sulu beamed. "I wouldn't have it any other way, sir."

Everyone clustered around to congratulate Sulu, with Uuvu'it offering to take bets on how long it would take him to become captain of the *Enterprise.* Cella DiFalco in particular seemed to have gotten over her crush on Kirk, judging from the way she was looking at Sulu. Chekov drifted away, not begrudging Sulu the attention and celebration. He recognized now that he and Sulu were growing apart as they followed their own paths. They might not even remain on the same ship in years to come, he realized, especially not if Chekov continued his pursuit of the command track. Which, despite his pain and guilt at the loss of Zaand, Chekov knew that he would. Because he was too much of a cynic to think the galaxy could get by without starship captains—and too much of an idealist to resist the challenge.

Kirk gave McCoy a dirty look. "So you're telling me that the only reason you're staying with the *Enterprise* is because Natira turned you down?"

He'd invited Spock and McCoy to share a drink in his quarters, something they hadn't done for a long time. Spock was abstaining from the drink as usual, but seemed to appreciate the company. But McCoy was fidgeting. "It's not like that, Jim. I just didn't want to walk out on her again. Not when things seemed to be working out." He quirked a brow. Kirk had always been amused that his two friends both had the habit of raising a single eyebrow, but each in his own distinct way—a smooth, sustained lift for Spock, a convulsive up-and-down for McCoy. Their whole personalities summed up in one facial tic. "Actually, I guess I'm feeling a bit relieved. Bein' married to a planetary head of state isn't exactly my speed. You know how I hate wearin' formal clothes."

Spock raised his own brow now, and Kirk stifled a chuckle. "And being chief medical officer on a Starfleet vessel?" the Vulcan asked.

"I seem to be gettin' the hang of it again," McCoy said with a hint of smugness. "Spring Rain's going to make a full recovery. The brain damage was limited, maybe a slight loss of memory and motor function, but"—he looked at his Saurian brandy—"no worse than drinkin' this stuff for a few decades will do." Kirk froze with the glass at his lips, and nonchalantly set it down as McCoy went on. "And I think I learned more from those crew physicals than I thought. Crewman Kick came in with a digestive problem this morning, and I had him fixed up in no time. And I tell you, a seven-foot-long caterpillar's got a *lot* of digestive tract." Kirk cleared his throat, grateful he'd already put his drink down.

"So what about you, Spock?" McCoy asked. "If you're still havin' trouble with your meditation, I'd be happy to take another look under the ol' hood."

"Thank you, Doctor, but I am meditating satisfactorily once again. I found many answers during my meld with Dovraku."

McCoy stared. "*Dovraku* gave you answers? Don't tell me you're gonna start burning incense in front of the computer core." He grunted. "Not as if you don't already worship the blasted thing."

"He provided only a negative example, Doctor. But it did force me to confront certain issues of my own." Somewhat to Kirk's surprise, Spock went on to tell them some of what he'd experienced in the meld, about Dovraku's father and his own. The old Spock would have considered it a private matter. Hell, the old Spock would have avoided it altogether, which seemed to be the point. "I believe this is what lay at the root of my difficulties with control and meditation—my subconscious guilt and fear over how Sarek would judge my recent decisions."

"Hell, isn't that what I told you three weeks ago, Spock?" McCoy asked. "That you were nervous about tellin' your father?"

"It is not the same thing at all, Dr. McCoy. You suggested that I was failing to confront the question of how to inform Sarek. I replied that I was in fact confronting that question, but had not yet reached a decision. What I now recognize is *why* I was unable to do so. It is a crucial distinction."

"Hunh. You haven't changed that much at all, Spock. You're still too stubborn to admit it when I'm right."

"I am still awaiting an opportunity to discover how I would react to your being right, Doctor." Before McCoy could parse the insult fully, Spock turned to Kirk. "In any case, Captain, I would like to request a leave of absence once we return to Federation space. I . . . am somewhat overdue for a talk with my parents."

Kirk nodded. "Of course. Sulu can stand in as acting first officer—it'll be good experience for him."

McCoy shook his head. "Parents. Fathers. It all comes down to them, doesn't it? The things we do in life . . . most of the time we're either runnin' toward or away from our parents. Hell, if you think about it, even V'Ger was basically just tryin' to feel a parent's touch. Even without any emotion at all, it knew on some level that it was missing that."

Kirk pondered the thought for a moment, then looked at Spock. "Speaking of which . . . have you had any further mental contact with V'Ger? Or . . . the Voyager?" he corrected, remembering Spock's nickname for the evolved entity.

"None, sir. I was never entirely sure whether I was sensing the Voyager itself or merely an echo in my own mind. But I no longer have any sensation of contact at all. If it was a genuine contact, then since it occurred, the Voyager has either traveled or evolved beyond my ability to detect. And . . . I believe I have gotten all I needed from the contact." At Kirk's thoughtful look, he added, "Did you have a specific question?"

"I was just wondering . . . could you tell if Decker was happy?"

Spock pondered. "Insofar as he still existed as a distinct being . . . I believe so, Jim."

Kirk smiled just a bit. "Somehow . . . I figured as much."

"And you, Jim?" Spock asked. "Are you satisfied with your current situation?"

After a moment, Kirk replied, "I'm not sure, Spock. I no longer doubt that I did the right thing in taking the *Enterprise* back." He glanced at McCoy, but the doctor didn't challenge the statement. "But . . . I'm still not sure the crew feels that way. I don't think I managed to do very much on this mission to win their confidence. You stopped Dovraku, Sulu kept the ship safe, Bones saved Spring Rain. What did I do?"

"You ordered me to research Yonada's history and find a common ground to unite the factions—a decision which proved instrumental in resolving the crisis."

"He's right, Jim," McCoy said. "Maybe it wasn't the kind of flashy, last-minute heroism that interstellar legends are made of, but it was the right call at the right time." The doctor tilted his head. "As for the rest . . . well, Jim, you did one of the most important things any leader can do. Something Natira finally learned how to do, too."

"What's that?"

"You trusted your people. Gave them room to use their own judgment. And if you want to win their trust, I don't know a better way to start."

Kirk pondered his words, remembering what he had said to Zaand back on Yonada. "You have to give trust to get it," he murmured. "It's always a risk."

"And aren't you the one who always says risk is our business?"

"I never say that."

McCoy glared at him. "Do you mock me, sir?"

"Never. I'm a captain, not a comedian."

Spock raised a cutting brow, and there was a twinkle in his eye. "I am forced to agree, sir."

Kirk laughed. After a moment, McCoy joined him. Spock contented himself with a serene smile—but that was enough.

ABOUT THE AUTHOR

At the age of five and a half, Christopher L. Bennett discovered *Star Trek,* and it changed his life forever by introducing him to space, science, and speculative fiction. Spock became his childhood role model, which didn't work out so well; but he came to recognize the value of emotion at about the same time Spock did in *Star Trek: The Motion Picture.* That personal resonance helped make TMP his favorite *Trek* movie, and has made *Ex Machina* a tale very close to his heart. The fact that it's his first published novel doesn't hurt either.

Christopher has made two separate passes through the University of Cincinnati, thereby putting off real life as long as possible, and earned a B.S. in physics and a B.A. with high honors in history in the process. His published works include "Aggravated Vehicular Genocide" in the November 1998 *Analog;* "Among the Wild Cybers of Cybele" in the December 2000 *Analog; Star Trek: S. C. E. #29: Aftermath,* available in eBook form; and ". . . Loved I Not Honor More" in the *Deep Space Nine: Prophecy and Change* anthology. More information and cat pictures can be found at http://home.fuse.net/ChristopherLBennett/.

The author is not the same Christopher Bennett whose father is *Star Trek* movie producer Harve Bennett, though he is apparently a cousin of paleontologist Chris Bennett. You can see why he uses the "L."

KNOW NO BOUNDARIES

Explore the Star Trek™
Universe with Star Trek™
Communicator, The Magazine of
the Official Star Trek Fan Club.

Subscription to Communicator is
only $29.95 per year (plus shipping and handling)
and entitles you to:

- 6 issues of STAR TREK Communicator

- Membership in the official STAR TREK™ Fan Club

- An exclusive full-color lithograph

- 10% discount on all merchandise purchased at
  www.startrekfanclub.com

- Advance purchase preference on select items
  exclusive to the fan club

- ...and more benefits to come!

So don't get left behind! Subscribe to STAR TREK™
Communicator now at www.startrekfanclub.com